Copyright © 2023 by Emma Lee-Johnson

All rights reserved.

No part of this publication may be reproduced, distributed, or transmitted in any form or by any means, including photocopying, recording, or other electronic or mechanical methods, without the prior written permission of the publisher, except as permitted by U.S. copyright law. For permission requests, contact Emma Lee-Johnson directly via emmlee-johnson.com.

The story, all names, characters, and incidents portrayed in this production are fictitious. No identification with actual persons (living or deceased), places, buildings, and products is intended or should be inferred.

Book Cover by GETCOVERS

Edited by: Stephanie Cosgrove

*To, Mia, Football all the way! Love, Emma Lee Johnson*

For all the years of loyalty, passion and thrills, many thanks
To,
Sir Kenny, Rushy, Fowler, Steve Macca, Owen, Stevie G, Gary Mc, Carra, little Luis, Alonso,
Barnes, Hypia, Kuyt, Dudek, Suarez, Lucas, Moreno, Salah, Mane, Bobby, Hendo, Milly,
Robbo, Gini, Ali, Jota, big Virg and the greek scouser.

Special chants to: Trent A.A, C.Jones, little HarveyE: The future of our team.

Mostly, thank you to Jurgen, the normal one. You're a fucking mad genius!

**YNWA**

# Contents

| | |
|---|---|
| Title Page | VII |
| Synopsis | IX |
| Playlist | XI |
| 1. Chapter 1 | 1 |
| What is football? | 19 |
| 2. Chapter 2 | 21 |
| 3. Chapter 3 | 33 |
| 4. Chapter 4 | 49 |
| Substitution Definition | 57 |
| 5. Chapter 5 | 59 |
| 6. Chapter 6 | 75 |
| 7. Chapter 7 | 93 |
| Headline News | 107 |
| 8. Chapter 8 | 109 |
| 9. Chapter 9 | 125 |
| 10. Chapter 10 | 141 |
| 11. Chapter 11 | 155 |
| Match Definition | 169 |
| 12. Chapter 12 | 171 |

| | | |
|---|---|---|
| 13. | Chapter 13 | 183 |
| 14. | Chapter 14 | 201 |
| 15. | Chapter 15 | 215 |
| | Players Positions | 225 |
| 16. | Chapter 16 | 227 |
| 17. | Chapter 17 | 241 |
| 18. | Chapter 18 | 259 |
| 19. | Chapter 19 | 273 |
| | Fouls | 289 |
| 20. | Chapter 20 | 291 |
| 21. | Chapter 21 | 307 |
| 22. | Chapter 22 | 325 |
| 23. | Chapter 23 | 343 |
| | EEFL League Table | 351 |
| | BONUS MATERIAL | 353 |
| | Claire's PDF | 355 |
| | About the Author | 363 |
| | Also By Emma Lee-Johnson | 369 |

AN ENGLISH ELITE FOOTBALL LEAGUE ROMANCE

# SUBSTITUTION
## *Clause*

**EMMA LEE-JOHNSON**

Leila Monrose has a life many would envy. In her prestigious career as an injury specialist in Elite English Football, she meets interesting people and travels the world. Beautiful and clever, she has a nice car, a stylish home and has made plenty of friends since she moved up north for her job. Sooner or later, someone will come along to share it all with her.

Could it be the younger footballer Jack Cardal, who Leila helped regain form after a nasty injury? Handsome, rich and confident, Jack always wants what he can't have. When Leila declines his invitation to dinner, he sees it as a challenge.

Or maybe it will be his older brother, billionaire property and technology tycoon turned football club investor, Nate Cardal, who is a perfect gentleman with a massive skeleton in his closet.

When one brother hurts her, the other helps her seek revenge, but with conditions attached.

In a world of high-stakes contracts, will Leila activate the Substitution Clause?

## SUBSTITUTION Clause Playlist
### AN ENGLISH ELITE FOOTBALL LEAGUE ROMANCE

1. Fire- Kasabian
2. Lionheart (Fearless)- Joel Corry, Tom Grennan
3. Anti-Hero- Taylor Swift
4. One Kiss (with Dua Lipa)- Calvin Harris
5. Kiss Me- Olly Murs
6. Allez Allez Allez- JAMIE WEBSTER
7. Watermelon Sugar- Harry Styles
8. Once in a Lifetime- Talking Heads
9. World in Motion- New Order
10. Until I Found You- Stephen Sanchez
11. The Winner Takes It All- ABBA
12. Leave a Light on- Tom Walker
13. Forget Me- Lewis Capaldi
14. Nothing's Real but Love- Rebecca Ferguson

# CHAPTER 1

## ~ Leila ~

My phone beeps, indicating that it is time for my next appointment. I quickly change the sheet covering my examination table and wash my hands before pressing my buzzer, which will alert the receptionist that I am ready for my next patient. My room is white, clean and airy with an underlying smell of disinfectant. Apart from the charts on the walls showing the varying sports injuries I help players rehabilitate from, you would never guess that my office is part of a multi-billion-pound training complex for elite athletes at the top of their field. In this case, Harringwood: the training facility for Redvale City Football Club, one of the top Elite English Football League teams.

Before I am settled back behind my desk, my door swings open abruptly, and a portly man in a shirt, tie and suit walks in, his shoes squeaking against the linoleum on the floor; the boss, Mr McAllister. He is followed by my patient Jack Cardal, last season's superstar signing, who rather distressingly dislocated his ankle after making his debut. He has been side-lined ever since, and I have been working closely with him to assist in his recovery. At twenty-two years old, he has youth on his side, and although the road to recovery has been a long one, it is now the start of the next season, and he is hoping to be a part of the team.

"Is he cleared to play?" Mr McAllister asks me, the desperation and anticipation bouncing off him. You'd think, after two years of being here, I would be used to the pressure of clearing an injured player. As a professional sports physiotherapist, I take my position very seriously. This isn't just a matter of a man playing football; it's his whole career. If I clear him too quickly, he could reinjure himself or worse. Needlessly preventing someone from playing is the last thing I want, but I need to be sure.

"Good afternoon, Mr McAllister, Jack," I say in greeting, purposefully using my manners to show him he hasn't used his. When I was a little girl, my dad always told me, 'Remember where you come from and that manners are free.' It's an ethos I have lived by.

"Yeah, yeah, good afternoon. What's the verdict? Can he play?" Mr McAllister replies quickly, as impatient as always. He always seems to be in a rush and acts like no one has ever had a dilemma or problem like him, as though the weight of the world is on his shoulders.

"I don't need to tell you how serious Jack's injury was. Many others have seen their careers ended over something like this. However, Jack has worked hard and fully participated in his rehabilitation. I see no reason why he eventually won't return to his peak." They both stare at me in confused silence, so I cut to the chase; this is what they are here for after all. "He is cleared to come off the bench for twenty minutes, thirty at the most." Before I finish my sentence, the player in question, Jack Cardal, jumps up out of his seat.

"I'm cleared? Did you hear that, Macca? I'm cleared. I did it!" The two men jump and whoop with joy. Mr McAllister even shakes my hand.

"Thank you, Doc. I'll go and let the manager know," McAllister adds. No matter how much I tell them I am not a doctor, they still insist on calling me 'Doc'. At least I got a thank you out of him this time.

Standing up as Mr McAllister leaves, I point to my examination table, and dutifully, Jack jumps up and removes his shoe and sock, his leg already on display in his training shorts. "If I am ever not there during a match, you need to ensure the physiotherapist tapes you up here and here to support your ankle. You already know it's a weak spot now. All we can do is try to prevent any further damage."

"Yes, Doc. Look, thank you for everything you've done. I don't know where I would be if you hadn't took over my care." When Jack first suffered his injury, the higher ups went over my head and took him to another specialist. Their star signing needed the best care. Most other therapists treat the injury but not the mind and soul. Jack came back under my care angry, frustrated, and disillusioned. Jack needed to know that this was a setback and that with his dedicated work, he could have a career in football again. Over time, he learned to trust me and my methods, and when his form began to return, he put all his faith in what I was teaching him. Luckily, it's all working out. I have asked for a staggered return to the game for him so he can slowly adjust to being back in top flight. "I think you're incredible. Now that I'm fit again, how about I take you out for dinner sometime? I was thinking tonight after the game?"

Jack takes hold of my hand and pulls me closer to him, looking into my eyes with his smouldering grey ones. Heat rises in my face, but as flattered as I am, I cannot date him. "That's not necessary; it's my job, Jack, and it was a pleasure helping you get back to the game you love." I try to step back, but he moves along the bed, swinging his legs over the side and trapping me between them. "Besides, I already have plans tonight," I add nervously. It's not that I don't find Jack attractive, because he is very handsome and fit. I don't want to mix business with pleasure.

"Tomorrow night then?" he murmurs, and my skin prickles and pimples as his breathy words wash over me. "It's been a pleasure working with you too, and I think we could be something special."

Having heard enough, I pull away forcefully. "No. Thank you. You're lovely, but I'm not interested in you in that way." His crestfallen face almost makes me regret my decision, but not quite.

"Well, this is embarrassing! I'm not used to people, especially women, saying no." I smile at him, because I know he isn't. 'Jack-the-lad' the newspapers call him because of his off-field antics. He has no shortage of female company, and that's not a life I want to get wrapped up in. "Please think about it. I'll see you after the game, hopefully."

Smiling tightly, I return to my desk and pretend to type up his report until he leaves my office. He has got absolutely no chance. Tonight, I'm going dancing with my girlfriends.

My next and final patient of the day is the team captain, Lucas Jones. 'Jonesy' as he is known to his teammates and fans is one of the older and more experienced players in the team. He suffers from a recurring groin injury, and as he enters the latter stage of his career, his injuries take longer to recover from and happen more frequently. Jonesy will stay at Redvale until he retires at the end of next season. Until then, it is my job to support him in staying as fit as possible.

"Watcher, Doc. How are things?" he says as he walks into my office, dropping his shorts and sitting on my examination table without any prompts. We do the same routine every match he is selected to play, and to be fair, as his therapist and colleague, I've seen it all before. That's the hazard of working in football. "I just heard Jack got cleared," he adds, resting his head back and closing his eyes.

After washing my hands, I pull on a pair of disposable gloves. There is nothing as smelly and sweaty as a man's groin after a day of training! "Yeah, he can't do the full ninety minutes but he's on his way. Any pain or pulls?" I ask him before adding, "May I?" Jonesy nods his head to consent to me touching him, and after probing and prodding at him and finding no issues, I tell him to get dressed again.

He stands up, wearing just his briefs on the bottom. I don't even bat an eyelid now, but when I first started working here two years ago, I would blush whenever one of the players stripped down in front of me. Now, I unfortunately have as much knowledge of these men and their bodies as their significant others do. We are like one big dysfunctional family and privacy is a luxury that doesn't extend to the players. "When I was jogging earlier, I felt a burning sensation in my groin, but it went away as quickly as it started. Should I be concerned about that?"

Shaking my head at him, I respond, "No, everyone will get sensations like that. Obviously, if it starts to hurt, make the signal to the bench and we'll get you out of there as fast as we can." Signing off on his wellness passport, I pass it back to him. "Good luck for tonight, Jonesy. You're free to go."

"Thanks, Doc, I'll see you later," he shouts over his shoulder as he gets to the door. "Here's to a new season and hoping I stay fit for it."

As fast as I can, I fill out Jonesy's care sheet, shut down my computer, water the plant and then lock up my office for the weekend. It's not unusual for me to be working on a Saturday afternoon. In fact, I work most weekends with matches often taking place then. I split my time between consultation and treatment at the training ground and then match days I am on hand for anything that may be of concern.

Showing my identity card as I exit the main foyer so the security team can sign me out, I head over to my new car. Now I must make this incredibly clear. My car is my baby! This car is the first car I have managed to save for and buy outright. And I adore it. Sat next to the Audis, Mercedes and BMWs that belong to the players, directors, managers, and coaching staff, it looks like a kid sister of a car.

But my yellow VW Beetle is everything I have ever wanted, and I don't care what anyone else thinks about it.

It's a warm August day, and the roads of Redvale City are busy. It takes me around twenty minutes to drive home. Last year I finally bought my first home, a small two-bedroom end terrace house in a quiet residential area on the outskirts of the city. After sharing an apartment for a year with my friends Claire and Louise, I appreciate the space, quiet and privacy I now have.

Parking straight onto my driveway, I wave to my neighbour, who looks at me sourly. Apparently, he still hasn't forgiven me for having a housewarming party a few months ago. However, I know he is a massive Redvale City Football Club fan. "Arthur? Young Jack Cardal should be on the bench tonight!" I shout as quietly as possible, relishing the look in his eyes as he realises what I am telling him. "Will you be at the game tonight?"

"Nah, I'll be listening to it on the radio. My grandson will be coming to listen to it with me," he tells me. Arthur used to be a staunch supporter who went to a lot of football matches. Since his wife died, he doesn't seem to go as much.

"I have a couple of spare tickets if you'd like them." We are all given tickets for family and friends; however, my family aren't really football fans and live on the south coast. My friends did take me up on the offer a few times until they realised they wouldn't be getting anywhere near the footballers.

"You'd do that for me?" He looks at me, surprised and in awe at my offer.

"Of course. On one condition. Will you forgive me for my housewarming party, please?" I say to him bluntly. His ears and the back of his neck turn bright red, and he looks abashed.

Nodding quickly, he concedes, "We'll say no more about it. You seem like a good girl; I don't think you meant to be so loud." I smile at him as I open up my bag and take out the tickets that I hand to him over our shared fence. "Thank you. You're an angel!"

"Have a great time with your grandson, Arthur. I must dash; I have to get to the grounds for the warm up."

Leaving him smiling at the tickets, I let myself into my home. Discarding my uniform, I have a quick shower, before putting on my official team clothing: The Redvale Medical Team uniform in the team colours made by major clothing brand Projection. With it being warm, I opt for the shorts, t-shirt and zip up lightweight jacket, teamed up with my matching running shoes. I pull my long chestnut hair into a high ponytail and grab my dress bag with my clothes for this evening.

Just in time, I arrive back at the training ground to meet the team bus. I no sooner embark, and the bus begins to move. "You're cutting it fine; I saved you a seat." I look up and find Jack sitting near the front, with a spare seat beside him. Internally, I groan. I hope he doesn't want to continue the same conversation we had earlier. Jack quickly proves I am needlessly worrying. He hands me a spare set of earbuds. "It's how I chill before the match. Listen with me." I accept the buds and place them in my ears and tranquil music fills my head.

With the excitement of the game and his potential return to playing, Jack has probably already forgotten all about his offer to take me out.

## ~ Jack ~

Although I'm riding on a high at being cleared to play today, I'm still smarting from Leila's knock back. I had been convinced she would be flattered. It was embarrassing the way she recoiled from me. I just don't understand it. I'm fit, healthy, successful and rich as fuck. I'm a catch. I don't see what her problem is, but I intend on breaking down all those barriers and finding out.

The first game of the season is full of tension. Both nerves and excitement war inside every player because today is a fresh start. It doesn't matter what happened last season, or the season before. The slate is wiped clean for everyone. The fans are full of optimism, and the players are rejuvenated after a holiday and rest. There is everything to play for. There is everything to prove, especially in my case.

Every match day, the whole team and support staff travel together on the team buses. Knowing that Leila will hop on the second bus with the rest of the staff, I opt to sit on that bus too. I sit near the front and pretend to be engrossed in my music when she finally arrives, looking out of breath and flustered. Leila is older than the girls I usually go for, but there is something about the way she carries herself, her quiet confidence, and the way she never seems impressed with any of the players. Her ability to reassure us all and yet remain distant at the same time leaves me craving her attention. I want to be her favourite. I want her to prioritise me over the others. Is it so wrong that I want to matter to her?

She sits next to me, looking at me warily at first and then relaxing when she accepts I'm not going to pounce on her or persist in trying to persuade her. This is not my style at all. We listen to music together; another word doesn't pass between us, and that's the way I want it. I want her to be thinking about what I said back when I asked her out; I want her to doubt her response and question if she's made the right decision.

The closer we get to Fielding Lane, Redvale's stadium, the more nervous I feel. My leg jitters; however, I only notice how bad it is when Leila places her hand on my knee. "Nervous?" she asks me simply, and I instinctively want to scowl at her for seeing my weakness. "It's a massive day for you. I know that you're going to have mixed emotions, especially when it comes to the reminders of your injury, but you've got this, Jack. You can do this, and you can do this well." I nod stiffly to her, trying not to notice how my body reacts to her touch. For fuck's sake, she's only touching my knee and I'm throbbing for her.

"I'm nervous that the fans have forgotten about me. The manager needs to bring me on as a substitution today so they remember I'm here and I'm the best player in our team."

"They haven't forgotten you, far from it. Even my grumpy neighbour is coming out to see you tonight," she whispers to me, and I'm glad that we are sharing this intimate moment. Perhaps it'll help her see me in a different light. "Try not to worry. At least try to enjoy your moment."

"Thanks," I say to her, before looking down at her hand, which is still on my knee.

"Oh, goodness! I'm so sorry, I forgot it was even there!" she mutters as her face turns puce. She snatches her hand away as though she has been burnt, and her reactions make me smile. Fuck, she's already seen me naked, seen everything I have, and touching me on the knee has her blushing like a new bride. "Do you want me to sort you now or at half time?"

My mind instantly moves to the dirty things she could do to me at half time. Maybe a quick blowjob in the stalls? Or she could strip and dance for me. "What do you have in mind?" I murmur to her, my body already reacting and buzzing with anticipation.

"Well, I don't want you going on too early, so I think you should wait until half time." Now I have no idea what she is talking about... My cock just wants to know if it's getting sucked! The innuendo and suggestion, mingled with the vibrations from the moving bus, have my body tied up in knots.

"What are you talking about?" I ask her, frowning in frustration.

"Strapping your foot, Jack. Do you want me to do it once we get in the changing rooms or at half time?" Oh FUCK! She's talking about my ankle; I am so glad I didn't say anything inappropriate!

With a spark of inspiration, I reply to her. "Actually, Doc, would you mind doing me a favour? Could you do it at half time, but check it before I go on? It'll get the crowd excited." All the other girls who I date love being photographed and speculated about in the tabloids and on social media. Hopefully, it'll appeal to Leila too.

"I don't think that's a good move, to be honest, Jack. The last thing you want is to draw attention to your weakness. No one needs to know you're wearing strapping." Another stone wall. What the hell is wrong with this chick? I'm offering her the chance at stardom and exposure, and she's not even considering it. She is the most confusing woman I've ever met. What is it she actually wants?

When we pull into the grounds, right beside the players entrance, the flashes and shouts of the paparazzi fill the bus. The first bus has already arrived, and the reporters scramble in a greedy frenzy to get the best photograph of the other players arriving. "Are you ready?" I ask her, adrenaline coursing through my veins. I love this part. It's been a while since I arrived as an eligible player, and I know the press will be feverishly looking for a sensationalised headline to include in their rag tomorrow.

"You go ahead. I'll see you inside in a few minutes," Leila says to me distantly. I had hoped to walk in with her on my arm. I wanted to show her how adored and important I am. To have some sort of angle I could tease her over, but she's declining every opportunity I offer.

Shrugging, I wait another minute before stepping off the bus and basking in the glory of the media vying for my attention. I'm back, and this time I will stop at nothing to make a success of myself.

## ~ Leila ~

Jack steps off the bus with such ease and confidence that I shudder in reaction. The limelight has never appealed to me and is probably one of the barriers to me doing this job. It angers me that there are people who think that they have a right to my privacy just because I work with people who earn astonishing amounts of money. Why are people so nosy and interfering? Don't get me wrong, I've seen the flip side, the footballers and their spouses who want to be in the public eye, ones who even behave outlandishly to improve their celebrity standing. The ones who court the media and try to grow their 'brand' as it is promoted are not the reason I became a sports injury specialist.

Well, one could question why on earth I even work within such a media driven arena, but that wasn't even a consideration. Ignorantly, I believed I would be below notice. No one knows the supporting staff. No one wants to know about the mundane and even negative side of football. They all want the glamourous and glossy insights that they aspire to replicate in their lives too. The beautiful, insanely huge homes, the flashy cars, the expensive clothing and jewellery, the star-studded events and exotic holidays, and the harem of stunning partners, who seem to throw themselves at the footballers. That's what people seem to want to read about. Not injuries or treatments that my oath as a care professional prevents me from discussing anyway!

None of that side of the game has ever mattered to me. I want to make a difference, and although it might seem arrogant of me to have presumed, when I applied for this job, I knew I had the skills and expertise to truly help the professionals whose careers are blighted by injury and inadequate recovery. I never in a million years thought I would actually get it; football is notoriously a male dominated sport, and yet, against the odds, I managed to secure one of the most prestigious jobs within my field. Working with English Elite Football league team Redvale City as the lead rehabilitation sport injury specialist. It is the job of dreams: the one you want but somehow seems just out of reach.

I sit in the team bus, waiting for the vultures, as I call them, to get bored and move to another place. Before picking up my bags, I pull the hood on my jacket as far over my head as it will go and make my way to the changing rooms.

"That's her, the physiotherapist! Ask her. She'll know if Jack will be playing." I'm startled by a sudden flash that is followed by a flurry of dazzling lights. "Will Jack Cardal be returning to action tonight? Can we expect to see his name on the team sheet? How is his ankle? Are you concerned about him potentially reinjuring himself?"

Like a rabbit in the headlights, I'm initially stunned into silence; however, a warm hand pushes me into the entrance of the grounds, and the changing rooms are now in my sight. Looking up to shout my thanks to my rescuer, I catch a flash of grey eyes before he turns and walks away. Probably to admonish the press. He must be part of the security team.

The changing rooms are so much more than the name insinuates. It's a whole complex of facilities, built up over time. What once started as a room with benches for the players to change into their kits is now a collection of high-tech amenities. Showers, bathtubs, massage tables, relaxation spaces, consultation cubicles, treatment room, medical room, cryotherapy chambers, sauna, meeting room, dining facilities, and so much more. Although I spend most of my time in the consultation and treatment areas, I'm no stranger to the other spaces too.

The thing with working with a group of young men is that they have no shame and if I intrude on their space, I am likely to see things I may not be counting on. This is something I accepted a long time ago. I've seen ninety percent of them completely naked, and I've heard crude jokes and language that would make a sailor blush. When they realise I'm in the room, they do stop and most of the time apologise, but this is their area, and if I truly felt they were disrespecting me, I would say something. The fact that they treat me like they would treat their male staff makes me feel like they see me as one of the team. That is more important to me.

Most of the players take advantage of the facilities, either relaxing in a massage chair, or eating the high carbohydrate dishes on offer that help with their energy levels during the match. Each player has his own space in the changing room: a small amount of bench to sit on with their kit hanging above them and their boots already laced and polished in the basket under the seat. Their lockers are concealed into the walls. I walk through and smile at the new kits. Every year their kit sponsor, Projection, designs and releases a new kit. Redvale, as their name would suggest, play in red, and this year's kit is a deep red, almost burgundy, with a white collar. Each shirt is displayed with the player name and number facing out, and under the spotlights, they dazzle as though up on a billboard.

The team manager, or 'Gaffer' as the players call him, is a Spanish man called Juan Carlos Diaz. He has been the team manager for three years, and under his regime, the team have made great improvements. It is hoped that this year is 'Our Year'. And with Jack returning to full fitness, and the new players that have joined over the summer, we are all positive this is possible.

"Time to group together the team. Everyone in their places. I have a few last words before we go out there," the gaffer shouts out, and the rest of the staff round up the rest of the players using the other facilities. Once they are all in their places, the gaffer gives his parting speech. "The past doesn't matter. The future still hasn't been written. All that matters right now is the present. This game, this score. You want to win trophies this year? Then go out and win! Play as a team, support each other, and the rest will fall into place. You can do this. It's our year, I can feel it!"

The players all stand and huddle up to each other; they have some pre-match rituals that include chants and songs that motivate them and unite them together against the opposition. Some of the chants are ones that the fans themselves have made up. This show of unity and the positivity buzzing in the air excite me, and I suddenly feel enthusiastic about the impending game too.

Even though I push my ear defenders in before I follow the team out to the pitch, the roar of the crowd still startles me. The vibrations, stamping and floodlights still overwhelm me. I don't think I will ever become accustomed to the sound of sixty thousand fans celebrating the return of the football season!

## ~ Jack ~

Adrenaline pumps through my veins because my body and soul know they are home. Although I am starting on the bench, the buzz of the crowd when they see my name on the list of available substitutions is insurmountable. I could live off their excitement alone. I shake hands with the referee and other officials in the tunnel and face up to our opposition, Westcastle United. As they file up in the tunnel too, I size up their starting eleven players. They have a striker who has a lethal left foot, and their goalkeeper is a world cup winner. This isn't going to be an easy game.

The crowd, at least sixty thousand strong in the stadium alone, sings our club songs, and when I hear them singing 'Redvale are on fire', anticipation and excitement bubble up in my chest. I cannot wait to get out there, playing, scoring, winning. I've never wanted something more. The roar of the crowd as we walk out is electrifying; the whole team is motivated and energised to play to the best of its ability. I see a couple of flags and banners with my name emblazoned on them. Leila was right; the fans haven't forgotten me. They are eager for my return. How I wish I was in that starting side. However, I know I will get my chance. I am positive that Gaffer will call on me to play, especially seeing the crowd cheering for me.

Once I'm settled on the bench, I keep a watchful eye on Leila. I'm scared she might vanish before I can get my ankle strapped up. Once or twice, I look up at the executive box and notice my older brother, Nathan, watching me, watching the game. When Westcastle scores against us, he shakes his head and sips from his glass. It's probably bourbon; that's his drink of choice. His condemnation angers me, so when the first forty-five minutes are up and we return to the changing rooms for half time, I immediately ask Leila to strap up my ankle.

The gaffer looks like he could breathe fire at this moment in time, and when he is angry, his English becomes broken and incoherent. Occasionally, he will shout at us in Spanish, and only a few of the guys will understand what his actual words are, but we know exactly what he has said from their reactions alone. Every wince and gasp is palpable and tells us that our boss isn't happy.

"Jonesy, wake the fuck up, man. That goal would never have happened if you hadn't lost your man. We are losing at home — you need to lead your team. Jack?" Juan shouts so quickly I almost miss that he has moved on to me. "Warm up when we go out. Doc, I'm bringing him on for the last half hour. We need him." Leila nods to him and applies the last piece of adhesive strapping.

"How does that feel, Jack?" she asks as her fingers press the blue tape to my ankle.

"Incredible," I say simply, hoping to see a drop of desire before I leave the room again, but she throws my sock at me, not even taking me and my comment on.

"Good, see you out there. We'll get you warmed up on the side lines and wait for the substitution to be made. Good luck, Jack." Before I can help myself, I admire her ass as she walks away without a backward glance at me.

Leila is in fantastic shape. You can tell from her physique that she works out and takes care of herself. Most of the women I have been with are enhanced in some way; the norm seems to be at least Botox or lip fillers. However, Leila is completely natural. She has a nice round ass, well cut, long, brown hair, pretty blue eyes and lips that drive me to distraction. She'll never be all over the covers of the popular magazines but she has a certain 'girl-next-door' quality that I find intriguing.

"Jack?" My older brother, Nathan, walks into the changing room as I pull on my boots. "Is your ankle okay? Is the gaffer bringing you on as a substitute?" I roll my eyes at him.

"You know you shouldn't be back here," I tell him, hating that he is here interfering in my glory.

"It's my fucking club; I'll go wherever the fuck I want, Jack." Yeah, and don't I know about it.

"Forty percent of it is your club, Nathan. Just leave me to warm up, will you?" Nathan shakes his head at me. At twelve years older than me, he knows better than to start an argument.

"I'm just making sure your ankle is okay. No need to bite my head off. The fans are screaming for you," he shouts over his shoulder as he walks out.

"The Doc cleared me for the last twenty to thirty minutes. I'll be called on soon," I call to him before the door closes.

He turns back around, his face beaming with pride. "Good luck then, kid. I'll be watching you." I suppose, for thirty-four years of age, Nathan doesn't look too bad. He's taller and broader than me, but I am definitely more sculpted. We have the same eyes and face shape, but he is obviously more aged. His hair is turning silver at his temples. I suppose it helps that he is a billionaire.

After warming up with Leila, the gaffer calls me over and tells me the strategy he wants me to implement. After spotting a weak spot in Westcastle's defence, he thinks he's found a way through for me to score. After telling him I understand, he calls the official over.

"We would like to make a substitution, please." And, with these few words, my heart pumps with joy. I'm back. I'm finally back in action.

# FOOTBALL
(NOUN)

A game (sometimes referred to as soccer) played between two teams of eleven people, where each team tries to win by kicking a ball into the other team's goal.

(SOURCE: Cambridge Dictionary)

## CHAPTER 2

### ~ Jack ~

The crowd swells and roars when they see my number on the substitution board. I applaud my fellow team member as he leaves the pitch so I can substitute him, and we shake hands before I run out to take his place. The atmosphere is thumping, humming with excitement and nerves, and my body drinks it all up, bathing in it, loving every millisecond of this moment that might never have happened if my injury had been worse. Signalling to Jonesy so he understands the gaffer's change in tactics, it doesn't take more than a couple of minutes for the pace of the game to change. The fans buzz off the energy my substitution has brought to the game, and belief, almost tangible, emanates from them like never before.

One of the rights of passage for a footballer signed to Redvale is the assignment of a nickname from the fans and a song that the fans make up, usually adapted from popular chart songs. My nickname, very imaginatively, derives from one of the first newspaper articles written about me when I signed to Redvale. 'Jack The Lad' they called me on account of my blatant womanising and penchant for extracurriculars such as threesomes, orgies, and sex clubs. I had to try it all. My song is called "Jack's our Lad", and I can't help but feel like the world of football is welcoming me back as "Jack's our Lad" rings from all four stands of fans.

My opportunity to reward the fans for not giving up hope on me comes roughly seven minutes after I came on the pitch. Taking advantage of that weak spot the gaffer highlighted for me, I manage to get around the defenders. As the ball leaves my foot, I already know in my gut that it's a goal. However, with the recent introduction of Video Assistant Referees, I wait to celebrate.

While everyone else waits with bated breath, looking at the screens dotted around the stadium and watching the referee like a hawk, I accept a bottle of water from one of our support team, trying to keep my cool. In this moment, three things flash through my head. The first is that the gaffer is a genius. A mad, fucking genius! The second is that, for a period of time, I thought I might never get back to full fitness, and look at me, seven minutes after I am brought on, I have scored. The third and final coherent thought is that I have Leila to thank for making this a possibility. Sanity and reason desert me as the referee blows his whistle and points indicating it is a goal, but instead of celebrating with my teammates, I run all the way back to the halfway line, right in front of the team benches. I point at Leila, who looks back at me shocked and embarrassed, and mouth to her, "That was for you. Thank you."

The crowd lap it up, and as I continue to play football, I see from the corner of my eye that the press are frantically trying to get a photo and information from Leila. If I have done this right, Leila will be known to everyone by tomorrow morning. It's a tabloid's wet dream. Brands and power couples have been built on less than this.

Full time approaches and I'm desperate for another goal; one more will ensure we get the win. Westcastle is throwing everything at us. They have the goalie and at least six other players defending. However, that little sweet spot presents itself again at eighty-nine minutes, just one minute from full time. This time, there is no hesitation. I hit the ball with all my strength, instinctively aiming for the top left corner, and bask in the screams of joy all around when the ball hits the back of the net. My teammates all crowd around me, cheering and jumping like we've won the world cup, not just the first game of the season. When I make my way back to the semi-circle for the final restart of the game, I glance over to see if Leila is courting the press. However, she isn't there. Scowling, I wish for the next couple of minutes of added time to pass quickly so I can find out where she is and why she left.

The full time whistle blows, and while I join in the initial celebration, I don't waste time clapping fans or giving interviews. I want to know where Leila has gone. The gaffer collars me as I am about to walk down the tunnel. "Jacky, come on, we must celebrate with the fans," he instructs me as he wraps an arm around my shoulder and redirects me back over to my teammates.

"Where did the Doc go?" I ask him. There is no point in trying to hide from the gaffer that I'm interested in her. "I need to ask her something."

"She has gone home; the photographers and reporters annoyed her. She was very embarrassed," he tells me in his thick accent, before he realises this might be something relating to my injury. "Is your ankle sore? Do you need the physio?" he asks me with concern, looking at my foot and legs to observe any obvious signs of injury or pain.

"No. My ankle is feeling good," I add quickly. Leila's gone home because she's pissed off. I officially do not get it. I don't understand her! "Was she annoyed that the press wanted to take her picture?" I ask him incredulously.

The gaffer laughs. "You are in big trouble, Jack. The Doc - ella esta enojada!" he says, chuckling as he jogs the final stretch to the rest of the team.

Well, what the fuck does that mean? I don't have a chance to dissect what the gaffer has said as the press pounce on me like a swarm of locusts, all wanting a piece of the action.

"Jack, over here: Ollie Wright, Redvale Gazette. Tell us: how does it feel to be back after such a long absence? How long have you been romantically involved with the club injury specialist? Tell us all about her, Jack. Does it pose any issues of favouritism or are the rest of the team cool with it?"

"Jack? Are your 'ladding' days over now? What did you say to your physio when you scored? Did you plan it before you did it?"

The questions, mostly around Leila and our possible relationship, all pile in, firing at me from all angles. "Look, you've got the wrong idea. I was just thanking her for helping me–me–" But having formed their own, more favourable, story, they don't listen, brushing me off with a wink and insinuating that I am covering up. I just hope this doesn't affect my chances of picking up a girl tonight. There is only one remedy for the come down of such a high like tonight. Getting laid! And seeing as Leila has abandoned me after I made that nice gesture to her, I'll need to look elsewhere to get my rocks off.

"Jack, will you spare a quick word with Sports News Channel before you leave?" Knowing this is the ultimate in sports reporting, I accept. Leila may not appreciate the importance of media in the game, but I do. It would be a crime to pass up such an incredible opportunity!

"Yes, of course. I always have time for SNC," I tell them, flashing my most charming smile. Oh, how I love my life!

## ~ Leila ~

As the flashes of the press continue to burn my retinas, I tell the gaffer that I am leaving early. I cannot stand the thought of trying to leave the match and my every move being under scrutiny. The gaffer thanks me and tells me the rest of the team have everything under control. I grab my bags, throw on some oversized sunglasses and go to get dressed for my evening out with my friends. It's the only way to get away from the grounds and as far away from Jack Cardal as possible until I cool off. I have never felt as annoyed as I am right now. I dress as quickly as possible into my slinky black dress and apply some makeup while I wait for my cab to arrive.

"Where are you going?" the driver asks me.

"Sully's place, please," I tell him. While we drive, I text my girlfriends Claire and Louise, and they tell me they are in our usual booth waiting for me.

The bar is loud and noisy, and it smells overpoweringly of booze and disinfectant. It's a small, underground place that my friends and I visit every time we hit the town. It's not an extravagant place, but it's comfortable. They sell drinks we like and play music we enjoy, and we can dance until we wear holes into the soles of our high-heeled shoes.

However, this evening, I am in no mood to dance and enjoy myself. I am raging! How dare Jack draw attention to me like that. He might enjoy being the centre of attention, but I don't! I never have. So while I find it sweet that he wanted to thank me, the fact that he felt the need to do it in such a public manner has irritated me.

After telling Claire and Louise what happened, I'm disappointed that they don't share the same indignation that I have about it.

"I can't believe you are complaining about this, Leila!" my friend Claire tells me. I met Claire at the gym I used to work out at when I first moved to Redvale. She is a female bodybuilder and model with a perma-tan and bleach blonde hair. Despite being a strong independent female, she tells me frequently that she would love to meet a rich footballer and settle down. "He's obviously interested in you and is showing the world too. You should go to dinner with him. This could be it, your path to an easy life of fame and fortune."

Louise rolls her bright green eyes at Claire dramatically. "You are so crass, Claire. You know Leila isn't interested in mixing business with pleasure. Though, Claire does have a point, Ley. You should at least give him a chance." She smiles when I begin to object to her suggestion. "Ley, what if he is 'The One', but you are too stubborn to give him a chance?" Louise, who I met through Claire, is usually the more rational of the two, but obviously sanity has left the building!

"He isn't 'The One', Louise. He's an arrogant playboy who is used to getting everything he wants. Well, he'll have to look elsewhere; I am not interested in the likes of Jack Cardal." And the truth is, I find Jack too young, emotionally and mentally immature, and we don't seem to have a lot in common. Going out with him for dinner seems like a waste of both of our time. I would like to meet someone; I just know in my gut that it isn't Jack.

"Can you say with one hundred percent certainty that he isn't 'The One'?" Louise asks me. She sips delicately at her wine before placing it back onto the round table we are sharing, staring at me with those serious green eyes. Before I can make my argument, she adds, "If there is even a one percent chance he could be 'The One' but you just haven't realised it yet, don't you owe it to yourself to find out."

Could I be wrong? Should I at least give Jack a chance? He is attractive and can be incredibly sweet at times. I just don't know if I feel *that pull*. You know what I mean, right? That totally indescribable feeling of meeting someone and knowing almost instantly that you have a connection. Butterflies in the tummy, incessant thoughts of that person, and a desire to spend every moment with them. I've been close to that feeling on a couple of occasions, but obviously, it wasn't the whole package because the relationships didn't work out. Is it a feeling that can grow over time? Am I being too dismissive of someone who could have genuine feelings for me and could make me really happy?

"You don't have to sleep with him. It's just dinner. You could even pay if it makes you feel better about it. Just promise us you won't just rule it out." I groan as I make my promise. There is no way I'm going on any sort of date with Jack until he apologises for making a public spectacle of me.

"If he apologises for the circus he created and promises to not do it ever again… maybe I'll consider dinner." Even as I say the words, it doesn't fill me with any building excitement or anticipation. As a matter of fact, a small part of me believes that he will not apologise and I'll be let off the hook anyway. There is nothing for me to be concerned about.

"And if it doesn't work out, you could always send him in my direction. Tell him I'll definitely put out for steak and chips," Claire adds with a smirk and a raised eyebrow. Louise and I laugh at her even though we both understand she is speaking the complete truth. "I would make that boy a man and then let him ruin me."

"Claire!" I squeal at her. The thought of her and Jack defiling each other is too much!

"Hey, you can afford to be picky. I haven't been laid since we went to that festival in June. I'm gagging for it," she confides with big, brown, puppy dog eyes.

Sometimes I wonder who is the crudest: the footballers I work with or my friends when they are horny!

"Come on, let's dance," Louise says as she drains her wine glass. As she stands, her long, bright red hair cascades down her back in luxurious curls. In her burgundy catsuit, she has no shortage of admirers. She is stunningly beautiful and graceful. "My feet are itching; I just want to dance with my girls."

Laughing, I stand too and drain my first glass of wine. "I'm ready. It's what we came for." Tonight, I am dancing. Tomorrow is soon enough to worry about Jack Cardal.

---

As I wake up at 6.30 A.M., everything that happened last night continues to run through my mind. Flashes of Jack grinning as he points to me. The heat of sixty thousand faces bearing down on me, attempting to look at the woman their boy wonder has drawn attention to. Then the constant snapping and flickering of cameras. All I want to do is cringe about it.

Then I try to consider all the things my girlfriends said. They sincerely believe I should give Jack a chance and that I'm being too harsh or picky. With all the damning thoughts cluttering my mind, I have no option but to get up out of my bed; there will be no lie in today, even if it is my first day off in ten.

After a quick shower, I tug on my running gear. Maybe pounding the pavement will make things clearer. With my phone strapped to my arm and my earphones blasting out my favourite tunes, I pick up my bottle of water and open my front door.

Blinding lights, and the constant click of cameras that sound just like the little crickets that live in the trees in hotter climates. I slam my door closed again and go to look from my upstairs window. The paparazzi line the pavement outside my house. Rage flares up inside me once more at the audacity of them and the stupid idiot who caused all this frenzy.

I quickly call into work, following the guidance that is continually given to us all from human resources.

A sleepy voice answers the call. "Martin Baker," he says, and if I didn't recognise his name, I probably would've just slammed down the phone.

"Hi, this is Leila Monrose. I'm the injury specialist at–"

However, Martin gruffly interrupts me. "Yeah, yeah. I know who you are; the phones have been ringing off the hook about you. It would be easier if you had told us you are in an intimate relationship with Jack first, you know?" He admonishes me, causing my cheeks to pinken under his chastisement.

"I'm not!" I squeak, realising how feeble my protestation is in light of Jack's display last night. God, I could kick him in the balls right now. "I have a bunch of reporters and photographers camped outside my house and I don't know what to do!"

"Confirm your address, and I'll send security and a lawyer as soon as possible. Do not speak to them or engage with them. Have you informed Jack? Is Jack with you?"

"No, I haven't told Jack. We aren't together! And he most definitely isn't here with me either. We are not together."

"Well play dead, and they'll get bored and leave you alone. Once they realise Jack isn't there, they'll leave you alone. Just don't let them get any photographs of you." Well, it's too late for that.

"They already did. I was going for my morning run; I didn't know they were there." I hear Martin's groan down the phone and the squeak of what I think must be his bed or sofa at least.

"I'll let the board know. We might have to move you somewhere else until this dies down." Damn Jack Cardal, the big, stupid airhead!

"Move me where? This is my home!" I shout down the phone, incredulous that my life is taking on this whole new agenda.

"Calm down, princess. It's just until this all dies down. You'll be living in luxury in some swanky house, no doubt. Don't sweat it. Just pack a bag for the next week or so, and security will come and get you soon." He hangs up without saying goodbye. The asshole.

Pulling out a suitcase from my wardrobe, I consider my plans for the next week. We have a mid-week game in France, so I will need different clothes for that. My work clothes, both treatment and game ones. My work out clothes, underwear, pjs, casual clothes, all my shoes. One case isn't going to be enough.

Zipping up the first case, I carry it downstairs, straining as I reach the bottom. Then I run back up the stairs, throw the rest of my belongings into the second slightly smaller case, and add it to the first one in the hallway.

Then I pick up a large, oversized handbag and put in my laptop and charger, my kindle, my phone and charger, my makeup and toothbrush, and a collage photograph.

Within minutes of making my call to Martin, there is more commotion outside, and I hear a rather stern man informing the paparazzi that this is private property and to leave. I watch from the window as the vultures grudgingly move onto the public pathway, still waiting to get a photograph of me.

Once they've all moved off my property, the doorbell rings, and when I open my door, the man I presume to be the lawyer stands at the front gate, ensuring no one attempts to come closer. Two huge men stand at my front door, dressed in black suits that stretch across their enormous shoulders and chests.

"Ma'am, we are here to move you to safety. Where are your bags?" the fair-haired guy asks. His straight to business, no nonsense attitude reassures me.

Unable to speak, I point to my cases, which he picks up with ease and takes them out the front door.

The second guy, almost bald, asks for my keys and tells me he will be adding additional security measures. "The name is Jameson," he tells me as I hand over my keys. "And my colleague is Damon. We will be looking after you until this dies down, Ms Monrose."

Damon returns as Jameson is securing my house. My mind whirls in panic at how quickly everything is changing. "Do you want to cover your head or face?

The car is ready for you, but the paps aren't leaving." Pulling up my hood over my head and as far down over my face as I can, I push my sunglasses on.

"Okay, we are ready, let's go," Jameson adds as he returns to the room. Sandwiched between the two man mountains, with one in front of me and one behind, I step out of my safe haven, and almost immediately, the onslaught begins.

"When did your relationship with Jack begin?" "What are your long term plans?" "Will you continue to work at the club?" "What do you think of the photographs of him emerging from a nightclub with another woman last night?"

Are they actually kidding me? I literally woke up thirty minutes ago. Right now, Jack Cardal wants to stay as far away from me as possible because I want to seriously hurt him for sending my life into an uncontrolled spiral.

## Chapter 3

### ~ Nathan ~

Usually, on a Sunday, I wake up early, work out, have brunch and work on one of my cars. Sunday is my one day of self-indulgence. My one day when I don't usually allow work to interfere. However, following on from Redvale's victory last night, my phone has been ringing off the hook. Goddamn that younger brother of mine. How come *he* gets laid, and *I* get all the aggravation? That boy could cause trouble in an empty room.

The fact that his exploits now involve an employee of the club is cause for concern. Not only could their relationship reflect on the reputation of the club, but the ethical doctrine of therapists brings moral and legal issues into play.

We normally don't have to deal with these sorts of issues that often but trust my brother to find a way. At twenty-two years old, twelve years my junior, I have hoped and prayed that Jack would have grown up by now, but if anything, he is more immature than he has ever been.

Technically, we are half siblings. Jack's mother, my father's third wife, died when Jack was a baby. Our father passed away when Jack was still a boy, making him an orphan, and if I'd listened to everyone around me, he would have been passed off to some distant relative, or a boarding school. But not while I had air in my lungs and a multi-million-pound business to support us. Granted, I have leaned on friends and my staff more than I should have along the way, but he is my kid brother, and I will never leave him no matter how much he annoys the shit out of me.

Now, it's Monday and the shit storm continues to brew. Jack is painted as a fun boy who is dipping his wick in every candle he can while Leila has been built as some pathetic woman, broken hearted at being cheated on by a man she should know better than to attempt to tame.

Sitting behind my desk in my office, while I waste my time waiting for my wayward brother to show up and explain himself, anger at his attitude and lack of regard for anyone but himself simmers inside me. This is getting beyond a joke. It's time for me to finally teach Jack a lesson. I simply need to figure out a way to do it.

"What are the headlines this morning?" I ask our public relations officer, Kym, as she walks into my office. "And what can we do to calm them down?" I add.

"It's not looking great. Jack's really outdone himself. I feel bad for the Doc; she'll be so humiliated. I mean, there is no evidence of a relationship between them, but he dragged her into this and made her look stupid." She throws down a pile of newspapers. Jack has made the front page on several of them. The worst of the speculation is online. The technological advances my own company contributed to now bite me on the ass. All the gossip channels and all platforms of social media spew a plethora of stories, memes and discussions around Jack and his assumed infidelity.

Jack stumbling out of a nightclub with two women, Jack opening the door to another woman with just a towel around his waist, not to mention more than a few 'kiss and tell' stories from his past conquests. Added to the debauchery is the photograph of the pretty brunette with her hair tied back and her running gear on, her skin glowing and clear and her eyes bright and sparkling. How the fuck has Jack managed to get her to go out with him? I will never understand women and how their minds work.

"What has Ms Monrose said about it all? I believe she is staying in my apartment on the docks?" For some unfathomable reason, the woman intrigues me. She's beautiful, intelligent and successful. She doesn't strike me as the type of person who would hang around assholes like Jack in the pursuit of fame and fortune. But what the hell do I know?

"She is fuming about Jack. She maintains that she has never been involved with your brother and that he has made a laughingstock out of her. She is not wrong." I wait for Kym to add something else, but she holds back.

"So, what does she want? How can I fix this?" She will obviously lose her job; her integrity has been brought into question, and although I feel bad for her, there is nothing else I can do. "Money? A reference? What can I do to make this more palatable for her."

Kym looks up at me from the seat facing mine. "All she wants is to get back to work. Her job means everything to her. It's going to crush her if you let her go. This isn't something you can throw money at, sir. She isn't that type of woman."

Fucking Jack!

"I'll go and speak to her myself and explain why she cannot continue to work with us. If she's telling the truth, then it's unfortunate, but I don't have the power to change the public's perception or the media's narrative on what has or hasn't happened."

"There are other clubs interested in her; she'll have no issue getting another job," Kym adds as I stand to leave. The way she raises her eyebrow at me tells me without words that she thinks that information is significant.

"She's that good?" I ask as I pull on my jacket.

"Yes, Mr Cardal. One of the best, if not the best, sports injury specialists in the country. She'll be a hard act to follow. I'm going out on a limb here, but it doesn't set a good precedent releasing one of the only female members of staff. The media will have a field day with that too."

"So, what do you suggest I do?" I stare at her, but Kym isn't intimidated by me. She worked with my father for years and is excellent at her job.

"Talk to her. Let me come with you to see if we can salvage something. Leila is a sweetheart, and it doesn't sit right with me to dismiss her if she sincerely hasn't done anything wrong." Deep down I know she is right; however, I know better than to let personal feelings interfere with business negotiations. And that is exactly what this is.

"Do you sincerely believe she isn't involved with Jack?" I put to Kym one last time.

"There were no connections in their personal contacts, no messages or phone calls, no sightings of them together outside of work. She says he asked her out when she cleared him and she said no. She isn't interested in him in anything but a professional manner." That does sound as though she isn't involved with him.

"Okay, let's go and talk to Ms Monrose. Jack obviously isn't coming. I will have to deal with him later."

## ~ Leila ~

Since I was lifted from my life over twenty-eight hours ago, I have been holed up in this apartment with no explanations. I am going to throttle Jack when I see him. I cannot believe what his actions have caused.

On our way here to the docklands, my minders, Jameson and Damon, explained that my phone would be tracked, so after extracting the numbers I would need, namely my mother, work, Claire and Louise, my phone was switched off, and they provided me with a brand-new iPhone. I've never felt more out of my depth. Jameson and Damon take turns to stay with me, never leaving me alone, and whilst I appreciate their support, I also need some space to clear my head.

It comes as a shock when I discover that my hiding destination is The Redvale Docklands. The docklands were once derelict and disused, left to ruin once the import and export industry developed, leaving no need for ports. However, a decade or so ago, a massive regeneration program brought the area back to life. Now, it is a tourist attraction, and an affluent and influential area full of prestige and trendy assets such as an arena, shopping centre, museums, fine dining restaurants and bars. This is where you'll find the celebrities and sports stars local to or visiting Redvale. The apartment itself is in a block that was once an old tobacco factory. Though old, it has been sympathetically restored with all the original features still in place. It may be an old factory but they sure as hell don't make buildings like this anymore. With its unique architectural flair and fittings from when it was first built, this is one special building. The apartment itself is tastefully decorated, incorporating the original features with a timeless elegance. It's smaller than my house, and yet it's probably worth ten times the amount.

I could be comfortable enough in this apartment, but with my whole career and private life under scrutiny, I haven't felt able to relax and enjoy my time here.

Roughly four hours ago, I was due to start work back at the training ground, but Jameson said I have to stay away for now.

"When can I go home? When can I go back to work?" I ask him impatiently. The men are polite but distant, and with a lack of other human contact, they are suffering the brunt of my frustrations.

"I'm sorry, Ms Monrose. Our orders are to keep you safe here until further notice," he replies stoically. I can almost see a tinge of pity in his eyes.

"Can I at least go for a walk? Go and get some fresh air and stretch my legs—"However, before I've even finished the sentence, Jameson shakes his head at me.

"You'll be spotted. The paps will be here before you know it, and then you'll have to move again. Just be patient, and I'm sure you'll get some answers by this evening," he adds bluntly, knocking my request back flat out without even thinking about it. In frustration, I storm away and slam the door to the bedroom I am staying in. I miss my life. My boring, predictable life that is mine to do as I please.

Throwing myself on the unmade bed, I cover my mouth with the pillow before letting out a scream of disappointment. This cannot be happening, but it is.

Allowing myself a couple of minutes to calm down, I take control of the situation. I make up the bed and adapt my morning workout so I can do it in the bedroom. I'm about halfway through when a light tap on my door interrupts me.

"Come in."

Damon pokes his head through the small gap he makes when he opens the door. "I'm just letting you know that Mr Cardal is on his way, and he would like to speak to you."

As surprised as I am that Jack has the audacity to come here after what he has done, I am also thrilled that I will get some answers and will get to tell him exactly what I think of his behaviour. "Thank you, Damon. I do appreciate what you and Jameson are doing. Tell Jameson that I'm sorry for freaking out. I just feel trapped and I'm worried about my job."

"That's understandable; we civilians don't live in 'their world', and you've been thrust into it. Hopefully, Mr Cardal will straighten this all out for you." Thanking him as he closes the door, I pack up all my stuff in the hope that Jack sorts this out and I can go home and resume my normal life.

However, a mere twenty minutes later, I get the shock of my life when a man and woman arrive. Looking at Damon, I hope he will take mercy on me, but when he doesn't, I say, "Damon? I thought you said Jack was coming to sort this all out."

The older woman, the handsome man and my two guards all look at me like I'm an alien. The handsome man steps forward. Dark hair, a chiselled jaw, brooding grey eyes that I want to get lost in. "I think you may have misunderstood. I'm Nathan Cardal. I'm the man you've been waiting for."

The double entendre isn't lost on me. Nathan Cardal is a fine specimen of a man. In his thirties, established in his career, and as hot as the day is long. I've been waiting my whole life for a man like him alright. He is also the biggest shareholder in the club making him... my boss? And Jack's older brother.

"Mr Cardal, I can only apologise. I thought Damon was referring to Jack, seeing as he started all this mess," I explain as quickly as I can, flustered and embarrassed. I'm acting like a hot mess. It begins to dawn on me that this is a bigger deal than even I knew it was. If one of the club owners is here, this isn't good. This is not good at all, and I tremble inside, my stomach spinning like a washing machine as I realise I could actually be losing my job.

"It's been a tough time for you. An apology isn't necessary. I would like to talk to you about what has happened. Jameson, take Kym and Damon for a coffee. I'll call you when I'm done here." Despite my concerns, my body defies me by reacting to Nathan Cardal's deep tone. I bet he could make anything sound sexy. I shiver in reaction to my thoughts and quickly try to cover it up but not quick enough. Nathan Cardal eyes me suspiciously. "Are you cold, Ms Monrose?"

"Yes!" I blurt out, despite the August sunshine and evident heat. "It must have been a breeze taking me by surprise." I bluster, making a complete ass of myself. Nathan smiles back at me, amusement dancing in his eyes. Beneath that steely persona is a man who likes to have fun. I can tell from his reactions to mine.

As the others file out, the older lady throws a stare at Nathan before she leaves. I can't help wondering what is behind that warning.

"Firstly, I wanted to apologise for not coming to see you sooner, Ms Monrose. I want to hear your side of things. Are you in a relationship with my brother?"

## ~ Nathan ~

The photos that have been splashed all over the place don't do her justice. The grainy, somewhat pixelated images failed to capture her beauty. There were decent shots of her, but none have quite captured her glowing skin, the mischief in her eyes and the grace she has when she moves. Having only seen her on a screen and in a photograph, I never knew there was such a beauty right under my nose.

Now that I have met her, an overwhelming need to help her takes over inside me. My father used to call me "the champion of the beaten and damned", and while I personally think that is drastic, something about Leila's 'damsel in distress' plight sings to my heart. I want to fix this for her. I could strangle Jack right now!

"I am NOT, never have been, and never ever will be associated with Jack in any way apart from our patient-client way. We aren't even friends, not really. He is a patient, that is all." Although the passion is evident in her voice, I can tell from her eyes that she is telling me the truth. The outrage, the anger, and the indignation are all genuine as each emotion flashes through her eyes. She is no actress, but maybe if she had to be, she could put on a stellar performance if she realised how telling her eyes are.

"So, why are the press running with this story? What did Jack say to you after he scored?" I ask her. I just want to understand, but already, I can see her shoulders rising defensively and she uses her hands more to express herself as she speaks.

"I don't know why! I don't understand how it all works. I have no interest in the press or in Jack. And, as for what he said, I think he mouthed 'that was for you, thank you!' But he had no reason to thank me, and I didn't know he was going to do it." Her voice rises an octave, and in a bid to soothe her, I place my hand on her arm. She looks startled when I do. "You do believe me, don't you?"

"Yes. Kym tells me Jack asked you out before the match. Can you tell me why you said no?" I add in a lower, soothing voice, enjoying the way Leila reacts to my voice. Her skin puckers involuntarily. This sort of reaction cannot be denied or faked. She is wonderful.

"I'm not interested in him in that way; he's far too young and immature. We have nothing in common. His lifestyle outside of the game doesn't appeal to me." While her stance is unusual, I can see she is genuine. She doesn't want to ride someone's coattails to be a celebrity. "It seemed pointless wasting both our time when I already knew I thought of him as more of an annoying younger brother than a potential lover."

"Oh, he's annoying alright. I'm sorry that his actions, no matter how well intended, have turned your world upside down, Ms Monrose." Despite her woes, she smiles at me; a smile that lights up her whole face.

"Please, call me Leila," she tells me, and I smile at us becoming more acquainted. Maybe that will help soften the suggestion I'm about to make to her.

"Then I'd like for you to call me Nathan. Actually, I'd prefer it if you called me Nate." Her pupils dilate as I lean in and whisper to her. "This is the position I find myself in, Leila. The press believe you're in a relationship with Jack, and while they continue to believe that, your position at the club is untenable." She tries to interrupt me with her protestations about how she's done no wrong, and I understand it. She is set to lose her career over a crumb of information that has been blown out of all proportions. "Just hear me out. The press don't care if their narrative is wrong; they will continue to run this story until a better one comes along." Her shoulders slump, and she leans forward, resting her head in her hands. "That is unless we give them another story, a better one."

Her head snaps up, her face full of determination. "What kind of story?" she asks, her voice still thick with emotion.

"I think we need to make a simple substitution. One brother for another. I propose that we pretend we are an item, that we are engaged, for the rest of the season, and then we will amicably break up but remain friends at the end of the season." Her eyes bulge out at my suggestion. She stands up and paces, muttering to herself the whole time.

"Will I get to keep my job?" she enquires first.

"Yes, I see no reason why not."

"How? Why is it okay to be involved with you and not with Jack?" she adds, squinting inquisitorially, and to be fair, it's a great question.

"I'm not your patient; Jack is and will potentially be again." I think I've won her over when some of the tension leaves her face.

"What do you get out of this?"

There are many ways I could answer this. I get to pose with a beautiful, intelligent woman on my arm. I get to experience some sort of domestic bliss for a short while, even if it is fake. Or I could be brutally honest and tell her that I find her attractive and I'm not ready to let her go just yet. However, there is another truth that I think will be more palatable for us both. "Jack needs to be taught a lesson, and this seems like the best way to do that, plus you'll get to keep your job."

"A simple substitution. So we tell the press they have it wrong?"

I shake my head at her. "No, we show them. Showing is always better than telling. We will draw up a contract, and once you move in with me, we will not speak of a contract or arrangement again. We will live as an engaged couple."

"A contract?" she whispers.

"Yes. A contract. We will need to start with a non-disclosure agreement. But then we will need to agree on a set of terms about our Substitution. We have to both agree to our Substitution Clause," I add. I like the sound of that. The main clauses in our contract will centre around me substituting Jack as Leila's significant other in a bid to save her job and teach my wayward brother a lesson.

Casually she leans towards me. "Okay, when can we start?"

"Right now."

Leila looks at me with wide eyes. "Seriously? Are we going to do this?" she asks as she wrings her hands anxiously. "What about the contract?" she adds as I pull out my phone and call Kym.

"I need an NDA for Leila. Bring it back to the apartment alone and be ready to take notes for our contract. Tell the boys, I'll take it from here," I murmur down the phone, watching my new fiancée as she gulps and trembles. I end the call and instinctively go to her, knowing I have just sprung this on her and wanting to ensure she is really okay with doing this.

"Talk to me, darlin'. Have you changed your mind?" She shakes her head at me vehemently. "Then why are you shaking?" I ask her with concern.

"I'm so relieved I'm not going to lose my job. This is all unexpected and a bit crazy," she answers honestly, ending with a small laugh. With tension leaving her body, she seems younger, more carefree and even more irresistible. As my thoughts turn more carnal, I know I'm going to have to be careful. This woman, this enigma of a woman, could steal my heart if I don't protect it. "So, you want me to move in with you? How is this going to work?"

Without waiting for Kym, I help myself to a bottle of water from the fridge and toss one to Leila too. "Yes, I would like you to move into my house today. I will collect your belongings from your home for you, and once we leave this apartment, there will be no mention of this contract. You are my fiancée, we are engaged, and we are deeply in love." I think I've made my position clear, but Leila is still full of questions.

"Will we share a bedroom?" she whispers. Sincerely, I want to grin. We will be sharing a fucking bed; that is what engaged couples do, right? "Listen, I really appreciate your help, but I-I can't just have sex with some random guy. I can't do this." As she talks, she walks backwards away from me; that's how passionately she feels about this. Well, hell no! I've come this far, there is no way I can let go of her now.

"Leila, chill out, will you? Sex will never be part of our contract. If we fuck, it will be because we both want to. We will be sleeping in the same bed, in the same bedroom. There is only going to be sex involved if that is what we both want. Got it?" She nods to me, her cheeks flushed with colour once more. "There will be public hand holding and kissing, though. Sorry! We have to make this convincing after all."

She laughs this time. "I think I can live with that, Nate. So, tell me, what is this plan of yours?"

"The press will be tipped off that you have been spotted in a restaurant at the docklands with a man. We will have our first official outing as a couple before returning to our home. Tomorrow the press will swarm to our home and we will tell them that they had the story all wrong and that you couldn't say anything because of our non-disclosure agreement."

"And then we will live as an engaged couple for the rest of the season? How will we *show* that?" she enquires. I hadn't thought about it beyond the next couple of days, but now that she's raised such a valid point, I must consider this.

"How about one dinner date a week, plus one mundane activity a week such as shopping, visiting family or friends together, going on a hike or testing out a new car? We will go on holiday and... maybe we could get a dog." A cute desire fills her eyes once more when I mention a dog, but it quickly dissipates.

"I'd love a dog, but I don't think I'll be able to leave it behind at the end of the season. It would break my heart." Her sense of awareness leaves me in awe. I wonder if it's a natural instinct for her to think about the consequences of her actions or if that has been bred from something else. I'm not going to lie, the fact that leaving a dog will break her heart but leaving me doesn't, chafes so badly, but my own ego is pushed aside to assure Leila.

"Then you can keep the dog. It can be one of the clauses." Her face lights up once more.

"Really?" she asks, and when I nod, she almost knocks me over as she hugs me in thanks. "Thank you, Nate. I've wanted a dog for so long. Thank you." Her humble gratitude and the ease at which she feels completely at home in my arms leaves me stunned. "Sorry, I got carried away," she adds as her face burns bright red and she backs away from me.

"Hey, come back here. This is good practice; we need to look genuine, and I'm glad you felt comfortable enough with me to hug me." I pull her back to me, her cheek pressed against my chest, and I am man enough to admit I like this a whole lot more than I ever thought or intended to. "I'll get you a ring – I'll have to ask your father's permission–"

"My dad's dead. You can ask my mom, though." Her abrupt answer startles me. I really don't know much about Leila. If we are going to pose as an engaged couple, we need to rectify that.

"How about a quickfire round of questions so we can learn more about each other?" I ask her as I stroke her arm. It's amazing how quickly we have relaxed in each other's company. I don't think this has ever happened to me before.

"Dad is dead, mom is alive. Only child. Mom remarried about four years ago, when I was at university. My best friends are Claire and Louise. I have an allergy to bees and carry an epi-pen. My favourite fruit is strawberry. Once a month I become a chocoholic. I love my job and I want a dog."

Following her lead, I try to follow the questions she answered with my own answers. "Dad's dead, my mother is alive. I have two half brothers, Jack and Sam. Jack lives with me. My mom and stepdad live in Spain with my stepbrother Sam. I have two close friends, Otis and Hugo, but due to work commitments, we don't see each other that much anymore. I don't have any allergies, and I'm terrified of needles. My favourite fruit is also strawberry. Once a month I intend on bringing my fiancée chocolate so I stay in her good books. I also love my job, and I like dogs, and I'm happy to share one for a season."

She giggles at my final answer, and I tickle her to make her giggle even more. "That wasn't so bad, Nate. I think we can do this," she says between little laughs.

"Yeah, I think so, too!" I reply, as I notice someone in black shoes standing at the door.

"My, my, my! Don't we look cosy!"

## CHAPTER 4

### ~ Leila ~

It would be an out and out lie to suggest that I am a shrinking violet, or still as pure as the day I was born; however, I have never felt as comfortable with another man as I do with Nate. He is sexy but also reassuring and powerful, and yet he doesn't use that against me. It shocks me to admit that I feel safer with him than I've ever felt with anyone. That's the stuff of fairy tales, right?

When he suggested the Substitution, I initially thought he must be mad, but as he spoke to me, my body responding to his words and nearness, something just felt right about the whole situation. I know this isn't real, but the fact that he would go to so much trouble to ensure my career won't be taken away from me showed me the heart of Nate Cardal. He is a good and decent man, and if I'm not careful, I could end up falling for him for real. The thought of leaving a dog behind is bad enough. I must remain on guard so I don't end up falling in love with a man that isn't truly mine.

A deep female voice catches me off guard, and with my arm wrapped around Nate and him tickling me, we do appear to be closer and a lot more intimate than two people who met thirty minutes ago.

"Kym! Good, you are here. Leila, Kym is my personal advisor on Public Relations and a fully trained and qualified lawyer. She will help us with our contract."

I smile meekly at the other woman, who must be in her fifties. "Kym, I'm getting married. Well– *engaged*. I will take the place of Jack in the stories and show the press they have the wrong idea. We've agreed on a season-long arrangement and Leila gets to keep the dog at the end."

"There's going to be a dog, sir?" she asks him with amusement in her eyes.

"It was either a dog or a baby, Kym. A baby isn't an option in our timeframe and future plans," Nate informs her nonchalantly. "I'm going to Leila's house to get her stuff. I need you to prep her and have the agreement printed and signed for when I return. Leila, I'll call you when I'm at your house; tell me what you need so you don't have to go back for a few weeks."

I hand him my keys and blush when he winks at me before he leaves. "Well, I've got to say, I don't think I've ever seen him as smitten as he is with you," Kym remarks. There is something warm about her manner that makes me feel at ease. "Shall we have a cup of tea and get to work?" she asks, and although I don't relish the thought of spending the afternoon thrashing out a legal contract, the fact that my job is now safe thanks to that contract rejuvenates me.

"I can make the tea while you set up. How long have you known Nate?" I ask the older woman as a means of starting a narrative between us.

"Since he was a boy. I worked for his father for years."

Once I have the teapot, milk, sugar, teaspoons and teacups, I place them nicely on the round, marble dining table that has sat unused all the time I've been here. Then I go back to the open plan kitchen in search of some biscuits that I am certain I saw Jameson and Damon eating.

"This all looks divine. Thank you. Now, are there any financial agreements you've previously agreed with Mr Cardal, or any that you want him to consider?"

I'm taken aback by the question. I don't want his money. I have a job and my own money. "No, and I don't want money. My job safety and the dog are sufficient. And if he's wanting money from me, tell him I'm broke." I serve us both tea and sit down next to Kym when I am finished.

"The first form I have for you is a non-disclosure agreement. Mr Cardal will also sign the same document. You will both essentially be agreeing to not divulge anything around this substitution arrangement. It is legally binding and enforceable."

Without reading the form, I sign it. At this point I would sign my life, my soul and my first born child if it meant my career was still mine. As though a large, uncomfortable weight lifts from my shoulders, I feel lighter and more carefree as I dot the i's and cross the t's.

"The contract will have to be agreed in principle by both you and Mr Cardal. A verbal agreement that will activate the physical contract after a pre-agreed amount of time. This gives me time to write it up, and you both time to make reasonable adjustments or seek clarifications."

Kym whirls through the basis of the contract: the time frame, the agreement, the intent to form a contractual relationship, the end period and the stipulations. While some of the jargon seems familiar, most of it is gobbledygook. When Nate calls me on my new phone, it's a welcome reprieve from the dull paperwork, and I quickly excuse myself to take the call.

"Hey, I'm at your house. I've packed up your clothes and some personal effects. I need to go into your underwear drawer to get out some essentials for you. Is that okay?" His consideration warms my heart.

"Yes, of course, just bring everything in there, please." Too late, I remember my Rose Toy is safely hidden away in there.

"Even this pretty pink thing? What is this?" Nate asks, and I want the ground to swallow me up whole.

"Just put it in the bag, and I'll explain later!" I tell him. As much as I'd love to front this out, I know that I cannot survive the whole season without my treasured sex toy, especially if I'm going to keep a respectful distance from my fiancé.

"Is there an off switch? The damn thing just attached to my hand and is sucking the life out of it!" Nate shouts down the phone. Oh the SHAME! My sucking clitorial stimulator is more acquainted with my new fiancé than I am!

"There should be a switch at the front," I tell him frantically.

"Darlin', which way is the front? Oh, I've found it, it's okay." The gentle purring of my Rose stops abruptly. "It's a powerful thing, isn't it? Are you sure you want it?"

"Yes. I definitely want it, Nate!" Another double entendre. I'm going to hell!

When I return to the dining table, I try to look as relaxed as possible. "Why are you blushing?" Kym asks, eyeing me with interest. Under no circumstances am I discussing what just happened with another living soul. It's going to be torture discussing it with Nate later. To distract her, I pick up the document and tell her the end date is incorrect.

"The last game in the English League is May sixth, but if Redvale makes it to the European finals, there is another game on May twenty-fifth. To account for possible celebrations, if they should then win, the contract should run until around June first." Just as I surmised, Kym quickly swipes through the offending words with a red pen and adds the corrections in. She is smart and conscientious, and she will not like that she didn't consider this.

"I will add a clause that will end the contract early if Redvale don't make it to the European final. Is Mr Cardal on his way back?" she asks when she's finished splashing red all over the documents. "I think I have enough to work on now. I just need to get both of your verbal agreements and his signature on your NDA too."

"Yeah, I think he was almost done when he called, so depending on the traffic, he should be here anytime now." I smile at Kym but feel at a loss of what to say to her. "What will happen now?" I ask. Maybe she will know, because I certainly don't.

"Mr Cardal has never done this before. If you look through his history online, he's had a few relationships that have lasted weeks or months, but he has never made a commitment to anyone before." She pauses while I shift in my seat. "I believe there will be a media storm, especially because of the rumours about you and Jack, but also because Nathan is a very wealthy and important businessman. There will be a lot of interest in the person he is settling down with."

"So, there will be more media, not less?" I ask desperately. Maybe I have been naive in thinking that once the press gets the 'true' story things will die down, but it seems I'm going to be under more scrutiny.

"It will be a shitstorm for a couple of weeks, and then it should settle down. You'll get to keep your job though, Leila. Surely that will make a bit of pap intrusion worth it?"

The door clicking open prevents me from answering. My stomach jolts nerves and anticipation at seeing Nate again. "Hey!" he calls from the doorway, making me smile. "The paps are still outside your house. I allowed them to take a few coveted shots of me. They will be used as evidence once the news of our relationship breaks, I'm sure."

"Sir, I think we are all wrapped up here. You need to make a verbal agreement with Leila and sign her NDA," Kym interjects from the table. Nate nods to her before striding over and glancing over the agreements. He signs the NDA with as much thought as I gave it, but when it comes to the main contract, he frowns. "What's wrong?" Kym asks when she sees his displeasure.

"There is no monetary compensation mentioned. This isn't acceptable. I must insist that Leila is given an allowance to at least cover the cost of the events we will be attending and the extra clothing and stuff she will need," Nate replies bluntly while looking at me.

"What's wrong with my clothes?" I ask defensively! How dare he!

"Nothing is wrong with them. You're going to need a lot of gowns and couture and sparkly things for the events we will attend. And there can be no reusing. We need to look genuine, and the press knows *I* wouldn't let my beloved wear the same dress twice or wear anything but the best." Although it rankles to be reminded that we live in different worlds, Nate's fiancée will wear dresses that cost more than my annual salary, but I agreed to play my part and so I acquiesce.

"To look genuine, I will accept your compensation, as long as I can resell the items and repay you once we are done?" He shakes his head. No, he isn't going to agree to that. "Okay, can I donate the money to charity at least?"

"What you do once the contract is over is up to you, darlin'. Keep them, donate them, throw them on a bonfire. I don't care, but this is all irrelevant unless you agree to the compensation to begin with." He continues to stare at me, those deep intense grey eyes scorching my skin so much that I do believe it will be permanently marked.

"Okay, I agree to your compensation." His dazzling smile makes me grin back at him like the Cheshire Cat. What the heck does this man do to me? "And I verbally agree to the clauses. I have discussed them with Kym. I'm happy to proceed."

"Awesome! Me too. Are you ready to grab some dinner? I'm starving!"

Before I nod to agree, I think about my appearance. Never before would something like not wearing makeup or dressing casually be a cause for concern for me, but I don't want to embarrass Nate. "I think I best change," I say as I head to the room I have been sleeping in.

"No, Leila! You look fine. We need to try and blend in and look natural. You look perfect just as you are. You'll need to add a cap to try and hide your face a little, but they do need to get a clear shot of you and me together."

His approval means a lot, and that's a new development too. The approval of the men I date has never bothered me before, but then maybe that's why I have never had a long term relationship. However, I know, at this moment, I want to please Nate. I want to make him happy. Fuck. How did one hour with a stranger turn into me wanting to satisfy him?

With all the emotions running through my body right now, I'm so relieved sex isn't part of our contract. All temptation in that department has thankfully been removed.

"Okay, Kym. Let the vultures know where we are. This Substitution is active!"

# SUBSTITUTION
(NOUN)

The action of replacing someone or something with another person or thing.
(SOURCE: Oxford language Dictionary)

In an Elite English Football League game, a maximum of three substitutions can be made by each team.

# CHAPTER 5

## ~ Leila ~

It's still warm and bright outside, so although early evening is approaching, I don't wear a coat. Nate stops me at the door before he opens it and gently places a black cap on my head, leaving me to pull it low. "If at any point it gets too much or you want to leave, just remind me you have to call your mother. I will know you want to go home and will have us out of there as fast as possible. Okay, darlin'?"

"You're sticking with darlin', then?" I ask him as I adjust my cap in the mirror. It's not very imaginative, but it feels nice to be someone's darlin'. He raises his eyebrows at me, as he pulls on his own cap. "Yes, I understand, *honey*."

"I can see you are going to be trouble! You'll be my darlin' until we get to know each other better and I find a name that suits you," he says with a twinkle in his eye. He looks even more dashing with his cap on. A day's growth across his jaw leaves him looking rugged and dangerous.

When we exit his apartment, he holds my hand, threading his fingers through mine. It shocks me at first, but once I settle, striding in sync with Nate, it actually feels quite nice.

As I walk beside him, the wind blasts his scent at me, and he smells incredible. Masculine, strong and undeniably sexy.

To distract myself from thinking about how good Nate smells, I ask, "Where are we going, Nate?" He brings my hand to his lips and kisses it instead of answering me. Butterflies tickle the inside of my tummy until I remind myself this isn't real. This is all for show.

"There is a lovely little restaurant on the river. We have reservations there, darlin'." He points out to the floating restaurant on the river. It's a very well known and prestigious restaurant, and I have only ever heard of others eating there. The Helm is an eating experience renowned for its fresh fish and elegant decor and location.

Surrounded on all sides by a veranda that looks like something straight from a magazine, with its abundance of trees and flowers and the glint of twinkling lights, visible only because of the shade cast by the roof of the restaurant, it looks magical. Like a romantic hideaway that has just emerged from some other realm.

"It's beautiful, Nate. But how do we get there?" With a lack of bridge or jetty in sight, I don't know how we actually get to the restaurant. I look up at Nate, who points to a few steps ahead. On the dock is a waiting speed boat, providing me with my answer. I've never even been in a speed boat before. "Oh my! Nate! You shouldn't have," I say sincerely, as I turn, stepping really close to him. He places his hands on my waist as I lean up on my tiptoes and kiss him lightly on the lips, tilting my head to the side so our caps don't collide. As I attempt to move away, Nate holds me tighter.

"You're doing so well and I think a photographer is just behind us. How about a proper kiss, give them something to stew over?" However, the mood is zapped. I had momentarily forgotten that this is all a show, a game. Nate is my Substitution, and I can't get carried away. The concern in his eyes as I pull away leaves a knot in my stomach.

"Sorry, I'll be smoother next time," I cover. I don't know why I find it so hard to focus when I'm around him. He sends my brain to mush. "How on earth do I get into the boat?" I ask, changing the subject as quickly as I can and leading us to the dock. The man sitting in the boat, noticing our arrival, tips his hat at us both.

"I'll help you. Wait right there," Nate says as he simply steps over the ledge of the boat. Turning back around to me, he holds out his hands, so I move closer to the edge, trembling at the thought of falling in, but when Nate's strong, warm and assured hands hold me around the waist again, I know he won't let me fall. As I land with a thud in front of Nate in the speedboat, my hands land on his shoulders. "See, that wasn't so bad," he whispers to me, and my body reacts once again. Does he feel it? This connection between us? Or is this all in my imagination?

I've never been a fanciful person. All the stories of instant connection and even love at first sight sound cheesy and unrealistic. The way I feel, the way my body reacts, and the desire that swirls around my entire body is foreign to me. I've never felt this way about anyone, ever before. Not until I met Nate. Now, I'm in a contracted fake engagement with him and will be forced to spend the next nine and a half months with him, whether I like it or not. I'll have to spend that time pretending to be hopelessly and irrevocably in love with Nate, whilst holding back and protecting my heart from him, because Nathan Cardal has some sort of power over me. For him, this is a game, a farce, and I need to keep that at the forefront of my mind.

We glide over the water, covering the short distance to the beautiful restaurant in a matter of mere minutes. At the front of the restaurant, the veranda meanders down to a mini mock dock. I worry needlessly yet again about disembarking, but Nate is a perfect gentleman, stepping out first and holding out his hand for me.

Upon noticing Nate's arrival, the waiter opens the double doors to us and invites us inside. Nate laces an arm around my waist and rests his hand on the small of my back. Try as I might, I cannot help the shiver that emanates from where his hand is to every single nerve ending in my body.

This is going to be torture.

## ~ Nate ~

Even though I know Leila isn't mine to keep, what is the danger in playing the part? She is attractive and funny, and we are both adults. Who knows... This could be fun. She's made it clear that my lifestyle, which is similar to Jack's, doesn't appeal to her, and while I tend to agree with her on matters such as press intrusion, I've never known a different life. I was born with a photographer's lens directed on me. My life has been documented, for the most part incorrectly, in more columns of gutter rags than I would care to remember. So while Leila has the privilege of walking away from this life at the end of our contract, I never will.

Her refusal to accept financial compensation shows me what sort of person she is. The more she resisted my money and the benefits of a life with me, the more I wanted to shower her with it. Her joy at seeing the little restaurant made me want to cause that reaction again and again. A saner man would distance himself, uphold the contract and walk away without any mess. But I want to be involved. I want to get to know more about her. It's safe to say I want this woman to be a part of my life, even if it is just for the duration of our contract.

Pride washes over me as I walk into the restaurant with Leila beside me. Due to the time of day, there are only a few other diners, but they all turn and acknowledge me, and then attempt to get a look at my date. Before I can calm myself, I hide Leila from view. They can fuck off if they are going to make her feel uncomfortable, staring at her all evening... Then I remember, that's exactly the effect we want.

I don't like sharing. It seems that will extend to my temporary fiancée. I've never felt this way with any of my ex-girlfriends. I think my lack of possessiveness is ultimately what drove them away. They wanted someone to fight for them, and I just wanted a bit of fun. But it's different with Leila. I want to protect her, keep her safe and enjoy all her looks and smiles, all her feminine actions, and secrets. Anyone else having that twists my insides uncomfortably.

Leila smiles as she looks around, and I'm glad that I chose this place. Designed to replicate the dining room of the Titanic, this is one of the classier places to eat at the docks, and yet the reason I picked this place was to show Leila the extent the press will go to in order to get her photograph right now. "Would you like a secluded table or one by the window, sir?" the waiter asks, and already, I know we would both prefer a private table, but we need to be seen together.

"Darlin', are you okay by the window?" Leila nods to me shyly. She looks delicious, exactly how I imagine she would look in a post-coital glow. Pulling out her large, ornate chair, I wait for her to sit before pushing her closer to the table and taking my next seat next to her. In the distance, I can see the braver and more savvy paps approaching the restaurant on their jet skis and speedboats. A couple have improvised and sent drones. Kym really didn't waste any time.

The restaurant manager comes over to greet me. I'm used to this sort of attention when I eat out. I'm well known not only in the local area but also around the world. The manager gives us a full breakdown of their menu, including their specials menu, most of which includes fresh fish and seafood. We both order the daily special of whiting and scallops that the manager assures me was freshly caught this morning. After consulting Leila, I ask for a bottle of white wine to accompany our fish. The waiter hasn't even finished pouring our wine, when the first distinctive click of the camera sounds, startling everyone. More clicks follow, as well as several flashes. A couple of the other guests leave, but we sit and wait as planned.

"So, darlin', I could do with a laugh right now. What was the pink thing in your drawer? My imagination has been running wild since I found it." Just as I thought, Leila almost chokes on her wine, her face turning crimson. I guessed it was some sort of self-pleasure device but I've never seen anything like it before. "Why are you so embarrassed? Is it something naughty?" I tease her. I want to see what she'll tell me.

"If you must know, it's a very special family heirloom," she tells me solemnly. "It once belonged to my great-great grandmother and has been passed down the generations ever since. It's meant to bring good luck," she continues without even changing her facial expression, and I burst out laughing at her and her obvious lie.

"Oh, is that right? Your great-great grandmother is how old?" I ask her through my laughter. "I didn't realise they had USB charging ports back when your great-great grandmother was a young woman. I have an idea of what it is, Leila. I've never seen one like that before, but you don't have to be embarrassed."

Although she glances at me and huffs in exasperation, she eventually joins me in laughing. "I was mortified when you found it and it sucked your hand. But yes, it's my special toy to… relieve my stress," she adds demurely.

"I had a feeling you were a naughty girl!" I murmur to her, watching for her reaction, and just as I had thought and hoped, she shivers again. "I'm looking forward to finding out exactly how naughty you are, darlin'." Her eyes shine brightly at me, desire swimming around in those big blues. How easy it would be to completely lose myself in them.

"We have to go; I need to call my mother," she tells me, using our secret code just as I instructed her. I don't know if I feel disappointed at the abrupt end to our date, or happy that she wants to go home with me.

Not wasting a second, I ask the manager to arrange our food to take away. "Mr Cardal, I am so sorry. We never usually have problems with the press thanks to our location. I hope you won't hold this against us." Guilty of being the reason the paps are here, I quickly reassure him that I will return in the future.

Pulling out my phone, I call for my car, and when Leila is ready and standing, I place a protective arm around her shoulders and swiftly move to the veranda, to our waiting speedboat. However, Leila freezes when the flashes and clicks begin again, as well as the shouting, the demanding, rude, overbearing shouting.

"Look this way, Leila. Where is Jack? Have you spoken to him about his womanising? Will you forgive him? Is it the first time he's cheated? Leila, how about a big smile? Can we get a side profile of you? Will you be returning to Redvale after Jack has humiliated you like this?"

Inexplicable anger rises in my chest. How fucking dare they hound *my fiancée* and make her feel vulnerable. Stepping in front of her, I raise my hand. "Stop it. Now." I shout out. I know I called them here, but for fuck's sake, she is a woman, not a piece of prized beef. She should have some right and say in whether they photograph her and the questions, the many questions and assumptions, are ridiculous!

"Mr Cardal?" Finally, they recognise me, but after the way they have just hounded Leila, I don't want to give them the scoop. I don't want to reward their intrusive and vile behaviour. "Tell us why you are here with Ms Monrose. Is this about your brother? Where is Jack? Would you and Ms Monrose pose for us?"

Reaching the end of my patience, I shout at them all. "I said ENOUGH! Give me your names and tell me what rag you work for. If you are not out of here in five seconds, I am going to ensure you NEVER work again." Just as I suspected, every single one of them speeds off without telling me their name. They've got their photographs; they'll add whatever story they want to it now.

Leila applies a little pressure to my shoulders, needlessly reminding me that she is still here. Like I need a reminder, the woman is beginning to consume my every thought. "Thank you, Nate," she whispers. "No one has ever stuck up for me like that before."

"You're my fiancée. Mine. I protect what is mine. Come on, darlin'. Let's go home and settle for the night." Her warm hands are still on my shoulders, so although I can't see her face, I can feel her reacting to me.

"Yes, let's go home. It's been a long, weird day, and I'm ready for bed."

Fuck. Leila in my bed. Leila in my bed with me. Me in bed with Leila. A throb of desire and need starts with my cock and balls but then radiates throughout my whole body. What have I let myself in for? This is going to be torture!

I am on guard for the journey back to the dock. These few seconds seem to last a lifetime as I scan the area looking for rogue photographers. A million thoughts begin to swirl in my mind as the reality of this whole situation finally dawns on me. I have a fiancée, for at least the next nine months, and it's safe to say, I want her. How do I stop myself from falling for a woman who is in a fake contractual relationship with me simply to save her career? Sex is not part of our deal, but could it be? Would that be enough to get Leila out of my system?

My driver waits for us as we climb out of the speedboat. "Jeremy, could you take us home, please?" He tips his hat in agreement after opening the door for Leila. When I take my place next to her in the car, I watch her in fascination as she tries out a couple of the features of the car.

"What does this do?" she asks, pointing to a larger black and grey button that seems to shine like a beacon to her.

"When you press it, it will eject you through the roof!" I tease her, and she looks so adorable as she initially absorbs what I say, her eyes wide with interest and growing alarm that she almost pressed it. "You're so cute!" I laugh as the realisation washes over her that I'm teasing.

"I can see you are going to be trouble too, Mr Cardal," she adds through a self-conscious giggle. She is as sweet as honey when she giggles. "Where do we live?" she asks, finally leaving the button alone, relaxing back into the comfortable seat and closing her eyes.

"Not far. I prefer to live in a manor house on Sandybank." Her eyes dart open again. "As I mentioned, Jack has been living with me while he was injured, but he has mentioned moving back permanently to his own apartment."

"You live on Sandybank? Jeez, isn't that where all the celebrities live? There will be no running to put out the bin in my pjs there!" I chuckle at the disappointment in her voice, disappointment that stems from losing a part of her normal life. Leila is a one of a kind woman, and I will not impress her with my fancy house. If I want to impress her, it'll be something I have to work at. The thought of trying to impress her is becoming more and more appealing.

"When we get home, there will be press outside. When I kiss you, you need to kiss me back like you really mean it. Okay?" I could be wrong, but I am sure her pupils dilate, and my pants become uncomfortably tight as I swell in reaction to her. How the fuck did I start the day looking at firing someone and now ending it with a hot woman I want to impress?

"Nate? Do you have a mint?" She interrupts my thoughts once more. "My mouth feels horrible after the wine, and if I'm going to kiss you like I mean it, I don't want your lasting memory of me to be stale wine!"

The fact that she is thinking about our first proper kiss sends a thrill of desire down my spine. I would be a fool to deny it, she is under my skin alright. "Press the button," I instruct her harshly, my voice thick with pent up frustration at being so close to her, and yet so far.

Before pressing the button, Leila looks at the ceiling of the car, questioning if she does indeed press the button, will she be ejected? However, she still presses the button.

"Yes, sir?" The voice of Jeremy, my driver, comes through on the intercom.

"The lady would like some mints, Jeremy. Do you have any?" I ask him, drinking in Leila's look of exasperation that it is simply a communication button.

"There are some in the arm rest, sir. We are three minutes from Sandybank," Jeremy replies.

"Thank you, Jeremy." I lift up the arm rest, and sure enough, there is a tube of mints nestled against some other essentials. "Here you go, darlin'. Mints." My body is aware of the familiar road now. The bumps in the street, the roundabout, the sharp turn and then the security gates. The flashes from the press start almost immediately. When Jeremy pulls up outside my garage, I tell Leila to stay seated.

I open my door to a tirade of blinding lights and questions. There must be about a dozen paps waiting outside my house. However, I ignore them. I'm not here to tell them what is going on. Leila and I are going to show them. I walk around the car and open her door. "Allow me to lift you," I request, and when she gives her nod of consent, I try to ignore how right it feels to have her in my arms, how nothing has ever seemed quite so perfect.

Leila wraps her arms around my neck as I carry her bridal style, then she surprises me by initiating our kiss. Ever so gently, like butterfly wings, she places one hand on the side of my face and directs it to hers. Her cheeks are flushed, her rosy lips just begging to be devoured.

Although I know I stand here with her in my arms for mere seconds, it feels as though the world stops turning just for us. When our lips finally meet, I swear the ground moves and stars shoot across the sky. A kiss so impassioned, deep and carnal that I never want it to stop. My hard lips crash over her soft ones, and our tongues dance. When I hear a low moan in the back of her throat, I know I have to pull away or I'll be giving the press a show they'll never forget.

"I'm taking you to bed, darlin'," I murmur to her as I continue to pepper her face in kisses, and gods be damned if she doesn't shiver in response. Sex was never part of the deal, but it's clear it's on both of our minds. Finally, I let Leila stand. Though I keep her near to me, not wanting to lose our connection. "Welcome home, Leila. I've got a feeling we are going to be really happy here."

## ~ Leila ~

Everything seems to flash by before my very eyes so quickly that I cannot keep up. My overwhelming feeling is to run and hide. Being photographed and talked about is my idea of hell. I don't want this. I crave to be invisible.

Nate is as dependable as a rock for me, though. He is protective, courteous and strong. A real man in my eyes, and despite the fact that our relationship is based on a contract, I can't help but be in awe of him and of how it would feel to truly belong to a man like him.

He told me to kiss him like I meant it, but as he walks me to the large double doors at the front of his house, I wonder if he meant to *make it look like I mean it*. Because that is totally different. Isn't it?

What a kiss it was. A perfect first kiss. Nate kisses like he owns me, like he knows me on a level that no other man has even glimpsed. It's both arousing and absolutely terrifying. I don't consider myself as an easy ride; there is no long list of sexual conquests in my past, but enough for me to know that this... whatever this is with Nate, could be incredible. We would be incredible together in bed.

But, it doesn't matter how much I want to see if that is true. Sex isn't part of the deal, and it is bound to overly complicate an already confusing arrangement. With me, sex never stops with just sex, and the very last thing I need now is to fall in love with a man who is going to walk away from me. That is guaranteed.

Someone inside opens the doors wide for us. Large ornate wooden doors with a brass knocker and letterbox on the frame to the left. There are little stained glass windows in the doors that glint in the fading August sunlight, casting blues, reds and greens across my skin.

"Welcome home, darlin'," Nate says simply. The hallway is light and fresh. Marble covers the floor and stands in columns in the open space, giving it a grand Grecian feel.

After the staff has closed and secured the doors, Nate thanks them and quickly introduces us. Mrs Claybourne is the housekeeper and Baxter is the assistant. Both in their fifties, the two of them look startled by my sudden appearance. "Mrs Clayborne and Baxter have been with us since Jack came under my care. You've met Jeremy, my driver, and Damon and Jameson are my security detail. Apart from them, Giovanni, the chef, is the only one left to meet."

Having never had household staff, this is quite an adjustment, but I wave to them, happy to make their acquaintance. "It's really nice to meet you," I tell them both before they return to their duties.

Once we are alone, Nate pushes me up against the doors, his hand grazing my throat before settling on my chin, holding my face in place. "That was some kiss, Leila. Did you mean it?"

Unable to nod, and not wanting him to let go, I whisper my reply. "Every second of it," I tell him, and his eyes darken. Maybe he wants this as much as I do? Maybe we can just get it out of our systems and then go back to the arrangement. Maybe I'm most definitely kidding myself. "Want me to show you again?" I ask him, deliberately provoking him to see where this is going.

However, it seems Nate doesn't like to be goaded, because before I can finish my sentence, his hard, unyielding lips crash over mine once again. My hands rest on his chest, a firm, toned chest that makes me want to see what is under the shirt.

Before I get carried away, I link my arms around his neck and allow myself to be completely consumed by another amazing kiss. Nate's hands are at my waist, and he lifts me so my body is flush with his. I've never felt as though I belong as much as I do right now. His body, his sexy body, fits perfectly with mine. As our kiss continues, I wrap my legs around his waist and revel in the groan of satisfaction that Nate makes when I do.

With only our clothes in the way, it's clear what Nate and I both want. My panties are already damp and cling to me as I press against Nate shamelessly. Although it's difficult to tell, I think he's equally aroused, if the hard, generous bulge pressing against me is anything to go by. He skims his hands over my ass, hips, waist and up further in the direction of my breasts; however, he stops just on the under cup on my breasts, not actually touching them. "Fuck, baby girl. You're fucking perfect. So amazingly perfect. I just want to carry you to bed right now."

I bite my lip to suppress my smile. Nate sounds in awe but also in pain. What if I told him I want the same? I could brazenly tell him, 'take me to bed then, big boy!' like they do in the soap operas. But this isn't a soap opera; this is real life. If he rejected me, I'd have to live here with him for another nine months, and that would just be too uncomfortable.

"How about we eat first. I'm starving now, and I was really looking forward to the fresh fish."

Taken aback by the change of subject, Nate misses a beat before replying, "Yes, food. You need to eat. I need to eat. And we have food… somewhere." He's flustered! He's adorable flustered. This man, who just completely possessed me and almost had me begging to be fucked in the foyer less than thirty seconds after he brought me home, is flustered. Pointing to the box that contains our food, I remind him where our food is. "Yes, of course! What was I thinking?" he jests.

"Nate? You'll have to put me down if we are going to eat," I tell him, unable to keep the laughter out of my voice.

"Shit, yeah, sorry!" He stutters, and my heart melts a little more for him. "Let's eat, and then I'll show you around." He picks up the box and instructs me to follow him.

## CHAPTER 6

### ~ Nate ~

At the tender age of twenty-four, I inherited my father's businesses and millions, save for the amount he had put aside for Jack. Within a year, I had turned that lucrative business into a multi-billion-pound empire. That was all while coping with being a pseudo-parent to my little brother and mourning the loss of my father. I had business acumen running through my vein and nerves of steel they said, the Midas touch.

It was all a load of bollocks. If I have nerves of steel, then why am I shaking like a leaf after kissing Leila? As I stutter and stumble, I want the ground to swallow me whole. What the fuck is happening? No other woman has ever affected me in such a way. Not even close. I don't think I was this bad as a teenager, never mind now as a thirty-four-year-old, relatively experienced man. As I will myself to concentrate, I find myself thinking about her and the way she responded to me. No, scratch that. The way *I responded to her* is more accurate. There is no way, not a cat in hell's chance, that sex is off the cards for us. I'll be damned if either one of us can last the night. There is simply too much electricity between us.

Leading Leila into my kitchen, I feel like an absolute fool. I open several drawers and still cannot find the cutlery. What is this woman doing to me? I'm a mess!

"Nate?" she calls in her cool, smooth accent. Her mother might live in the midlands now, but this girl has a proper English accent. "Are you okay? Don't tell me you can't even find your way around your own kitchen?" She teases, and although I should feel embarrassed, the familiarity and ease between us allows me to relax enough that I can at least get out dishes and glasses so we can eat.

"Do you like to cook?" I ask her, wanting to know more about her.

"Not particularly. I cook mostly because I have to; it's not a passion of mine. Do you?" I burst out laughing, thinking of my last mishap, as I pull out plates from the cupboard and utensils from the drawer that eluded me a couple of moments ago. Who on earth can burn boiled eggs? Me, that's who.

"I like watching cooking shows and trying new food, but I'm an absolute disaster in the kitchen. If Jack does move out, I'll miss his chef. He's kept me healthy and well fed this past year." She looks at me, assessing me, reading me, figuring me out, and for the first time in my life, I feel self-conscious. While I pour the wine, Leila dishes out the food. From the steam, I can see that it is still warm.

"Jack has a chef. My, my, isn't he a pampered pooch!" she adds scathingly. I get the distinct impression that Leila will take a while to forgive Jack. "I knew most of the players have dieticians and nutritionists but his own chef. Wow!"

"Talking of pooches…" Trying to subtly change the subject, I find the ideal time to bring up our joint venture. "What kind of dogs do you like?"

"A girl one," she adds simply. Her eyes widen, and she blushes as though the words fell out involuntarily. "Sorry, I didn't mean to sound rude. I've always wanted to have a dog called Lady. Like Lady and the Tramp," she says in between eating her food. I'm so distracted by her that I haven't even noticed the taste of my food.

She looks so sweet and honest when she gives her explanations that the urge to go to her and sweep her off her feet once more almost overwhelms me. "Then, that's what we will have. A little Lady. What is she? A King Charles Spaniel or something?" She nods to my question, still blushing. "Are you feeling okay about everything? I know this has been a roller-coaster, but I'm so glad we are here, doing this." Taking the empty plates, I load them into the dishwasher while I listen to Leila.

"I'm happy too. I'm just feeling a little stressed and overwhelmed."

Her talking about feeling stressed has my mind returning to her face in the restaurant when we discussed her little toy. Fuck, I want to be the one to relieve that stress for her. I want her to bask in glory and sleep like a baby afterwards and know, deep down in her stomach, that she has just been worshipped for the goddess that she is. "Let me do something about that?" I ask her, hoping she will catch my train of thought, but if she does, she gives me no indication that she has.

⚽♥⚽

After cleaning up, I take Leila by the hand and give her a short tour of our home. She gasps and murmurs admiration for the gym, the bar and the living areas, letting me know that she likes the place well enough.

"Do you spend much time in here?" she asks me when I show her the games room.

"Not particularly. There is a poker table out back that I use with my friends sometimes, and occasionally the bar comes in useful if I am entertaining." I reply to her honestly. "There is an outdoor football pitch as well as an indoor one and we have a decent garden area and some land all around us. I'll show you the rest tomorrow."

As I lead her up the wide wooden staircase, Leila whispers her appreciation for the artistry in the banister. I've never taken much notice, but now, I have a new appreciation for my own staircase. Now, I see it through her eyes. "These are all our rooms. There is another room through there that I will make your dressing room, your space just for you. Our bathroom is through there, and this one is the master suite. Our bedroom." I push open the door and wait to see what she does.

She tentatively walks past me and peers inside. "That bed is massive! I was worried about us sharing, but I think we could both stretch out our arms and not touch. Well, unless we wanted to, of course."

"Unless we wanted to," I repeat, soaking in the undertones of meaning. "You can decorate this room however you want. I know it's very masculine," I add awkwardly. My room, usually so familiar, feels different with Leila in here. Next to her, the room looks dull and cold. My bedroom is functional but bland; it fails to reflect me and my personality. I'd failed to see that until now.

"Nate, it's perfectly fine just as it is. It is your bedroom. I think I'd be more freaked out if it looked like a couple's room already. What side is mine?" she asks, looking up through her eyelashes. "I don't think I want to be closest to the door, especially tonight."

Giving her a lopsided grin, I open my arms and offer her the side away from the door. "Don't worry, precious. I'll keep you safe."

"You'll keep me safe, will you? And who is going to protect you from me?" she says as she spins around to me, placing her hands on my shoulders once more.

Seizing the opportunity I've been desperate for since I set eyes on her, I push her back until she falls back onto the bed and drop down on top of her. She giggles as I do so, assuring me without words that this is okay.

"Do I need protecting, Ms Monrose? What are you planning on doing to me?" She responds in earnest by leaning up and brushing her lips delicately across mine. It's over in a millisecond, leaving me craving even more.

"I'm going to drive you crazy, Mr Cardal. Of that you can be certain!"

Drive me crazy? Thanks to her mere presence, I'm already halfway there.

## ~ Leila ~

Things are moving so fast between Nate and I, but I like it. I've never, ever felt as comfortable or as turned on as I do right now. If I was a coward, I would hide behind the whole 'we are engaged and meant to be living as an engaged couple.' But the truth of the matter is, I want Nate, even if it is only for this one night. I want to be with him. This is not your conventional one-night stand, but nothing about my 'relationship' with Nate could be classed as conventional.

We just need, or rather, I just need to get this out of my system. I can do this. I'm sure of it. As I lie on my back on Nate's massive bed, with him pressed against me, and the two of us kissing, all rhyme and reason leaves me, and what remains is a ball of desire that sits heavily in the pit of my stomach. I roll over, sitting astride him, and tug off my top, aiming it at one of the plush chairs that sits there, judging me and my loose morals.

Nate sits up, resting on his elbows. Looking at me, drinking in my toned physique. I am actually quite proud of my body. I work hard to stay in shape, but also work at maintaining my natural womanly curves. "You look fucking incredible. I knew you were going to be a naughty girl," he whispers gruffly at me with passion clouding his eyes. I'll show him exactly how much of a naughty girl I can be.

Nate kisses down my neck and over the straps of my bra. How glad I am that I thought to wear decent underwear. I don't even know what possessed me; I was moved to somewhere strange and thought I best not have holes in my underwear and socks! It's all worked to my advantage now. I might even shake Jack's hand for leading me into the path of his big brother. He may have actually done me a favour.

I tug at Nate's shirt, telling him without words exactly what I want. I want to feel his skin next to mine, and he doesn't disappoint me. Once he has discarded his tie, he unbuttons just his cuffs and collar and pulls his shirt over his head, throwing it at the judgemental chair too.

"I wasn't expecting this when I woke up this morning, but I'm delighted this is how my day ended up. You are so beautiful," he says to me in between kisses. He kisses my cleavage, causing my skin to pimple in reaction. "May I?" Nate asks me when he lowers the straps on my bra. I give a swift nod and within seconds, I am spilling out of my bra.

"A bit of a professional at this, are you?" I murmur to him with a grin. He throws my bra with the rest of our clothes and finally palms my breasts like I've wanted him to since we kissed in the hallway. I moan in my throat and throw my head back as he sucks each of my nipples, and grind against him as the heat and need between my legs continues to grow.

"I may have done it once or twice before," he mumbles back to me in between mouthfuls of my breasts. "You are perfect in every single way, Leila. I'm so glad you're my fiancée." I laugh out loud and eventually he joins in too. The whole situation is preposterous and it's about to get a whole lot trickier.

Unwilling to wait any longer, I stand up. "Do you have a condom?" I ask him as I wriggle out of my pants. When he shakes his head at me, annoyance flares inside me. Claire always tells me I should carry protection, and every time I have told her that I'm not that sort of girl; I don't sleep about, not on the first night any way. Look how that little gem has come to bite me on my ass. "Shit. I don't either."

"I'm clean, are you?" And although I could take him at face value and accept that, I can't. I can't take that risk.

"I'd rather not take the risk, Nate. We've only just met, and the women in my family are like super fertile. We settled on a dog for now, remember?!" I'm glad to see he looks as disappointed as me. That ball of desire is quickly turning into frustration. Pent up frustration that is foreign to me. It has never really bothered me all that much if full sex was off the cards, but with Nate, I'm wound up without any outlet, and logically telling my body that we can't go any further doesn't seem to work; it's as though it has a mind all of its own! So much for our one night to squash the tension between us!

"So, I'll pick some up tomorrow, but for now, there are many things I can do to relieve your stress for you, if you consent of course." He still wants to continue even though he knows I won't be sleeping with him at the end of it. It's like music to my ears. This could be our test drive, then tomorrow we can bash it out and get rid of all this tension between us.

"I consent. I'd like to relieve some of your stress too," I say to him, and my little slut of a body thanks me silently that we will get a little action with Nate after all. The traitorous little bitch. Nate puts his hands out to me, and I walk back to him, my knees already weak and trembling.

"Just let me take care of you, precious. That's all I want to do: look after you." He runs his hands up my body from my thighs all the way up to my breasts again. I moan involuntarily, and Nate chuckles as he pulls me back onto the bed with him. "I love that you're so honest in your responses. If you need me to do something else, or go harder, or softer, or faster, just tell me. I want to give you whatever you need."

"Nate, shhh, let's just see how it goes," I say to him, my hips bucking against his body. The ache in my stomach and the throbbing between my thighs hits a peak, and I'm concerned I might combust if he doesn't touch me soon.

"Okay, darling," he says, and for the first time, I realise he said it properly. I pull him closer to me and kiss him deeply. I'm shivering with need and drunk on desire. Just as I begin to feel desperate, Nate takes full control.

Slowly but surely, he strokes me from my navel all the way to my knee. He spreads my legs wide and then trails his hand back up to my tummy again. My pussy pulses, and the heat of my need hits fever pitch. Finally, Nate's fingers slip down into my panties and connect with my clit. Thank fuck he knows where it is. The first time being intimate with someone can be challenging, and I think if Nate didn't know his way around a woman's body, I would be crying right about now. Instead, I groan in pleasure as my spine begins to tingle; a sure sign that I am so far gone that my orgasm won't be far away.

"Nate!" I call out when he fingers me, pumping just one finger inside me before adding a second, stretching me, while he continues to rub my clit with his thumb. He plays my pussy like a fiddle, and within minutes, I am coming.

"Next time you come, it'll be around my cock, darling. Promise me," he demands as waves of pleasure wash over me. "Promise me, Leila."

"I promise," I shout. At this moment in time, I would promise him the world and more.

"You promise what?" he whispers harshly against my ear, as the last wisps of pleasure are running through my body. "I want you to promise me properly, Leila."

"Nate, I promise the next time I come, it'll be around your cock." He smiles back at me as he takes away his magical fingers, but then he surprises me once more by licking my come off them.

"You taste delicious. So sweet, so fuckable. My naughty girl. Say it." he demands again, and this time, I am so invested in this roleplay, so turned on by the man who has instigated it, I have no qualms in playing my part.

"I'm your naughty girl, Nate. All yours."

## ~ Nate ~

As Leila falls to pieces in my very hands, a feeling of pride fills my chest. She fits me like a glove and responds to me perfectly. The last thing I want is to stop. I want to see her come again and again, but I don't have condoms. I actually cannot remember the last time I had to wear one. I do regular sexual health checks, especially at the beginning and end of a relationship, but I completely respect and admire her decision to not take needless risks. She has more restraint than me.

Her little moans, the way her body trembles as she surrenders to the release, and the scent of her very arousal and orgasm fill my room, and nothing has ever sounded, appeared or smelt sweeter. I need more. More of Leila.

Just as I am about to suggest asking Jeremy to get us some condoms, the security alarm beeps, letting me know that Jack has returned home. Damn it. I had hoped he would continue to stay away so I could prepare Leila for seeing him, but Jack has a knack of turning up when you don't want him to.

"What's wrong, Nate?" Leila asks me, as she strokes my bare chest. She doesn't look like she wants things to end just yet either. Unable to resist her, I kiss those swollen rosy red lips again.

"That beeping was Jack coming home." As Leila stiffens against me, I know our tryst is over for now. "Just ignore him, we will deal with him in the morning." She nods to me, pulling the sheets up to her chest, shielding herself from me.

"Where is my stuff, Nate?" she asks cooly. "I'd like to change for bed." I can't believe this is the same woman that just came in my hands and promised me she was my naughty girl. She is now very business-like. Almost cold.

When she doesn't make eye contact with me, I grab her by the face, hooking my fingers under her chin, forcing her to look at me. "This doesn't change anything," I tell her firmly, but she pushes me away.

"It changes everything. This was a mistake. We went too far. I went too far. I need to clear my head." She stands up, taking the sheet with her when the sounds of Jack and the women he is entertaining filter through.

"Leila!" I say, raising my voice, hoping I get through to her. "What is this about? Do you regret me touching you? Because, you consented, sweetheart. You wanted it."

She stumbles as she lifts her top up. "I did, Nate. I don't regret what we did, but this... us. It is all a big mess. We should try and remain... friends.

"Friends? Friends my fucking ass, Leila. Don't pretend this means nothing. Don't pretend you don't feel... the energy between us." That's when I realise, that's when I notice the fear in her eyes. "I've never felt anything like it before. Have you?"

She shakes her head side to side and murmurs her answer to me. "No. It's scary. I–" I kiss her once more before she can finish or object. "But, Nate, I worry about the line."

"What line?"

"The line between us pretending and what is real." As she says it, I realise she's worrying that she may forget this is make believe, temporary. It shocks me that I also forgot until she brought it up. This is as real as it comes; we're forgetting the boundaries because everything between us is so easy and natural. I should be wanting to keep to the conditions of our contract, but fuck it all, life is too short to pass up opportunities like this.

"Please don't push me away. We're in this together. Fuck, I want to make you come again. I want to feel the way you just made me feel when you splintered apart in my arms. I'm not sure where the line is either, but I'm right here toeing it with you, Leila." I open my arms to her, and she returns to me.

Sitting between my outstretched legs with her back against my chest, she leans on me, and with her back in my arms, my chest loosens ,and I can breathe freely again. How can she mean so much to me in so little time? It's scary, but not scary enough that I'll let her walk away from me.

"Sorry. Jack returning reminded me of why I'm here in the first place. I got carried away; I don't usually do this kind of thing, Nate. It's confusing!" I kiss her shoulder over and over and smile when her skin puckers again.

As she relaxes against me, I hold her close and rub her back, never stopping the hot kisses I lavish on her. "Forget about Jack, forget about everything else. Let's just concentrate on you and me. I didn't relieve all your stress. Let me try again?" I ask her in-between kisses, and it intrigues me that she smiles before shaking her head no.

"I can't. I made you a promise, and I never break a promise," she tells me earnestly. I almost wonder aloud if Jack has condoms, but I think better than to suggest it.

"Please don't make me beg. I will. But I'd rather just use all my energy into giving you the best orgasm ever." I trail my fingertips down her body and to the waistband of her panties. "Take them off for me, precious, and let me make you feel amazing."

Even as she lifts up her ass as I help her tug down her underwear, she protests. "But what about my promise? I don't like breaking promises, Nate."

"Make me a new promise. When I have condoms, you'll come around my cock twice. Promise me now. I need to touch you again."

She makes her promise, and so I push my hand further down between her legs. She is already wet. Probably, some of it is from her last climax, but I can tell she is turned on again. I can smell it! She feels perfect under my fingertips, and I look forward to making her pussy all mine. With my other hand, I tweak her nipple, palming her ample breast, kneading it until her nipple stands to attention. "Will you go on the pill so we can do it without condoms too." She freezes in my arms. I sink my fingers into her tight pussy as a distraction, but in-between her light moans, she resists the pleasure I inflict on her.

"I thought this was going to just be a one-time thing," she says breathily, biting down on her lip. Like fuck it is. "Are you thinking we could keep this as an additional benefit for the duration of our engagement?"

"Why not. If we are compatible, it makes sense. We can't sleep with anyone else, and I don't know about you, but nine months of celibacy sounds like hell." I know I'm stretching the truth, but the thought of not being with her or of her being with someone other than me is unacceptable.

"Okay. I'll think about it."

I hope she does. I want her to think of nothing but me and her in bed together. I know I'll struggle to think of anything else.

## ~ Jack ~

It has been a fabulous return to football, to the game and to the lifestyle that I love. The girls have been throwing themselves at me, my form continues to improve, and the press cannot get enough of me and what may be happening between me and the Doc, as well as lavishing me in praise and adoration for my brave comeback.

It came as a disappointment that the Doc didn't show up for work on Monday morning. Although the headlines became more and more outrageous, I had hoped she'd front it out and even consider our dinner date, seeing as she will probably lose her job anyway. Guilt does try to edge into my mind, but I remind myself I do not control the media or its stories. What I did was a nice thing to thank the woman who got me back to full fitness.

Nathan left several messages for me to contact him as soon as possible. He sounded very contained and business-like on the first few; however, his tone became more and more clipped as the number of messages rose. Then all of a sudden, during the afternoon, he stopped calling me. I take the win for what it is. Nathan has given up on trying to parent me. I am a grown man, no matter what he might think, and he isn't the boss of me. Well, not completely.

Once I finish training and check in with one of the other physios, I have a shit, shower, shave and get ready to hit the town and look for more pussy to pull. One of the younger academy players asks to come along, and I promise him he will get laid tonight. My friends Tyson, who is another midfield player for Redvale, and Sancho, who is a heavyweight boxer, are coming along too.

The four of us manage to create a storm of paparazzi as well as available and willing women with one thing on their minds. Getting photographed with us.

We start off in the Hotspot, one of the trendiest and upmarket lounge bars in Redvale City Centre. The door staff immediately lets us in and ushers us to our very own roped off VIP section with our own bar and staff. From the comfort of our seats, we can invite who we want to join us.

I spot a popular soap actress and beckon her to me. She isn't the prettiest, but she is most definitely the most confident. "Jack," she says, addressing me even though we have never been introduced before. I like that, let's not pretend.

"Alana," I say back to her, tipping my head to her. "Would you and your friends like to join us?" Giving me a wide smile, she nods and calls over her girlfriends. All of them are minor celebrities and actresses. I think I recognise one of them as a past conquest of one of my teammates. She makes no reference to it, so I don't either. With my nod, the security lifts the red rope to grant them admittance to our area.

Alana's career has really started to take off. She has had several massive storylines in her soap and has done some charity work for domestic violence off the back of one of her most prominent storylines. I know she must be getting offers for reality shows, product endorsements and modelling. "How did you manage to get your own area? They told me there was none left and you arrived after us."

I shrug in response to her question. Wherever I go, people bend over backwards to accommodate me. There is no secret to my privilege; it's just the way it's always been. "You know, you and me, we could cause quite a stir in the media. News of our romance would probably get us our own spread in the glossies. Think about it," I tell her, offering her a flute of booze–it could be prosecco, but it is more than likely champagne.

"What about your nurse? I heard you're in love with her?" she asks, jealousy flaring in her eyes.

"The Doc? Nah, she's no one. We aren't involved," I add quickly, brushing a strand of her blonde hair away from her face.

"Well, in that case, you've got a deal. Are you taking me home tonight?" she asks, before downing her champagne.

You bet your fucking ass I am.

"Will your friends be joining us?" I enquire, looking at them, admiring them. The one who has already slept with my teammate is now cosied up to Kelvin, the academy player. Tyson has his arms wrapped around her other two mates, grinning. Sancho is dancing with a civilian, just like he normally does. He doesn't like dating or sleeping with celebs. He prefers to be the centre of attention and therefore, always makes a beeline for the ordinary folk.

"I think my friends are all taken care of for now, but who knows? Make this a night worth remembering, and they might be game to join us in the future. If you like that sort of thing, of course."

Well what sort of question is that? Who doesn't like that sort of thing? "Challenge accepted. Come on, blondie, let's get out of here." I wave goodnight to my friends and take their jibes good naturedly. I can't help my prowess. They are used to me by now.

I am making my way to my car with Alana, flashes and shouts from the waiting paparazzi assuring me that they're getting the shots of Alana and I that I want them to, when Kelvin shouts out to me, "Jack, wait."

"What's up? I'm about to leave!" I say to him impatiently.

"Can we come to yours? I still live with my mum," he requests with a red face.

"Get in, for fuck's sake," I tell him, pushing his head down so he can get into my car. His girl follows, and for dramatic effect, I take Alana's hand and kiss it before holding the door wide for her to get inside too. A frenzy of flashes and clicks confirm to me that Alana and I will make the front pages tomorrow.

Once I am seated next to Alana, I tell my driver to take us to Sandybank. I'm still living with Nathan, although I'm fit and healthy again now, so I could move back to my apartment, but I like living on Sandybank. I've been thinking of persuading Nathan to let me keep the Sandybank property and getting him to move elsewhere. A long shot considering it's his home that he has renovated, but still a shot worth taking in my opinion.

The press has been camping outside the house since the first game, but tonight their number seems to have swelled threefold. Surely the news of me bringing Alana home for the night hasn't got out this fast.

After posing for their photos, I place my hand on the base of Alana's back and direct her into my home. There is no doubt why she's come back to my house, and the press will make a meal out of that. I'm sure we could capitalise on it.

Alana is very forward, so after showing Kelvin to my guest bedroom, I take her to my own bedroom. Within minutes, she is riding me, shouting and moaning as I bang her. It doesn't take me long to come, and afterwards we discuss us stepping out together and building a brand, but the truth is I think I'm bored of her already.

A few hours later, long after Alana has fallen asleep, the housekeeper opens the front door as usual, bringing in the newspapers. I run down in my shorts, greet her and take the newspapers from her, expecting to see my own face splashed all over the front of the papers. Instead, it's a photo of Nathan kissing a very familiar brunette outside the house. What the fuck! Why is the Doc kissing my brother?

Wasting no time in finding out, I bound across to his wing, noticing he's closed his door. He only usually does this if he has female company. In any case, his door isn't locked, so I don't think twice about barging in to demand answers.

"What the FUCK is going on, Nathan? Are you seeing Leila? Is that why she turned me down?" I shout until I'm at the side of Nathan's bed. The curtains are drawn and the room is in complete darkness. The bedside light turns on, and Nathan looks at me, sleepy and squinting. In his arms is the brunette, the Doc.

"We've been seeing each other for a while. I asked her to marry me last night, and she said yes. Don't ask her out again. She's mine!" I stand in shock. I had no idea they were seeing each other, but now her rejection makes sense. "Now get out of my room. I'm not ready to leave my bed yet." He winks at me and pulls Leila closer to him. Her back is uncovered and her creamy, flawless skin is visible through her hair. She is completely naked. It must be true.

"I want to talk to you before I leave for training," I say as I leave his room. I'm going to look like an idiot now. I need to know how to fix this so I can save face. This could change everything for me. Goddamn my brother.

# Chapter 7

## ~ Nate ~

Knowing that it is highly likely we made the newspapers and that Jack always checks the newspapers early when he is likely to feature in the news, I text Kym to see if anything has dropped about Leila and I. When she confirms that we made the front page on several publications and a middle page spread on another, I know I have to wake Leila.

After informing Leila about the newspapers and warning her that Jack will barge in once he sees them, we hatch a plan to make our relationship more believable to him. She suggests undressing so he knows we are naked together in bed, but my face must give away all the positions I imagine Jack walking in on.

"I mean I could *look* naked but he isn't seeing anything. Like I could be asleep on you, and he could see my bare back. Nothing else!" I chuckle at her but inside I am gloating. She allowed me to see her and will lie naked with me, but no one else.

"No chance of a shag then? I was thinking you could be on top riding me when he walks in," I counter suggest in jest, just to see her face turn puce. "Missionary is fine. Maybe you could dangle your head over the edge of the bed and wink at him while I fuck you."

"NATHAN!" she shouts at me. "Seeing as it would be our first time together and we still don't have condoms, *are you out of your fucking mind*? I think I'll decline." As I laugh at her reaction, she realises I am joking with her again. "You're such an ass. Do you know that?"

"Aww, come on, gorgeous, I'm only messing about," I explain gently to her, as she lifts off her top and lies down next to me. "Come closer," I encourage her, lifting my arm so I can embrace her. She scoots closer, and her bare flesh presses against mine. Fuck my life. It feels incredible to hold her in my arms. My cock begins to stir – I no longer have any control of it. It seems to spring to life every time Leila even breathes in my direction, and my lack of discipline disgusts me.

Leila exhales as she rests against me, and I wonder if she could be feeling content? I don't know how to describe the feelings I already have for her. It's scary as hell, and once I get a few moments alone, I will need to think about what the heck is going on. This is a contractual arrangement. I can't forget this.

When Jack finally barges in, Leila tenses next to me, and suddenly the thought of him seeing any tiny bit of her has me ready to choke him. She is mine, not his, and the sooner he accepts that, the better for me.

Jack tells me he wants to talk to us before he leaves for training, and I know Leila will be eager to return to her work too. As reluctant as I am to leave this little cocoon, the promise of us returning here tonight with appropriate protection is the only thing that encourages me to get up.

Once Jack leaves my room, I let Leila know the coast is clear and gaze down on her proudly. "Would you like to see your dressing room?" I ask her, wanting to share everything with her.

She smiles and nods to me, so I open up the double doors and show her the room I have earmarked for her. I promise her that I will have everything in place for her this evening, meaning her belongings will all have places, extra clothing will be selected by my team to save her the trouble and her security detail will all be in place.

She, however, misconstrues my words. Standing on her tiptoes, she kisses me lightly on the lips and murmurs to me, "I'm looking forward to it, Nate." Within milliseconds, my wayward cock is straining in my pants against my will. The traitorous bastard.

After showering and dressing, we go downstairs, and I hold her hand, half because I want Jack to see we are together and half because I simply want to. Jack's eyes widen when we walk into the kitchen together. He whistles. "Here they are. The lovebirds. You could have just told me, you know. Now I know why you weren't into me," Jack says to Leila, over jovially and somewhat uncomfortably. "So, what are we going to do about the press? I mean, they seem to think we are either in a triangle or a throuple. As much as I love you, bro, my image means more."

"What do you want me to do, Jack? As far as I am concerned, you started this with your unneeded display at the match. What the fuck was that all about? Had you become suspicious of us? Were you playing with us to see if we would crack?" I am giving him a clear way out of this, where he can save face, and it also helps add weight to my relationship with Leila. Vital evidence that all accumulate in making us look more authentic.

"Yes, erm… yes, of course, I was suspicious. You're great and everything, Leila, but you're not my type. I knew you wouldn't just come out and tell me: you always have a non-disclosure in place." When he winks at my fiancée, I step towards him. A growl begins in my chest, but I manage to stop it before it is obvious. "Nathan, you must have a plan. You always have a plan." He throws one of the newspapers onto the breakfast bar. "I mean, look at what your kiss has already snowballed into."

The headline is cringeworthy, but the photograph is truly magnificent. Leila in my arms, holding my face while I kiss her. "Look at us, darlin'. We look fucking amazing!" I turn to Leila, but instead of a beaming smile, her face looks like thunder.

Snatching the paper up off the counter, she scans the first few paragraphs. "Is this what they are saying about me? That I have somehow strung you both along and now I'm stuck in the middle of you both, unable to choose?" She doesn't mince with her words. "And what the fuck has my father got to do with anything? They have no right bringing him into this!" She slams the paper back down on the counter and paces away.

Walking to the counter, I pick up the paper and read the first paragraph aloud.

*"Leila Monrose, daughter of the former footballer Frankie Monrose, has taken revenge on her toyboy lover, Redvale city star Jack Cardal, by hooking up with his older brother, Nathan!"*

Although I know Leila is not going to be happy it is suggested that she is going between me and Jack, the fact that her father used to be a footballer too is news to me. "You never said your father was a footballer." Despite my best intentions, I know my voice sounds defensive. It brings home that I don't really know Leila, not even a tiny amount.

"It has got nothing to do with anyone who my father was and what he did for a living," she shouts back at me, anger simmering in her big blue eyes. She is absolutely raging.

"Woah, lovebirds. Calm down all the emotions. How about I drop in that I just wanted to thank my future sister-in-law. Are you okay with the press getting wind of your engagement?" I quickly agree to Jack's suggestion and turn back to Leila, who refuses to make eye contact with me. I don't understand why she kept the information about her father quiet or why she is so upset about it now.

"Are you okay with our engagement being leaked?" I don't know what I'll do if she says no, but I have to at least give her a final opportunity to walk away.

"It doesn't matter what I think. The bastards will get a hold of it somehow. Can I go to work now?" Without taking any breakfast, she walks out of the kitchen and into the garage.

"She is going to run rings around you, Nathan! I'm happy for you, though. I'm glad you found someone to share your life with." He looks at me meaningfully, but this time, I refuse to meet his eye. I know what he'll want to talk about, and I have no idea how I'm going to avoid the world and its dog finding out more about me, especially Leila.

"I've gotta go; I promised to drive Leila to work so she can collect her car. Will we see you for dinner?" Jack shrugs at me noncommittally. "Well, call or text and let me know. Now that I have a fiancée, we need to have some stability in our home."

Jack stares at me, surprised at my outburst. I don't blame him. What the fuck do I know about stability?

"I can drive her. I'm going that way too, remember?" Jack offers, but I don't want to leave Leila just yet. Besides, her going to work with Jack will raise even more questions.

"No, I want to make sure she's okay before I leave her," I say as I follow her path to the garage. Leila stands in between two of my cars. "Do you have a preference?" I ask her, extending my arms to the cars, but she shakes her head stiffly.

"Nathan? Why do you always have a non-disclosure in place?" Oh, fuck! Jack was right. Leila is going to run rings around me. The morning started so idyllic, I should have known it wouldn't last. "What is it you're hiding?" She looks at me accusingly. Already our bubble has burst.

"Leila. Stop prying! You've got such a suspicious mind. Would you like it if I snooped into your life before me?" Just as I suspected, she steps away from me. I saw how touchy she was about her dad being mentioned in the newspaper. She doesn't want anyone spying on her. "I have non-disclosures because I need to have them. People have used me in the past, have told my secrets and extended the truth for their own gain. I must protect myself and my business."

Although she nods in acceptance of my explanation, there is now a chasm between us. The familiarity we managed to create last night has been replaced with doubt and suspicion. I don't know if we can go back to how it was, and now, we are stuck with each other for the next nine months.

## ~ Leila ~

My blood boils in unspent rage, and my despair tastes like ashes in my mouth. The audacity of the reporters to go digging into my past like that. Is nothing sacred? How dare they pry into my private affairs. I share a surname with my father, but I was sixteen months old when he died. I don't remember him. I spent enough of my adolescence wondering about how my life may have been different if he had been a part of it, his absence weighing heavily on me during my teenage years.

The press have no right to not only open that can of worms, but empty the can everywhere without any care.

"Which car?" Nate asks me, and I shrug. I don't give a fuck about cars at this moment in time. I feel violated. To Nate, this might be the norm, but for me, this is tantamount to someone breaking into my home. They've abused my space, my information. Something that was mine.

The mysterious air I found attractive in Nate now glows like a beacon. He may as well be waving a big red flag. And I am stupidly tied to him until the end of the season. Nine and a half months to be exact. What the fuck possessed me to be so rash?

We travel in silence. It's uncomfortable and stifling. "You could have given me the heads up about your dad. I can do without these little surprises. I know this has upset you, but I don't know why, Leila." I scowl at him. "Talk to me. Why haven't you told anyone who your father is?"

My anger breaches my control, but I don't shout or lose my composure. Very calmly, I talk at Nate. "I didn't tell you or anyone else, because it has got nothing to do with any of you. What don't you get? He was my dad. Mine." The press, the football association, and the clubs didn't give a shit when he was alive, or in the twenty-four years since he died. Why now? None of them had any sort of right to know I'm his daughter.

"Okay," he replies bluntly, clearly not expecting the response I gave, but I'm past caring. I've had enough taken away from me. I'm mad about it all. "Just tell me if there is anything else they are going to drag out. You don't have to give me details but don't leave me open to looking like a fool when I get asked about you."

He drives through the city traffic and into the residential area surrounding the training ground. My stomach churns as I worry about what to say in response. I'm not ready to share that part of my life, not with Nate, not with anyone.

"This is fucked up and I don't like it," I explain as openly as I can. "These past few days have been crazy. My life as I knew and loved it is gone, and now, I live in a fishbowl without any sort of protection or armour. I don't think there is anything else they will drag out, Nate. You see, for me, dragging my father into this is bad enough. That's the most invasive thing anyone could have done."

He keeps driving, but when we stop at the traffic lights, he turns to me. "You can keep the parts that belong to you. I don't want to violate that, Leila. But if we are to pull this off, we need to trust each other. Can you trust me?" He looks at me intensely, demanding something from me that I sincerely want to give, but there is a part of me that holds back.

"I hope so. I want to. But I'm frightened at the same time," I reply, and once the lights turn back to green, he moves off again. I can tell he isn't completely happy with my response, but there's nothing he can do about it. He can't force me to trust him; forcing me would cause the opposite effect.

The matter is pushed aside once more when we arrive at the training ground. The paparazzi flock outside and descend on us like a swarm of locusts with their clicking and flashing and intrusive shouting of questions. The muscle at the side of Nate's jaw ticks and jumps again. I don't know why I find that both amusing and sexy. We have to stop at the security gates, and the vultures take advantage of this. They attempt to take photos through the blacked-out windows, and a few try to open the doors on Nate's car.

"Right, that's it. Stay here. Do not move." He gets out of his own car, and I can hear him through the door. "I will have you all removed if you continue to put the life of my fiancée in danger. This is way over the top. She is an injury specialist, and she wants to go to work. We are a normal couple. Leave her alone."

"Mr Cardal, if you'll just answer a few questions and pose for a photo or two, we'll leave you to your day," one of the cheekier ones suggests.

"I said NO! Damn it, leave her alone. Back away from here now, or I will call the police. That is your final warning." He climbs back into his car, a storm brewing in his intense grey eyes. "You'll need to call you mum. I just let it slip that we are engaged."

What he just did has lightened my mood. No one has ever stood up for me like he has. "Thank you," I say to him. It seems so little compared to what he just did, but I want him to know that I am grateful for it.

Nate, however, thinks I'm being sarcastic. "It just slipped out, damn it. I'm sorry." After the morning we've had, I don't have the time or energy to correct him. This just all confirms that we are best keeping this as a professional arrangement.

Spotting my own car, I thank him for the lift. "I'll see you at home tonight. The condoms are no longer needed." He gawps back at me open mouthed.

"Leila, wait! Kym will be coming by to talk to you about social media protocols this afternoon." I look back at him once I reach my car. "Is that your car? Fuck me, you can't drive around in that!"

"What's wrong with it?" I reply back defensively. I love my yellow beetle. It's my pride and joy!

"You'll be followed everywhere, Leila. And this is hardly inconspicuous. You may as well have 'follow me' on your registration plate! Damon will pick you up after work. I'll arrange a more generic car for you so you can blend in a little." Great, another part of my life that is ripped away from me. Taking my belongings from my car, my indignation simmers away inside me.

When I stand back up, I bump into Nate. I didn't realise he had gotten out of his car. "Have a nice day at work, honey." He cups the side of my face and pulls me into a kiss, but before our lips touch, he whispers, "We are in love, remember? Kiss me like you mean it, darlin'."

Why do I want to kiss him and punch him in the eye at the same time?!

As soon as I step inside the training centre, Mr McAllister spots me and orders me into his office. The dread that has been steadily building all morning suddenly hits a peak, and I want nothing more than to curl up in a ball and forget the world around me. With my head bowed like a naughty schoolgirl, I answer his summons and make my way through his open door.

"You should have been at work yesterday. Jonesy needed you. Your team needed you, and you let them all down without so much as a phone call." I definitely called into work to explain the situation to them; however, disappointing people and letting them down when they need me is one of my pet hates. Guilt fills my gut, making me feel nauseous. "I understand that you are in a relationship with Mr Cardal – Nathan Cardal – but I will not make allowances based on your current boyfriend."

"Mr McAllister, I can assure you that I do not and never have expected special treatment. I could not come in yesterday as advised by our public relations team," I inform him as calmly as possible. "I actually resent your accusation. I am one hundred percent dedicated to both my work and my patients. My relationship with Nate – Mr Cardal – has nothing to do with it." Looking fiercely at the man who has insulted me over his clutter desk, it occurs to me that I signed a contract to save my job and I could lose my job anyway.

"Leila? Sweetheart? You left your phone in the car." Nate barges into Mr McAllister's office, and although we didn't leave on good terms, I'm so happy to see him. "What's going on? Is there a problem, Shane?" Nate surprises me by using Mr McAllister's given name. Having never heard anyone call him Shane before, I'm taken aback at first, wondering who on earth Nate is talking to.

"Mr Cardal, I was just having a word with the Doc about the situation and ensuring…" I look incredulously at Mr McAllister as he bumbles and stutters like a little boy, using a simpering tone to cajole Nate. It is sickening and absolutely hilarious at the same time.

"Cut the crap, McAllister. I'm warning you now. Back off and let her do her job, or you'll be the one looking for a new one. Am I making myself clear?" Nate looks down on Mr McAllister, snarling at him. As I watch him from the seat to the side of him, I can't help but be in awe and slightly intimidated by him. "The reason we kept our relationship a secret is so Leila could go about her job without interference. Now that we are getting married, you will respect her as the CEO's fiancée as well as a valued member of our team."

"Of course, Mr Cardal, Ms Monrose. Congratulations on your engagement."

"Yeah, yeah. Whatever. Can she go and do her job now?" Nate retorts rather rudely, and Mr McAllister practically falls over himself as he opens the door to the office for me and sends me on my way. Nate doesn't follow me, but I wait to say thank you to him.

Around thirty seconds later, Nate stalks out of the office. I smile at him, ready to thank him for rescuing me, but Nate frowns at me. "I'm not going to be here to support you every minute of the day, Leila. You are my fiancée. Do not let anyone talk down to you. Do you understand? You need to stand up for yourself." I stand staring at him like a goldfish with my mouth opening and closing in shock at his outburst.

Once I regain my composure, my outrage at his assumption also returns with a vengeance. "I'm sorry I disappointed you, Nate. It won't happen again. I'll see you at home." Turning on my heel, I stomp away from him. As grateful as I am, I am also a proud, independent woman, and no one, not even Nate Cardal, will take that away.

"Leila?" he calls after me as I walk away, and in the interest of keeping up appearances, I turn and blow him a kiss that seems to take him by surprise. I smile to myself as I make my way to my clinic.

"Thank god you're back!" Jonesy shouts to me from the chair outside my clinic. I can't ignore the worry lines on his face, nor the measured way he gets to his feet.

"What's happened?" I ask him with genuine concern. We have been trying to keep Jonesy as fit and healthy as possible so he can stay active as captain within the team. Although he is older and not as fast as he used to be, his wisdom as a player and his natural leadership ability is essential to the team and its success.

"Don't be mad! I sort of fell off a table," he tells me sheepishly. "Put the kettle on, and I'll tell you all about it. And you can tell me all about your engagement. You know Paris will want to know the ins and outs." I try to be jovial about sharing my details. I like Jonesy, and his wife, Paris, has always been an ally of mine.

"What the hell were you doing on a table?" I ask him suspiciously, while I open my clinic. Getting back to my natural habitat, to where I am capable and in control, is all I need to create some normality.

"Well, it all started after the match. Paris wanted to help me celebrate. We ended up shifting quite a lot of champagne, and then we carried the party on back to my house. I lost a snooker match, and the forfeit was dancing on the table." Having heard all about Jonesy and Paris' parties, I know what is coming next. "So, I got up on the table and was giving it the biggins, and the next thing I know, I'm spread eagle on the floor. My groin is killing me, and I think the hernia is back."

It feels amazing to be back doing what I do best. "You silly man! I'll get you booked in for an emergency scan. You know what this means, though, Jonesy."

"I'm out, aren't I?" he says starkly. The words no footballer wants to hear, closely followed by the amount of time they will be out for. "I'm such an idiot. I should never have gotten up on that table."

"I'm so sorry. Depending on the extent of the damage, you may need surgery this time. And you know the recovery period." This is the most difficult part of my job, but at least at this point I can offer him some hope. "There will be no more drinking, Jonesy. I'll be calling Paris and telling her too. And I'm going to be working you hard to get you back as soon as possible."

"Thank you, Doc. I told the others, 'if anyone can help me, it's Leila Monrose.'"

Sports News

# THE DAILY GALAXY

09 August, 2023                                        Celebrity News

## KEEPING IT IN THE FAMILY!

### Jack-The-Lad loses his girl to his big brother!

Leila Monrose, daughter of the former footballer, Frankie Monrose, has taken revenge on her toyboy lover, Redvale city star Jack Cardal by hooking up with his older brother, Nathan!

After news broke of the budding romance between Jack and Leila, Jack was spotted up to his usual tricks of womanising.

However, Leila didn't waste any time on getting even. She was spotted dining with billionaire business mogul Nathan, 34, and the couple were photographed kissing and cuddling before retiring to Mr Cardal's Sandybank home.

**For more juicy details turn to page 46**

# Chapter 8

## ~ Nate ~

Well fuck it all. That did not go how I wanted it to. The morning had begun perfectly. Leila in my arms in my bed and the promise of what was to come later. Mainly me and Leila, of course, but then the reporters threw a spanner in the works, and I can tell it spooked her. It spooked me too.

After the story about Jack and Leila broke, I obviously looked into her personnel file and found nothing that suggested she or her family were football alumni. Not even a whisper about her father being a former footballer had been found. Yet the paps found that information in less than a day, and as surprising as it was, it has also piqued my interest. Why did she hide it, and when confronted with the information, why did she become so prickly?

The easiest thing for me to do would be to conduct my own search now I am armed with her father's name. I have resources that your average Joe doesn't, but as my hands hover over my keyboard, I know deep in my heart that I can't and shouldn't pry into Leila's private information. She evidently found the whole topic of her father deeply upsetting, and as much as I want to understand her, I also want her to freely share that part of her life with me. Snooping would make me as bad as the reporters that I condemn.

As I think back to the hurt look in her eyes as I chastised her, regret and guilt ebbs away at me. I shouldn't have been so harsh with her. I was frustrated at the way things were running out of all control, but that is no excuse for taking it out on Leila. She deserved better than that.

Eileen, my head Personal Assistant, hovers around the outer atrium of my office. At fifty years old, she is usually like a mother hen, fussing over me, but today, I stormed into my office without greeting anyone. The news of my engagement has now made the rounds, and I know she'll be surprised to hear that I managed to woo a woman without her knowledge. I call her into my office.

"Morning. I'm sorry I didn't say hello. The press followed me and I was annoyed." She smiles at me, understanding lining her kind face.

"Don't worry about that. I hear congratulations are in order?" I smile back at her and raise my hands. "You kept that one quiet!"

Having dated in the past, I had leaned on Eileen to keep up with my affairs. I needed table reservations, she arranged it. Flowers? She was my first port of call. "It hasn't been easy without you, Eileen, but Leila, my fiancée, made me sign a nondisclosure agreement too."

"Ooff!" Eileen makes a noise and laughs, highlighting her astonishment. I'm liking this story and so that is the official line I am keeping to. "It seems you've finally met your match, sir."

"Yes, it certainly seems that way. I'm in the doghouse already. I was rude to her this morning. I said something but it came out way harder than I meant it. I was angry, but not at her. Anyway, I need to say I'm sorry."

Eileen is nodding at me, having seen this play out several times before. "I know, nothing says sorry like flowers. Leave it to me." However, this doesn't sit right with me, not this time.

"No. I want to send them myself. I just have no idea what I'm doing. It's important that I do this. I want to buy her flowers." Although her eyes widen, I sense that she feels proud that this is something I could pass off to someone else to do but that I want to do it. Doing it myself seems mature, honest. Like something a fiancé should do.

"Here. Type this website in. I like this one because it's all locally sourced and they have some unique styles." She writes down the website, and I tap it in as she continues to talk to me. "They do all styles of personalisation, gifts, messages. Have a look through and pick what you like, and your order will be done in a couple of hours. I guess this one is special?"

Nodding my head, I smile sheepishly. "Yeah, she's... something else alright!" Eileen chuckles as she retreats back to her other work. For a few minutes, I sift through the numerous flowers of all shapes and sizes until they all blend into one. I don't really know Leila that well, and picking flowers for her now seems like such an intimate task. The things I do know about her give me no insight into the type of flowers she likes.

With no other ideas and inspirations, I think about what flower might remind her of me, but I don't think she would appreciate a thorny rose bush. I'm just about to give up and ask Eileen to send a generic bunch when a blush pink rose catches my attention. A similar shade to the one I found in her drawer. Smiling, I know I've found what I have been blindly searching for. Placing an order for two dozen long stems, I type a short but heartfelt card out online and complete my order. She should receive them just after lunch. Hopefully, the condoms will be needed again, if she forgives me, of course.

Looking at the mountain of work I have to catch up on, I know while my mind is tormented and preoccupied I'm not going to make much progress, and so, as the boss, I do something I should do more often. I take the afternoon off.

Now, I could happily go and play golf, or watch the football, but I still have to secure Leila's ring and adopt a puppy, and even though I accept I won't get that done in one afternoon, I can get the ball rolling so I feel as though I am making progress.

Kym calls me while I drive to my jeweller. "I've spoken to Leila. She knows the protocols, and I don't think we will have any issues with her leaking to the press. She hates them even more than you do." I smile to myself. It's my good fortune that Leila isn't a fame crazy wannabe. "She has given me a list of safe contacts that she will want to connect with as soon as possible." I give my consent to her authorising Leila's contacts. I don't want her isolated or cut off from her friends and family.

"Good, maybe once everything settles down, we can have a dinner party and invite them over," I say before I even remember we aren't a real couple. I don't have to get to know her family and friends. Not properly anyway.

"Save it for your engagement party. You need to get a task team together to organise that by the way."

What? What does she mean... Engagement party? Surely we can just announce it and that's it?

Unsure of what to pick, but knowing that Leila is a simple and practical person, I select a classic engagement ring that isn't too big and encumbering. Money isn't an issue, but that doesn't mean I want to give her an overly elaborate ring just for the sake of looking like I'd paid a lot of money for it. Of course, if she wants to swap it, I won't be offended. As it goes, I don't believe Leila will have any complaints about the ring I've chosen for her, but I could be wrong.

I've never bought an engagement ring before. In fact, if I am being honest, I have never bought an item of jewellery for a girlfriend before. I had always left it in Eileen's capable hands, and she had always excelled, but I want to buy Leila's ring myself. It didn't sit right with me sending Eileen to get something as important as an engagement ring, and as much as I try to convince myself that it is to maintain façade, a very small voice insists on reminding me that no one knows I'm at the jewellers and that maybe there is more to my motivation to doing the task myself. Pushing down the nagging voice, I continue to accept this is to maintain my charade and nothing more. This is all I'm comfortable with addressing at this moment in time.

Lunch time comes and I call Damon directly to give him the details of where Leila works and when she finishes for the day. He will arrange a vehicle for her, but he informs me it'll be a couple of days before it is ready with the additional safety features I insist on.

A notification shows up on my phone from the florist, telling me that my order has been delivered. As the afternoon progresses, I gulp down my disappointment that Leila doesn't reach out and thank me for sending them. Maybe she is busy, or is waiting to tell me at home? I'm not sure, but I had hoped my peace offering would sway her into forgiving me for being an ass this morning. Perhaps I am being too optimistic.

Kym calls again, just as I am about to call a friend who is high up in the Kennel Club to ask for puppy advice. "Sir, you are required at the grounds ASAP. There is a last minute star signing about to happen, and as majority shareholder, they need your permission."

Although I had an inkling this may happen, with the club captain staying uninjured and healthy, the board had been swayed into not breaking the bank on another new player just yet. Something must be going on for this to be rushed through now. "Why the sudden change of heart?" I ask her as I change direction in my car.

"Jonesy needs surgery for a hernia repair. They don't know how long he'll be out for or if he'll be coming back at all," she tells me. Fuck, that's a blow for Jonesy and Redvale too. "How long will you be?"

"About twenty minutes. How did Leila seem today?" I cringe as I hear myself, but I can't help asking; I genuinely want to know if she is okay.

"She's had a busy day. She's coping okay, but, yeah, it's been hectic for her today," Kym says back to me, telling me everything but giving me no clue as to what made Leila's day busy and hectic.

"Okay, tell me about this new player. He is from Poland, right?" Changing the subject back to the matter at hand temporarily stops me brooding over my fiancée and what she may or may not be feeling, and in turn, I don't have to address the same issues about myself either.

"Yes. His name is Piotr Mankiewicz. He is nineteen years old, and the club is negotiating the fee for him right now, which is in excess of one hundred and twenty million pounds." Excitement and exhilaration bubbles up inside me. The guy must be something special to be considered for such a deal at his tender age. This is what attracted me to football, long before Jack's obsession. Long before I had to become a businessman. The thrill of building a team and winning trophies.

"Please tell me he is worth it, Kym," I tell her, remembering all too late that she is opposed to footballers' wages.

"No fucker is worth that amount, but you lot still insist on paying it, so good on the boy for using his head." Kym believes that footballers' salaries are tasteless and unnecessary. "Your fiancée does actual good work, helping people, making a difference to the quality of their life. Do you know that kid will earn more in a week than she does in ten years on her current salary. That's food for thought for you, Nathan."

I'm going to suffer for rattling Kym's cage, but her words certainly do get me thinking about Leila. What is her rate of pay and why, given her sensitivity around her father, does she work with footballers?

"I'll be there in ten minutes. Has Damon picked up Leila yet?" I ask. Maybe I could swing by and say hello before she leaves.

"They left five minutes ago, Nathan. Get your business head on." She hangs up, and I smile. Anyone else and I'd drag them over hot coals. But not Kym. Kym has been like a surrogate mum for both me and Jack and has no issue telling me exactly what her view is on certain subjects.

Even though it is still summer, by the time I have finished welcoming our new player and agreeing to the financial terms of the contract, darkness has fallen across the city. I drive home in silence, glancing at my clock and cursing being so late. It's almost midnight.

The house is silent when I finally get home, and my heart pounds as I walk directly to my room. I worry she won't be there, then I worry she will be and I will have to explain my lateness. All my worries are for nothing. She's here, fast asleep in my bed. My chest eases as I watch her sleeping. Part of me wants to wake her up and apologise, and part of me never wants to stop watching her sleep. In the end, I lie down next to her on the bed, intending on just resting for a minute. I am still fully clothed, and in the peaceful silence, I close my eyes for what feels like a moment. But when I open my eyes again, the room is full of light, and my fiancée... Well, she's already left for work.

## ~ Leila ~

After arranging Jonesy's scan and follow-up appointment, he seems to be feeling better. Especially when he and the rest of the team playfully tease me and my recent scandal in the press.

"So, Doc... can we still call you Doc? Or will we have to address you as Ms Monrose, future wife of the CEO?" I take their mocking in the good faith it is intended. "Show us your ring, then! How big a rock does a billionaire buy?" they ask, looking at my hand.

I raise my hand, luring them in, and then flip them the bird, making them laugh. "I don't have one yet, and to be honest, I don't think I'll wear it to work. It'll only get in the way." From the looks on their faces, they don't seem impressed by my statement. From bulging eyes to muffled laughter and looks of incredulity, all of them look back at me as though I've grown a second head. "What?" I squeak out.

"As if Nathan Cardal is going to let his fiancée just trounce around without a ring on her finger. You're crazy if you think he doesn't want everyone to know you are his now." As a few others laugh, I bite back my retort. I am walking around without wearing a ring right now. Nate said he will get me a ring, but if I choose not to wear it, I don't think he will care.

"Come on, you gang of gossiping old ladies, get out there and warm up," the gaffer shouts at them, chasing them out into the training field. Jack waits until everyone else has gone before he approaches me.

The silence between us is awkward, stilted, unnatural even. "Are you okay, Jack?" I ask him. In the capacity of the team injury specialist, enquiries about his health and well-being seem an appropriate way to open a conversation with him.

Giving me a stiff nod, it appears Jack is feeling as uncomfortable as I am. "I just wanted to clear the air between us. We are going to be family, and no matter what anyone else says or thinks, I love my brother. He hasn't had it easy, and I want him to be happy."

Smiling at Jack and his genuine love for his brother, I mentally ingrain the information he has just given me. Something about it makes my spine tingle, and I don't know why. "I'm happy we're going to be family, Jack. Nate makes me happy, and I want to make him happy too." Although I am fabricating the facts, I concentrate on the fact that I am bound by contract to say such things and that Nate did make me happy by helping to save my job. As difficult as I have found being his fiancée for less than twenty-four hours to be, I do want him to be happy and for him to know that I am grateful for his help.

The feeling of wanting to make Nate happy quickly evaporates when I return to my clinic and find Kym waiting to give me instruction. I like Kym, but she is like an elephant in a china shop. By the end of her session, I have basically been trained to keep my mouth shut. To reply 'no comment' or simply make no comment and to be absent online until they get me a Public Relations Specialist all of my own to handle things. How outrageous! After she leaves, I rush through lunch, opting for a sandwich and fruit from the canteen, which I take back to my office. I am ravenous after no breakfast this morning and vow to be more prepared in future.

Then I finally get a few moments alone to call my mother, Claire and Louise. My mother, as always, becomes disinterested when I mention that Nate is involved with the football club. "I'm not interested in hearing about a load of grown men who run around chasing a football," she abruptly replies, and her rudeness stings my pride. My mum has very fixed opinions about footballers, and that didn't soften with the choices I made in my career. If anything, she has become more vocal about her 'indifference' of the sport.

"What about the man who has asked your daughter to marry him? Are you interested in him?" My relationship with my mum can be strained at times. I used to think it was because of the pain of losing my father, but even now, years after she remarried, that bitterness seems as potent as always.

"I am interested in you. Are you happy, Ley? Does he make you happy?" Tears brim my eyes, threatening to overflow. I wanted her to congratulate me, to be happy for me, but even that seems a stretch.

"He makes me happy. I've gotta go. I just wanted to let you know before you see it on the news." Ending the call, the same empty, flat feeling swirls around inside me. She has been all I've had for all my life, but at times, I feel completely alone. Not two members of the same team, but two strangers forced into close proximity. Not unlike Nate and me, I suppose.

As soon as my call connects to Claire, she begins screaming down my phone. "How could you have kept this a secret? No wonder you didn't want to date his brother. Is he hung like a donkey? Does he make your eyeballs roll to the back of your head and your toes curl up like a piglet's tails? What's your engagement ring like? How did he propose? When is the wedding? Can I be your bridesmaid?" As Claire continues to have a one-sided conversation about my love life, I log into my workstation in the clinic. A couple of times I type out Nate's name and then abruptly delete it. Even if he does pry into my private information, I can't do it. It's not right to invade his privacy. Sure, he has had numerous girlfriends, but he has never hidden that from me. He has the right to keep this information about his nondisclosure agreements from me until he feels like sharing, if he ever does.

"Are you still there? Will you be coming then? On Saturday? I wanna get papped too!" I have no idea what she is talking about, but I already know I am not going to be around this weekend anyway.

"I can't, Claire. I fly out to Paris tomorrow afternoon with the team, and then we are straight home to play down in London on Saturday afternoon. I won't be back until late Saturday night. Claire groans down the phone and makes me promise we will meet up soon. I'm absolutely mind-fucked by the time I hang up on her.

Calling Louise, I know she will be calmer and more collected. "Leila? Oh goodness, I'm so glad you're safe! Where are you?" As we chat more generally, she takes her time getting to the news of my engagement. "So, you had a contract that meant you couldn't tell us? How long has it been going on?" she asks me.

Quickly, I try to remember the last time I had another date or hookup. It's been a while, probably April time? "It's been a couple of months," I improvise, not committing to an exact date. I will have to consult Nate to ensure our timelines are legit.

"And you're getting engaged already? Are you sure about this, Ley? Don't rush into anything, okay?"

"I won't. I promise. Nate makes me happy, and I want to be with him." I try to assure her; however, maybe Louise knows me better than I give her credit for.

"As long as you're happy, that's all I care about." I gulp down the guilt I feel. I hope the truth never gets out after this. "Ley, Claire and I thought you had become fussy, not hooking up with anyone or calling guys back. And all this time you've had Nathan Cardal in your bed!" I end the call after promising to give her a call over the weekend, but the guilt of lying to my friends continues to attack my conscience.

Will they ever forgive me if they find out I'm lying to them?

⚽♥⚽

At the end of my working day, I quickly greet the club's new signing. His medical will be completed by the real club doctor, and I will only become involved in his care if he suffers an injury. There is nothing else for me to stay at work for, and so, as reluctant as I am at returning to Nate's, there is nothing to stall me. As I walk out, I admire the blush pink roses the receptionist has behind her desk. The colour reminds me of my own Rose, and my face flushes with embarrassment. Luckily, no one else will understand my reaction, if they even notice that is.

Damon is waiting outside for me, looking like one of the Men In Black in his black suit, sunglasses and dark, sleek car. I almost laugh at him.

"Damon, can you take me to a supermarket, please? I would like to pick up some food. I could do with porridge oats, yogurt and fruit for my breakfast, and I would like to cook something for dinner," I tell him, and although he is reluctant, he takes me to an M&S food just off the motorway. "Thank you, Damon. Do you want anything? I will literally be ten minutes, I promise."

He tells me he is okay but refuses to wait in the car for me. He stands at the joint entrance and exit points, intimidating the couples and families running in for an impromptu shopping trip. I waste no time browsing, speedily picking up a basket and quickly filling it with berries, bananas, oats, almond milk and yogurt. The couple's meal deal attracts my attention, and I quickly select steak, vegetables, desserts and wine from the array of available dishes.

While at the till, I spot cashews and chocolate covered raisins and cannot resist a sweet treat too. Less than seven minutes and I'm back in Damon's car. He chuckles as he tells me he didn't believe I would be quick. "My wife would go in for bread and come back an hour later," he tells me, his eyes twinkling as he describes his wife.

The house, though lit up, is cold and quiet. No one else is here, and an overwhelming sense of foreboding settles within me. Like I'm an intruder in someone else's life.

Nate didn't say what time he would be home, so after locating my belongings in my dressing room, which is large and filled with boxes and bags of all sizes, I manage to find my work out clothes, nothing too revealing but certainly not my flannel pjs or my silky nighty. Then I quickly shower, washing away the day's frustrations and disappointments.

Checking the time as I return downstairs, it's already way past seven, and still Nate isn't home. Does he usually work late? I check my phone. There are no messages from him, no indication of any issues. My stomach growls again, reminding me that food has been thin on the ground.

To pass the time, I return to Nate's cavernous kitchen. Modern and sleek, it has everything hidden away out of immediate sight, giving it a minimalist effect.

I'm not fond of the concept, especially as I go in search of a chopping board and a bowl. I prepare my oats for the following morning, chopping and slicing the fruit before layering it in between oats and porridge in a Tupperware I find in a cupboard. As I do it, I wonder if I should make Nate breakfast too. That seems like something a fiancée would do.

Then indignation flares inside me. He hasn't called me or met me at home. He's sent no messages to say he'll be late. He's left me waiting without any consideration. I'm not making him breakfast and I'm not waiting any longer to cook our evening meal either. If he wants me to treat him like my fiancé, he best start acting like one and give me some consideration too. I place my assembled breakfast in the fridge and take my cashews, raisins and a banana up to bed with me. I still don't know my way around the house, and without Nate here, I feel uncomfortable snooping.

With nothing else left to do, I pack my overnight bag for my trip tomorrow. The team is playing in the European tournament, and our first match is against Paris. I will be leaving directly with the team after our morning conditioning session and then will return with the team the morning after the match.

Two nights in Paris sounds wonderfully romantic and adventurous; however, this will be my third trip to Paris with the team and I still haven't seen the Eiffel Tower. There is no leisure time, especially not this early on in the season when we have to get back to England in time for our weekend match too.

Packing for my trip is quite easy. I have to wear the official training clothes, like the rest of the medication and response team, and I have official clothes for travelling in too. Apart from underwear, toiletries and nightwear, everything else is covered.

Setting my alarm and sending Damon a message to confirm what time I'd like to be picked up in the morning, I try to relax. The bed is comfortable enough, but my frustration and confusion about Nate and his absence prevent me achieving any sort of peace of mind so I can sleep.

After imagining him in a bar with Jack, laughing and joking at my expense, being pictured without me, and further speculation being made about me, it all accumulates into a massive ball of annoyance and irritation. I have no doubt I will be grinding my teeth in my sleep tonight. Finally, after tossing and turning, I must fall asleep. I hear Nate come home and quickly check my phone, which tells me it's almost midnight. He doesn't smell of liquor or seem inebriated, and he's still in the same suit he was wearing this morning.

Wanting to know what he will do if he thinks I am asleep, I feign my slumber. Nate surprises me by standing near me, just looking at me. He pulls the sheets up over me and mutters under his breath, "I should have called her. I forgot to call her. I won't forget again." As much as I want to sit up and forgive him, Nate thinking about his actions and the consequences is a positive thing.

When my alarm wakes me up, I'm surprised to see Nate still on top of the sheets, fully clothed and fast asleep. He looks younger, more vulnerable, like this. To show him what I class as consideration, I leave him a short note on his bedside table.

***Nate,***
***I am travelling to Paris this evening for work.***
***I will call you to let you know I'm safe.***
***There is food in the fridge.***
***Be back on Friday.***
***Love, L x***

Collecting my breakfast from the fridge before I leave, I wonder if Nate will even realise I am not here. I chuckle to myself as I imagine him suddenly remembering he has a fiancée. "Oh shit! Where did I put her?!" he would shout.

Somehow, the thought lightens my mood.

## CHAPTER 9

### ~ Nate ~

When I wake up, my mouth is as dry as the Sahara desert. It takes me a moment or two to remember why I have been sleeping on top of my bed with my clothes on. Then I remember! I look for Leila, but she's already left, and I still haven't had a chance to apologise to her. Maybe she is still here, I think to myself, dashing down the stairs while calling her name.

However, there is no reply. I check my watch and curse when I realise it is already past nine. Fuck, she's probably been in work for a couple of hours already. Annoyance creeps up over me that she didn't wake me to say goodbye, but then I know I'm being a hypocrite. I didn't wake her last night to apologise either. My internal calling system is all set up, so after fixing myself a coffee, I sit at the breakfast bar and call Leila. She answers on the third ring.

"Isn't it customary to wake your fiancé and kiss him goodbye before you leave for work," I say to her brazenly. I'm hoping my stab at humour will soften her.

"Isn't it also customary for fiancés to call their fiancées to tell them they are working late?" she bites back sharply, and her quick wit impresses me. "At least I left a note, Nate." What note? I didn't see any note, but then I ran so fast out of my room she could have written me a novel and I would have missed it.

"I didn't see your note. I'm sorry about last night. It won't happen again," I tell her contritely, but Leila isn't satisfied with my apology.

"Do you even know what you're apologising for, Nate? Because if you want this to work, you need to learn from the things that piss me off, or you will keep pissing me off." She is so mad that it tickles me. My past girlfriends have pretty much let me get away with anything and everything. But not Leila. She will not tolerate my poor behaviour, and she is willing and able to stand up to me and make me accountable. I have never felt as turned on or awed.

"For working late–" I begin but she cuts me off.

"We all have to work late. I will work late on occasion too. But you left me waiting without so much as a phone call. Is my time not as important as yours? Is that what you think?" Her voice raises an octave, and I recoil from her outrage.

"That's not what I think. I simply forgot, but I realised when I got home that I should have called you. The contract exchange with Piotr's agent ran over until almost midnight. I didn't realise I was going to be so late. I'm sorry." I try to placate her, but she still hasn't finished chastising me.

"I have to work late this evening. Would you like it if I didn't tell you or let you know I'm safe?" I shake my head as I protest loudly that I wouldn't. "Then show me the same courtesy, Nate. Treat me how you expect me to treat you. I have to go."

"Wait!" I shout to her. "Did you like your flowers? I thought you would have called me when I sent them. Can I take you out to dinner tonight to make it up to you?" I ask with an edge of shyness. How ridiculous I must sound, asking my fiancée out on a date!

There is a pause on her side, and I begin to think she's hung up when a little voice squeaks. "You sent me flowers? Where?" she replies to me. She didn't even get my flowers. No wonder she is so pissed off. I should have called to ensure she got them.

"I sent you two dozen long stem pink roses to the training ground. They reminded me of your family heirloom, and I thought you would appreciate it. I even wrote a note," I confess to her, wondering how it all went wrong.

"I didn't get them, Nate. But thank you. If I would have known, I–" She pauses, as if she recalls something of significance. "I did see some flowers at the reception as I was leaving last night, but no one mentioned them being from you."

"I'll call the florist now and see what happened. Will you go to dinner with me this evening?" I add hastily. I have some serious ground to cover here.

"No. I'm sorry, Nate. I told you in my letter, I'm leaving for Paris this afternoon with the team. I will call you when I get there. I really do have to go now."

"Leila!" I call before she hangs up again. "Be safe, my love." I can tell from her stutter that she is shocked by my display.

"I-I will. You too, Nate," she says before she finally hangs up.

As I said I would, I call the florist, who assures me they delivered as far as they were permitted. "The lady on reception told me that I couldn't go any further but that she would let Ms Monrose know. I even asked her to call her down while I was there, but she said no on account of the media invasion she's been suffering with. It seemed legit enough."

"I agree," I concede, so having not found my answer with the florist, I decide to go down to the training ground and find out why Leila wasn't given her flowers.

It's a long shot, but maybe I can make things up to her before she leaves.

Less than an hour later, I am showered, dressed and at the training ground in search of answers. Like a red rag to a bull, the sight of Leila's flowers behind the receptionist's desk fuels my anger even more.

"Those flowers were for my fiancée, and I want to know why she didn't get them," I say politely yet firmly to the receptionist while pointing to Leila's pink roses that look so much more glorious in the flesh as they sit idly on the shelf behind the front desk.

"I'm sorry, Mr Cardal. I wasn't on duty yesterday. There is no note on it, so I just assumed the management had brightened up the area," the redhead replies to me, not meeting my eye but remaining professional and polite.

"Okay, who was working the reception yesterday?" I ask her more gently, and she smiles her appreciation at my consideration. "It would have been around 2 pm," I add.

"Oh, that's usually our shift changeover time. Maybe it was lost in translation. Are you sure there was a card, sir?" I nod to her slowly. I know there was a card. I fucking typed it out myself. If the press has got a hold of that, I am not going to be happy. "Jenny was on duty yesterday morning, and Abby took over from her at 2 pm. Jenny will be in this afternoon if you'd like to talk to her," she adds, when an idea hits me. The CCTV. I can check to ensure the press didn't come onto the site and take the card.

"Don't worry, I'll check with security," I tell her as I walk over to the security station. "Hey, Mike," I greet the older man sitting behind the Perspex screen.

"Nathan! How are you? I heard you're finally settling down, my man!" he says to me jovially. I've known Mike since I was a child. He worked for my father, and when I took over, I made him head of security."

"I certainly am! Why are you working the security desk?" I enquire. It's not like him to be doing the manual work; he's more of a coordinator and organiser now, with an office and everything.

"I'm covering my son's shifts. My first grandchild is on its way. I'm keeping busy because my Judy is driving me crazy with all her worrying and fussing." I grin and congratulate him on his growing family. "How are you feeling now, Nathan? Everything good with you?" I nod quickly and change the subject back to the matter in hand.

"Was there any press inside the lobby yesterday? I sent my fiancée flowers, but the note mysteriously disappeared and she didn't receive them." Mike frowns, as he picks up his keys, ushering me into the back office.

"There were vultures outside, but I told my team to ensure they stayed behind the barrier that marks the beginning of our private property. We had a few lightweight drones coming over recording and there is nothing we can do about that. But no one has physically been on site that I am aware of. But let's check," he says, pointing to the screens.

Pulling out my phone, I identify the exact time the confirmation came through from the florist, and Mike quickly finds it on the screen.

"Okay, so here is your florist, and you can clearly see the card attached to the outside. That's Jenny on the reception. She is probably informing her that no one can be admitted past that point because of the media intrusion." He squints as he watches. "Jenny picks up the phone but replaces it mid dial when Mr McAllister approaches her."

In disgust, I watch for myself as Mr McAllister sends Jenny home ten minutes early and mans the reception himself. We both observe him looking around to ensure the coast is clear before he removes the card from the flowers. He then places the flowers on the shelf behind the reception and arranges other items around them, making it look as though they are part of the décor.

"That fucking snake! What is his game?" I say louder than I should. "What's he done with my card? That was private for Leila." We continue to observe him, and when Abby arrives for work a few minutes later, he taps his watch and chastises her despite her not being late. Then he walks off into his office with the card firmly in his hand. That rat bastard!

"Now, Nathan. Think about this. Don't go wading in. Play this cool. I'll make you a copy of this clip as evidence, and from now on, we will keep a closer eye on him." I know he is speaking sense, but I want my card back. I want nothing more than to scrag Mr Fucking McAllister by his throat and scare the living day lights out of him.

"He took my card. He stopped Leila from getting her flowers and her card. He's getting a kicking for that, Mike." Mike smiles at me, and I shift uncomfortably at what he sees in me.

"She means a lot to you, doesn't she?" I nod stiffly. "That will never go away; she'll always be right there at the forefront of your mind, deep in your heart and soul. Ingrained in your bones. You've caught the bug, my son."

Although he smiles at me with a knowing twinkle in his eye, it seems at odds with what he has told me. Not only am I doomed, but if Mike has seen it, everyone else will have too.

Against his counsel, I storm into McAllister's office. He is talking on the phone, so I cut the call. "You are one slimy little shit. You do know that I could fire your ass right now?"

"M-Mr Cardal. What is the p-problem? What c-can I do?" he stutters, his face and neck turning a delightful shade of scarlet as I uncomfortably stare at him.

"Flowers," I say to him bluntly. "Fucking flowers!" I shout.

"I don't know what you mean, Mr Cardal. You're not making any sense–" I slam my hands down on the desk, making him jump back. If looks could kill, the man in front of me would be as dead as a dodo.

"I've got you on camera, you fucking little slug. Where have you put the card?" His eyes widen and his mouth opens and closes. "What's your problem, Shane? Have you got an issue with Leila?"

"You know who she is, don't you? Is she really interested in you, Mr Cardal? Or is there something else at play here?"

"What exactly are you suggesting, Mr McAllister?" The cool, sweet sound of my fiancée's voice breaks the red mist that descended on me when I discovered who had taken the card. "Nate, darling. Calm down. I'm sure Mr McAllister has a very good explanation for his appalling behaviour."

Turning around to face Leila, I immediately know I am mistaken in thinking she is calm. The fire in her eyes tells a totally different story. She is absolutely raging.

We are finally on the same page.

## ~ Leila ~

The morning has been sad and challenging. I am sitting in my office after breaking the news to Jonesy that he does indeed require surgery and will probably be out for the whole season. Although he was aware this could be the case, it is devastating all the same to have it confirmed.

One of the academy players, a young sixteen year old, comes to see me on the request of the academy coach, Julian Britton. The young man introduces himself to me as Tyler, and I quickly discover that he has been experiencing some pain in his back. After a thorough assessment, I notice a small curve in his spine, probably caused by a consistent muscle strain, and suggest he have an MRI and take up Pilates.

As I am stretched for time, I try to take a moment to eat my pre-prepared breakfast to stop my stomach from growling and rumbling; however, I'm interrupted after one mouthful. "Doc, the gaffer wants to speak to you about Jonesy's recovery," the assistant coach tells me, but as I go to follow him, my phone rings, and the caller display shows me it's Nate trying to contact me.

"I'll catch you up in a minute; I need to take this," I tell him, closing my door between us.

Nate calling me takes me by surprise. His casual tone melts me in a way his anger or over sweetness never could. And the fact that he is apologising for his lack of thought softens my annoyance at him. However, when I realise that he thinks I am rude for not acknowledging his gift to me, my frustration fills my gut again. He sent me flowers, the very flowers I admired on my way home last night, and I didn't receive them. No one has ever sent me flowers before. I light up inside at the thought of his kind gesture, but the irritation at having not actually received them or enjoyed them tarnishes my sweet moment.

Once I end the call with Nate, I go straight to the gaffer, who asks all the questions I expect him to ask about Jonesy; alternative treatments, what will happen if we delay or 'watch and wait'. "The team will suffer greatly without him on the squad," he adds solemnly when I explain that although I would get a second opinion, to play with this sort of injury would be catastrophic to his physical health.

"What about bringing Jonesy on board in a coaching or supporting capacity while he recovers from his injury? The team would still feel his presence, and he can pass on the wealth of experience he has to younger players, who will benefit from it." I make my suggestion, and embarrassment at my forwardness colours my cheeks.

"It's a nice idea, Doc. But the board would never go for it. If Jonesy has to take time to recover, they will not want him coming into training; he will move on to rehabilitation." My heart sinks. I knew it would be a long shot, but I didn't expect my idea to be completely shut down.

"Leila?" someone calls out to me from outside the gaffer's office. Samantha, one of the receptionists, steps into the office. "I'm sorry to interrupt. I just thought you should know that Mr Cardal is downstairs, and he is very unhappy. Would you come and speak to him, please?"

Nate saves me from further embarrassment and disappointment. "Sorry, I have to go. I'll ask for a second opinion if you really want it," I shout back to the gaffer as I follow Samantha down the clinical corridor into the bright reception. I can hear Nate shouting and don't hesitate in following his voice to Mr McAllister's office. I slowly open the door and hear Mr McAllister's assassination of my character.

"You know who she is, don't you? Is she really interested in you, Mr Cardal? Or is there something else at play here?" he spits out at Nate through gritted teeth, his ruddy face ready to explode in rage.

A quick glance at Nate confirms he is ready to lose his cool. That tick in his jaw that I find ever so attractive is doing overtime at the moment. His defence of me is admirable, but I am quite capable of guarding myself. "What exactly are you suggesting, Mr McAllister?" I say to him, breaking the stare off between the two men. Mr McAllister looks bad at me, shock mingling with disdain on his face. I have never noticed him looking at me with such hatred before. "Nate, darling. Calm down. I'm sure Mr McAllister has a very good explanation for his appalling behaviour," I say to my fiancé, mostly to give myself time to process why Mr McAllister suddenly despises me but also to lean on Nate for support too.

"Why did you lie to get this job? If you had told the truth, you would never have been given this prestigious opportunity. You are here by deception," he accuses me.

"How dare you. I'm here because I am qualified and the best candidate for the job. Are you suggesting otherwise?" I shout back at him. How dare he! I have worked hard for every single qualification I have presented to my employers. I have never lied or expanded on the truth.

"You should have been honest about who you are. Do you know who her father is? Do you know what–" Mr McAllister stops mid-sentence when Nate descends on him.

"Apologise to her, now. I know who she is and who her father is. It's got fuck all to do with anyone else. Leila got the job because she is the best sports injury specialist in the country. She is an asset to our team," Nate states fiercely, and although I don't know the extent of what he knows, his blind support of me assures me that he believes in me and my ability to do my job, regardless of who my father is.

"No. If she stays, I am going. I am not working with Frankie Monrose's daughter. I am not letting that man pollute my life any more than he did when he was alive." I honestly have no idea what McAllister's problem is.

"Fine. Have it your way, Shane. I'll call security now to escort you off the premises. Leave your ID and your access passes. And while you wait, if you wouldn't mind handwriting your ultimatum, I will deliver it to the board myself."

Mr McAllister splutters in exasperation. "You're choosing her over me? After everything I've done for this club?"

"She is going to be my wife. You are the only one who has an issue and has made unreasonable ultimatums, Shane." Nate steps closer to me and threads his fingers through mine. "Your service to the club is appreciated, but I will never allow anyone to speak to my wife in such a derogatory and insulting way. So, if you want to stand by your ultimatum and refuse to apologise for offending and upsetting Ms Monrose, I'll accept your resignation with immediate effect."

"You're making a mistake. A big mistake. She's her father's daughter through and through. She'll be the end of you, Nathan, and the end of Redvale too."

As he continues to spew his venom at me, I begin to tremble. He really hates my father. I didn't even realise he knew my father. There was no space on the application form to put *Oh and by the way, my dad once played professionally*. I wanted my job on my merit, not on who my dad was.

"Mike, ensure Mr McAllister is escorted off the premises without his access passes, and he is not to be granted admission again. Then, once he's gone, I will need you to secure all the data and information in this office." Mike, the head of security, smiles at Nate and nods to me, while Nate tugs on my hand and directs me outside to his car.

"I should get back; I'm leaving for Paris soon," I tell him, avoiding eye contact. The incident has left me shaken up, and my emotions are very close to the surface right now.

"Come to Paris with me. I'll clear it with… Well, I'll clear it with the gaffer and the board right now. You can join the team for training in the morning, and if there are any emergencies, they can get you on the phone," he says, rubbing his thumbs over the top of my hand. It is such a small yet comforting gesture. "Have you ever been up the Eiffel Tower?"

Shaking my head, excitement grows in my tummy as I think of Paris with Nate. This could be epic. "Okay, if you can clear it with everyone, I'd love to see the Eiffel Tower."

"And spend time with your fiancé!" he pushes, with a glint in his eye that is becoming all too familiar.

I roll my eyes at him, and a blush creeps up over my face as I concede. "And spend time with my fiancé!" Nate smiles at me in approval.

"You're such a good girl when you want to be of course," he says through a chuckle, which is surprising considering the naughty thoughts that are running through my mind right now!

Nate insists on me waiting in his car while he ensures Mr McAllister's office is secured and so he can call the board of directors to tell them of his resignation. I'm glad for the reprieve. The hatred Mr McAllister rained down on me shocked me to the core, and I am not entirely sure where it came from. My father never played for Redvale, and I was unaware until today that Mr McAllister even knew him.

Although I know my mother will be annoyed if I ask her questions, there is no one else to turn to. My grandparents on my father's side are no longer with us. There is no one else I can ask. I wait for her to answer my call, nervously biting the inside of my cheek until I taste my own blood seeping onto my tongue. I wish it wasn't so difficult to talk to my mum. She is all I have left, and I don't mean to hurt her. I'm sure she doesn't intend on hurting me either.

"Leila, how are you, my darling?" my mother asks when she answers the call. It should comfort me that she is in a cordial mood, but the nerves still rage in my body. She never talks about my father, but from the photograph I have seen, they were really happy together before he died.

"Hey. I'm okay. Listen, I've just been involved in an altercation at work. Someone read the papers and found out who my father is and verbally attacked me because of it," I explain to her. Tears sting the corner of my eyes, but I will not disgrace myself or Nate by crying out here. Not when the press could be spying. "Nate stepped in when it became personal, but I need to talk to you about it."

"They put your father's name in the paper?" she shouts at me incredulously. "What do you want me to say, Leila? I warned you about working in that industry. Who attacked you?" she asks me, anger lacing through her every word.

"The club manager, Mr McAllister. He said I obtained the job through deception. That if he had known who my dad was, he would never have worked with me." As I think about what he said once again, I question why that hurt so much. Sure, Mr McAllister had never been a massive fan of mine. Most of the time we seemed to be on opposing sides when it came to injured players and their return to the game. However, I had always believed that there was a mutual respect between us in our joint concern for player welfare. Now, it's clear that it was based on certain conditions that I had no control over.

There is a deathly silence on the line, and then my mother squeaks out, "Shane McAllister?" In the surprise of her knowing his name, I fail to answer her. "You work with Shane McAllister? Leila. I want you to come home. Now," she adds forcefully.

"No, you can't tell me to come home! I'm a grown woman. My home is here. How do you know Mr McAllister and why does he now hate me?" However, she doesn't answer me. She slams down her phone on me, leaving me with more questions than I started with.

"Are you okay?" Nate asks as he returns to his car. His look of concern causes my upset to rise again. I quickly nod to him and look out the window so he doesn't see how much the entire situation has affected me.

"Let's go and pack an overnight bag that doesn't consist of work clothes, and then, we will be taking a private jet to Paris. Where else would you like to see? We could go to the Louvre too?" I expected him to grill me about my father and Mr McAllister. But Nate acts as though nothing has happened. I know I owe him some sort of explanation, but there are things I don't want to share, and then there is apparently plenty I don't know too.

"I've always wanted to see Notre Dame or the Palace of Versailles. There has never been enough time before when I've travelled with the team," I say meekly.

"I'd love to spend a few days there with you and show you everything." I try to interrupt him because I can't stay for a few days; I have to get back for work. "I know, I know. You have to work, so for now, we will choose two places and we can plan to return in the future."

The way he talks troubles me and soothes me at the same time. We have a temporary arrangement, yet he talks about the future. We aren't a real couple, but he still treats me with the consideration of a fiancée. It's nice to have someone to share the new experiences with and to make plans for the future with, but it's concerning that I might get carried away when this has to end.

"Thank you, Nate. I know I owe you some answers, but I'm still working through them right now." He takes my hand from my knee and presses his lips to my knuckles, while he continues to drive.

"There is no rush. I'll be here when you're ready. Until then, we should have some fun," he tells me, and for the first time since I walked into Mr McAllister's office, the knot in my tummy eases. "Are you going to try frog legs? I'll be so disappointed if you don't at least try them!"

"Eww, no way! Are you?" I reply to him in disgust as my laughter bubbles up in my chest, lifting the remnants of guilt, confusion and shame that has been plaguing me.

"No, I like the garlic snails better. You'll definitely try them, won't you?" He continues to tease through a laugh.

"I'll try whatever you do. That's my promise," I tell him straight, as we arrive on the driveway.

"I'm going to hold you to that, Ms Monrose."

# Chapter 10

## ~ Leila ~

We arrive back at Sandybank, and my growling tummy tells Nate I still haven't had breakfast. "I think I'm feeling hungrier because I didn't eat a proper evening meal last night either. But look, I got us steak and stuff. Maybe I could rustle this up before we go."

Nate looks on as I pull the steak and vegetables from the fridge. An expression affects his face, one I've never seen before. "You went shopping for us?" he asks in a low voice, pointing to the food I bought yesterday.

"Well, yeah. It seemed like something a fiancée would do. I was going to cook for us." He closes the space between us, pacing towards me with purpose, and butterflies dance in my tummy when he reaches me.

"I'm sorry, Leila. Can we start over. I fucked up. I should have been doing what a fiancé does too." He leans his forehead against mine, and his cologne, woody and masculine, fills my nostrils and feels familiar now. "Why don't you go and pack your pack for Paris, and I'll cook for us. In future, we will plan our evening meals together, and if there is an issue, we will work it out." He peers into my eyes with sincerity until I nod my agreement.

Placing my hands on his chest, I run them up over his shoulders before fully wrapping my arms around his neck. "I'd like that too, Nate." All thoughts of food leave my mind as his lips take possession of my own. His kiss is hard, fiery and intoxicating. I moan into his mouth as he bites my bottom lip and lifts me onto the countertop.

"If I were to get on my knees right now to beg your forgiveness, I would be just the right height to show you how sorry I truly am," he murmurs into my ear in between kissing my throat. My tummy clenches as shots of desire spiral throughout my body. We are interrupted by my rumbling tummy again. "Go and pack while I cook," he instructs me firmly.

"What about you, Nate? Don't you need to pack?" I ask him as he lifts me back to the floor.

He shakes his head. "I always have an extra bag prepared just in case. I just need to slip a couple of things into it." The final part intrigues me.

"What things? Did you get condoms?" I enquire, my mouth engaging before my brain can intervene.

"Amongst another couple of essentials, yes, I did. Should I bring them?" My mind literally explodes with curiosity… What other essentials and how many condoms is he bringing? Of course, I do want him to bring them. I just don't want to seem overeager.

"If you have room in your bag, there's no harm in bringing them, just in case," I say to him in a flushing bluster. He laughs at my reply, a deep, booming sound that fills my body with joy.

"Just in case? Come on, Leila. You're a big girl now. Tell me what you want." His whisper caresses me, sending a bolt of longing throughout my entire body.

What do I want? It seems such a stupid question because the answer is blatantly obvious to me. "We're starting over, remember. I want to get to know my fiancé better. So, bring the condoms in case I like what I see." I can see the passion burning in Nate's eyes and know my own reflect back the same way. I need to remind myself intermittently to not fall for Nate. That would not be a good thing. I want him. I know that for sure, and hopefully, a few nights together will be enough to get him out of my system.

My dressing room has even more bags inside than it did this morning when I left for work. Thick, expensive card bags with silk ribbons as handles and gold leaf on the logos at the front contain the clothes, shoes, bags and other expensive items that Nate's personal shopper has deemed necessary for me. It's a little overwhelming, so I try to make a mental list of everything I may need. "Underwear, let's start with underwear."

Sure enough, I find three bags with two from Victoria Secret, and another from Fig Leaves that contain everything I might need. There is also a little silk nighty in one and a baby doll. I pick the nighty and decide I'll leave the baby doll for when I return home.

Home. This is actually starting to feel like my home. In one of the long suit covers is an evening gown, a deep blue with one shoulder made from roses and two slits up the skirt at the front. "Wow!" I whisper to myself as I stroke the material. It is exquisite. Far too fancy to take tonight but my oh my. I wonder what occasion Nate could have in mind for such a beautiful dress.

Eventually, I find a sexy black dress for tonight, and some casual jeans and tops for sightseeing. It's usually still warm in Paris this time of year, but the wind can be strong.

I add my stuff to a large holdall I find in my dressing room, and leave my bag on Nate's bed before the scent of food pulls me back downstairs.

As I approach the kitchen, I can hear Nate talking to someone on speakerphone. I wait by the door, unable to tell if it is a private call or if he is okay with me overhearing.

"Reschedule it. I don't care. I'm going to Paris for the night with my fiancée to celebrate our engagement. Tell Dr Singh I will see him when I return."

"Nathan. You know you cannot ignore this. It's important. Go and celebrate your engagement, but you need to go before the weekend." Kym's stern voice, fiercer than I have ever heard it, chastises him.

"Reschedule then for Friday. I've gotta go. I'm cooking for Leila, and everything is looking charred. We're flying in forty minutes as it is." Making a noise to announce my arrival, I call out to Nate.

"Babe, do you want to add anything to my bag? There's loads of room left." I push open the door to the kitchen and smoke bellows out at me. "What the hell? I didn't know we were having a barbecue."

Suddenly, the front door opens, and a short man in his mid to late twenties runs inside, shouting in a language I don't not recognise.

"Oh mio Dio. Signor Cardal, lei sta bruciando di nuovo la mia bella cucina. Ti ho detto di stare lontano da tutto ciò che ha bisogno di riscaldamento. Sei un incubo. Il mio povero cuore non ce la fa!"

"SHIT!" Nate shouts. "Can I get you a subway? We have to go now, or Giovanni is going to kill me. I am banned from the kitchen after last time."

"My bag's on the bed," I tell him as Giovanni, dressed in the chef's whites, continues to exclaim and dramatically throw down pots and pans in distress.

"They're the keys to the car, gorgeous; go and get it. I promise I will feed you." Peering back into the kitchen again, Giovanni wails out loudly as he throws away the lovely vegetables I picked with care only yesterday. It seems my fiancé could do with some lessons in the kitchen.

"Hello. I am Leila," I shout out to him, and he turns abruptly.

"A-ha, the new fiancée? Did you know about this? Mr Cardal is a bad man. A very bad man... look at my pan, look at the beautiful food he has wasted," he tells me with tears in his eyes. "You must tell him, I cannot work like this. This is torture."

"I will. I will tell him he is a bad cook and to stay out of your kitchen." His face lights up at the thought of an ally in his camp. I need him as my ally too. "Giovanni? I am so hungry. Can I please get my fruit from the fridge before I go?"

His expression changes immediate as he passes me the punnet of strawberries and blueberries from where I left them. "Oh mia povera dolce signora. Certo, certo. Devi mangiare. Quando ripristinerò l'ordine nella mia cucina, farò in modo che tu non abbia mai più fame. Tieni il tuo uomo fuori di qui. È un cuoco terribile," he says to me, and although I don't understand his words, I feel like he is telling me the saddest story ever.

"See you soon, Giovanni. And thank you," I say to him as I run out to the car with Nate hot on my heels.

## ~ Nate ~

My lunch for Leila is all going to plan, then my phone rings, and I groan internally when Kym begins to chastise me for skipping my appointment at the hospital. I had sent her a short text when I decided to go to Paris, asking her politely to clear my schedule for the next few days. She sent a string of replies expressing her displeasure, and after the second or third one, I stopped reading them. I'm a grown assed man. I am allowed to celebrate my engagement with the one person I want to know better, and nothing will get in the way of that.

The vegetables are looking perfect, the steak sizzles away, still pink through the middle. I go in search of plates and cutlery when Kym's voice changes. "I'm worried about you. You're taking on so much. You need to take care of yourself." Her softened tone reaches me far more than her stern words of reality. "As much as you like to think it, you are not invincible. I'm begging you to see reason."

"Kym, I am well aware of the importance of this appointment. Trust me, I am. But life is too short, so I'm taking this trip. I am going to Paris and I'm celebrating my engagement. Everything else can wait for a couple of days," I tell her as reasonably as I can. I don't want her to worry about me, especially not more than is necessary.

"Nathan. You know you cannot ignore this. It's important. Go and celebrate your engagement, but you need to go before the weekend." She relents; however, she returns to using her stern voice once more, and it only takes a couple of seconds for me to lose interest and resume cooking.

"Shit!" I exclaim while wondering if I can pass the food off as well done. The perfect vegetables now resemble charred fingers in the pan, and when I flip the steak, I am presented with a completely black side. This is a disaster. Leila is going to waste away into nothing if the poor soul has to rely on me.

"Reschedule then for Friday. I've gotta go. I'm cooking for Leila, and everything is looking charred." Checking my watch to see how much time I have left to rustle up something, I am alarmed when I realise we should have left for our flight already. "We're flying in forty minutes as it is," I say before I cut off the call.

Leila walks in just as the pan holding the steak begins smoking. I have forgotten to turn off the heat, and the charred meat now resembles chunks of tree bark. For fuck's sake, is there anything I can do? I don't know what she says to me, because as the door swings, I catch sight of Giovanni, Jack's chef.

That's it, we are out of here. I throw the car keys to Leila and promise to buy her a subway or something. And then dash out the kitchen through the other door, avoiding Giovanni before he can shout at me again 'for using his kitchen'.

Taking the stairs two at a time, I quickly throw the condoms and the small velvet box that contains Leila's engagement ring into my open bag and pick hers up from our bed. As I thunder down the stairs again, I hear Giovanni on the phone complaining loudly about me.

Leila sits in the passenger seat of the car, eating fruit. She laughs at me as I speed away from the house. "Are you scared of Giovanni, Nate?" she asks as she plucks a plump strawberry from the punnet she holds possessively in her hands. "I don't know what he was saying to me, but I can tell he is not a fan of yours."

"He was telling you that I am a terrible cook, that I ruined his pans and that I am banned from his kitchen." Laughing out loud at my words, my mood lightens and I grin back at her. The anxiety that filled me earlier eases as I share this moment with Leila, her finding it as funny as I do.

"He's not wrong to be fair. What the hell did you do to the food? It looked incinerated. I swear I went upstairs for five minutes." We laugh together and eat her fruit as I take us to the airfield. "The fruit will be enough until we get to Paris, but I swear to god, Nate. You best make it up to me once we get there. I want a proper meal and a dessert," she tells me, making me eye up my own dessert and fantasise. This irresistible woman, spread wide all for me.

"I concede. I owe you big time, gorgeous. I promise I will fill you up tonight," I reply cheekily, and she smacks my hand in outrage at my crass joke. "I have everything planned. You will not be going hungry," I tell her as I park the car. Already I can see my valet and pilot approaching the aircraft. I pick up the last strawberry from her punnet before I step out of the car.

"Hey, that's the last one!" she shouts to me. She follows me to the rear of the car to get our bags, which I lift with one hand and place by my feet.

When she is close enough to me, I lift the strawberry so it's level with my face and slowly lick all the way along its seeded exterior. Her eyes widen as she watches me, and the seconds seem to pulse between us. The strawberry is sweet, but not as sweet as I imagine Leila to taste like.

"I licked it, and now it's mine, gorgeous." Thinking I have sufficiently riled her, I grin at her, all the while hoping she is as turned on about this as I am.

However, Leila is always one step ahead of me. She leans forward, and I think she's going to kiss me, but instead she leans closer to my ear and whispers to me, "I like the game you want to play. So yes, you licked it and now it is yours." She leans back, smiling at me, before licking the strawberry too. A rush of blood shoots straight to my groin, fuck! I want that tongue; I want that mouth. I want her! Then out of nowhere she bites the strawberry, leaving me with only the stem, and in between chews she adds, "And whatever is yours… is mine now. Remember?"

She walks towards the jet, chewing the strawberry, with a grin on her face, leaving me to pick up the bags and chase after her.

And what a chase it will be!

## ~ Leila ~

My body is humming in anticipation of what is to come. The atmosphere between Nate and I is on fire. He has the innate ability to make me laugh and want to tear his clothes off in lust at the same time. By the time I reach the steps for his jet, Nate is right at my heels. His firm warm hand sits on the small of my back as he introduces me to the flight team.

Having never been on a private plane before, I'm unsure of what to expect. The doorway leads to a comfortable and stylish seating area with a table to one side. It reminds me of the inside of a limousine, only bigger. "Where would you like to sit?" Nate asks from behind me when I stall. "Window? Aisle?"

Knowing the flight attendant is watching from a curtained area, I take an opportunity to play up to my role as Nate's fiancée. "On your knee," I say as I step aside to let him through. Taking my cue, he pulls me close to him. His hard body crashes against my own, and I throw caution to the wind as I wrap my arms around his neck and kiss him deeply. It's all for show, well maybe fifty percent for show, but boy does it feel good.

"That's just for a start," he whispers to me as he kisses over to my ear, causing me to lose track of my thoughts. "You can sit on my knee now, but later you will be sitting on my–"

Aware of where his dirty mouth is going and that we have a small audience, I kiss him again to prevent him from finishing his sentence, while yearning bubbles in the pit of my stomach, and Nate chuckles into our kiss. He pulls me down with him as he sits in his seat, allowing me to sit on his lap as requested. This trip is going to be so good. I can feel it already. "Do you like to play cards?" Nate asks me while pulling a deck from a concealed drawer.

"I can't play poker, never mastered the face. But I like blackjack." He places the cards into his bag and encourages me to lean closer to him, so I rest my head against his shoulder and soak in the feel of being in his strong embrace.

"Blackjack it is then. I will teach you how to play poker, though, if you want." I nod to him in response as a few additional ideas pop into my head. The possibilities are endless.

The flight is short and pleasant. We are served snacks and drinks but again, still nothing substantial, and I have to admit that the whole procedure is a lot easier and more enjoyable than flying commercial. We spend most of the time in the air kissing and fondling each other, and once the staff member has served us, they retreat and leave us in relative privacy.

"Thank you for all this, Nate. It's more than I could have dreamed of. I've always wanted to see Paris, like properly," I thank him shyly, and he kisses my temple when I do. My skin puckers and a shiver of desire runs through my body as he rubs circles into the base of my back, slowly finding his way under my shirt.

"Hopefully, we have plenty more adventures and experiences to look forward to," he murmurs back to me as he nips at my earlobe. "There is so much I want to show you. So much I want us to share." Warmth spreads throughout my body. This is what happiness must feel like. Although I remind myself that this is temporary, I don't see any harm in enjoying what we have right now. In fact, I see it as my reward for having to put on this show in the first place.

"What do you want to show me?" I ask him curiously. There are a lot of places in the world that I would like to see and explore. I just hadn't anticipated it being this year and definitely not with someone like Nate, but this just makes it all the more thrilling.

Nate leans close to me, bringing his mouth to my ear again. "What I want to show you, if you want the same, is everything." I shift slightly on his lap, and he groans low as though in pain. "You're driving me crazy, Leila, wiggling that sexy ass all over me. Can you feel how hard you make me?"

The evidential bulge pressing against me confirms that my unintentional teasing is having a profound effect upon him. One I want to see more of. "Do you want me to sit in my own seat?" I put it to him straight, but as he hugs me closer, I giggle. "You're driving yourself crazy, Nate. Don't go blaming me! Anyway, I'd like to change into something nice before we land, so I will leave you in peace."

He groans aloud this time. "You leave me knowing the state I'm in over you, and tell me that you're going to be getting naked, and then claim you're not torturing me!" He moans as I stand, before lightly smacking me on my butt as I walk away. Another jolt of arousal passes through me. Dear god, how am I going to last the whole evening without jumping him?! "Anyway, don't take too long, gorgeous. We're almost there."

Rushing so that I look nice for our trip, I slip off my work clothes and change into my jeans with a dressy top. I run a brush through my hair, swipe lipstick on and pinch my cheeks for colour. I am just spritzing myself with perfume when Nate knocks on the bathroom door to tell me we need to be seated for landing.

"You look pretty. I almost forgot, I have your ring." He pulls out a little velvet covered box and opens it to me. A beautiful, classy solitaire diamond ring sits nestled against the contrasting black satin inside.

"You're not getting down on one knee?" I press him, arching my brow in disapproval. He rolls his eyes and kneels in front of me.

"Leila, shall we get engaged?" he says very seriously, with laughter dancing in his eyes, contradicting him.

"Why not? It would be a shame for this ring to stay hidden away." He slips the ring on my finger, and I'm surprised to see it fits. "It's beautiful, Nate. Perfect."

"A perfect ring for my perfect fiancée," he adds. We sit together for the landing, which is smooth. Once Nate gets us both clearance, we hold hands as we walk together to a waiting car, complete with driver. It is warm and muggy, but not uncomfortably so. Paris is wonderfully warm in late August, and every time I have visited has been as glorious as today.

"We'll go straight to the Eiffel Tower. Jean-Paul will take our bags to the hotel. I want us to make the most of the time we have." I have no objections to that. "Leila?" he adds, as he wraps his arm back around my waist.

"Yes?" I say with a small smile, enjoying how much the feel of his arm around me still affects me. Nate is masculine, strong and assured. I am proud to be on his arm as it is. I am proud to be his fiancée.

"Welcome to Paris, gorgeous. This will be the first time you've seen Paris this way." He kisses me slowly this time, lazily, a sultry kiss that leaves me begging for more. Especially when he bites my bottom lip as he pulls away. "We best make a move, or I'll not want to share you."

The feeling is mutual! Do I really need to see the Eiffel Tower? Or eat? Right now the burning fever between my legs seems to be in more imminent need of attention. However, I came all this way for a reason, and my lustful yearning will have to wait for a short while. Nate opens the car door for me, and I duck my head to sit in the back of the car.

"Can we please eat something proper, Nate," I say as my tummy growls again. He nods to me, taking out his phone and tapping it.

"On it. We are eating at Madame Brasserie," he says with a smile.

"Is that on the way?"

"No, gorgeous, it is one of the restaurants in the tower."

Oh my goodness!

## Chapter 11

### ~ Nate ~

The area around the Eiffel tower is all pedestrianised. We therefore get out of the car a few minutes' walk away and stroll across the Pont d'Iena that offers tourists passage over the Seine River. I watch Leila in fascination. Everything she sees brings wonder to her eyes; even the boats cruising down the river bring delight to her face. Her reactions bring a whole bunch of emotions right to the surface; feelings that I didn't know I had the capacity to experience, ones I certainly haven't felt before. When the Eiffel Tower finally comes into view before us, Leila grabs on to my hand, her engagement ring biting into my skin in a comforting reminder that for now she is mine.

"Nate! It's so pretty! Look how big it is! I can't believe we are actually going to the top." Her appreciation and wonder stuns me. I can't help pulling her to me and kissing her in full view of everyone around us. They don't call Paris 'the capital of romance' for nothing. "What was that for?" she asks me when I finally let her go.

"Can't a man kiss his gorgeous fiancée?" I deflect, but her answering smile lets me know that she enjoyed our kiss, even if more than a couple of people stopped to stare at us. "We need to hurry, or we'll miss our tour time," I tell her, changing the subject.

Knowing there are always queues and thousands of tourists, I paid for a VIP guided tour that gives us priority access to all areas. The young guide, a French woman called Antoinette, greets us both and passes information pamphlets to Leila, who seems to bounce on the balls of her feet in excitement.

Wanting her to have the best experience ever, I ask her what she wants to do. "I know your hungry, so do you want to eat first or–"

"No, I want to go right to the top and look out first. Please!" she replies enthusiastically. "Are there loads of steps?" she asks Antoinette with interest. I don't think the steps actually bother her.

"Non, mademoiselle. Vous êtes traité à l'expérience de l'ascenseur," Antoinette replies, but Leila doesn't understand most of what she says to her.

"She said, 'You are being treated to the elevator experience,'" I interpret for her.

"You speak French?" she inquires with a smile, and I nod to her. "Say something in French to me, Nate!"

Lowering my voice, I tug her closer to me and murmur into her ear. "Tu es tellement sexy. J'ai hâte de vous emmener dans mon lit ce soir," I say to her. She takes a sharp intake of breath, and her pupils dilate. "Did you understand what I said?" I ask her, my body physically responding when she wets her lips with her little, pink tongue. She shakes her head at me, but her reaction has been noted away. Leila likes dirty talk! And I can say anything in French and make it sound dirty.

"Ahem." Antoinette clears her throat; she is blushing profusely. I obviously wasn't as discreet as I thought, and unlike Leila, she understood every damn word

I said. With a heavily affected accent, she adds, "We'll go straight to the top and work our way down to the restaurant."

Leila remains oblivious to the awkward exchange, and I am thankful she is. She continues to hold my hand and chatters away excitedly until finally the elevator pings and we step out together.

Tears fill her eyes as she looks at the breath-taking panoramic view. "Wow," she whispers simply as she keeps a firm grip on my hand. "The world and everything else with it looks like a pinprick from up here, Nate. We could pretend no one exists while we are here. We could imagine we are the kings of the world from up here."

"It does remind me that we are all insignificant in the grand scheme of things," I say in response. Not really expecting any sort of answer or follow-up.

"No. You're not insignificant, Nate. Not to a lot of people. Especially not to me." Funnily, that is all that seems to matter to me at this moment in time. For this little amount of time, I can fool myself into thinking that this is real, that her feelings for me are genuine and that she is here with me because she wants to be, not because of our contract.

"You're so sweet, gorgeous," I tell her honestly.

We visit the second floor, and I tell her what I know about the city. The great monuments of note, the Louvre, Notre Dame, and all the bends in the Seine can all be seen clearly from this point. The area is busier, with other visitors milling around to the restaurants and shops. Before we leave to go to the restaurant I booked, we stop at the famous macaron shop and purchase a selection of sweet treats to take away with us.

When we approach the restaurant, Antoinette wishes us a good day, and I thank her for showing us around without too much waiting or intrusion.

Leila, upon smelling the delicious cuisine, looks wistfully at me. "Nate, I'm starving now. What's this place like?" I smile to myself. I chose this one because it's the mid-card place; it's not stuffy and pretentious like the Michelin star one I could have taken her to, and it isn't as informal as the buffet food. The restaurant itself has set service times, but I sent a message to let them know I am visiting.

"Don't worry, gorgeous. The food is delicious here." After giving my name to the maître d', we are escorted to the reserved area. To ensure no one further intrudes, I reserved the whole window area. The panoramic views from here are exquisite. Having never taken the time to fully appreciate it, I observe it through new eyes now I get to share the experience with Leila.

"Bonsoir, Monsieur Cardal. Le chef sait que vous êtes ici et vous servira personnellement. Vous ne serez pas dérangé une fois que nous vous aurons servi. Jouir," the Maître d' tells me after taking our drinks order.

"Merci, mademoiselle," I reply in response, and Leila smiles again when I do.

"How many other languages can you speak, Nate?" she asks me with intrigue in her eyes.

I hold her hand across the table before replying. "Spanish and a little Mandarin. But my French is the best. I am very good at French." The fine blonde hairs on her arm all stand to attention. I can read Leila like a book. She is so open and honest in every response. "What about you? Do you speak any other languages."

She takes a moment to respond. "I thought I knew a little French and Spanish too, but I can see now that I need a lot more practice." She holds my gaze, and for the first time, I notice the cutest little smattering of freckles across the bridge of her nose. She is fucking exquisite! "Maybe you could help me with my French."

"Ce serait avec plaisir," I reply to her and revel in the arousal that flares in her eyes. Dinner needs to be quick. I can't wait much longer.

## ~ Leila ~

It has been a fabulous day. One that I'll never forget, and as we sit looking into each other's eyes, surrounded by all the beautiful splendour, it's pretty easy to forget the rest of the world. Nate promises to help me with my French, but the innuendo is clear. This isn't stopping at vocabulary or even French kissing, although maybe I will give him an oral exam all of my own.

The chef introduces himself to me and shakes Nate's hand. "I'm honoured to have you here, finally, Mr Cardal. Your food will be served shortly. Please accept this bottle of champagne with our compliments," he says to us both as his servers bring both food and champagne to our table.

The food is simply divine, and although the portion sizes are on the delicate side, I still feel full and satisfied. With classical music playing softly in the background and the rest of Paris still bustling about their business below our feet, it's easy to forget we are anywhere other than at home. That's how comfortable I feel with Nate.

As he talks to me about his work and his plans this year within the business world, my mind slips into what my own plans are. I had hoped to set up a foundation by now, but the more I work as an injury specialist, the more I realise how insignificant my contribution is in comparison to what I want to offer. When I first began on this career path, I had high expectations of revolutionising the treatment and rehabilitation of injured players, but my impact has been more of a pinprick than the crater I was hoping for.

"Did you ever want to play football like Jack?" I ask him, as I finish my beef tartare, and I spot a fleeting look in his eyes of regret? Or maybe longing? It appears and disappears so quickly it would have been easy to miss.

"I did for a while, but my talents have always been business based. Investments and innovation," he adds modestly. "When my father passed away, the business needed a leader. I didn't have the time to go kicking a ball, and my investment into Redvale ensured I could still be involved in the football world in some capacity."

His comments intrigue me. Does that mean he was involved *before* his father's death? However, I have pried enough into his life, and he has been respectful of my tight grip on my own life. "I'm ready to head to the hotel. I've had a lovely day, and I intend on having a fantastic night too." I look him in the eye as I finish my sentence. I don't want to play about; I know what I want, and I think Nate should know it.

Smiling widely at me. "I'm glad to hear it, gorgeous. I'll call for the car now, and we can make tracks to the hotel," he whispers to me, pulling out his phone and tapping on it.

"I'm just going to use the bathroom before we leave. Are we staying with the team?" I usually manage to get a room all to myself simply because I'm the only female on the team. However, I am happy to share it with my fiancé.

"No, actually. I hope you don't mind. I took the liberty of checking us in elsewhere. You know so we could have a little space and privacy," he tells me while scratching behind his ear nervously.

I lean up and kiss him. "That's perfect. Thank you, Nate. I'll be two minutes."

As I walk away to the bathroom, I can feel his eyes burning into me. I like that. I quickly use the toilet and refresh my lipstick before running my brush back through my hair. I want to be as desirable to Nate as he is to me.

When I exit the bathroom, Nate is leaning against the wall, waiting for me. "Are you ready for a little walk? We need to cross the Seine again."

I nod to him, rubbing my tummy as I do. "I could do with the exercise. I'll be getting fat with all this delicious food and no running. That reminds me, when can I go running again, Nate? And where can I go? All my exercise has been on hold since we got engaged."

"Keep rubbing your tummy like that and you'll start pregnancy rumours." I immediately still my hands. I had forgotten that we may be followed, that right at this moment in time someone could be photographing us. However, the laughter in Nate's eyes suggests that he isn't upset about my mishap.

"Shit, I'm so sorry, I forgot this is–"

"Leila. I'd be proud to have you as the mother of my children. I'm just trying to save you some hassle. Come on, gorgeous. I have the perfect workout method for you," he tells me as he clasps my hands and tugs me to him, and my temporary attack of anxiety disperses.

The walk back over the Seine seems so different now that I have seen it from above. I know it is only a few paces, not the long stretch of bridge I initially chalked it up as. The black car we left a couple of hours ago sits waiting for us, right where we left it.

"I forgot to ask, Nate, where are we staying?" I ask him. I did mean to ask earlier, but my mind was muddled with the possibilities of what could happen tonight.

"The Peninsula. We have a rooftop suite. You're going to love it; you can see everything from up there." Having never heard of the hotel, I thank him as intrigue swirls up in me.

When I travel with the team, we usually stay in decent hotels, but as a member of the medical staff, and a lowly paid one at that, I always have the standard or basic room. It's always been more than sufficient. However, a glimpse into the players' rooms when one has been injured and they've required assistance has shown me what the difference is. I wonder if tonight's rooftop suite is as nice as the executive suites I have lusted after.

The drive takes less than five minutes through the fast and aggressive traffic of the French capital. I watch the city as it passes by my window, while Nate clicks away on his phone again. We stop in front of what looks like a stately home. A massive residence that is grand and majestic. Something fit for royalty. "What is this place?" I whisper in wonder.

"I told you I booked us into the Peninsula," he replies to me, unsure of himself. "Is this okay?"

"I'm wearing jeans, Nate. Will they let me in?" It looks like the kind of place where you wear a ballgown and lots of jewels. I'm going to lower the tone, strolling in wearing my jeans.

"They'll be honoured to have you here, Leila. Wearing jeans or not."

"The area has been checked, sir, and there are presently no paparazzi within the vicinity."

"Good. Thank you," Nate replies to the driver before turning to me. "Now, Ms Monrose. Kiss me like you really mean it. It's just you and me."

"And your driver!" I tell him, my voice rising. I've kissed him plenty of times already.

"I want to know before we go upstairs how much is for the cameras and how much is all for me."

Without further hesitation, I unclip my seat belt and straddle him. Then I take his face into my hands and kiss him as though my life depends on it.

## ~ Nate ~

Her every reaction fascinates me, but morbid curiosity makes me question how much is for show and how much is truly because she wants this. I don't want her to feel pressured into taking things further, even though I could actually combust with built up tension right now. I need to know if she feels the same connection that I do.

As she kisses me, I know this isn't just me and it isn't for our contract. She wants this just like me. The second bed in the rooftop suite will hopefully not be needed.

Though she sits on my lap and straddles me, the overwhelming need to take control is so powerful that I lift her and slowly lower her until she is lying across the back seat before laying on top of her and kissing her back with equal measure.

She's so sweet and pliable. Receptive and passionate. Everything I could ever want in a woman.

I want to shout in objection when she pulls out of our kiss. "Nate, as hot as this is, why the fuck are we doing this in the back of a cramped car when you've just told me we have a suite there?" she asks, pointing towards The Peninsula, and I can't help but laugh at her.

"Because I can't resist you; I want you so badly," I tell her honestly. She has been candid with me, and I want that to continue.

"I want you too, but can you want me in there, please?" she demands in exasperation. "I've got a seat belt up my ass, and it's not sexy at all!" We laugh together, but wanting her to be comfortable, I reluctantly move away. Lifting the privacy glass between us and the driver, I tell him we are going inside.

"Sir, your bags are in your room, and I have your fob here for the direct elevator access and door pass." He steps out of the car and opens the door for Leila, who shifts in embarrassment, fixing her dishevelled clothes.

"Thank you. I will call you tomorrow morning," I say to him, taking the fob he offers me.

Taking Leila's hand, I follow the signs for the elevator, and as soon as we are alone again, she kisses me. I like that she's forward, that she knows what she wants and is open to exploring this. I pull her shirt out from her jeans and finally touch the skin on her back, dragging her closer to me and pressing myself against her. This is torture, sweet, exhilarating torture, but fuck me, I have never wanted another woman the way I want her right now.

As we kiss, I beg to not be interrupted. I'd be happy to continue, but I know Leila would be mortified, and I do not want this moment to end. I slide my hands down over her ass, lifting her closer to me until her feet no longer touch the ground, and groan in pleasure when she gets the hint and wraps her legs around my waist. My cock, hard and constricted in my pants, presses up against her warm pussy, begging for just a peek at what is to come.

Finally, the lift arrives at our floor, and I pause only to dangle the fob in front of the sensor to open the door to our suite. I walk into our room, carrying and kissing Leila, and as soon as the door closes behind us, she throws her purse to one side and tugs off her top, revealing a black lacy bra and her flawless, creamy skin. Growling low in my throat in sweet satisfaction, I kiss down her neck, deeper into her clavicle, and nip at the hem of her bra, wanting more of the soft flesh.. "You are so fucking perfect, Leila. Gorgeous doesn't do you justice."

Unable to stop, I keep walking until I finally spot a bed, thank fuck for that. I lower her onto the bed and pull my own top off over my head and throw it to one side. When I turn back, Leila has unclasped her bra around the back, but the cups stay in place, the straps falling slightly to show it is loose and ready to fall. "Take it off. Let me see you," I murmur to her, my voice husky with arousal and desire.

She kneels up on the bed and slides the straps off her arms before finally exposing herself. I try to rush to her, but she stops me. "Take them off first, Nate. I can't wait much longer." She tugs on my belt, kissing down from my chest to my abs while she unbuckles my belt and undoes my button and zip.

"I can't wait much longer either, but I've got some work to do first, gorgeous. How about you sit on my face so I can eat your pussy until you come?" I watch in satisfaction as Leila squeezes her legs together, whimpering as she does. "Tell me what you want," I demand of her. I'm hoping I have the stamina to make all her wishes come true, but the need to be inside her, pumping in and out, is overwhelming me.

"I'll sit on your face later. Right now, I want to feel you. I want you. Where are your condoms?" she asks me, unbuttoning her jeans and flashing the tiniest hint of her matching underwear. "I just need to feel you in me. It's driving me insane, Nate."

Putting my two hands under her thighs, I pull her legs forward and push her back onto the bed. "My back pocket," I grunt out at her. She retrieves the condom before I step back and yank her jeans and underwear off. Finally, she is fully naked below me, wet, whimpering and wanting more. "You're sure?" I ask her, my voice thick as I struggle to hold on to my control.

"Yes, Nate. Please!" She tugs down my pants, and my cock slaps me in the abs when it finally escapes its prison. "Well, that's impressive," she adds, wrapping her hand as far as she can around my cock, making me sigh at finally being touched by her. She rips open the condom wrapper and quickly slides it down my shaft. She returns to lying down, pulling me with her so I lie on top of her, in between her open legs. My cock presses against her, and my natural instinct is to press into her and bang her as fast as I can, but I resist, wanting to ensure this is as good for her as it is for me. I slip my hand between her legs and smile when I find how wet and warm she is already. Using her own wetness, I slide my fingers over her clit, responding to her reactions, and when she whimpers at the back of her throat, I know she's enjoying it. Sinking two fingers into her and curling them up to reach her g-spot, I add to the sensations by taking one of her nipples into my mouth, sucking on it and licking it.

"Nate. Now. I need you, now," she calls to me as her legs begin to tremble, and unable to resist any longer, I thrust up inside her, almost up to the hilt. Her warm tightness squeezes me, and it takes all my strength and will power to not pour myself inside her. She feels magnificent. Perfection seems to fall short of how it feels to be balls deep in Leila. Her answering gasp and moan are all the encouragement I need to continue. I almost fully withdraw before burying myself inside her again. Her legs tighten around me, pulling me closer.

"Yes, Nate. Right there, just like that," she murmurs to me, her eyes shut tightly, and her body writhing for release. "Faster, I'm going to come, Nate. Faster." I put my head down and give her everything I have, fighting the urge to come for as long as I can.

"Fuck, Leila, you feel incredible. We fit together perfectly. I can't wait to do this again and again and again.

"Nate!" She calls my name as her body splinters apart, squeezing me and forcing my own release.

"Fuck..." I call out while I come too. This is so much more than just a sexual release. Our souls have just knitted together.

"Oh my god. That was... that was... wow!" And I couldn't have put it better myself.

# Football Match
(NOUN)

A competitive game between two teams from the same league, The winner is awarded three points. The loser recieves none. In the case of a draw, each team takes one point each.

Each match is 90 minutes long (a game of two halves that are 45 minutes each).

(SOURCE: Oxford language Dictionary)

# CHAPTER 12

## ~ Leila ~

After the most incredible date at the Eiffel Tower, I didn't think Nate could top it, but he more than excels at impressing me. I already know, of course, that he can push my buttons in all the right ways, but his skills transfer to full on sex too, as does his consideration towards me and my fulfilment.

As I lie beneath him, his breathing as heavily affected as my own, I try not to think too deeply about why this was probably the best sex I've ever had. My sex life has always been satisfactory. But sleeping with Nate… this is a whole new level. Satisfactory seems laughable in comparison. Satisfactory is somewhat unsatisfactory now that I know what satisfaction is truly like.

"Oh my god. That was… that was… wow!" I hear myself mumble the words and cringe when I do. I'm an adult, not some lovesick teenager. I sound like an idiot.

Then Nate murmurs back to me, returning my sentiment. "It really was wow. I mean I knew… I knew we'd be good together. But wow." He looks down into my eyes, and his grey eyes resemble a wild storm brewing, yet I know I will find safety there. "I think I quite like this being engaged business," he says, and it gives me a cool stark reminder that this is just a game. A game where we can both have fun while we play it out, but also a game of risk, because it obviously would be all too easy for me to blur the lines and fall in love with him. Then I'll end up with a broken heart, because I know this is just the here and now.

"Well, we have had all the arguments and misunderstandings. We may as well have all the good bits too," I reply to him, as he withdraws from me, leaving me feeling cold and empty. I'm unsure if it is time and space or his assured embrace that'll keep me grounded. As he moves away from me, I want to call him back and tell him to never leave me. But I also know that's not part of the deal. None of this is.

As he pulls off the condom and discards it, I sit back and watch him. "Well, yes. But it's more than that too, isn't it? It's never felt this way for me before. Ever." I want to tell him that it's never felt this incredible for me either, but my words seem to be stuck in my throat. "This was never part of our agreement, but I want to see where it takes us because if our paths hadn't crossed when they did, I'm sure they would have. I'm sure this was meant to be."

"You don't know that, Nate. Look, I'm not going to lie and tell you that wasn't amazing, because it was. But let's not get too carried away just yet." Hurt flashes in his storm filled eyes, and I hate that I caused that, but I'm trying to protect us both.

Sitting next to me, with his hands out in front of him as he talks, his voice takes a steely edge. "If that's what you want, Leila. I'll respect it. But I want to do this, all of this again. A multitude of times. With you." I throw myself at him, showing him without words that I want exactly the same. How do you tell a man who could have anyone that you want him to be yours for real? I can't even think about it without my heart beating out of my chest. "Let's check out the shower. I think I'm ready for round two, if you are too, gorgeous."

Biting my lip, I nod to him. It would be a shame to let the shower go to waste after all, and the thought of Nate already being ready for more has my own desire coiling back in my tummy, ready to spring with enough provocation.

My first proper glimpse around the room leaves me entranced. It is sleek and modern but with a lot of original French features incorporated. In addition to the bed we've just used, there is a second bed, exactly the same size with identical sheets and pillows. "I want to do it on this bed too," I tell him, and I get butterflies in my tummy when he chuckles back at me.

"Your wish is my command, but first, I wanna shower with you. You've been a dirty girl. Let me clean you up." The bathroom is bigger than my little house; the shower is probably the same size as my bedroom. The whole room screams of opulence and grandeur. Nate turns on the shower and looks about for toiletries, while I eye up the roll top, claw footed bathtub. I've never seen anything like it before. "Get in here," Nate calls out to me as he steps under the waterfall shower.

I seem to skip towards him, and while we wash each other, concentrating on certain areas more than others, we kiss once more. A French kiss, just like he promised me earlier. We might be under a shower, but the chemistry between us burns and scorches to a fever pitch. The whole bathroom could be on fire for all I know and care right now. All that matters is Nate and I and the need that builds between us.

Squeezing a generous amount of body wash into my hand, I rub it into a lather over Nate's chest and abs, then lower, into his dark pubic hair, and up and down over his cock that stands hard and thick under my fingertips, his skin there stretched and slick as I rub the soap over him. The water from the shower trickles down and washes away the suds revealing his cock in all its glory. An idea springs into my head, and I smile as I drop to my knees. Nate's head falls back as I wrap my lips around the head of his cock and release it with a large slurp.

"Hey, Nate," I call out to him, looking up at him through my eyelashes. Closing my eyes again once I know he is watching me, I then thrust my tongue out and lick him from the base of his shaft right up to the head of his glorious cock. I open my eyes and look up at him again. "I licked it. So now it's all mine!" I tell him confidently.

His eyes widen slightly as I quickly grin at him before taking him fully into my mouth, hollowing out my cheeks, waiting for his reaction. He groans in his throat and grabs me by the hair. "Yes, gorgeous. It's all yours now."

And for now, that'll have to be enough.

## ~ Nate ~

I watch in fascination as my cock thrusts into Leila's warm and welcoming mouth. Nothing has ever felt as good as this. She stakes her claim on my manhood, and I happily give her ownership of it. I would gladly do most things for her to make her happy.

Her reluctance to admit that this is more than our contract troubles me, but it also challenges me to ensure that she knows she is mine and that I will not let go of her without a fight.

She hums as she sucks me, rolling my balls in her hand at the same time, and when I grip onto her hair for stability, she moans low in her throat, giving me deeper access. Her throat squeezes me, pushing me towards a release I don't want to happen just yet. I want to claim her pussy too.

"Can we try out the other bed now, gorgeous. There is so much more I want to do," I say to her with my eyes closed, relishing the delight she inflicts on me with her mouth. "I don't want to come just yet, but if you keep going, I will."

She releases my cock with a pop and wipes her mouth with the back of her hand. "Why don't you want to come?" she asks me with a frown.

"I do want to come. I just want time to do more things with you before I am rendered useless," I admit to her honestly as I pull her back up to her feet. "I wanna eat your pussy, and I want you to ride me on the other bed." I growl against her ear, and when I see her reaction to my words, I can't hold back any longer.

I claim her, licking every single part of her that I can, and firmly repeat the word "MINE" as I do. Her skin puckers, her pupils dilated, and she begins to move against me, craving more of my touch. I bite her, leaving little marks to remind her later, tomorrow, the next day, that she is mine now. I have claimed her, and although this is just a game, a bit of fun, the tightness that settled in my chest when she told me to not get carried away seems to ease slightly.

She gasps as I push her against the wall for leverage. I am about to lift her leg so I have better access to eat her pussy when my gentlemanly instincts kick in. "The other bed, now," I command her, and she whimpers with need, knowing I was about to claim her pussy as all mine but now she has to wait. "I'll spank you if you don't move it, gorgeous." And I'll be damned, but desire flashes in her eyes at my threat. Who knew we could be so compatible.

Unable to wait any longer to taste her, I throw her over my shoulder and carry her to the bedroom. I can't resist smacking her across the ass when I do. Her answering yelp and then giggle all but confirms that Leila likes a little bit of rough. I can do that.

I throw her down on the bed and spread her legs wide, her beautiful pussy bare and glistening for me. Hooking her legs over my shoulders so I can hold her thighs in place, I swipe up over her clit and lay my claim. "MINE!" I tell her, and it brings me joy to hear her whimpers.

"Nate's! It's all Nate's." Yes, it fucking is. I get busy licking and sucking her. Her taste, so sweet and delicate, fills my senses, leaving me ravenous for more. I fuck her with my tongue, plunging it as deep as I can inside her, and smile in satisfaction as she writhes below me. When her legs tremble, I know she is close. She pulls on my hair, showing me where she wants and needs my touch. To push her over the edge, I add a finger, pumping it in and out of her before curling it up. "Nate!" she calls out breathlessly, and her body contorts, spasming in completion.

But I'm far from finished. I keep going. I want another orgasm from her, and I know with the right amount of coaxing, I can give it to her. She screams my name when I don't stop. Her sweet honey fills my mouth and makes me hungry for more. Her nails dig into my scalp, as the feeling becomes too intense for her until finally, she moans loudly, her body contracting once again for me.

"Yes, baby, come for me. Just for me," I say to her in between lapping at her softly and slowly, squeezing every last wave of ecstasy for what it is worth. Her body continues to shudder as I kiss and bite my way back up to her. "Are you okay?" I ask her once our faces are level again.

"I want you now, Nate. Fucking hell, I've never come like that before." I chuckle against her ear. "My legs are like jelly," she exclaims in shock. This is no act. It is evident from the sated look in her eyes and the rosy glow that covers her cheeks.

Looking around to locate the mini bar, I walk over to it and pull out a couple of bottles of water. "Would you like a drink?" I ask her before swigging deeply from my bottle. She nods her reply and accepts the bottle I got for her. "You seem to have gotten your breath back, are you ready for some more?" I tease as I sit next to her on the bed.

Looking excited, she springs up and straddles me. "You're not off the hook yet, Nate. I want you inside me. I wanna look into your eyes while I make you come." My hard cock presses against her wet pussy, twitching in eagerness. "Where are the condoms?" she whispers against my cheek as she writhes over me, just a touch more pressure and I would be in her. How I want to be there without the rubber in the way.

"In the bag. My bag." She writhes against me in frustration, but as willing as I am to accommodate her, I want to remind her of her own reservations. The last thing I want is for her to do something she'll later regret. "Leila, gorgeous. Remember, you wanted the condoms. It'll take ten seconds to get them, and then you won't have any regrets," I reason with her.

She kisses me with force and passion before hopping off and retrieving the box from my bag. She opens the box. "A twenty-four pack... are we using them all on this trip, Nate?" she adds with a coy smile when she hands one to me.

"If I have my way, then yes," I reply honestly, "although I would prefer without. However, I'll settle for anything as long as it's with you." I roll down the rubber on my throbbing cock. "Come on, gorgeous. Hop on," I tell her, and like the good girl she is, she obeys me and slides her wet and willing pussy over my cock, taking me inside her bit by tantalising bit.

She sighs and throws her head back once I'm fully embedded inside her. "I prefer it without too. Let me talk to my doctor and maybe he can give me some assurances."

"Fuck talking about your doctor and ride me, you dirty girl. Show me what you've got." She gasps at my barb, but her body responds to the words. Clenching me inside her and then riding my cock like her life depends on it. "That's my good girl, ride me just like that." As she rides me, her breasts swing in front of my face. I can already see the marks I have made on her, and they make me smile with pride. She is mine, and at this moment in time, I can't help thinking how perfect my life is right now. This little snapshot of perfection means more to me than anything ever has.

I am going to cling to us with all my might for as long as I can.

## ~ Leila ~

Paris in August is sweaty business, especially when you spend the night thrashing around with a sexy man. I wake up in a pool of my own sweat, my mouth dry and sticky. I feel revolting. I look over at Nate, who looks so young and peaceful as he sleeps. Gently, I run my fingers over his jaw, where fresh day old stubble is beginning to sprout, and warmth spreads throughout me. For Nate, and for us. Maybe this could be something more? Nate seems to think so. I want it to be so, but I worry that eventually he'll tire of me. If I just concentrate on the timeframe of our agreement and not fall in love, I might be okay. But it's so hard to close off feelings for someone like him.

Not wanting to disturb him, I creep out of bed, turn on the air conditioning and then move to the bathroom. I do want to try out the tub, but it is far too warm for a bath. Instead, I run the shower, step under the cool invigorating water and finish what we started last night. This time, I actually clean myself. Starting with my hair and then giving consideration to the rest of my body. As I cover myself in the rich, fragrant lather, I notice the marks Nate left all over my body. Little tiny bites and suck marks. Although I'm indignant, a shiver of arousal runs through me too. It was incredibly hot and sexy to have him claim me and my body the way he has. And if Nate and I both like it, what does it matter what anyone else thinks?

"You're showering without me?" Nate's groggy voice carries over the running water. "Let me in," he says, already naked, having not dressed after we finished in a tangle of limbs last night.

I step over so we can share the cool water, and he wraps his arms around my waist and kisses my shoulder. I lean my head back against his chest and melt into his strong embrace. "I missed you," he tells me, and I giggle as he tickles me with his whiskers.

"I've only been in here for five minutes," I remind him, turning to face him. "But I missed you too. All I've done is think about you the whole time I've been in here," I tell him, running my soapy hands over his torso, washing him.

"Did you touch yourself? When you thought of me?" I shiver at his words, and his voice hums throughout my body. I shake my head at him. "Didn't you want to?"

"I didn't need to. My man more than satisfied me. But maybe next time," I offer him as I continue to wash him.

He grabs my wrists and looks into my eyes. "Promise me you'll only think of me when you do."

I kiss him hard, and thoroughly, biting his lip as I pull away. "Last night just ensured that I'll never be able to think of anything else. Or anyone else. It was pretty amazing." This time he kisses me, taking possession of my mouth forcefully.

"I'm glad you agree. Best night ever. I mean that, Leila. You're incredible." I blush at his compliment, before shutting the water off and handing him a towel. "I know you have to work this evening and you'll have to check in with the team soon to check for injuries, but I was hoping we could spend a couple of hours together this afternoon?"

"I'm heading to the training ground so I can work out. The team should arrive by the time I'm done. I'll double check any niggling injuries, or new injuries, and then I should be free to go until the match tonight." Slinging the towel low on his hips, he passes me a robe to wear. "Won't I have to pay for this if I use it?" I squeak out at him.

"And? I want you to have all the nice things. I don't mind the cost," he says firmly as he wraps the robe around my shoulders. "Do we have to go back home tonight?" he asks as we go back to the bedroom, both of us organising our clothes and personal items for the day.

I nod to him. "Yes. I'm sorry, Nate. I have to travel to London tomorrow afternoon with the team." He nods to show his understanding, even though he is disappointed. "We'll have to make today count as much as last night did."

"Maybe I could bring you back sometime. There is so much more to do and see," he offers, and it's a generous offer, but I'm not sure when we will fit that in, not with the time we have. "I forgot to say Kym is organising the engagement party. It's during the international playoffs so you won't be busy at work. I hope that's okay." I give him a tight smile but nod my agreement. The information serves as a reminder that we still have a show to put on.

"What will you do while I work?" I ask him. I can't even imagine Nate relaxing or staying stagnant for too long.

He chuckles at me. "I have to work too. In fact, my first meeting starts in about twenty minutes, so if you want breakfast, you'll have to be quick."

Not feeling so hungry anymore, I wave him off. "Nah. It's okay, I'll get something at training. They always have lots of stuff for the players." I sip the rest of the water from the bottle he gave me last night, and once I pull my hair into a ponytail, I look like Leila the injury specialist again.

"You look so sexy in your work clothes. I mean, I like it better when you're naked. But there is something very cute about your shorts and training top." I tut at him, and he smiles back at me with a gleam in his eye. "I've sent the driver a message. He'll take you to the training ground, and I'll meet you there when you're finished. I'll walk with you to the car before my meeting starts."

I give him a little salute to his plan and place my bag on the bed. "Shall I leave this in the car? It's got my clothes for later." I don't want to go sightseeing in my work clothes. I want to try and blend in a little.

"Don't worry, I'll bring it with me." We walk together to the elevator, and I am somewhat emotional about leaving the hotel. As soon as we hit the doors to the outside world, the flashes and glares of a million cameras seem to descend on us. The black car from last night sits in wait for me, and we rush towards it, Nate opening the door as soon as we reach it. "Just go. I'll deal with this," Nate shouts to me. I kiss him chastely on the lips before closing the car door. I thought being in Paris would mean less press scrutiny, not more!

## Chapter 13

### ~ Leila ~

With the press now intruding, there is no way we can make it around in a couple of hours. Our plans for this afternoon will have to change and from the set of Nate's jaw, I know he must realise this too. I watch Nate disappear in the cloud of reporters, our little bubble bursting without fanfare or grace. Some of the reporters follow me on little electric scooters and bikes, but the driver speeds up to lose them. I'm taken by surprise when there is a knock on my window, followed by flashing lights. Their incessant behaviour troubles me. Is this what life with Nate will be like? Is this what he always deals with? I would hate that.

I arrive at the training ground, and as per my new usual, my stomach growls and turns, but after what just happened, I don't want to eat. "Hey, Doc! You're here. Will you take a look at my ankle please." Jack's sunny disposition and cheeky grin couldn't be farther away from how I'm feeling.

"Yeah, sure," I tell him as I walk into my temporary treatment room. "Hop on the bed and take off your socks and shoes, please." I close the door behind us and get the shock of my life when Jack grabs onto me and pushes my back against the doorframe.

"Shhh, listen to me. There are rumours flying around. About you. And your dad and McAllister. They are saying you got McAllister fired," he tells me under his breath. "You need to be careful. Does Nate know about your dad?"

Defensively, I push back against him. "Know what exactly? What do you think he needs to know, Jack?" I spit out at him. This is getting out of hand. My father has been dead for over twenty years. Why is this suddenly an issue?

"I don't know, Leila." He raises his voice. "All I know is, you're going to be my sister-in-law and I cannot protect you if I don't know the truth. There are already too many secrets in your relationship with Nate. Don't add to it." He looks into my eyes, challenging me, and I'm confused. Is he trying to stir up more trouble or is he trying to protect me?

"What secrets? What are you referring to, Jack?" I deflect, and he groans in agitation, holding his head in his hands, giving me the ideal opportunity to escape from his scrutiny.

"It's not my place to say. But you two… there are far too many skeletons threatening this relationship, and if you're serious about each other, you need to start being honest." His words seem heartfelt and sincere, but I'm still suspicious about his sudden U-turn.

"I don't know anything else about my dad or why McAllister hated me. He died such a long time ago. Nate knows who my father was. But I can't tell him anything else because I don't know anything else." Jack nods, accepting what I tell him.

"Then I suggest you do find out, because the vultures are already running amok with this story. Find out the truth before they do and run the narrative for you,

Leila." He lies on the examination table and takes off his sock and shoe from his recently heeled foot. "It actually feels okay, but I needed an excuse to talk to you."

"Your feet stink!" I exclaim truthfully, and he bursts out laughing. "What?"

"This is what they usually smell like when I'm not trying to impress someone. Get used to it, Doc."

I look closely at his stinking foot. "Yep, it's looking good, Jack. You're ready to play." He grins at me, while I wash my hands. "Now get out of my examination room with them honking feet!"

"I'll send your next victim in," he tells me cryptically.

The clinic room isn't empty for long before the gaffer comes in with one of the midfield players that I haven't treated before. "This is Reagan Graham. He is going to be taking Jonesy's position on field as captain–"

"Skipper. Jonesy is the captain; I'm going to be the skipper." He holds his hand out to me and smiles as I shake it. "The gaffer just wants me to have the once over before he appoints me."

"Congratulations, skip. This is a fantastic opportunity. If you just give me five minutes, I will get your notes up and we can begin." Without needing to be asked, he strips down to his underwear, ready to be assessed.

"I'm only here because we don't have a manager any more to oversee it. I should be developing plays and scouting new players," Juan Carlos complains in a heavily accented voice while glowering at me. Although I feel my cheeks heat up at his insinuation, I don't rise to the bait. McAllister resigned without giving me a reason for hating my guts; that's on him, not me.

I click into my work laptop, but my password is denied. I try again, but I cannot log into the system. Undeterred, I improvise. "So, skip, the system is down. Are you okay giving me a quick rundown of your physical health and any injuries you have had, please?"

The examination takes a little longer than usual, but I am able to give him a full bill of health and send them both on their way. I just settle into my seat, when there is another knock. I groan, because there seems to be no let-up today.

"Hey, hangry girl. I thought you'd appreciate some breakfast." Nate walks in with coffee and a brown paper bag I hope is filled with French pastries. He closes the door behind him, and I run into his arms once he's placed the breakfast items on the desk. "It's only been like two hours, gorgeous. Did you miss me?" He looks into my eyes; his intense grey ones seem to read me like a book.

"Yes, I sincerely did, Nate." I want to tell him everything, but as I look around the room, I'm worried about someone else overhearing. "My access to the players medical files has been cut. Do you think this could be something to do with McAllister?"

He frowns at me but picks up his phone and rapidly taps until he swears under his breath. "I don't know if it was McAllister, but you have been reduced to limited access. We will discuss it with the board when we return to the UK."

Nodding to him, knowing there is nothing more to be done today, I point to the takeaway breakfast he has thoughtfully brought. "What have you got for me?" I ask him, challenging and teasing him in equal measure. His hand travels to my throat, and I sigh into his hard, unyielding kiss, craving more, never wanting this to end.

"I've got everything you could ever want and need, Leila. You just have to take a chance on me."

## ~ Jack ~

Away games suck ass. Especially international ones. Sleeping in a poxy hotel, using someone else's mediocre training facilities. And less tickets are allocated to the travelling fans, so we are heckled more than we are cheered. We go two goals down, and during half time, the gaffer gives us all a good telling off. True to form, half of us don't understand a word of it, but the look on his face says it all.

His anger is well placed. Paris Football Club is not even a great side. On a normal day, we could score ten goals past them without breaking out into a sweat. But not today. Today, as my late father would often say... we can't find our assholes with both hands!

The new team captain, or 'skipper' as he insists we call him, stands and touches the gaffer on the shoulder. "May I, Gaffer? I think some people are having trouble accepting me as Jonesy's replacement. And I get it. But he's injured and the game goes on. Now, you can sulk that I have taken his place, or you can go out there and make our idol proud." The room seems to still at his words. "This is knock out football! If we lose, we are out of Europe for a year. I thought you wanted to win trophies and be winners?" he roars at us.

"We do! It's just weird. Jonesy has always been my captain. His boots aren't even cold, and you've jumped into them," I shout out on behalf of myself and my teammates. A few holler their agreement, but most of them lower their heads.

"That's a fair enough judgement, Jack. But let me ask you. Would you prefer no captain?" My shoulders sag, because of course I don't. Deep down, I know that me making Reagan's job harder won't help the team, but I feel guilty about Jonesy. And Macca is gone too. I don't like it. There is too much change.

"I wouldn't. I'm happy we have someone with your experience to continue to lead us. I know every single one of us would have been honoured to have been asked. I just feel like a traitor," I tell him and the whole team as honestly as I can. The ones closest to me pat me on the back and murmur reassuring words to me. Having released what was bothering me, I feel lighter, more optimistic and ready to win.

"Let's go out there and win this for us, for our fans, but mostly for Jonesy. Our brother, our role model, our friend." Reagan rallies us all, and the changing room erupts with our shouts and roars.

"For Jonesy!" "For our role model!" "Get better soon, Jonesy!" We all shout, and I'm not going to lie, a lump forms in my throat. While the rest of the team file out, I stay back, just a moment alone to regain my composure.

"Are you alright, Jack?" I jump, not realising anyone else is here with me. "Sorry, I didn't mean to make you jump. Your strapping has come loose, and I wanted to fix it before you go back out." Leila's voice is so sweet and soothing. After the way I ambushed her this morning, I had expected her to be cool and standoffish with me, but she is still professional and caring. Wiping my face so she doesn't see the tears that have left a trail down my face, I look down and see the tell-tale blue tape trailing on the ground, confirming Leila is correct. I do need retaping.

"If you think this is bad, you should have seen them last year after you got injured. They were heartbroken." I look up at her, and until this moment, I haven't even been able to imagine that they continued to play after my injury. I stopped playing and temporarily left the team and so, for me at least, everything stopped. "Tyson got a lot of stick for trying to fill your shoes. But Jonesy protected him and rightly told everyone, just like Reagan is, *the game must go on.*"

She kneels and re-straps my ankle, giving me a moment to respond. "I get that. I never imagined what was happening here. I was too absorbed in my own self pity to worry about the team. It was only when I came back from rehab that I realised that time had moved on without me. That I wasn't as important to the team as I thought." Getting to the root of the issue, I begin to realise this might be more about me and my own injury than it is about Jonesy. I felt brilliant about my return until he was ruled out for the rest of the season. It reminded me that my position here means everything to me, and that I could have a career ending injury at any time.

"You are important and so is Jonesy. But, right now, Jonesy needs to concentrate on his treatment and recovery, and we have to continue carrying the torch that he lit for us. He understands the game doesn't stop with him. But he is gonna be pissed if you don't try after all the hard work the whole team has put in to get here," she tells me in a matter-of-fact manner. I smile down at her. She'll keep my brother in line. Maybe she would have kept me in line too if things had been different.

"I know, you're right. Am I ready to go, Doc?" I ask her, and she nods and stands, allowing me to pull my sock and boot back on.

"You've got forty-five minutes to turn this around, Jack. Show them what you, and Redvale, are made of." She pushes me out into the players tunnel, and purpose and renewed meaning course through my body. I can do this; I have to do this. Jonesy deserves it. The whole team, including the gaffer and the Doc, deserve it too.

As I run out onto the pitch, the couple of thousand fans that travelled to support us cheer their support. This time I am able to block out the opposing fans, and I concentrate on the anthem our fans sing to me. I clap my new skipper on the back as I get into my position for the starting whistle. "Let's do this, skip. We've got this!" I tell him before shouting to my teammates, rallying them and supporting them. "Just like Jonesy showed us, lads. Let's do it for the captain."

Despite the terrible first half, we all step up. We communicate better, which makes us pass better, read each other more adeptly and move faster into spaces that seem to open up from anywhere. It isn't long before I assist Tyson with a glorious pass, and he scores a screamer of a goal from just beyond the penalty arc. Tyson runs to our fans, and the stadium erupts in their cries of euphoria. The whole team follows Tyson into the corner to congratulate him and celebrate too. The referee blows his whistle for the restart, and Reagan takes the opportunity to lead us.

"Come on, lads. We need two more," Reagan shouts, and excitement brews inside me. The home team fans have quietened down since our goal, and our fans are hyped up, sensing the change in pace and morale. I'm going to score, and I'm going to suggest that the Doc do all our pre-match pep talks from now on!

The game continues for another fifteen minutes or so, when one of our strikers is fouled by the opposition. We are given a free kick from just outside the penalty box, to the left-hand side. It's time for me to shine. This set piece is designed to trick the other team into thinking that Reagan will be taking the shot, but in actual fact, I run from the opposite direction, kicking the ball with force and precision, straight into the upper left corner.

The whole arena erupts, causing my ears to ring, and I search the bench for the gaffer. He is jumping up and down with joy. I don't even dare look at the Doc. I want to thank her yet again, but I know Nathan is here somewhere, watching my every move. He's made his claim on Leila clear, and I respect him enough to leave that well alone.

My teammates huddle around me in celebration. We are now two a piece. One side needs to score to go through, and there are still twenty-five minutes of game time. Anything could happen. I just hope we have it in us to win so we can continue on the path to becoming European champions.

## ~ Leila ~

Our afternoon plans are scuppered, but after the wonderful day and night we had, it's okay that we don't get to see more of Paris for now. Against my better judgement, the thought of returning here in the future with Nate sends fresh swirls of excitement throughout my body... maybe we'll get time to come back? And there are a whole bunch of places we can explore together before our deadline.

Although my job had been the main motivation for entering into this contract, the more bullshit that spews from the fallout, the less I seem to care about it. Perhaps, this just isn't meant to be. I've been so focused on making a difference and advocating for injured players that I forgot about what matters to me. Having this time now and seeing the little impact I am having in comparison to what I wanted to make has me doubting if this is the best path to deliver holistic care for the recovering footballers when they are injured or left unable to play.

"You're lost in thought," Nate comments, as we eat fresh croissants and hot coffee in my temporary clinic room. "Is something troubling you?" he adds, placing down his coffee cup so he can rub my knee.

"I'm just thinking about how far away this all is from what I actually wanted to be doing. The bureaucracy and red tape and pettiness of some just make things... difficult," I reply. I want to be honest with him, even though I'm now questioning the very reason we started this whole contract relationship. It's the one thing I don't regret at this moment in time. My time with Nate. I hope he knows that.

"So what would help get you from doing what you are doing now to what you would like to happen?" For someone like Nate, solutions just snap out of fresh air. But I don't come from that world.

"I don't think there is a sure way to execute the type of provision I want to make available. I would be the first person to do it and so I would be building the blueprint that I could desperately do with about now." The conversation is getting away from me, so I shrug it off. I'm not making much sense, because as of now, nothing is making sense to me anymore. "Anyway, what shall we do now? We aren't going to be able to go out there without being mobbed."

"We could go back to the hotel, darling," he whispers to me, tugging my hand so I have to sit on his lap or fall over. "There is lots more I want to do in the bedroom, never mind the outside world."

"Nathan!" I shout in mock outrage. "At my place of work, how rude!" He laughs with me, but wraps his arms around me, and kisses the side of my neck. My body instantly remembers his touch and unadulterated desire pulses throughout me.

"Kym left me a couple of messages about our engagement party. She took it upon herself to employ a task force to oversee it all. She needs your guest list as soon as possible." He doesn't even falter, not even for a millisecond.

"How big of an engagement party, Nate? A task force sounds pretty hardcore!" I answer quickly. Suddenly, us having this party, celebrating our fake engagement and inviting my friends and family feels all kinds of wrong.

"Calm down. We have a few weeks; it'll be in October. You have some time off work with internationals taking a lot of players away for a couple of weeks," he says nonchalantly, still trying to kiss me.

"You set a date without me?" It comes out as barely a whisper, but the hurt is overwhelmingly obvious. We are supposed to be in this together. His eyes widen, but then a defensive look takes over his expression.

"I thought you would be happy. It's one less thing for you to worry about." His body stiffens against mine, but not in the delightful way it did last night. "What's the problem, Leila? I thought you would appreciate the help."

I stand up, trying to put some distance between us, but he stands too and advances on me, holding me by my chin. I want to kiss him and smack him across the head at the same time. "Back off, Nathan. Please give me a little room to get my head around all this."

"I don't understand what the issue is. We need to show the world. I organised it. We are also doing an exclusive interview with Solar magazine; they've offered a massive donation to a charity of your choice for doing it."

"NATE! Damn it, will you stop? I need some space. Magazine deals, parties, the fucking press badgering me. Please just give me some time to get my head around all this." He looks back at me, wounded but also angry.

"Fine, I'll see you after the match," he adds, the tic in his jaw doing overtime as he contains his anger for me. "I didn't mean to upset you."

I nod to him, but don't say another word, waiting desperately for him to leave. He surprises me by kissing me on the top of my head before he leaves me in the empty room. His absence only makes all the doubts and uncertainties multiply and grow until I can't take the tormented silence any longer. Locking up my clinic, I head to the training facilities. Although it isn't as high tech as the one back at Redvale, I lift weights and pound the punch bag, before running a few miles on the treadmill. With each movement, all the tension that had riddled my body eases. With each moment that I have, and the time and space to think, my issues lessen until finally, it's time for the pre-match warm up.

---

Watching the final minutes from the bench, every member of staff, player, and coach moans and groans each kick, tackle and attack. It's thrilling football, but I'm sure from the pounding of my heart, the hum of my blood pumping forcefully around my body, that this match has knocked a couple of years off my life. My nails are bitten down to the quick, and my stomach twists in sick anxiety. With three minutes to go, a Paris player takes a shot at the goal; however, our goalie catches it and quickly rolls the ball out to Reagan, who presses a counter attack. The entire stadium is on the edge of their seats with bated breath, tension filling the air around us. Having caught Paris off guard, Jack has managed to get himself into a position with lots of room around him, and the Paris goalkeeper is out of the penalty box, but attempts to run backwards to his station. Jack is too fast for him, though. Reagan passes the ball to Jack, and with a beautiful first touch, Jack controls the ball before shooting at the goal. The seconds seem to take years to pass before the stadium erupts again.

"GOAL!" We hear over the speakers, and a lot of the staff and players run on to the pitch to celebrate with the rest of the team. Jack has tears in his eyes once again, but this time they are tears of joy. The cameramen get right up into his face, but Jack loves the attention. He kisses the camera lens and is talking to the fans through the camera. It is poetically wonderful to see.

The clock runs down to the final seconds, but the referee still has to conduct the restart. The game restarts, and we sit once again in twisted agitation in case Paris is able to score a quick goal in retaliation. Although only a minute goes by, it feels like an hour. Finally, the referee blows his whistle, and Redvale are through to the next round of the European championships. After congratulating the gaffer and a few of the players, I make my way back to my treatment room. There doesn't appear to be any injuries, but I like to make myself and my team available in the event that I have missed something.

My assistants quickly assess the players and bring back any reports of concern, but luckily, there aren't any. Passing on the good news to the gaffer, I reluctantly accept his dismissal for the evening, knowing Nate is waiting for me and that I need to apologise for flying off the handle earlier. I just hope he's in a forgiving mood.

## ~ Nate ~

It is killing me having to stay away from Leila. I want to respect her boundaries and give her the space and time she's demanded, but at the same time, the overwhelming need to be near her claws at my peace of mind. Fuck, being engaged is a lot more complicated than I anticipated!

After leaving Leila in her clinic, I wander aimlessly back to Jean-Paul, who drives me to my hotel again. I abandoned all my meetings when I saw the press following Leila. I couldn't stop thinking of her being chased, or scared. However, when I brought her breakfast, she was unaffected. She seems to have adapted to the intrusion faster than I thought she would. Pride filled my chest as I watched her, so beautiful and graceful with a wonderfully infectious laugh.

In all honesty, I never thought me organising the engagement party without her would bother her. Contrarily, I thought she would be thankful that she didn't have to worry about it. As much as her reaction rankled me, it angered me more that I don't seem to be getting it right. The flowers, not calling and now this. I have a lot to learn about being a considerate partner. For the first time in my life, it matters to me that she knows that I want to be considerate of her. No matter how much I try to hold back, there is no doubt in my mind that I am falling for Leila, fast and hard. It's alarming the rate at which she has got under my skin, without even trying to.

With no idea how to rectify this, I call Kym. "I need you to cancel the engagement party team. Leila is upset about it," I tell her, missing everything else that happened.

"Woah, hold up, why is she upset, Nathan? This party has to go ahead," she replies sternly. "What did you do?"

"I agreed to a date for the party without consulting her. She told me she needed space. I just need to make it better again." Kym groans in the background, and I want to join her to be honest. However, I would be a foolish man if I thought she would give me any sympathy.

"You didn't ask her first? What is wrong with you, Nathan? Of course, she's going to be upset about it. Just give her some time and tell her you can cancel if she wants a different date." Will that be enough? I think to myself. "I don't think she is upset with the date; it is you dictating to her, taking away her right to choose, that has more than likely upset her."

"Do you think?" I ask, and even I cringe at the desperate hopefulness that drips off my every word.

"I've never seen you like this, Nathan. You're falling in love with her, aren't you?" I take that as a rhetorical question, because I'm still having issues admitting to myself how strongly I feel for her. "Be careful, son," she says under her breath, cautioning me in a way no one else can.

"I will. I am," I promise her, and for her, I will. I'll try to approach this in a more business-like manner, and then maybe I won't keep making mistakes.

The game is exhilarating. I watch from the executive box, and occasionally, I think of Leila and smile, knowing she would love having food on demand and that she would find something beautiful in the view from up here. I can't even see her from where I am. My box is directly over the benches where Leila and the rest of the team sit. As soon as that last goal goes in, I shake hands with my fellow board members and make my way down to the changing room to wait for Leila.

I wait for around ten minutes before she comes out. "Hey," she says to me sheepishly. "Nate, I'm so sorry. I felt overwhelmed and I know I pushed you away, but I know you were trying to do a nice thing now."

My stomach unclenches, and nerves that she would shoot me down evaporate. "I'm sorry too. I got carried away trying to take away anything that might stress you out. I can cancel everything, and we can start over, if you like."

She shakes her head at me in alarm. "No! No way. You're right, it would stress me out. Just please include me next time, okay?" I open my arms to her, and she pleases me by wrapping her arms around my neck and returning my kiss.

We pull away, aware that we could be interrupted at any point. "Next time?" I murmur to her. "I'm only doing this once, darling." Too late, I realise, I've said something totally inappropriate that might scare her off again.

"I should think so too, Mr Cardal. It's until death do we part, remember?" she counters me with a twinkle in her eye. It worries me that she is joking, because in this moment, I am being completely honest.

---

We arrive back at Sandybank a mere three hours later. It's almost midnight, and Leila dozes in the passenger seat while I drive us home. She has to leave for London tomorrow, and this time, I can't go with her because I've neglected all my other responsibilities since I became an engaged man. I also have to see my doctor tomorrow or Kym is definitely going to do her nut.

"We're home," I whisper to my sleeping beauty, not wanting to disturb her, but equally wanting her in the middle of my bed too.

"That was quick. I must have fallen asleep!" she replies with what must be a contagious yawn; as soon as she yawns, I do too. "You looked tired, Nate. Do you want me to carry you to bed?" She teases me.

"I think I can manage it, can you?" I tease back. "Is there anything you need from the bags? We can leave them until morning if not."

She shakes her head at me but then reminds me to get the condoms, bringing another wide smile to my face. No matter how tired we both are, we can't keep our hands off each other, and I intend on getting my fill before she leaves for the weekend.

We are both so wound up and frustrated that we are barely in the bedroom before we are ripping clothes off each other. I'm just about to take her from behind when she strokes my calf. "How did you get that bruise, Nate? It looks nasty." I falter, not expecting her question or the subject matter.

"I knocked it on a chair. It doesn't hurt, baby. Don't worry," I say before pressing into her. Her tight and warm wetness completely envelops me, and while I bring her to climax, I lose myself in her too.

The following morning, I kiss her goodbye when Damon arrives to take her to work and get ready for my own appointment.

The private hospital just outside of Redvale is discreet and elite enough that I don't have to worry about who I bump into. However, I do not want this news to become public knowledge, so as always, I am booked in under a pseudonym. With my cap-covered head downcast, I enter the doctor's room when 'Joe Bloggs' is called.

"Hello, Nathan, thanks for coming to see us again. It's been two years since your last check up, but after your recent bloods and test, I felt it was necessary to bring you in and discuss your results." I nod my head, bile rising into my throat. "I'm afraid the markers indicate that there are some cell changes, and we feel you may be relapsing."

"The cancer's back?" I ask. Although, deep down, I knew this was a possibility, I refused to acknowledge it.

"It's very early days. But yes, the cancer is back."

# Chapter 14

## ~ Leila ~

Friday afternoon, we leave for London on the team coach and thankfully, once again, I'm just 'the Doc'. It is heavenly. A double seat to myself, and my own hotel room, which, I might add, is a lot nicer than any I've stayed in before whenever I've travelled with the team.

Once I am safely in my room, I call Nate. It's only been a few hours, but I've missed him. Thoughts about him have been playing through my mind, and I've decided once I return to Redvale tomorrow, I need to ask him outright if this is just the contract or if he feels more, like I do. He makes me feel as though this is more. I'm falling for him, and it is scary! I don't know if I'm heading for heartbreak or the ride of my life. I just feel, deep down in my gut, that this could be something very incredible. I'm starting to accept that Nate Cardal is the one. Having never believed that there is a special someone for everyone before, it's both magical and overwhelming. If I let my guard down, Nate would have full ownership of my heart and soul.

Nate doesn't pick up my call, but I know he has back-to-back meetings today, having dropped everything to accompany me to Paris. I type out a quick message to him, before going in search of the spa. This is not something I would usually do, but the facilities came as part of the room I have been allocated, and it seems like the perfect opportunity to look the part as Nate's fiancée. And hopefully I can bag a couple of essential beauty treatments while I'm there.

When I realise that some of the other wives and girlfriends (WAGs) of the players have also made the trip and are already using the spa, I feel very self-conscious. These ladies are preened and polished to within an inch of their lives. Perfect hair, perfect skin, perfect nails, perfect teeth. Just flawless perfection in every way. Then I roll up in my work gear and scabby nails that I bit off yesterday watching their significant others. However, the group is very welcoming and warm towards me and shows a lot of interest in me and my newly revealed relationship.

"Leila, come join us. We saved a lounger for you. And give us a look at that engagement ring." Usually Paris, Jonesy's wife, is the head of the gang, but with her absence, one of the more prominent WAGs, an ex-pop star in her own right and the wife of our goalkeeper Yusef, welcomes me to the fold. Gisele was a massive pop star around five years ago; however, her success and career is now clouded and her prominence in the world of celebrity is basically based on her marriage.

"Thanks, Gisele. Although you seriously don't want to look at the ring yet, I bit my nails watching the match in Paris and they look horrendous!" They all crowd around me. Peering over each other's shoulders to see my ring.

"Don't worry about that. We'll get your nails and hands and everything photo worthy," she replies, taking my hand into hers. "Wow! Look at the clarity of that diamond. Nathan Cardal is one classy man." I smile at her and her kind remarks. "You see, if I had left my Yusef to pick my engagement ring, I would have ended up with something the size of the moon. Absolutely no taste, he would just buy the most expensive one. Bless him!" she adds on a sigh.

Without meaning to, I notice that, up close, Gisele isn't as flawless as her social media profile would suggest. Although she wears a hefty amount of makeup, she has blemishes on her face and even a tiny scar on her eyebrow. She must edit them out before posting. Although seeing her in her 'normal' state allows me to see her as more human, I worry about the reasons why she feels the need to do that, and if other impressionable women, like me, feel the need to live up to the standard she falsely sets.

"Nate picked it. I wouldn't have a clue if this was a diamond or a piece of cut glass, to be honest. I do love it, though. He picked well." The other ladies tell me their varying stories of their engagement rings, some from a few years ago to the ones who haven't even got to that stage yet.

"I've had two babies with Freddy and still he hasn't proposed. My mami is crazy about it. 'You should be married by now, Aurelia.' He will marry me, won't he, girls?" A few of the others look uncomfortable, but one or two reassure her that she will get married soon.

The girls look after me and ensure that I have access to all the best beauticians. They insist on some treatments I've never considered, such as a body wrap to make my waist slimmer and cellulite treatment for my legs. Once I've had my nails, eyebrows and hair done, I feel like a mass-produced barbie doll.

A spa suggests rest and relaxation. Pampering even. However, I leave there feeling like an overly plucked chicken ready for the oven. I can't be doing this every week! It's torture!

I try Nate again, but he still doesn't pick up. I'm starting to worry now. Several times, I type out a text to him and delete it. I don't want to appear clingy or needy, but I am concerned that he hasn't returned my calls or texts. Finally, I decide to go for humour. Taking out my Rose Toy and picturing it, I send it to him with the caption...

*"Thinking of you xxx"*

Within two minutes, a reply bleeps back, and excitedly, I read it. To my horror, it's from his number but it's not from Nate.

**Nathan is in a meeting right now,**
**but he knows you've called,**
**and will call you back when he can. Kym**

Oh, my goodness. I hope Kym doesn't know what my Rose is! The shame!

After my time at the spa, I just want a little time alone, so I order room service and wear the towelling robe I brought back from Paris. I must fall asleep because I wake up sprawled on top of the bed with the television still on.

I'm so disappointed when I check my phone. It's 4 am and Nate still hasn't called. He still hasn't returned my text, and although I miss him, I know I need to be more sensible. I'm throwing my heart out to him, letting him into most aspects of my life, and as soon as I'm out of sight, I'm apparently out of his thoughts too. In the cold, bleak hotel room, it becomes crystal clear that I'm not that significant to Nate, and in order to keep some dignity and self-respect, I need to keep my heart safe from him.

A quick look on social media shows me that my friends are continuing with their lives. Dancing at the bar, living their best lives. My mother posts about walking on the beach with the love of her life. Everyone else is getting on with their lives.

Waking up early, I stretch and sip my water before turning on my phone. I am livid when I see there is still no reply from Nate. Well, fuck him! I've tried and I gave him another chance. He only thinks of me when I am right in front of him because I am convenient for him. Well, he can go to hell if he thinks that is continuing.

The team plays Central London FC just after dinner time, and then we catch the team bus home again. Everyone is subdued after the match. Maybe it's fatigue from travelling, but their performance was lacklustre, and they are lucky to have come away with a draw. It's been a heavy start to the season, but with multiple more matches planned in the coming weeks, they are going to have to learn to man it up and do the job they are generously paid to do.

Jack is waiting for me when I get off the team bus. "Doc? Do you want to catch a ride home with me? Save the planet and all that?" I didn't tell Damon what time I would be returning, and so I accept Jack's offer.

"Have you heard from Nate?" I ask him casually.

"Yeah, I told him I'd bring you home. He said he would be home later." I nod to him. Although disappointment and anger swirl inside me, I try to keep it in. "Didn't you speak to him?" he asks, his voice rising an octave, showing his surprise.

Shaking my head, I look out the window as Jack drives us home. I don't want him to see the bitter tears that are stinging my eyes. They will be the first and last tears I shed for Nate Cardal, the inconsiderate piece of shit.

The house is empty when I arrive back, and part of me wants to get my stuff and go back to my own house. I've never ever felt as insulted, and my mind goes into overdrive thinking about why he is acting like this. Is this because we've slept together now? He has no further use for me. Well screw all that. I have my dignity... somewhat. Nathan Cardal can kiss my ass if he thinks I'm standing for this.

"Giovanni has left us food; do you want something?" Jack calls to me, already pulling things from the fridge like he's never been fed. "I could kiss that man. Look at this, Leila!" he calls out to me.

"I'm knackered, Jack. I'm going to bed; I'll see you tomorrow," I tell him as I make my way up the stairs to the bedroom I still have to share with Nate.

"Are you okay, Leila?" Jack says from the bottom of the stairs. "You've been really quiet, and you've hardly ate anything. You're not sick, are you?" There is genuine concern in his voice, even as he stuffs some sort of savoury product into his mouth.

"I'm okay. I'm just tired," I offer him as an explanation.

"I can make you tea. I know how to do that. You get into bed, and I'll bring you a cup of tea." I smile at him and his consideration.

"Okay, thank you, Jack."

While I wait for Jack to bring the tea, I empty out my bag. I still haven't had a chance to sort through my new dressing room and don't have homes for my personal items yet. There are even more bags in here; designer labels, exclusive boutiques and every high-end name lavishes the unopened bags.

"Where shall I put it?" Jack calls from the doorway, where he stands with a silver tray in his hands, which sweetly carries a china cup and saucer, a mini teapot, a mini jug of milk, a sugar bowl and a silver spoon. To the other side is a plate of biscuits. I indicate to the dresser, lost for words at his thoughtfulness. "Do you need anything else, Leila? Medicine? A sandwich?"

Smiling widely at him, I thank him. "No, this is more than enough. Thank you, Jack."

"What the fuck is going on here?" Nate roars from the doorway. Neither of us had heard him come in. I spin around to face him and I'm shocked by his appearance. His head is closely shaven and there are bags under his eyes. He limps slightly as he approaches me. "Get out now," he shouts viciously at Jack.

"What do you think is happening here exactly?" Jack fronts up to Nathan, and my heart pounds against my ribcage. This is a simple misunderstanding, but it's escalating faster than the speed of light. "Your fiancée isn't feeling well, and you weren't here, so I made her tea. Nothing more, nothing less."

"If she needs anything. I will look after her," Nate shouts back at him.

"Well, why don't you look after her better, then no one else will have to step in. You look a mess, Nate," Jack roars back. The brothers reach an impasse, and Jack turns to leave. "I hope you feel better soon, Doc. Drink the tea while it's hot."

Silence reverberates around the room when Jack leaves. Not willing to make the first move, I pour my tea and stir the milk and sugar in the cup while I wait for Nate to say something. Anything.

"What's wrong with you? Is it the flu?" he asks me harshly, wincing as he sits down.

"I'm just tired," I reply simply. I'm not sick. Not in that way. Sick of Nate and his hot and cold attitude but not physically sick. I'm not willing to go into more detail. Not until he explains himself, and if he doesn't, then I'm not either.

"I'm sorry," he mutters with his head lowered.

"What for?" I answer, wanting to know if he understands why I'm upset, annoyed and disappointed. "What are you sorry for this time, Nathan?"

"Don't. Please don't. I've missed you so much, and I know I've fucked up again. But I am really sorry, Leila." I'm about to argue back with him when I hear whimpering outside the room. "You best go and get that; she won't shut up until you do."

Frowning at him, I walk to the bedroom door and peer outside. There is a small wicker carrier on the floor, and the whimpering is coming from the inside. Through the little door I see a small, brown and white puppy with a large pink bow on its collar.

"It's a dog!" I call out to Nate. "It's a puppy. Nathan?"

Without having made a sound, he has moved to the doorway and stands behind me. "One girl puppy, as requested. I am sorry, Leila. I should have called."

He places his hand on my shoulder, but when I look at it, his knuckles are red and bleeding. "What happened? Who did this?" I ask him, making eye contact with him for the first time since he walked into the bedroom.

"It's nothing. Look, this weekend didn't exactly go how I planned and shit happened—"

"Are you in trouble?" He shakes his head at me. "What happened to your hair? Did someone do this to you?"

"No. It's nothing like that. I'm okay. Well, I will be if my fiancée forgives me. I promise, no matter what, I won't do it again." The puppy yelps again, reminding us of her presence. "Are you going to let her out? She's eager to meet you." He smiles at me, and although I know I shouldn't forgive him so easily, I do anyway. If it happens again, I suppose that's on me.

"You can't keep doing this, Nate. We can't keep doing this. You're either all in and treat me with the respect I deserve, or we call this quits now. What's it going to be?" I ask him sternly. I want to forgive him, but an apology without change is meaningless. I need him to learn that this is not acceptable and despite forgiving him, I will not tolerate this behaviour again.

"I'm all in. I will never disrespect you or our engagement ever again." I nod to accept his commitment, before bending down to open the basket. My little puppy pops her head out first and yelps adorably. "You need to name her."

With her ear flopping over and her eyes wide, I finally coax her out of her basket. "Hello, girl. Welcome to your home. Oh, Nate! I love her!" I say to him as my puppy snuggles into me. "Hey, where are you going, little miss?" I ask her as she hides under my arm, climbing inside my jacket. I am hopelessly in love with her already.

I know when I look up at Nate with tears swimming in my eyes he knows the reason for my weepy state. My own puppy to love and to love me back. It's everything I've ever wanted. He kneels next to me and strokes my little girl as he whispers, "She loves you too. Look, she can't get close enough." He wraps his arm around me. "I know how she feels. What's her name going to be, darling?"

Leaning into his embrace, I answer him. "Missy. Her name is Missy." Nate gently kisses my temple as he repeats her name back to me. "Thank you for my puppy. But I swear to god, Nate, if you ever treat me like that again, I'm gone. I don't take shit from anyone, not even you. Do I, Missy? And you can go and apologise to your brother."

The dog gives another yelp before licking my face. At least I have her support.

## ~ Nate ~

Although my heart starts to beat more regularly when Leila gives me one more chance, the tightness in my chest doesn't ease, because I'm keeping a massive secret from her. It's easier to tell myself that my condition isn't serious, not yet, not like last time. However, from experience, I know that means nothing. This is as far as serious gets, and I'm terrified. I have finally found someone incredible, and life seems to be picturesque, and then cancer comes to shit all over it once again. Last time, I was still a child and my dad assured me everything would be fine, and I relied on that. This time, I've got everything to lose.

In a fit of rage, I punched the walls and doors in my office and shaved my hair off because if I have to start treatment soon, it's going to fall out. Selfishly, I was lost in a world of terror and pain. I'm a good person. I've never deliberately hurt anyone. Why me? Why me, again? Life isn't fair; in fact, it's fucking cruel. Why give me the love of my life and a glimpse of our happily ever just to snatch it away? If there is a god, he is one cruel bastard.

With Leila in my arms, I feel complete, but the lie I have created between us causes a fissure. A distance between us.

"Thank you for my puppy. But I swear to god, Nate, if you ever treat me like that again, I'm gone. I don't take shit from anyone, not even you. Do I, Missy? And you can go and apologise to your brother," Leila chastises me. I wish I could tell her, but all I could see when the doctor told me my dreaded diagnosis was Leila's face, and our future started slipping away. I need her to know and love the real me. Not sick Nathan, or Nathan the pretend fiancé. Just me. I need to know that what we have is the real deal for her as well as me.

"All Missy's stuff is downstairs. I need to call the vet to update her name on her registration and chip. But I'm going to talk to Jack first," I tell her, and she nods to me, although she is distracted with the little puppy. The joy on her face and the adoration in her eyes as she looks at the furry bundle is all I could ever dream and wish for. I'm not falling for her. I'm desperately in love with her. It's been days, a little under a week, since we got engaged, but she's very quickly become the centre of my world.

I walk along the corridor to Jack's wing. The place stinks of food and sweaty feet, as always. As a courtesy, I knock on his door before I enter and find him sitting on the floor playing on his PlayStation with a chicken drummer sticking out of his mouth. "I want to apologise," I tell him. He doesn't look up, but he does pause his game so he can take the bone out of his mouth. "I was out of order, and of course I appreciate you looking after Leila for me."

"So go on then... apologise," he retorts frostily.

"I'm sorry, Jack. I really am," I sincerely add, hoping my little brother will also forgive me this time too.

"You might be able to pull the wool over Leila's eyes. But I know you, Nathan. I know something is up, and unless you are honest with me, yourself and especially the woman you want to share your life with, you are going to keep fucking up." I stand silently; I will not share my secret with him. He will fall to pieces and within an hour everyone will know. "Whatever is going on, put a stop to it now. Or you will lose her. Trust me, she's different. She's not here for your money or fame. She won't stay for it either."

Although I know Jack is talking a lot of sense, it bitterly stings my fragile ego. I'm going to lose her. If I don't get my shit together, I'm going to lose her. "You're right. I'll talk to Leila later about what has been happening. Oh, and by the way… we have a puppy now."

"You got a dog?" he asks me incredulously. "You are terrified of dogs. What changed?"

I laugh before I answer him. "Leila. I'd live with a million murderers if it made her happy. Missy is actually quite cute. I think we can make it work."

"Nathan? You are okay, right?" he asks, and suddenly, the little boy, the one I had to tell our father had died, is sitting there with concerned eyes.

"Everything is fine, Jack. I just got fucked up this weekend and I messed up. But I'm going to get my shit together, I promise." I lie to him. I've told him little lies before but nothing of this magnitude. But how else can I stop him from worrying unnecessarily about me? He needs to concentrate on his game and his career. He has his own life to worry about. "Oh, we are having an engagement party in October. Keep your diary clear, okay?"

He salutes me as I walk out of his room and return to my fiancée. I've got this. I will start the low grade treatment in secret now, and hopefully, in a few weeks' time, when we have our engagement party, the oncologist will declare I am back into remission. The only people that know include me, the doctor and Kym. I know I can count on them for their discretion.

Leila is in the kitchen when I finally locate her. She sits on the floor with a dog bowl of water. "You thought of everything. Thank you, Nate. This is the best present ever." She cuddles her puppy like it's the most precious being to walk this earth. "I don't want to stay mad at you. I don't know how you can do all this but forget to call me back."

Wanting to offer further explanation, I attempt to interrupt her, but she shushes me. "Let me finish. Let's start over. No more mess ups or interruptions. Let's do this properly."

I sweep her and Missy up in my arms and kiss her. "I want nothing more than to prove myself to you. So yes, I'd love to start over. I can be better this time." Pushing all thoughts of my condition and treatments to one side, I completely absorb everything that is good and logical in my life. And Leila is top of that list.

"Take me to bed, Nate," she murmurs against my neck, her hot breath making me shiver in reaction. I want nothing more than I want this. "Can we take Missy for a walk tomorrow, please?"

"Anything, darling. Anything for you." And I mean every single word.

## Chapter 15

### ~ Leila ~

The days roll into weeks, and before I know it, Missy is getting her second round of vaccinations and our engagement party is upon us. True to his word, Nate has called and texted as promised, and we seem to be going from strength to strength. In-between our fun walks through the secluded forest behind our home in Sandybank to the star-studded events we attend together, we enjoy each other's company, and I'll honestly admit that I've never felt as comfortable with anyone as I do when I am with him.

Our nights are filled with passion and sweetness, and as the cold nights draw in, we take sanctuary in each other's arms. Everything has settled, and we have been able to create a bubble of domestic bliss.

Until today.

All hell broke loose when the press leaked the location of our meticulously planned engagement party. Though, who leaked it to the press to begin with remains a mystery. All I know is that Nate is fuming while he frantically arranges extra security for what was shaping up to be a beautiful affair.

The party starts in mere hours, and everything is already in place. It's too late to change anything, no matter how much Nate attempts to do so. I listen to him as he demands answers. "The reason we chose Lord Redvale's estate to host our engagement party is because of its gated location. Yes, I understand we have to open the gates for our guests and vendors. So, there is no way to stop the press entering the grounds."

Knowing there is nothing else we can do, I take Nate's face into my hands and kiss him. He looks tired and stressed, and I have the remedy to make it all better. "It is what it is. We just have to act accordingly. Let's leave it in the capable hands of our security."

He sighs after I finish kissing him. "I know you're right, but goddamn them all. I wanted this to be perfect for you. To be no press intrusion."

"It's already perfect. It's more than I have ever dreamed of, Nate. I'm taking the win." He laughs, and his shoulders relax. I think I'll be glad to get this engagement party out of the way and maybe Nate will relax a bit. He's stretching himself far too thin, and it's starting to take its toll on his physical health. "Zip me up, please?" I ask him, turning to reveal my bare back through my open dress.

Instead of zipping me up, he slides his hands inside my dress, touching me as though I'm his long lost treasure. "What are you doing to me? How can I concentrate when you're here, flashing your skin at me?"

Although I laugh, I turn to him and warn him. "I'm telling you now, Nathan Cardal. If you ruin my dress, I won't be going to any engagement party. Now zip me up."

"Damn, woman, you're hot even when you're telling me off!" He sulks, zipping my dress closed. "You look incredible, darling. The colour suits you." I bat his hands away, wary of him crinkling my expensive dress.

"Let me help you with your bow tie. Did all the extra clothing go to the estate already?" I ask him. He yawns as he nods his reply. "I think you need a vacation, Nate. You look knackered."

"I'll be fine. Did your mum return your call?" he asks as we walk down the stairs to the hallway. The blip for me tonight is my mum. I tried to convince her to come, but she refused. I know I shouldn't be bothered because this isn't real, but she doesn't know that. Her lack of support and concern has upset me. "No, but she sent a text inviting me to Mexico for Christmas."

He stops to look at me. "Are you gonna go?" He looks devastated at the possibility.

"No! I can't, and she knows that. The football season is one of the highlights of the festive period for the fans. I will be working, and she knows that. This is her way of politely inviting me to something she knows I won't accept."

"If you want to spend the holidays with your mum, I'll arrange the time off for you," he offers.

"I don't want to go, and she doesn't want me to go either. It's a little game she plays, Nate. Honestly, I think Christmas will be better here." He holds me in a tight embrace, one that I imagine would hold all the pieces of me together if I were to break down; however, I feel more anger towards my mother than I do sorrow. She hasn't even given Nate a chance, and that infuriates me.

"We'll make it the best Christmas ever. I promise," Nate assures me, and I know we'll have a decent try of it.

The drive to the country estate takes around twenty-five minutes. The estate itself is absolutely gorgeous. A huge manor house with an orangery and exemplary gardens. The house was once occupied by Lord Redvale's family, but now it is used for functions and events. We have hired the entire estate. There will be live music in the gardens, dancing, drinking and dining inside, and a selection of guests will stay the night too.

The theme, set by some pretentious party planner, is 'bow ties and ballgowns', and as the hosts, Nate and I fulfil the detail beautifully.

The colour scheme, the flowers, and the menu have all been taken care of by some higher up team. I have simply signed off on things that I like and vetoed the ones I didn't. Our guest list is over four thousand people strong. Most of whom have RSVP'd.

Besides my mum and stepdad, I invited my cousins and my friends. Oh, and my grumpy neighbour, Arthur, and his family. Everyone from work is invited, and a lot of Nate's business associates. To my friends' delight, there are several celebrities that have confirmed their attendance; even though I have never met them personally, Nate knows them all. Claire has designs on nabbing a celebrity and getting her own engagement ring. Her enthusiasm does make me laugh.

Jack has been very supportive and is even dog sitting Missy this evening. Our pampered pooch is of course invited to our party. She has become a celebrity in her own right, with the press photographing her as much as they do me. She will get a shock when I return to my normal life and she can't be a diva any longer.

We arrive at the gates to the estate, and after talking to the security, we drive through the gates and down the long driveway that is lined with trees on either side. The valet holds up the car when we near the house, and even though I have seen the place a couple of times already, I cannot help but gasp in awe.

"Congratulations on your engagement." The waiter greets us with champagne in flutes as he stands upon a red carpet that covers the stony ground, up the steps and into the grand building.

After weeks of preparation, a little hard break and frustration, it's finally time to celebrate.

## ~ Nate ~

The evening passes by almost without a hitch, which is nothing short of a miracle. The house looks nothing short of amazing. I wanted Leila to have the best of everything and ensured the party planners catered to her every whim. Not that she had whims. She respectfully asked for a place to dance, mini macarons on the dessert table and decent music. The whole place looks beautiful with its lights, flowers and tasteful arrangements. There is a starlit dance floor, just for Leila and her friends, and we have a live band, a popular one, that will be performing a private gig for us. The dessert table has all the sweet delights that I know Leila is fond of, but at the centre of the pile are the French macarons imported especially from the shop at the Eiffel Tower.

The pride that fills me that we have pulled the party off is nothing in comparison to how I feel having Leila here beside me as my fiancée. Proud doesn't seem enough of a word to portray just how in awe of her I am. She glows as though the source of life beams from within her very soul. She is beautiful. To me, she is perfect in every single way. She wears her dress with grace, and her hair glistens in the tiny rice lights that imitate stars in the night sky. Her smile lights up the whole room. Leila is everything I could ever want in a life partner. I know I've struck gold with her.

As the thousands of guests arrive, we end up separating to greet different people. Leila talks to the people from work and the staff I have introduced her to. I welcome the politicians, celebrities and business associates I am obliged to invite. After an hour, I go in search of her. This is our night to celebrate, and yet I've only spent around five minutes with her.

"Nathan!" my mother calls out to me as she walks down the red carpet into the hall. "This is all wonderful! And where is she? Where is my future daughter-in-law?"

My mum and Leila have met a couple of times over video call. Though Leila was shy, my mother, having finally secured a female in the family, is ecstatic and enthusiastically welcomes her to the family. The only fly in the ointment is that my mother despises Jack. The lingering hatred my mother felt for my father and Jack's mother for having an affair has always coloured the way she has thought of Jack. She still doesn't understand why he lives with me and why I looked after him when our father passed away. He is a child, and her treatment of him angers me. It wasn't his fault, and yet she treats him as though it is.

My other half-brother, Sam, accompanies my mother, but her husband isn't here. Not wanting to cause a scene, I don't ask, but I know I'll find out soon what is happening.

"I'll bring her to you in a moment; we are just greeting our guests," I tell her as she wraps me in her embrace. "Hey, Sam, you've got tall. How old are you now?"

"He's sixteen, Nathan. He's your brother; surely, you remember his age." The truth of the matter is, I hardly know Sam. I'd love to get to know him better, but with our mother hen pecking between us and him living in Spain, we haven't had the chance to bond. "Sam, grab us some drinks. I just want a word with your brother."

Sam stomps off, reminding me of Jack when he was that age. My mother would sprout grey hairs if I said that out loud. "What's up, mum?"

"You are probably wondering about Olivier. He's not going to be here, and we are spending some time apart." I nod to her, not wanting to pry. "We'll talk about it tomorrow. I just wanted you to know."

Uncomfortably, I don't know what to say to her about it. Olivier is fifteen years younger than my mother. He is a known womaniser and cheat, and this isn't the first time he's flaked on her. As long as my mother has money and influence, he'll never leave her, no matter what she says.

"Go and sit with Sam. I'll find Leila." I kiss her on the cheek before she re-joins Sam. The sadness in her eyes pulls at my heart. I'd love to wipe Olivier off the face of the earth for hurting my mum this way.

Finally, I find Leila, surrounded by ex-players of Redvale. Just as I reach her side, I overhear an older ex player, Tommy Hartley, talking to Leila. "I didn't know if you'd want to talk to me. I used to play with your dad. We were best friends before the accident," he tells her quietly.

Leila stiffens beside me, and I instinctively hold her hand. "I didn't know that. I wasn't aware of my father having many friends, if any."

"Well, once he passed, we all kept our distance. Just like your mother told us to," he explains to her. "I get it, she was in pain and mourning, but I promise you, Leila, your dad loved you. He just–"

Before he can finish, Leila interrupts him. "My mother told you to stay away? Why?" She keeps her voice low, but I can feel the desperation in her questions. There is a whole side of her life she knows nothing about.

"She blamed us, you know, afterwards. She said we had all abandoned him, and there is some truth in that." Tommy's light blue eyes fill with tears as he explains what happened. "As a young man, I was travelling around the country as a player. I was living a good life. When Frankie got injured, I called him a couple of times, but my stories reminded him of what he was missing. Soon, he stopped taking my calls. Then I stopped calling."

"I know players often do that after an injury. They retreat because it's painful to be close to the world you once belonged to but don't belong there anymore. I don't think that was your fault, Mr Hartley."

"I do shoulder some of the blame, though. I always have. If I had supported him better, would things have turned out differently?" he offers to her in regret before continuing. "When your mum sued McAllister for causing the injury, and then the club and football association for neglecting Frankie, and it was thrown out, she blamed us all and told us to stay away from you both."

Leila grips my hand tightly, and I pull her closer to me, wanting her to find comfort in my presence.

"I never knew. She just told me you all turned your back on him. That you weren't true friends." Leila sounds bewildered, and I want to intervene on her behalf, but I know she needs these answers. "She wouldn't even come today; she won't meet Nate. She's completely against me working in football. I always thought it was too painful for her."

"There is a lot you don't know. We set up a trust fund for you. So that Frankie's daughter didn't go without. She refused to accept it." Tommy stops abruptly.

"Look, I didn't intend on telling you all this, not right now. I just wanted you to know that I am sorry for any part I played and that not a day has gone by when I haven't thought about you and your dad."

After a few pleasantries, Tommy embraces Leila and gives her his card with his contact details. He shakes my hand before he moves on, and I thank him for giving Leila some insight into her past.

"Nate, I need a minute. I'm so overwhelmed. I need a little time to just get my head around all this." She's beginning to fall apart in a way I have never witnessed before. Not wanting to leave her alone, I pull her out of sight of our guests, through the voiles that cover the doors, and out onto a secluded balcony.

"Can I stay or do you want me to give you space?" I offer to her, silently begging her to not push me away.

"Please stay. Don't leave me. I need to talk to you. I need to tell you what I know about my father."

# Players Positions

A simple list of the standard roles within a professional football team:

- Goalkeeper
- Defense
- Midfield
- Attack

Roles are always evolving and interchanging.

(SOURCE: Oxford language Dictionary)

# Chapter 16

## ~ Leila ~

Nate takes me by the hand, and I'm thankful to have him anchoring me. The revelation about my mother and father has knocked the stuffing out of me. The pain of losing him has been hard enough to live with. The nature of his death has always been a bitter pill to swallow. Why couldn't he stay, if not for mum then for me, his baby girl.

When Nate asks if he can stay or if I need space, I hold on to him tighter. "Please stay. Don't leave me. I need to talk to you. I need to tell you what I know about my father." I end on a sob that I don't mean to release. I am not a crier, but through my blurry eyes, Nate's silhouette stays beside me, no judgement, no pressure to spill what I know, and that convinces me that it's okay to tell him. "I should have told you sooner, but I didn't know how. I was still worried about how much I could trust you."

He nods after he kisses my head. "I understand, Leila. It's hard opening up to people. But, I trust you. How about I tell you something personal first, something you've asked and I haven't answered yet?"

My intrigue is piqued; there are many things I still don't know about Nate, and what he wants to divulge is as interesting as the stuff that is still to be revealed. "Okay. If you want to. Don't think you have to, though, Nate."

He smiles before starting his explanation. I watch as he braces himself, leaning onto the balcony railing. We stand side by side looking out at the spectacular grounds from our privileged position. "I haven't had a relationship with a woman that wasn't protected under a non-disclosure since the first girl I slept with sold the story to the rags and made a mockery of me. I have controlled every relationship I've ever been in because she took away my control." He continues to look out into the distance once he's finished his explanation.

"Is that true? Someone did that to you?" I ask in barely a whisper. My heart breaks for him when he nods. "I'm so sorry, Nate. That's a horrible thing to do. How do these people live with themselves?"

"It was a long time ago. I learnt my lesson the hard way. But I learnt my lesson," he adds with a sad smile.

Nate confiding in me gives me the assurance I need to open up to him. I take a deep breath, and spill my deeply hidden secrets. "My dad took his own life. He was young and suffered a career ending injury early on in his career. He never got over it," I confess in hushed tones. Nate is the first person I have ever told. He listens and then pulls me back to him. Kissing my temple, then the bridge of my nose before moving to my mouth. "I'm not ashamed of him or what he did; I simply don't talk about it because it hurts me. It hurts that he couldn't stay for me. That he felt so desperate and alone that dying seemed like the only way forward. It horrifies me that the system I now work for is still as flawed for injured players as it was when my father played." I'm unable to continue because despite my best intentions, I begin to cry.

"That's why you became a sports injury specialist, isn't it?" I nod to his question, because that had been my driving force. In some ways it was my apology to my dad for being unable to do anything for him. I wanted to ensure that no other player felt as he did. "Your dad would be so proud of you, Leila. He wouldn't want you carrying his hurt and pain."

Although I agree with his sentiment, I have lived with this knowledge for as long as I can remember. "The thing with suicide is that the pain never ends. It is simply redistributed. My father may now be at peace, but his pain has spread to me, my mum, his parents, even Tommy Hartley carries the scars of my father's death."

"I know. I don't think a person who is that desperate to end things is capable of that sort of reasoning, though, Leila." I know he is right. As much as suicide is a taboo subject, I know that better understanding and intervention will only come with more people talking about it. Maybe a change has to start with me.

"Nate, you asked me once if there was anything more lurking at the back of my closet. I didn't know about it when you asked, but you heard Tommy back there. My mum sued McAllister and the club and the governing body. This could have implications for you. I'm sorry, I–"

Pulling me tightly to his chest, his voice is gruff and hard when he interrupts me. "Look at me," he commands, and I obey him immediately. "Do not apologise for something that wasn't your doing. We'll cross that bridge when we get to it. There is nothing that we cannot solve together," he tells me, and I just want to climb inside him and take sanctuary there. Nate is a tower of strength, a constant. He is everything to me now. I can't remember my life before him anymore. I don't know how I would have ever found these answers or coped with the overwhelming information without Nate by my side. "At least now we know what McAllister's issue was. Though how he can blame you is beyond me; you were a baby!" he adds, and I have to agree, although I do feel some guilt that my past has ruffled McAllister's world enough that he left his job.

"How is the party going, Nate? Do you think anyone has noticed we are missing?" He laughs at my question. "Yes, I have just remembered this is our engagement party and that we are supposed to be hosting, not hiding on the balcony." I join in his laughter, feeling lighter now I've shared my burden with him, and I can almost detect my feelings deepening for him.

"Everything is going great, and if anyone has noticed, they are probably wondering what room we're fucking in, darling. So, tell me... what room should we fuck in? We don't want to let our guests down now, do we?" I stop myself from responding in outrage, and instead, I raise the stakes.

"What's wrong with right here? I can look at the stars while you rock my world!" The quick change in conversation is just what I needed. We both giggle, the mood lightening as I get my game face back in order.

"As amazing as that sounds, it'll have to wait until later. My mother is waiting for us," he drops on me. I smack him on the arm. "Hey, what was that for?"

"Why didn't you tell me your mum had arrived? Nate, she's going to think we've been... doing stuff out here. Oh my god, I'm mortified." I can already feel my face burning in embarrassment. I wanted to make a good impression, but she's going to think I'm a sex maniac.

"We've only been out here for five minutes, calm down. Olivier didn't come. It's just her and Sam, and I left her to find a table while Sam got her a drink, so you're good," he reassures me. "Now come here, we need to straighten your crown."

Confused as to what he is referring to, I am left gobsmacked when he takes my face into his hands and smooths his thumbs over my face where my tears have probably left tracks. He looks deep into my eyes once he's done. "God, you're fucking gorgeous. Are you ready?"

With that endorsement, how could I not be?

⚽🖤⚽

The rest of the evening goes by in a blur. I meet Nate's mum, Drea, and his other brother, Sam, who is incredibly shy. He looks nothing like Nate, but I suppose almost being old enough to be the boy's father will do that.

Drea is glamorous and chic, in all ways except one. She speaks to Jack as though he is the dirt off her shoe, and having gotten closer to Jack and become friendly with him, my back goes up defensively. She shouldn't speak to anyone like that. Nate warned me about her and her attitude towards Jack, but nothing could have prepared me for the venom that woman directs at Jack.

"What's that raggedy thing he's carrying around? He looks ridiculous," she spits at the table as she watches Jack from afar.

"Actually, that's my dog, Missy. Nate bought her for me. I don't think she's raggedy... Do you, Nate?" When I look at Nate, I can see the anger bubbling below the surface, the tic in his jaw jumps erratically. I don't know if his anger is directed at me for questioning his mum and bringing him into it or because his mum insulted his brother and my dog.

"No, darling. She most definitely isn't raggedy!" he replies to me while never breaking eye contact with his mum. This isn't their first rodeo; Nate and his mum have butted heads over this many times before.

"Well, obviously the dog is an excellent breed, and she is well kept. It's just that street urchin carrying her like a bag of potatoes," she replies nastily while sipping her champagne.

"Mum. I am warning you," Nate says in a voice I have only heard him use once before. "I told you if you couldn't be civil, to not come. You can leave if you continue," he tells her in a no-nonsense manner that I would never have the balls to pull off against my own mother.

"And where is your mother, Leila? Are you going to introduce me?" My stomach turns to ice water at the mention of my own mother.

"Leila's mum couldn't make it, like Olivier," Nate interjects sharply. I can sense a war brewing between them when Sam chirps up.

"Nathan, would you mind introducing me to your brother, please? I would love to talk to him about football." We all stare at him, shocked for a millisecond, but then I am amused, and my respect increases tenfold for the young man sitting in front of me.

"Samuel. No. What are you thinking?!" Drea exclaims in disgust and panic.

"Calm down, mother. You might carry a grudge, but I don't. It has got nothing to do with me, and I can do what I like." He stands abruptly, and when he stalks away in Jack's direction, I encourage Nate to follow him.

"Never have children, Leila. Not that it'll be an issue for you. However, children are ungrateful, spoiled little swine's that generally take after their fathers." The point she raised about children is muted by the declaration that Nate is like his father.

"Are you saying Nate is like his father?" She laughs at me coldly before placing her hand on mine.

"Dear, the apple doesn't fall far from the tree. He is a workaholic like his father, and he disregards and disrespects me, which will show you exactly what he will be like as a husband." She keeps a tight grip on my hand with one of hers while she drinks her champagne using her other before continuing, "And as soon as he grows bored, which he will, his eye will wonder and his wealth and status will ensure he'll never be short of another woman to warm his bed."

Staring at her, stunned into silence, she continues to hold my hand. "Nate's nothing like that. But I suppose he was always going to take after the parent that actually raised him and stuck around during important events in his life." The words fall out, shocking even myself at my own willingness to take on Nate's mother.

"He was free to come to Spain with me," she counters back at me defensively. I snatch my hand away from her grip and stand up. I do not like Drea. She is not and will never be my ally.

"I suppose I should count myself lucky he chose to stay. Otherwise, he would be bitter and twisted like you." Spotting Claire and Louise, I leave her gawping at the back of me while I join my friends.

"Here she is, the woman of the hour, the engage-ee," Claire shouts loudly over the music and bustle of the crowd. "Our best friend, capturer of billionaire's heart." Her and Louise giggle and embrace me when I stop at their side.

"Thank you for coming! You don't know how much I needed to see a friendly face right now," I tell them both.

"What's up?" Louise asks, passing me a flute of champagne. "This place is amazing, Leila! Will the wedding be here too? It's going to be so fricken amazing."

"I-I... we haven't decided yet, still plenty of time. I think after all the trouble we've had with the press, we might even do it in another country." Although I initially stumble over my explanation, Louise is drunk enough to simply accept my answer.

"Ley, there are sooooo many celebs here. I'm like a dog with two dicks... All I need to do is bag one of them and I'll be set for life!" Claire contributes, in what I hope is jest. "Who should my first victim be?" she says as she begins to spin on the spot.

However, unknowing to her, Jack's friend Tyson stands behind her, his head cocked in intrigue at the whirlwind that is one of my best friends. "How about me?" he says to her seriously.

Without any grace at all, Claire spins back around to me and Louise and shouts, "Well, that was a lot easier than I thought. I'll see you girls later. Pray for me that he is a deviant, won't you?" Tyson smiles as he accepts Claire's hand.

"Goodnight, Doc, and congratulations," Tyson calls out to me as they walk away.

"Can you believe she's just left me?" Louise looks at me horrified. "Ley, you need to find me a friend, someone I can hang out with while you do your couple-y things," she tells me desperately.

At the same time, Nate returns to me with two men in tow. "Leila, darling, I'd like you to meet some friends of mine. This is Otis Levelle and Hugo Wallis." While Nate's friends look at both Louise and I appraisingly, I smile widely at Nate.

"You're just in time. Louise needs a friend; Claire has just left with Tyson." Nate's eyes crinkle in the corner as he laughs.

"Otis is here with his partner. Otis, where is Liam? But Hugo here is also in need of a friend." As another gentleman joins our growing group, Hugo and Louise smile timidly at each other.

Our party is officially hookup central!

"He's a decent one, isn't he?" I whisper to Nate as I sway in his arms, looking over at my friend, who dances a little uncomfortably with the man she just met.

"Trust me. He is one of the best. Very quiet, not very experienced with the ladies, but he'll look after her." Resting my head on his shoulder, I take his words to heart.

"I do trust you, Nate. I don't think I've trusted anyone as much as I trust you," I reply. Maybe the emotion of this event is getting to me, but a deep love and respect flows through me for the man I dance with. This may not be the real deal, but I am never going to forget the way he made me feel while I was his.

"I watched you storm away from my mother." Shit. I did forget about Drea and her attack on me and Nate. "What did she say? Don't say, 'nothing.' I've watched you long enough to know when someone has riled you."

"She told me to never have children and that you were just like your father. That you would..." I trail off, not wanting to speak ill of the dead and cause offence to Nate. "grow bored just like him."

"She told you I would cheat just like him, didn't she?" he adds, and I nod in answer to him "She's gone too far. I want her to leave."

"Nate, just ignore her for now. Let's enjoy the rest of our night. Your mother has no doubt in her mind what I think of her opinions." He smiles at me again.

"You are my perfect match, in every way, Leila Monrose." Thinking someone must be either photographing or recording us, I don't think too deeply about his words.

Instead, I reply, "As you are mine, my love." I add a kiss on his cheek.

## ~ Jack ~

As promised, I arrive at the party with Leila's dog. I think it'll be a talking point with the ladies at the very least, and my friends all think so too. I'm happy for Nathan and Leila, and the party is fun and full of interesting people I am eager to mingle with. However, when Nathan's mum shows up, I make myself scarce, attempting to hide away behind Leila's dog. That woman hates me with a passion and the feeling is mutual. She is very open about how much she abhors my very existence. When I was a child, I would often try to win her over, but I've long since let go of the notion of us all being a happy family. It's not going to happen, not like that at any rate.

As I watch my brother twirl his fiancée around the dance floor, a pang of longing rips through my body. Not only does it take me by surprise, but it also horrifies me. I've never felt the need for a long-term steady girlfriend, preferring the bachelor lifestyle I have lived by for most of my adult life. However, Nathan looks happy, settled, as though all his dreams have come true, and I do wonder if that could happen for me. Is there someone special out there for me?

Firstly, I worry it might have been the Doc and I fucked everything up. But one thing is for sure. As great as Leila is, she is perfect for my brother, and I see her more in a sisterly way now. Looking around the room, I no longer see potential targets for a one-night stand. All around me is a sea of potential women who could be 'the one' and I've never felt as intimidated or sick.

What if I've already met her but treated her badly. What if she knows me and doesn't want me because of my past behaviour? How will I know?

I need to talk to Nathan and soon. Missy, the dog, provides my perfect alibi. "Doc, Missy is pining for you. Do you want a little cuddle for a minute or two?" Leila instantly lights up and takes her puppy from me, chatting away to her. "Nathan, I need a quick word, please?"

"Is everything okay? What's going on?" he asks with concern, looking around to see if there is any immediate danger. I shake my head at him, and he pushes me into an alcove where we can speak in private. "Spill. What's got you all worked up, Jack?"

Looking at my big brother, really looking at him, I can see that he isn't as rested as I would expect. "You look tired, Nathan. That's not what I want to talk about, though. I need to know…" I stumble over my words, knowing what I want to ask but reluctant to show my vulnerability. "When did you know Leila was 'the one'?"

He looks at me confused, before scratching the back of his neck. "Honestly? Within thirty seconds of meeting her in the flesh, but it took a little longer to accept that is what she is to me," he replies. "Why do you ask?"

"Then if she was the one for me, I'd know already, right?" His face sets in a stony frown. "I know she's not mine. She's yours, but I saw you dancing with her and for the first time ever, I think I want something like that too."

"I don't know how it all works, Jack. But when you know, you know. I can't explain any better than that. I wasn't looking for Leila, to settle down or any of it. As soon as I looked into her eyes, the universe began to make sense." He falters, his cheeks turning red. "I know that sounds cheesy and corny, but that's the only way I can describe it. I feel complete now that I have her."

Thinking about his words, I smile back at him. "I'm glad you found her, Nathan. I want you to be happy. You're both so in love." Moving from the shadows of our quiet corner, I watch him as his eyes follow the Doc. "I never thought one woman, and kids and shit, would be for me. I think I'm growing up." We both laugh at that ridiculous notion.

"Well, I wouldn't go that far, but you've definitely surprised me." He ends on a yawn, and I try to look more closely at him.

"Are you okay, Nate? Something seems off with you." Instantly, I notice his stance change, and his earlier openness evaporates before my very eyes. "Oh, I get it. Leila has been keeping you busy in the bedroom, so you're not getting any sleep," I add to lighten the mood, and save myself from a chastising.

"Hey, what Leila and I get up to in our bedroom has nothing to do with you," he adds with a laugh.

"Would you mind keeping it down then. It's kind of sickening that my older brother is getting more sex than me at the moment."

He laughs again but shakes his head. "You can always move out. I best get back to Leila. What did Sam say by the way?" he asks almost absent mindedly.

"He's interested in training. He seems okay considering his mother is a dragon. A bit like you really," I reply.

He shoots me a warning stare. "That's my mother you're talking about. Though, you do have a point about her being a dragon," he says before he finally walks back to the Doc.

A few minutes later, my brother takes to the stage to toast his fiancée and thank everyone for coming to celebrate their engagement and then invites us all into the grounds for live music and fireworks. Leila keeps hold of the dog as prearranged, worried the dog may become scared of the fireworks.

While I stand with my friends, I look up at the night sky and bask in the excitement of what is to come in the next stage of my life. I want love. It may not be the kind of love that others dream of, because a sweet romance doesn't seem to be what is in the stars for me. I'm ready for the raw, the coarse, the rougher kind. I'm not expecting some big, perfect happily ever after because that's not me. I'm ready for the chase, for the courtship, the wooing, the fighting, the making up. I'm ready for it all. For the right girl, I now know it'll be worth it.

I think I'm finally open to meeting the one.

Kelvin, the young academy player, moves next to me. "Jack, are you heading out into town soon? Alana's friend sent a message saying they are at Hotspot again." Normally, a quick, cheap, easy fuck would be everything, but now I know what I want, and Alana isn't it. She isn't Mrs right. She was Ms right-now.

"Nah, I'm going to stay and help Nathan. Maybe next time." I gently let him down, despite knowing I'm more than likely cock-blocking him too. "Is it a thing with the girl you hooked up with?" I ask him, but he shakes his head.

"No. I haven't seen her since that night. She must have heard about the engagement party, because they were asking to come here, but I said no." It now makes more sense. I have seen Alana a couple of times since that night, but there was no media storm around us like I had expected and there was nothing special between us in bed. There seems little point in prolonging our interactions.

"Kelvin. You need to spread your net, don't put your eggs in one basket," I tell the younger player, imparting the wisdom I have accumulated, because I now have no use for it. "Until you're ready to settle down, you should have as much fun as you can."

Wow. It's unbelievable how much my whole ethos has changed within a few short minutes.

# Chapter 17

## ~ Leila ~

Our guests leave the building for the outdoor concert and firework display, but we stay inside. We are sleeping here tonight, and I requested that we watch the concert from our room. I also wanted to keep Missy close in case the noisy fireworks frighten her. As she settles into her crate for the evening and Nate practically collapses on the bed, I know I made the right choice.

We have our own personal balcony, so after discarding my high heels in favour of some fluffy socks and borrowing Nate's hoody, I sit out on the balcony alone. The sea of people below pose an intimidating sight; I find it hard to believe they are all here to celebrate my engagement. Especially seeing as my own mother didn't show up.

As my feelings deepen for Nate, the more outraged I become at my mother for refusing to acknowledge him. Imagine if this was real, would her attitude extend to our children? Would she attend my wedding? Would she just cut me off completely? At some point I know I would have dismissed all these concerns but not now. She has some dark secrets that I have the right to know about. The more she covers up to protect herself, the more she hurts me, whether intentional or not.

The little balcony I sit on has wrought iron railings all around, offering limited shelter from the biting wind that is beginning to pick up. Next week it'll be November and it'll be rainy, windy and cold from that point on. It almost feels symbolic. This may well be the end of our honeymoon period. Each day we spend together gets better and better, and part of me wishes for the next day to see what will happen, when another part of me wants to freeze time, because our time together is limited and precious and I don't want it to be over too soon.

"How's the band, gorgeous?" Nate asks me, standing in the open French door that leads onto the balcony. "Sorry I flaked out then, I needed a power nap," he offers me with a yawn.

"That's okay, you've taken on a lot these past few weeks. We can relax a little now. The band is awesome, by the way, and our guests seem to be enjoying themselves." I smile up at him, my handsome temporary fiancé, who still looks half asleep and dishevelled. "It's getting a bit cold here; I might come back inside in a minute or two," I add on a shiver.

"I'll bring you some blankets and order hot chocolate, extra marshmallows?" My heart warms at his kind gesture, and I nod to him. He returns from the room a few minutes later with blankets. "Room service will ring when they are outside. They are bringing you cake too."

"Cake? Our cake?" I ask excitedly. One of the very best perks of being engaged to a rich man is his ability to procure any cake in any shape and size at any time of the day and night. The highlight of our engagement party has been picking out our cake, or should I say cakes. It is four tiers, each one a different flavour and design.

He chuckles at me and raises his eyebrows, widening his eyes in what I know is his mock excited face too. "Just the little one. The carrot cake."

I groan out loud in delight, making Nate laugh even harder. "I could kiss you right now, Mr Cardal. You're an absolute gem," I tell him, carefully assessing every word. I am so close to saying the forbidden words. The words that I know will change everything, because those feelings were never part of the deal. As affection and respect bubble up inside me for Nate, I admit to myself, if no one else, that I am in love with him. As much as I want to berate myself, I can't, because even if this ends as contracted, it is totally worth it. Every moment, every memory is worth my broken heart come June time when this all ends. It will be a reminder of what we had, and what we shared together, and I could never regret that.

Once our cake and hot chocolate arrives, we return to the balcony for the firework display. "Let me snuggle you close and keep you warm," he murmurs against my cheek, and without any reservations, I completely melt into his embrace. I've never felt as safe or as wanted. I've never felt so loved.

"Let's stay like this forever," I say, skirting very close to the edge of what is truly on my mind.

"I would, but we'll need to pee eventually," he quips back, making me laugh again. "Can we discuss Christmas, please?" he adds, catching me off guard.

"What about it?" My heart sinks because I know Nate will want to revisit the invitation from my mother and I don't want to ruin this wonderful evening with any more talk about her.

"Well, since our father died, Jack and I haven't really celebrated Christmas. But I'm thinking we should this year. We should host, and if people come, then good and if they don't, well screw them, it's more turkey for us," he explains to me, and for the first time in a long time, I get butterflies when I think about Christmas.

"We will of course extend the invitation to your friends and family, and to mine too. And Jack can invite whoever he wants. What do you think?"

"I think it's a perfect idea. It's my turn to invite my mum as an act and her's to not accept. It's wonderful," I tell him, smiling at him. He kisses my temple, and I shiver, only this time it's not because of the cold. "I've always wanted a proper traditional family Christmas," I admit wistfully.

Pulling out his phone, he taps in a few words before putting it back in his pocket. "It's a plan then. We are hosting Christmas. If my girl wants a traditional family Christmas, that is what she'll have. We need another task team; it's only eight weeks away."

I'm starting to think that Nathan enjoys all these parties. "Another task team? Can't we just use the same one that did the engagement party?" It seems pointless getting to know another new team when we already have one.

"Noooo. That's a totally different project. We need a Christmas team." He assures me, and with no idea what he's talking about, I let him take the lead once more.

Missy begins to yelp in distress at the loud bangs in the sky, and so we move back inside, closing the doors shut tight to lessen the sounds outside. She quickly resettles, and once I finish fussing, I look up and find Nate lying naked on the bed.

"Come on, gorgeous. Don't keep me waiting."

Not needing further encouragement, I strip off my clothes. Nate is already hard and sits with his back against the headboard of our large bed. Despite the cold outside, the room is the perfect temperature. I take everything off except the fluffy socks. "Well, these are very sexy, Ms Monrose. I think I prefer them to the stockings you wore a couple of weeks ago."

I giggle as I sit next to him on the bed. "Want me to take them off?" He shakes his head at me before beckoning me towards him.

"No, my precious girl. You're perfect as you are. You were amazing tonight. Everything was beyond perfect. I am so proud that you are my fiancée and that we got to enjoy this party together." His words, so sweet and thoughtful, catch me off-guard.

"Nate... I-I..." I'm going to say it, I'm going to tell him my true feelings. I'm going to admit that I've fallen in love with him and damn to the consequences.

"Shhh, let me show you how much tonight has meant to me." He interrupts me, and my thoughts scatter as his lips connect with mine and pure electricity and frisson pass through us. "I want you to get up here and take a seat."

My mind is clouded with the kiss we just shared and the loving words he spoils me with. "Where? What do you want me to do?"

He slides down the bed until he is completely flat and tugs my hands. "Take a seat on my face. I'm going to show you how proud of you I am. I'm going to demonstrate what I want to give you, what I think you deserve."

"On your face? What if I smother you?" I question. He has asked before, but we didn't get around to it. Now I know him better, I am able to say the things that are running through my mind.

Nate chuckles before he answers. "Jesus, Leila. I can think of no better way to go." He closes his eyes momentarily and then he reopens them. "Nope, I just imagined that was the way I died, and I have no regrets. Sit on my face, gorgeous. I wanna make you come all over my face."

The need that started in my tummy reaches a fever pitch right between my legs; his words alone and the promise of what is to come already sends me on my way to oblivion. I hold onto the headboard and kneel while Nate scoots under me, practically wearing my legs as earrings. I whimper as his nose brushes over my clit. "I need you so bad," I tell him straight.

"Then stop being shy and lower yourself onto my face. I promise, I'll pinch you if I can't breathe." With a plan in place, I sit on his face. He wraps his arms over my thighs, preventing me from moving too much, and eats away at my core like he has been fasting for weeks. I cling onto the headboard for dear life, my legs trembling with every swipe of his tongue, but with each lick, suck and bite, I edge closer and closer to fulfilment.

Suddenly, I have an idea I want to try. "I have a hole that needs filling," I tell Nate cryptically. "I just want to face the other direction, is that okay?" He loosens his grip on my legs, allowing me to move, and when I look at his face, evidence of my pleasure glistens all over it. I begin to feel embarrassed until Nate licks his lips and groans in pleasure.

"I'm not done here, Leila. Hurry up," he tells me firmly, and I bet he is pouting about waiting for his supper.

Turning around to face the other direction, my target is now in my sights. I lower my pussy back onto Nate's face and moan when he rolls his tongue over my clit, the sensation varying now I have shifted positions. My legs tremble again as I climb higher. Shivers run up and down my spine, and my skin goose pimples in reaction to all the delightful feelings building up inside me.

My time comes to take Nate by surprise. I lean down and lick the tip of his cock, his salty precum sitting like a welcoming dewdrop. Nate gasps against me, blowing against my pussy, adding even more sensations. I raise my hips slightly giving him a little breathing space if he needs it, but Nate simply raises his head to follow me, burying himself back between my legs. Happy that he is comfortable, I get to work on getting my fill too.

Every time I go near his cock, it jumps and twitches in excitement all of its own accord. I blow on it, and it pulsates. I rub the tip of my tongue across the top of it, and it bounces off my face, searching for more. I do not deny his cock what it desires. I build up to sucking him dry, first with my tongue, then my lips, before finally taking him as far as I can into my mouth. His groan of pleasure as I give his dick the attention it deserves spurs me on, and I stroke his balls while I suck him, hollowing out my cheeks and humming in what I hope is added sensations for him.

Nate grabs me by the top of my thighs and pushes me forward, I take more of him into my mouth, almost gagging as his cock hits the back of my throat. "Fuck!" he growls out behind me "Leila, did you bring any toys with you?" he asks me breathily. He now pumps his fingers inside me, pushing me right to the brink of euphoria.

"No. I don't want toys. I just want you."

"Then ride me, baby. I don't want to blow in your mouth, and you're sucking me so good that I'm ready to go." I can tell how good it is for him from the way his cock is tensing and throbbing in my mouth. It feels good that I can give him what he gives me.

Releasing his cock with a pop, I move down the bed. Nate sits up and guides my hips while I line us up before dropping my weight back, sliding down his cock and rocking my hips as he hits the sweet spot deep inside me. My entire body begins to shake as I ride Nate. My movements become sharp and jagged, and my mind loses control to my body as it instinctively seeks the fulfilment it desires. Nate helps me by biting and sucking on my neck. One of his large hands palms my breast, while the other continues to work my clit, pushing me harder and faster until I squeeze him tightly inside me. Waves of pleasure crash over me, my limbs turn to jelly, and my eyesight blurs until all I am is a ball of climax. Nate ups his pace, thrusting up into me with the same ferocity as before, and another orgasm hits me as I feel him pump his load in me.

We fall in a tangle of satisfied limbs, still connected to each other. Nothing has ever felt more like home than how I feel in Nate's arms. At least I didn't tell him I'm in love with him. I get to pretend for a little while longer that what we have is the real deal.

⚽♥⚽

Nate is a very passionate lover; every encounter gets better each time. I keep expecting things to go stale between us, but the longer we spend together, the more satisfying our sex life becomes. As Nate dozes off, I take a quick shower and dress in my pjs. He snores softly, while I take out my phone and text my mother to tell her about Christmas. When she doesn't reply, I call her instead. She answers on the fourth ring.

My mother doesn't even mention that this evening is my engagement party; she doesn't ask about it, or my fiancé. She declines my invitation to Christmas, and her indifferent attitude chafes me. "My engagement party was amazing by the way," I tell her in a clipped tone. I have had enough. Nate has been nothing but adoring and respectful, and it's high time my mother stopped being a childish little brat and treated my partner with the same respect she expects me to treat her new husband with. "You know, I was speaking to some old friends of Dad's tonight, and let's just say, I think you have a lot of explaining to do."

"I think it's best if you don't call anymore, Leila. I told you I didn't want to be a part of that lifestyle. That world sickens me," she replies in a cold voice, so far removed from the mother I have known all my life. "And as for you expecting an explanation, I am not required to explain anything to you. It was me that went through it all, not you."

"He is my dad. My flesh and blood. I'm the one who grew up without him, not knowing him or why he left me," I shout down the phone at her. How dare she think she can hide this information away. She is the adult in this situation. I am her child, and if not knowing something about my father and our past hurts me, shouldn't she want to help me understand? I must have woken Nate with my shouting, because he wraps his arms around me and holds me close to him. His touch calms me, allowing me to regain my composure.

"He was my husband. My best friend. What happened, happened to him and me. Just let go of it, Leila," she spits back at me. "Leave the past where it belongs."

"No. I can't. I need to know the full truth of what happened, and if you don't tell me, I'll have to find out for myself," I tell her as calmly and rationally as I can.

"Then there is nothing more to say. Please, don't call me again, Leila. Goodbye." The line goes dead, and I look at Nate in shock.

"If you want answers, I'll help you. Your mum is... a complicated woman. Just give her time to cool off." I nod to him and roll back into bed with him. Within minutes, he's asleep again. However, sleep eludes me. Images of my father feeling alone and desperate haunt me, and resentment builds against my only living parent. Eventually I must fall asleep, because when I wake, I can hear Nate hurling in the bathroom, and morning has crept up on me.

"Are you okay?" I ask him, wondering if he overindulged last night or if he is getting sick. "Do you need anything?" I call out to him, but I don't think he can hear me over the flushing toilet. I hear him running the taps, and then he finally comes out of the bathroom, wiping his hands on a towel.

"Well, that champagne did not want to stay in me, darling," he tells me with a smile. He still looks tired even after a good sleep.

"Are you sure you're feeling okay, Nate?" He smiles at me, a stunning smile that makes my heart leap into my throat.

"Honestly, I feel so much better now that I've puked. I want you to get up and get ready. I've arranged a little treat for you." He stands at the foot of the bed, waiting for me.

"A treat that requires my clothes on. I don't like the sound of that!" I joke with him.

"After last night, I thought you could do with some moral support. You and your friends are having a brunch party. Claire has loads to tell you apparently." I think back to last night and Claire walking off with someone, but I can't remember who.

"Who was her victim again?" I ask him, while I select clothes to wear.

"Tyson. She called him a 'cotton candy man' and said you'd know what she meant." My mouth actually drops open, and I look at Nate incredulously.

"She said that... to you?" I stumble out my words. I can't believe Claire. She has no filter or shame. Nate bursts out laughing at me and my obvious embarrassment.

"She said you'd be mortified. What does it mean?" How do I explain Claire's rating scale to him? I barely understand it myself. "Is it good or bad? Am I a cotton candy man?"

"NO. You are not; you have cotton candy moments that I enjoy. Just remember that this is Claire's stupid list. A cotton candy man is one that strokes your face, constantly asks permission in bed and treats you like you're fragile and precious. Fluffy, sugary sweet, completely lickable, but he's not going to hold up in a storm." Nate continues to look at me with interest. "You don't fit into a category; you're an all-rounder, a decent amount of a few categories."

"What categories may that be, then?" I'm going to strangle Claire for putting me in this position. "Tell me, it's very interesting and insightful."

Fuckkk! I groan as I hide my face. "I don't have time to go through them all right now. I have to meet my friends, remember?" He looks crestfallen, and my overriding want to please him kicks in. "But if you're sure you want to know, I'll ask Claire to send me her PDF."

He bursts out laughing. "She has a PDF?" I laugh along with him because it is completely ludicrous.

"Some people have a bucket list; Claire has a checklist menu of sexual conquests," I tell him through my laughter.

"This I have to see. Tell the girls, brunch is on me if I can see the PDF. And, Leila?" I turn around to him, half undressed. "If there is anything on the list that you want to try, will you just leave a star by it?"

"Nate, trust me, there is nothing in our sex life that you have to worry about. I am more than happy. Claire's a deviant, that's all," I reply jovially to him, and I am being completely honest; Nate more than fulfils all my deepest desires. "But the same for you too. If you want to be dumbbellboy or the sprinter, that's okay too."

His eyes light up as he howls with laughter again. "I can't wait to see this. Go and have fun with your friends. I'll see you here later."

"We're staying another night?" I ask in surprise; we had only planned one night here.

"Yes. Lord Redvale has invited us for dinner this evening and to keep the room for another night. I'll take Missy for a walk while you have some girl time." I lean up on my tiptoes and kiss him on the nose. He's being incredibly thoughtful.

"Nate, thank you. For everything. I would have been lost without you last night." He kisses me on my forehead and pulls me closer to him.

"It's my pleasure, Leila. I would do anything for you." He whispers against my head so softly that I wonder if he meant for me to hear. I know all I'm going to think about during brunch is if he means what he says, or if it's just for effect.

Claire and Louise are waiting for me in the orangey, which has been transformed into a beautiful dining area. It still has all the trailing flowers, exotic bushes and foliage growing, but in the centre is a large sundial on the floor, providing plenty of room for tables and chairs and other furnishings.

As soon as they see me, they stand up. Claire waves her arms in the air like a child, like I might not see her. Louise rushes to me and hugs me tightly. "Thank you so much for last night. I had the most amazing time."

"I can't wait to hear all about it. Nate tells me you caught a cotton candy man. I guess they aren't extinct after all." Claire slaps her leg as she laughs hard at my remark. "By the way, Nate said if you let him see your PDF, he'll pay for brunch."

The standing rule is that no men ever get to see her rating scale. She worries that it may impact on her findings. Never once has she considered how misogynistic it is. "That dog, he said it was his treat anyway. I'm going to let him off because he has access to lots of beautiful boys."

"He's not a pimp, Claire," I retort in outrage, which makes her laugh even more.

"Will you lighten up; it was a joke. Okay, he can see the PDF but I want a verbal agreement that he doesn't pass on the information to anyone. Agreed?" I nod to her. "I'm allowing this one concession because Nathan Cardal is officially taken by my lovely best friend and will never be a victim of mine."

Thinking about her words, I wonder if that'll change once Nate breaks off our engagement. "What if we split up?" I blurt out before my courage deserts me.

"You and Nate? Oh no, girl! You are the real deal. You two are so in love, you're going to be together forever." A heavy stone drops into my stomach as guilt plagues me about my deception. "But say you were to die, or god forbid, change your mind about him, he'll always belong to you. You're bound together for life now, and so even if we were both free and single, he is off limits forever."

Louise bursts into laughter, and we both turn to her to see why. "Claire said if you die or god forbid, change your mind on him… like changing your mind is worse than dying." She cackles, and eventually, we all laugh too.

The brunch is overindulgent and excessive, but the girls seem happy enough to be spoiled today. Louise tells us tamely about her night with Hugo. "He walked me to my room and held my hand, and when I got to my door, he leaned in and kissed my hand and said 'sweet dreams.' It was amazing," she tells us both, and I can practically see the love hearts filling her eyes as she tells us.

"Quick, alert the church elders," Claire yells, causing Louise and I to jump. "Whatever will they say, holding hands and saying goodnight. Didn't he even try to kiss you?" Claire asks in disgust. Louise shakes her head, and a blush rises quickly on her cheeks. "Well gods be damned! We've got ourselves the monk too!"

"He's not a monk. He was respectful and a true gentleman. We are going to dinner tonight," she tells us excitedly. "Anyway, little miss judgemental… spill all your juicy details; I'm ready to judge you now too," Louise demands with a self-satisfied look on her face.

Claire groans dramatically. "Well, Tyson, as I'm sure you've both observed, is sexy, fit, full of stamina, and extremely strong. But, I was duped, girls. He's a cotton candy man," she declares in disgust. This very rarely happens; in fact, I don't remember it ever happening to Claire before. "He was so gentle and considerate. He kept stroking my face and asking me if I was okay, telling me how gorgeous I am."

"That doesn't sound too bad," I tell her honestly. "It was your first time with him. He was probably being polite."

"The first time was the first time, all the times after were exactly the same. At one point, I didn't even know if he was in me because he was being so delicate." She sounds forlorn, and it's clear that it's a different stroke for different folks. We all have our preferences, and incompatibilities are par for the course. "He said, 'it doesn't hurt, does it?' I wanted to shout, 'hit me with a brick or something.'" She wails quietly and rests her head in her hands. "He is perfect in every other way. But it was like being fucked by a feather duster."

A waitress walks by as she says it, and so I scold Claire. "Careful. The walls have ears, remember?" Claire's ears pick up in hypervigilance. "So, you won't be seeing him again then?" I ask her, because it doesn't seem likely that she will continue to see him if she is that unsatisfied already.

"Are you crazy? Of course, I'm seeing him again. I'm going back to his room after brunch. Maybe I need to be a bit more vocal about what I want?" I shrug at her; I have no words of wisdom because her logic makes no sense.

"Well last night was so epic that Nate has decided that we are hosting Christmas this year. You are both very welcome to join us." Claire instantly agrees, telling me her father will just be drunk anyway.

"Will Hugo be invited?" Louise asks me coyly. "I mean, I don't want to be rude and invite him if you don't want me to."

"Everyone is invited. Hugo, Tyson. We are going to have our own family Christmas." It hits me suddenly that with my dad gone, and my mother flaking on me, this is my family now. My family with Nate.

It's going to be amazing.

Despite the late October drizzle, the day is as beautiful as the summer's day we got engaged on. Once brunch is finished, I talk to the girls and explain that I have back to back matches from here until Boxing Day, but I'll be in touch when I can.

"Maybe, I'll see you there, if Tyson wants me to cheer him on of course," Claire adds, making us all giggle. "If he hasn't tickled me to death with his massive cock, that is," she further adds, demonstrating using her forearm to show us how big Tyson is, and I chastise her again.

"Claire. Did Tyson make you sign anything?"

"Like what? I can't remember, I was plastered. So, if I did, it doesn't count," she tells me with a massive grin.

"Just be careful. If you're genuine about wanting a relationship with Tyson, you need to be extra careful about what you put out there." I try to warn her. "The last thing you want is you being quoted in the press describing sleeping with Tyson as being fucked with a feather duster. Imagine how that'd make him feel."

We part on a hug before I return to Nate. We spend a lovely evening in the company of Lord and Lady Redvale and return to our room for another night of passion.

When I wake the following morning, Nate is already awake and talking loudly to someone on the phone. "I'll ask Leila, but why didn't he get the non-disclosure signed? Well, he's fucked himself up. This has nothing to do with Leila. Claire is an adult and should know better." He notices I'm awake and rolls his eyes at me before passing the newspaper to me.

On the front are photographs of Claire, Louise and I in the orangey with the headline "I was duped, he f***s like a feather duster". My eyes widen in horror, as I reach for my phone and turn it on. Message after message ping up on my screen. Requests for a comment regarding the matter come in by the dozen. "Oh for fuck's sake. This is never ending," I call out, but Nate is right beside me. He takes away my phone and pulls me close to him.

"Claire's got herself into a right pickle. Tyson is furious. He kicked her out of his house when the story broke. I'm just dealing with the media intrusion now," he tells me, kissing my temple in between sentences.

"I warned her. I'm so sorry, Nate. Is this going to be another PR nightmare for you to clean up?" I ask him, feeling really bad that my friend's big mouth has caused so much upset.

"It's okay. It's not your fault. Tyson should have got the NDA signed. His fuck-up." I climb into his lap and wrap my arms around his neck. "Christmas might be a bit awkward now, though," he says, bursting into laughter.

"How do you stay so calm, Nate? You take everything in your stride," I whisper to him in a pride-tinged voice.

"These are the little things in life. They mean something today, but in the grand scheme of things, they are insignificant. No ones going to die, or be arrested. It's a social slur at best, and it will all blow over. Like our engagement is now fully accepted and everyone knows they were wrong to think you were seeing Jack. It took, what? Eight to ten weeks?"

I nod to him, hoping he is right. I am already really excited for Christmas and I don't want it to be ruined before we've even started planning.

\*\*\* The story of Nate and Leila's Christmas together will be available soon as a novella \*\*\*

## CHAPTER 18

### ~ Leila ~

Days quickly fade into weeks, and before I know it, we are in January. There are no matches as the whole league rests for three weeks, which couldn't have come at a better time for the team. Injuries and fatigue have begun to plague the players, and their form has been less than desirable.

Nate and I decide to go on holiday, and I bite the bullet and begin researching my father and his injury and death. My mother has completely frozen me out. She hasn't returned any of my calls or acknowledged the Christmas card I sent her. My resentment towards her grows and fuels my desire for answers.

We spend two weeks on the Italian Riviera, watching sunsets from the glorious alps that spill into the Ligurian sea. The Mediterranean coast is simply magnificent, an area of outstanding beauty, and I can think of no better place to spend my last completely free time with Nate before the end of our contract. Once we return home, it is full-on matches at least twice a week during February, March and most of April. If the team makes it through to the European finals, there will be a couple more matches in May, but if they don't, the season will die down and complete by mid-May.

It is the trip of a lifetime. We visit Genoa, take river cruises, eat fresh handmade pasta and indulge in authentic tiramisu and locally made Limoncello. Part of me never wants to leave. However, the media have managed to find us and our last two days have been marred by intrusive photographers and reporters. On our final night here, we take blankets out to the rocky bed to watch one final sunset together. We hold hands under the blanket and cuddle close to one another.

"This has been the most amazing holiday of my life, Nate. I love it here. Thank you for bringing me," I whisper into the wind, but look up at him too, ensuring he hears.

"Thank you for coming with me. Nothing has ever felt as good." He seems troubled, but I'm not certain why. Out of nowhere he seems to become more serious. "Leila? I want you to marry me. I want us to get married."

Taking the hint that we are being watched and it's time to perform, I follow his lead and climb up on top of him. "We're already engaged, silly," I tell him before leaning down to kiss him. Secretly, I could want nothing more than for Nate to propose for real, but I'm mature enough to know that he is maintaining the act we agreed to.

It would be unfair of me to expect more, no matter how much I've fallen for him. That is on me. A reaction I can't bring myself to regret.

Holding my face gently in his huge hands, he looks into my eyes. "But I want us to be married. I want us to belong to each other for all eternity. I want all my lasts to be with you and you alone." The heat of his stare melts me. I want to be his last, his everything. "I'm in love with you, Leila. You are everything to me, and I want to be everything to you."

Panic begins to rise within me. I'm not sure what is real anymore. Will it make it weird between us if I say yes, but then find out that he's just playing a part? The contract brought us together, but now it sits like a concrete block between us.

Constantly reminding me of why I'm engaged to Nathan Cardal to begin with. "Ley? Are you still with me?"

"Yes. I'm just thinking. We can talk about all this once the season is over," I say rather more bluntly than I intended to. I have completely dismissed his declaration because it's too much for me to take. I can't give him my declaration too only to later find it was all an act on his behalf, because it's not an act for me. I am in love with Nate, and I do want to spend eternity with him. It's too close to the truth.

"Promise?" he asks, finally conceding. Though, I hope it's a flicker of disappointment I see in his eyes. I nod to him and smile to reassure him. "Good, okay, I can live with that for now."

Leaning up, I stroke his face, over his tickly stubble and strong jaw. "You know how much you mean to me, Nate. How precious our time together is to me." He kisses the palm of my hand, before pointing towards the horizon.

"Look, the sun is setting on our romantic getaway. I only hope we can come back here one day."

"Me too," I admit honestly, blushing at the truth in that statement.

⚽♥⚽

The cold and rain greets us when we land back in England, reminding us both starkly that the holiday is over. I shiver as cold water runs down the back of my dress, having left my coat in the car. "I want to go back now," I complain to Nate, who chuckles good naturedly.

"Soon, maybe for our honeymoon." He assures me, and it at least gives me some hope. Once we return home to Sandybank, my phone pings several times. "Welcome back to the madhouse, gorgeous," Nate says to me, catching my attention. When I look at him closely, he is pale, not golden brown like me from our trip. He still looks tired, and if I'm not mistaken, he has lost weight. Why is it that I put on half a stone and he loses weight? It's not fair.

"Are you sure you're okay, Nate?" I ask him in concern, but he brushes me off.

"Yes, I'm fine. I'm a bit jet-lagged." He assures me, and with no reason to doubt him, I tap on my phone and read my messages.

There are a bunch from Claire, starting off calm and measured but escalating quickly into full on frenzied panic. There are also some documents from the ancestry investigator I hired to look into my dad. Sensing that Claire's need is more urgent than my dead dad's, I call her first.

"Where the fuck have you been? I've been calling all day. Leila… I am up shit creek without a paddle," she tells me dramatically.

"What?" I ask in surprise. Now is not the time for riddles. I can't help her and work out her slang at the same time; I'm jet-lagged too.

"Can I come over or will you come to me? Please, Leils, I'm really scared." I've never heard Claire as frightened or vulnerable as she is right now.

"I'll be there in twenty minutes," I tell her before ending the call. Then I try to find Nate again. "I need to go over to see Claire, are you okay here?"

"I'll miss you, but I'm just going to hibernate in bed," he tells me. "Call Jeremy. He will drive you so I know you're safe." I kiss him quickly and promise him I'll be back soon.

Claire lives in a small apartment that she usually shares with Louise; however, Louise has gone on a weekend break with Hugo. She flings open her door before throwing herself at me in floods of tears.

"What's wrong?" Her snot and tears soak into my new silk scarf. "Claire? You're scaring me. What's up?"

She looks up and down the corridor before letting me inside and closing the door firmly behind us. "I'm a fuck up, Leils. I've fucked everything up." She wails in between, but these aren't the usual amateur dramatics that Claire likes to present us with. "You're settling down, Louise is settling down, and if I hadn't been such a bitch, I could've been too. Instead... I'm single and I think I'm pregnant!"

Well, shit has just got real!

## ~ Nate ~

After Leila leaves, I make the call I've been avoiding. Kym answers almost immediately. "You've missed your last two appointments. You're going to kill yourself, Nathan. This isn't a laughing matter anymore. Get your head out of your ass and get treated now."

"Get treated for what?" I spin around so forcefully I almost give myself whiplash and recoil in horror as I see Jack standing behind me. He is dressed in training gear, so he must have been out on our personal football pitch out the back. I didn't know he was home.

"Thank you for that, Kym. I will do what is needed," I say sarcastically down the phone, even though I know it's not Kym's fault I had her on speaker or that Jack overheard. "Jack... it's not what–"

"You're sick again, aren't you?" The fright and horror etched on his face is the reason why I didn't want him to know. "Why are you missing appointments? Have you got a death wish or something?"

"I just wanted some time to think about my options," I answer lamely.

"Bollocks. You are lying to cover up. Do you think it's going away on its own?" he retorts incredulously. "Is Leila okay with you missing treatments? I would have thought she would be frogmarching you to the hospital."

"She doesn't know," I shout at him, frustration and worry finally spilling from me.

"She doesn't know you skipped? Or she doesn't know, full stop." He lowers his voice and looks around as he says it.

"She doesn't know anything. She doesn't know about any of it. And I want it to stay that way."

"Why? She is going to be your wife; how can you keep this from her? Don't you think she'll notice when your hair falls out and you're puking up all the time? Or I don't know, she turns over and finds you dead in bed because you refused treatment." I cringe at the portrait he paints, despite the glaring truths within it. "She could have been mine, Nathan. But you love her and want to marry her, and

I accept that. But what you're doing is wrong. You need to tell her. You need to tell her soon or I will."

"This is my illness, Jack. You can't force me to tell anyone until I'm ready," I yell as he storms away from me. I know he's hurt and upset that I kept this from him, but I resent that he has made an ultimatum of me.

From the staircase, he turns around to me. "I suppose you're right, Nathan. But I'm not covering for you, and if she asks, I'll tell her no lies."

I accept his position, because there is no way I can justify taking any further action than I have. "I am sorry, Jack," I say to him sincerely. This isn't how I wanted him to find out, if at all.

"Sorry for what, Nathan? Being caught in a lie? We said we would always be honest with each other. And not only have you lied to me, you've duped Leila too."

"I haven't duped her. I just needed to know if she was here for me and only me or if I was kidding myself."

"She's head over heels in love with you, you stupid idiot. I told you, she's different. The money, the houses, the exotic trips away, she can live without that. She's here for you and you alone. I would kill for that," he tells me sternly. "She cooks for you, checks you're okay, leaves you little notes. She worries about you. Don't dare use your uncertainty about her feelings for you to justify your actions."

It's true that Leila still insists on cooking once a week. She has been pictured in the press a couple of times picking up Waitrose and Marks & Spencer meal deals. They call her the normal WAG and comment on how money hasn't changed her.

She still hasn't worn ninety percent of the clothes I bought her. Hell, I found out over Christmas she didn't even know there was a steam room and indoor football pitch in the house. She waved me off as if it were nothing. She hasn't asked or demanded anything overly indulgent. Her Christmas present to me was so sweet that it melted my heart. Having never met anyone I couldn't win over with money and gifts, Leila is different, just as Jack describes her.

The only doubt I have is the contract. She is contracted to be here to save her job. Though if we were both being honest, would the contract still be needed? Leila's job is more than secure now. We aren't contracted in having a loving and fulfilling sexual relationship, and there is no requirement for emotional attachment. The only thing that puts me off is that she pulls away when I try to discuss the future.

"I'm sorry for all of it. For getting sick, for lying about it and not telling you. For you to find out as you did," I tell him as tears sting my eyes.

"Are you going to die?" he asks me, and I shrug because this time, I don't know. I sincerely do not know how the cards are going to fall. "Is there nothing you can do? You're a billionaire for god's sake; there must be something."

My phone rings, interrupting us. I check who is calling, and when I see it's Leila, I tell Jack I'll be back soon. "Hey, are you missing me already?" I say as I answer. My heart pounds in guilt, as though she has witnessed my whole conversation with Jack.

"Hey, handsome, yes, of course I am. Listen, Claire really needs a friend right now. Would you mind if I stay with her tonight?" Although I wonder what Claire, the loudest, crudest woman I've ever met, could be going through that she would need a friend, I'm too relieved that Leila still has no idea about my illness that the curiosity doesn't last long.

"Sure. Do you need anything?" I ask her, wanting to ensure that she has everything she needs.

"Nah, we are going to order takeaway and talk." She lowers her voice. "Did you know that she and Tyson hooked up again at Christmas in our house?"

I chuckle before I answer, "I sure did. Everyone knew. Don't tell me you didn't realise?" I tease her.

"I didn't. I honestly had no idea. The emergency is that Claire is having Tyson's baby. We are going to spend tonight working out how she is going to tell him about it tomorrow." She continues to whisper, and I can tell from her voice that she is excited about her friend having a baby.

"I love you, Leila." I interrupt her ramblings. I don't mean to tell her, but I'm glad that I did. She should know that's how I feel about her.

"I love you, too. See you tomorrow, Nate," she says before she hangs up, and I fall to my knees at the foot of the stairwell.

I have to tell her the truth.

## ~ Leila ~

Our holiday ended with a bang. As serenely as I can, I try to calm Claire down and support her while she takes a pregnancy test. A positive result brings fresh tears, and it's hard seeing my friend so scared and vulnerable.

"Who is the father, Claire? Can you contact him and let him know?" She gives me the stink eye as she side glances at me.

"Ha ha, very funny. You know who the father is; we hooked up in your house." Well this is news to me. "Tyson doesn't want anything to do with me, and he's going to think I've done this deliberately." She cries all over again.

"You hooked up with him at Christmas?" I ask. She never said, and I never realised.

"Well, you were too loved up with Nathan to realise, and Louise was with Hugo. When I apologised to Tyson for the things I had said, one thing led to another." She sniffs after she takes a deep breath. "Then I woke up the following morning and he was gone. I thought we were going to make a go of it, but he made his feelings clear."

When I think back to Christmas, which was only a few weeks ago, I struggle to remember the finer details. I was wrapped up in my Nate bubble, and it had been the best Christmas ever. "Is that why you left on Boxing Day? Not to go and see your dad, but to hide from Tyson?" She nods before erupting into fresh sobs.

"I felt stupid and rejected and cheap. Of course, he would want to humiliate me; I humiliated him so badly. I just thought he had accepted my apology and we were moving on from it." It's all such a mess. I feel bad for my friend, so we decide to order takeout, get in our pjs and watch a romcom while we discuss her next move.

"I guess, from the way you are talking, that you're keeping it?" I ask her almost rhetorically. I smile at her when she nods before hugging her tightly. "Aww, Claire! You're going to be a mum. I hope it's a girl!"

"You haven't got it out of your system with the dog then?" She teases me. "I hope it's a girl too. God only knows what name Tyson has in mind… Lennox, Bruno, Foreman." She smiles sadly at me as she places her hands on her tummy.

"When are you going to tell him?" I ask her, knowing I'll see Tyson in training tomorrow and I am dreading keeping this a secret from him.

"I'll phone him now." We hold hands while she rings him, but when there is no answer, Claire looks dejected. "He knows it's me and he's blanking me. I don't think this is going to work, Ley."

Not to be deterred, I take out my own phone and call him myself. "Hey, Doc, is something wrong?" he answers on the second ring.

"Hey. Don't put the phone down. I'm with Claire, and she needs to talk to you. Just hear her out, please."

I stand to walk away and give them some space, but Claire grips my hand and mouths to me, 'please stay.' So I sit back down and support her with my presence.

"Hey," she says meekly. It's a shock to see and hear Claire so vulnerable.

"Hello, Claire. How can I help you?" Tyson replies solicitously and professionally.

"I-I… I didn't plan this, and I don't need anything from you. I just thought you should know."

"Know what?" he replies in a clipped manner, and I can feel the impatience rolling off him and Claire's courage waning as he continues to speak to her in such a cold fashion.

"This is so hard. Tyson. I'm having a baby and you are the father."

The line is deathly quiet. We sit here holding our breath as the shock of Claire's announcement penetrates. "Are you kidding me?" Tyson finally responds. "We can't have a baby. We can't even stand being in the same room together."

"I'm keeping it. I don't need anything from you. I just thought you had the right to know. And now you do."

"Wait, you can't just drop this on me. What if I don't want it? You're just going to take away my right to choose?"

"You're right to choose? You had the right to choose when we slept together, Tyson. You could have used protection, but we didn't." I can see Claire is getting upset and wonder if I should intervene. "You don't have to be involved. I'm not asking for anything from you. But I'm keeping my baby, Tyson. With or without you."

She ends the call and then bursts into fresh tears, and all I can do is comfort her. "I'm going to be alone. I don't know anything about babies."

"You won't be alone. You'll have me and Louise. I'll be your birthing partner." She laughs through her tears as I make my promise.

"You will?" she asks me with an open expression that I very rarely see on Claire.

"Yes, one hundred percent. I'll be with you every step of the way." She hugs me tight, and we resume watching our movie and eating ice cream straight from the carton.

As long as we have each other, we will never be alone.

The following day, after leaving Claire's apartment early to go home and change, I head to training. My tummy churns uncomfortably, wondering if Tyson is going to bring his grievance with Claire into work.

However, Tyson acts as though I am not even there. He keeps his head down and walks straight past me, not talking to any of his teammates. Jack also avoids me, and I wonder if Tyson has told him about Claire too. I'm sure I'll find out eventually. Nothing stays secret for long in the changing room of a football team.

The training session goes terribly, with both Tyson and Jack playing appallingly. The team seems to be falling apart, and the break hasn't helped improve their form. If anything, it's made the issues even deeper.

"No. No. No. We are playing Barcelona in two days; we will be annihilated." Is the extent of the gaffer's rants that I understand.

Knowing that personal issues can spill out onto the field and detrimentally affect performance, I approach Tyson after training and ask to speak to him in my office. He reluctantly agrees, and I'm sure I see Jack sigh in relief that I didn't ask to speak to him. Well, now I do want to talk to him to see what his problem is.

"I wanted to clear the air between us. Claire is my friend, and I know that yesterday was hard for you. But here I'm the injury specialist. Nothing from outside will spill over into my professional work. I hope you know that." He nods stiffly to me. "I don't want things to be awkward between us."

"It won't be. She said she doesn't need me, and that's fine by me. I just didn't know if you were going to bring it up in front of the team. I'd rather they didn't know."

"It's not my place to say anything, and as far as I am concerned, my friend's private life has nothing to do with anyone at work." He nods stiffly at me. "Did you tell Jack?"

"I didn't tell anyone. I'm not telling anyone. This is such a fuck up."

He leaves in a ball of frustration, and despite him assuring me he is fine having nothing to do with Claire and the baby, I think that might change once he cools off. What intrigues me even more is Jack's behaviour. Why is he avoiding me?

## CHAPTER 19

### ~ Leila ~

Having spent last night apart, I miss Nate desperately, and I thought and hoped he would feel the same. However, I arrive home late from work, and he isn't here. He's left a note telling me not to wait up, that he has to work, which is disappointing but understandable. Between jet lag, work, and Claire's non-stop crying, tiredness catches up with me, and I fall asleep after my shower and wake only briefly when Nate comes home. Missy sprawls on the bed next to me until Nate undresses and takes his place back. I lie in his arms, falling back into a dreamless sleep.

When I wake up, it's past six and Nate is already out of bed again. I dress and get ready for our European match. I grab my kit bag before going downstairs, ready to grab my breakfast and take Missy for a walk, but when I approach the kitchen, I can hear Nate and Jack arguing. Not wanting to intrude, I leave my bag in the hallway and take Missy's lead from the coat rack.

The grounds of Nate's house sit within two acres of land, and over the past few months, we have managed to indent our own trail for walking Missy. I follow the familiar pathway, allowing her to run ahead and explore the vast farmland. It's bitterly cold and barely light at this time of day. The sun is trying to rise, but the heavy veil of potential rain clouds prevents it from shining too much, and as I walk, I think about everything that has happened in my life over the past six months. So much has happened and yet there is still more to come. I think about Claire and her baby, and how in awe I am of her strength. I think about Louise's blossoming romance with Hugo. It's about time that girl got a man who'll treat her the way she deserves. Missy barks, and I automatically think of her and the joy she has brought to my own life. Then I think of Nate. Each day we spend together brings us closer to the day we walk away from one another, and a hollowness I've never felt before fills me at the thought of him not being a part of my life.

I wonder if we will remain friends afterwards. It'll be weird if Louise and Hugo get married and both Nate and I are there, but not together. Will he talk to me? Would I want him to? Our not so fake relationship seems to have spilled over into all aspects of my life.

By the time I return to the house, I'm famished and distracted. I only notice Nate and Jack looking at me when I approach the sink to wash my hands. "Leila? Are you okay?" Nate asks me with a cautious look.

"Yes. Why, what's up? Have you had breakfast? I'm starving now. I shouldn't walk Missy until I've eaten." I turn to dry my hands and find Nate and Jack just staring at me. "What's going on? You two are acting very strange!"

"You went straight out with Missy," Nate says simply, not so much a statement or question as it is an observation.

"Well, yeah. I could hear you two 'talking' and didn't want to intrude, so I decided to walk Missy first, which was a bad decision because I could eat a whole cow and still be hungry." I exaggerate, but it's my uncomfortable defence mechanism. Something feels really off, and I don't know what it is.

"I've put your oats and fruit in the fridge, and Giovanni has left you pancakes too." I groan in delight; his pancakes are the best. "So, you didn't hear what Jack and I were discussing?"

I shake my head at him slowly. "What were you talking about? I didn't want to pry, so I didn't listen. I wish I had now. Maybe it would explain why you're both acting so weird." Nate continues to look at me with horror in his eyes. "Are you coming to the match later?" I ask him, hoping the change of subject will calm the peculiar atmosphere. This match has a lot pinned on it for Nate and I and our contract. If the team loses, our contract will end earlier, a whole three weeks earlier.

"No, I can't. I have a meeting." My heart sinks; Nate never misses a home match. I had hoped his presence would bring us more luck. The fact that he isn't bothering to be there shows me that he isn't bothered about us, not really.

"Fine. I'll see you later, or whenever," I tell him, leaving behind my oats, fruit and pancakes in my haste to create some distance between us. I knew this would happen, but naively, I thought it might not. "Don't forget to walk Missy before you go," I shout over my shoulder before slamming the door shut. If Nate wants to act cold and aloof, well so can I.

My car is parked in the garage, and when I open the door, Jack looks up from his car guiltily. I march up to him. "Are you going to tell me why he's acting so weird?" Jack lowers his head, and I want to shake him and his stupid brother. "What's going on? Have I done something wrong? Has something happened?" I scream at him, but he still refuses to answer me. Instead he starts his car and begins rolling towards the exit until I jump in front of it.

"Leila, get out of the fucking way. I could have hurt you!" Jack roars at me, and for the first time, I notice the tears clinging to his eyelashes.

"You can't just avoid me, Jack. Please tell me what's going on." My voice breaks, and knowing I'm about to lose control, I step aside to let him leave.

His car moves forward so his window is level with me. "I'm sorry, Doc. I don't want to get caught in the middle. Speak to Nate. It's up to him to tell you if there is something you need to know. Not me." He drives off, his tyres screeching against the flooring as he does. Once his car is out of sight, I rush to mine before I lose all composure.

Once I'm out on the open road, I find a safe place to park and allow myself a couple of minutes to cry and scream. I've never felt so helpless and as though my life and future is no longer in my control. This is further compounded when an email pings from my private investigator, who is still looking into my father.

As page after page of evidence presents itself, I feel ill. My father was injured and depressed and was all alone when he died. My mother had told the press they were separating on the grounds of irreconcilable differences, and my father rented an apartment not far from our family home. Two days before his death, my mother was pictured with another man. Moving on with her life. Then the coroner's report stated that my father was low in mood at the time of his death, and that his requests to spend time with his daughter being denied, as well as dealing with his divorce and the end of his professional career as a footballer all contributed to his feelings of hopelessness. He left a note that read, 'tell my baby girl I'm sorry.'

My heartache overwhelms me. As a gut-wrenching cry echoes around my car, I picture my father in his desperate state and apologise to him. I wish I could have been there for him. Everything builds up into a ball of pent-up agony and despair. I am completely alone.

I think of contacting my mother to tell how disgraceful her lies are. She should have told me the truth. She should never have allowed me to find out in this way. I am on my own with this. Claire has her plate full. Louise is still on her break with Hugo. And Nate. Well, who knows what the hell is going on with Nate, but bringing this information to him just doesn't seem right at this moment in time. This is something I will have to deal with by myself.

Although my hands shake, I drive to work and lock myself into my office until my first appointment. I can't wait for this day to be over.

# ~ Jack ~

The tension at home is palpable, and Leila looking at me only amplifies my guilt. I cannot in good faith look her in the eye while I know what I do. She should know, and I hate Nathan for not telling her. She deserves to know what she is dedicating herself to, which is a man with a serious illness, who isn't getting the appropriate treatment, which means he could die at any point.

How can I talk to her like nothing is going on when I saw it first hand the last time Nate was sick. It was miraculous he survived then, when he was accepting every and any treatment going. His fear of upsetting Leila or losing her over this is going to be the death of him, and I'm not standing for it. She has agreed to be his wife, and that means he needs to start being honest with her. She should know the full picture before she makes such a huge commitment to him. I don't know how he has the gall to lie to her. Doesn't he feel bad that she'll be marrying him under false pretences?

Nate and I were convinced Leila had overheard us arguing this morning. When he realised she had left, taking the dog with her, he thought she had heard everything and had stormed out. Emotionally distraught is not a description ever associated with my older brother, but that is the only phrase that closely depicts what he looked like when he thought he had lost her. Devastated and lost also come close. I have never ever seen Nathan like that, and it scares me.

Then when Leila returned to the house after walking Missy, acting as though nothing had happened, we were both thrown off our game. Is she bluffing? However, the anger in her eyes when she asked me what was going on confirmed to me that she had absolutely no idea. Not a clue. I tried to reason with Nathan. Leila loves him and will want to support him. She is also a healthcare professional and may have more knowledge to impart about his treatment, but he wouldn't listen to me, told me it is none of my business and that he is dealing with it.

I escaped the house and went straight to the steam rooms before my cryotherapy. Now I am hiding out in the fitness suite, working on my cardio and strengthening my core so I can defend better on the pitch. "Who are you imagining is your victim, Jack?" the skipper, Reagan, asks me in concern. I must look like a mad man. "He concedes!" He jokes with me before sitting down on a bench facing me.

"I was in a world of my own then. Want me to spot you?" I deflect, pointing to the weights above him.

"Do you want to talk about anything, Jack? You know you can talk to me. You don't seem like yourself. Maybe talking about it will help clear your mind before the match." He pushes me too far.

"Stop being so nosy. I don't want to talk about it. There is nothing to say. I wish everyone would just leave me alone!" I shout, picking up my towel and water bottle. "I'll go and get some peace elsewhere," I roar as I storm out of the fitness suite and head towards the dining room. However, I see Leila sitting quietly in the corner by herself, and swiftly turn around and walk to my car instead. I need space from everyone and everything.

My phone rings about thirty seconds after I leave the training ground. First off it's our new team manager, Pepe. Then, a couple of minutes later, Nathan calls me too. Using my hands free, I answer and scream at him, "FUCK OFF!" before disconnecting my call again. Then the messages start.

**Call me**

**Jack just calm down, come on let's talk**

**Come home Jack. Don't do anything stupid now.**

**Jack. The team needs you. Go back to the training ground now.**

I drive for about an hour, and before I know it, I'm lost in the English countryside. In the middle of nowhere, I step out of my car before screaming at the top of my lungs. Tears roll down my face, and I do nothing to hide my despair.

"You're going to scare all my daddy's cows if you keep making a racket like that, sir," the sweetest voice in the world tells me without anger or judgement. I quickly wipe my face and look up to find that the voice belongs to a young woman, late teens to early twenties, who wears jeans and a checked shirt as she sits inside a big dirty tractor. She is beautiful. Wholesome. And familiar, like I know her already. "I don't know what is troubling you. But why don't you come down to the house with me? We'll have a cup of tea and a slice of cake. I made a lemon drizzle just last night."

At a loss, I nod at her and accept her offer to drive in her tractor. "How long have you been driving tractors?"

"Since before I could walk. That's what my daddy tells me anyway. I'm Lucy O'Dowell. I'm still training to be a farmer so I can take over from my father in the next couple of years," she tells me, chatting away as though she sees screeching and wailing men every day of the week.

"Nice to meet you. My name is Jack," I offer her, not wanting to be rude but not really in the mood to expand on myself and my profession.

"Nice to meet you too, Jack. The farmhouse is just ahead. It's nothing much, but it's home," she adds, not put off by my unenthusiastic response. "Are you having car trouble? Jared would be happy to take a look at your fancy car."

"Jared?" I ask her, my jealousy already poking its head up where it's not wanted, not by me and certainly not by Lucy.

"Yes, he's my younger brother. He likes to tinker in the barn with all the vehicles. I think he would be in heaven with your car, though. What on earth are you thinking driving something like that around here? Your suspension will be shot." He's her brother. My green-eyed monster sighs in relief.

"My car is fine. I just needed to clear my head." She smiles at me again. She turns her attention back to driving the tractor that rumbles and jerks as we roll across the rough farmland.

We pull up outside the farmhouse, which definitely looks as though it needs some repairs, and an older gentleman, wearing a flat cap and a green jacket, waves to Lucy and openly stares at me. "You found another stray, Lucy? You need to stop bringing home every Tom, Dick and Harry that drive down our lane." He shakes his head at her, and she laughs loudly.

"Stop being a big grump and turn the kettle on. Jack here is parched," she instructs her father, not even a smidge put out by his hostile attitude.

Her father looks me up and down before opening the front door. "Is he now?" I smile at him meekly. Something tells me he is going to be a tough nut to crack.

Lucy invites me to sit at a scrubbed wooden dining table in the large country kitchen. She sets the table, and I sit looking at her in awe at the ease at which she's switched from being a farmer driving a tractor to a domestic goddess. Mr O'Dowell sets a large teapot down on the table, earning a scowl from his daughter, who quickly lifts it back up and places a mat under it.

"Had some bad news, son?" Mr O'Dowell asks me as he assists his daughter. "Sugar?" he adds at the end while holding the sugar bowl and spoon in his large, calloused hands.

"No sugar and yes. I found out that someone I love is sick." Lucy places her hand over mine after she pours my tea and places a slice of cake in front of me. "He won't tell his fiancée, and he isn't getting the proper treatment he needs, and I'm scared he's going to die."

The father and daughter listen to me and don't pry, and I can't tell you how nice it feels to just be Jack for a while. Not Jack the lad, not Jack the star signing, Jack the footballer, or Jack the brand. Just Jack.

Using the little dessert fork Lucy gave me, I take a bit of the lemon drizzle cake, and it melts in my mouth. "This is good. This is really, really good," I tell her as I take a bigger mouthful, smiling when I see her eyes light up at my praise.

"It was my mother's recipe. I've been trying to perfect it. She died last winter after a long illness," Lucy tells me, and my heart aches for the loss she has experienced. I barely remember my own mother, and yet I have always felt her loss acutely. "Sometimes talking about things helps, especially when it's to people who aren't involved. Sometimes a slice of cake and cuppa help too."

After finishing my cup of tea, I thank the O'Dowells for their hospitality and tell them I best make my way back.

"I'll take you back to your car; I still have my chores to do," Lucy offers, and I thank her. I try to help her into the tractor, though she assures me she is capable. The need to be closer to her is overwhelming. As she passes me, I catch another waft of her alluring scent: earthy, sweet, and floral. "We seem to have a beacon here, calling the souls who are troubled to our farm for a chat and a pick-me-up. You are welcome to come and visit again. I'll leave the light on for you, so you don't lose your way."

When we pull up beside my abandoned car, I pluck up the courage to ask for her details. "Can I call you or add you on social media?" I ask her desperately, wanting to stay connected to this alluring woman, who is so far removed from every other woman I've ever known. My heart sinks when she shakes her head.

"I don't have time for phones and social media, sorry, Jack. All my time is invested here in the farm and with my family, but you know where I am if you want to talk again." I stand frozen to the spot, scared that if I leave, I'll never find her again.

"Thank you. I really needed a friend, and you more than stepped up to the plate, Lucy. I'll never forget that." She smiles at me as she starts the tractor again. Like a besotted man, I stand watching her until she becomes a dot on the horizon.

When I return to my car, I feel like a changed man. I finally understand why Nathan wants to protect Leila by not telling her, and I know I have to support him through this, despite my own fears. As soon as I turn my phone back on, Nathan tries to call.

"Nathan, calm down. I'm on my way. And I'm sorry. Everything got on top of me, and I ran, but I'm okay now, and Nathan... I've got your back one hundred percent." My brother stutters down the phone. "I'm about an hour away, I'll be there as soon as I can. Tell the gaffer and the team, I'll be there soon."

"Okay, Jack. Drive safely. I love you, little brother."

As I drive back, I really think about my life of excess and frivolity and how it's slowly sucking out my soul. It's time for a change, and that change starts with me. I need to be better, more mature. I need to become the man I should be.

When I arrive at the training ground, the team coaches are parked up outside. I've made it back in time for the match. However, the gaffer is not happy. He is not happy at all. "You are benched, and we are fining you for being AWOL, missing the pre-match meeting and for being an inconsiderate, spoilt little brat. Two hundred thousand pounds. You can pick what charity it goes to, but trust me, boy, any more of your stunts, and I will have you transferred to the middle of nowhere... Understand?"

"Yes, sir," I reply, and more than half of the people here look at me in surprise at my easy acceptance of my punishment. The old me would have argued and sulked, but the new me, the more mature, responsible me, accepts the punishment and the telling off.

"You will report for training tomorrow morning, and you will do extra training until you earn your spot back in this team. Do you understand?"

I nod to him. "Yes, sir. I apologise to you all. I've had a few things going on privately, and unfortunately, that spilled out here. I know you deserve my commitment and I promise I am dedicated to you all and to our team." Everyone seems to accept my apology, and we move to the coaches.

As I go to take my place on the coach, Leila stops me. "I'm sorry, Jack. I didn't know you had your own stuff going on. I promise I won't bring you into my issues with Nate. If you need anything, you know where I am."

Guilt bubbles up like lava in the pit of my stomach. It didn't take long to be torn by my decision to keep Nathan's secret from Leila. The sooner that Nathan opens up to his fiancée, the faster I can become the better person I know is deep inside me somewhere.

## ~ Leila ~

Nate calls me in panic, though he didn't need to. The whole team is searching for Jack, and my own guilt leaves me feeling partially responsible.

It surprises me that Nate doesn't immediately rush to find Jack. "I'm stuck in a very important meeting. I'm sure he'll turn up, but I feel really bad about our disagreement this morning." I sigh because I feel the same. It seems, between us, we've broken Jack.

"I'll go and look for him. Can you track his phone?" I ask Nate, knowing he has better resources than the club and police combined.

"I was, but he's turned off his phone. I have no idea where he is. I need your help, Leila. Jack will self-destruct if we don't find him soon." I reassure Nate and tell him to keep his phone close, that I'll text him if I hear anything.

With a plan in mind, I pull on my jacket and head to my car. "Doc? Where are you going?" Reagan, the team skipper, calls to me as I open my car door.

"Nate's in a meeting, so I'm going to try a few places to see if I can find Jack," I tell him. "Do you have any idea where his friend Sancho lives?"

Reagan shakes his head. "I don't, but I'll ask Tyson and text you the details." I thank him before driving off. Using my handsfree, I contact Damon and Jameson to help join the search. Then I call Giovanni, who keeps in close contact with Jack too.

No one has heard a peep from Jack, and after a couple of hours hunting him, I am about to give up when I spot Sancho returning home. I shout out to him and hope he recognises me.

"Oh, hey, Leila. What are you doing here?" he asks me with a puzzled look on his face and looks behind me into my car, probably looking to see who is with me.

"Hey, I'm sorry to just ambush you like this. Jack's gone AWOL. I was just wondering if you had seen him today." He shakes his head, and as he had been my last hope, I don't know what else to do. "Thanks anyway, Sancho. If you see him, tell him we are all worried about him and to just come home."

He nods at me. "I will. Sorry I couldn't be more of a help."

Not wanting to further intrude on Jack's friend, I drive away and pull into a layby while I gather my thoughts. "Come on, Jack, where are you?" I shout to no-one in particular. As if on cue, my phone rings and it's Nate. "Have you found him?" I ask, no hello or anything.

"He's safe. He's on his way back home now. I traced his phone to somewhere near Yorkshire. He said he needed to clear his head." I burst into tears with relief that he is okay. "Baby, are you okay? Look, I'm so sorry for the weirdness this morning. Can we talk tonight when you get home?"

"Yes. I'm sorry too. I don't know what happened. Whatever is going on, we can sort it out together, Nathan," I tell him, and just as I'm about to tell him what I found out about my father, an unfamiliar female voice carries over to me.

"I'm ready for you, Nathan. If you just lie back–"

The phone goes dead, and I'm left sitting in my car feeling like I'm a human boomerang. Who the hell was that? I guess I'll have to wait for this evening to get some answers from Nate. His phone is now unreachable.

With the leaving time for the match coming up, I return to the training ground, ready to take my place on the team bus, and breathe a sigh of relief when Jack shows up.

His apology seems sincere and from a decent place, and a part of me is proud of him, like a big sister watching her little brother become a man. It almost seems harsh that he'll miss the match because of his behaviour.

The night is bitterly cold and wet. The rain doesn't stop, and rather than putting off the opposition, who are used to playing in the warm sunshine, they are resilient and play well. Our team falls apart at the seams. Tyson is sent off after twenty minutes for a bad tackle on another player. He storms off to the changing room, not wanting to talk to anyone. His display is completely out of character for him. The team are also given a penalty, which they score, and the atmosphere drops into the boots of everyone present. When another two goals are scored by the opposition, the players look dejected, and their energy seems to dissipate into nothing.

"This is my fault. The whole team is rattled. I shouldn't have run. I should have been here," Jack says to me, and I have no words of comfort for him. My eyes are glued to the train wreck that our team has become. Right before my very eyes, my time with Nate is cut short because if Redvale lose tonight, they are out of the European championship.

"There are two minutes of extra time. Two minutes," the stewards announce over the speakers. The time is trickling away, and it's taking the silverware with it. The referee blows his whistle for full time, and everyone on our side sits dejected and shocked at the turn of events.

There are no celebrations. The mood is sombre and quiet. Jack leaves almost immediately, and although I don't want to be here, I don't want to face Nate yet either.

Claire calls me, and I try to discreetly take her call without giving anything away. But there are too many people still around. "I'll call you back in a minute," I tell her, though she can't hear me; she is too busy ranting about 'the father of her child acting like a tit' as she so eloquently puts it. "Claire. Give me five minutes." I put the phone down and have no doubt she'll still be ranting until I call her back.

"I want everyone, players, staff, catering, cleaners, doctors. I want every single one of you to report for training at 6 am tomorrow. That was a disgrace," the gaffer announces to the whole changing room. "The lot of you ought to be ashamed of yourself today."

Standing up, I don't need to listen to Juan Carlos' harsh words. They are nowhere near the ones that rattle around my head, punishing me for my failings.

"SIT DOWN," he roars at me, and his disrespect annoys me.

"No! This is your failing too. We are a team and you are ripping us all apart. What about you? You're the team coach. You benched our best player. You failed this team too."

I walk out of the changing room. It looks like everything Nate did for me to secure my job was for nothing. I have most likely just got myself fired for that outburst.

# FOULS

Are acts that go against the rules of the game. The referee has the power to punish foul play and is encouraged to do so to maintain the integrity of the game.

Punishments include: a free kick to the fouled team, a penalty if the foul takes place in the penalty box. There can also be individual sanctions for the offender, such as yellow and red cards, depending on the severity of the foul.

(SOURCE: Football Collective .org.uk)

# Chapter 20

## ~ Nate ~

The words I have been dreading from my oncologist's mouth echo around the consultation room, eerily repeating over and over, bouncing off the walls as if they are a tangible thing. "I'm sorry, Mr Cardal. Your results indicate that the leukaemia is back, and you have now entered a full relapse of your condition. I am recommending six weeks of daily chemotherapy and a bone marrow transplant." I stare at her, unable to comprehend how I could be so sick when my life finally feels complete and satisfying. "You need to comply with the prescribed treatment regime, or your survival rates are not favourable."

After avoiding my oncologist for far too long, I surrender myself to their cocktail of potent drugs that drain me of enough life that they can kill the cancer. Medicine is supposed to make you better, but this stuff is slowly and torturously ripping me apart. I stopped going for the treatment because I was finding it hard to hide the side effects from Leila. It takes days to recover, and then I would have another session.

"When do I have to start?" I ask, wondering how much time I have to tell Leila and show her that I'm still me. My greatest fear is that she will stay with me and support me, however, it won't be through the same love I feel for her but through pity and guilt.

"What I propose is that you go home and get your affairs in order. You will need to start a two-week course of steroids." I wince at the thought of steroids. It's only two weeks, but I hate needles and can't stand having to inject myself. "Then in two weeks' time, you can either come daily for your treatments or you can isolate and spend the six weeks in hospital to give yourself the best chance of fighting this and not picking up infections that will weaken your immune system." The choice is mine, yet I stumble over my inevitable decision, knowing committing to treatment will basically put an end to the contract with Leila.

"I will ensure all my affairs are in order, and I will have my secretary call you to confirm my plans once I know what my prior commitments are."

The doctor nods her head solemnly at me. "I'm so sorry, Mr Cardal, but the maintenance regime just wasn't enough to stop this progression. Now, we must act, and it needs to be as soon as possible." I nod to her, indicating that I understand that my life is in mortal danger if I continue to disregard her advice. "I also highly recommend that you freeze your sperm, as this treatment will be gruelling and will likely leave you sterile."

This final blow is what pushes me to the edge. We haven't even discussed children yet; I haven't wanted to push the issue, knowing it might not be a possibility and that Leila is frightened to talk too far into the future, whether that is because she doesn't see me in hers or because she worries that I don't mean what I say when I tell her that I want her, that I love her. Now, if I survive, and she feels for me as I feel for her, and we want a family, that might never happen; the path to achieving it will be a hard one.

Leila knows something is wrong, but I cannot find the words to tell her about my condition. I've lied to her, kept this information from her so that she would know me as me. Maybe that's manipulative, but I wanted to be more than a billionaire or a patient to her. I wanted her to feel for me the way I feel for her. She is the love of my life, the one, and I can feel her slipping away from me.

My life is spiralling out of control and nothing I can do can stop it. Jack knows I'm sick and he isn't happy that I haven't told Leila. So, when I'm told that Jack has left training without permission, I know my secret is about to come out. I try my best to stay calm and tell everyone I'm in a very important meeting that I cannot get out of. I frantically try to call Jack to reason with him while the nurse tells me that stress and overworking is bad for me. I try to trace the last location of Jack's phone before he switches it off, but he is nowhere to be found. Speaking to Leila reassures me that people are trying all they can to find him, and even though I'm not there contributing to the search, I feel confident that, sooner or later, they'll find Jack. They must.

Relief floods through me when I finally make contact with Jack. He sounds different. Changed. I don't know how exactly, but he seems contrite. Although I'm mid treatment, I throw caution to the wind and call Leila to tell her Jack is on his way. After we both apologise to each other, we finally have the breakthrough we have needed. It's all shattered moments later when the lead nurse approaches me. "I'm ready for you, Nathan. If you just lie back–" I drop the call, not wanting Leila to hear what she is saying.

"What did you do that for?" I shout at her in frustration, while shutting off my phone. I don't know how I am going to explain this to Leila. "Do you know what you just did?"

"Mr Cardal, we are ready to start your scan. You need to hand in all your electronics now please," another nurse instructs me, and reluctantly, I surrender all my means of contact for the next hour at least.

The horrible smell of the hospital treatment room clings to my skin long after I leave. After collecting my prescription, I book an appointment at the fertility clinic before heading home. I need to do my first self-administered steroid injection, and I am sick in anticipation. My phobia of needles stems from the last time I became ill. My father would have our private nurses pin me down to inject me when I would refuse. In his eyes, he was doing the necessary thing to keep me alive; however, I found the whole bizarre situation traumatising.

After preparing the steroids and cleansing the area I am going to inject, I falter. I'm terrified to even remove the sheaf from the needle, never mind sticking it into myself. I'm so absorbed in my own terror and the task I have to perform that I am not thinking about anything else; my mind is in its own little bubble, where nothing else exists anymore.

Finally I expose the needle. My heart hammers in my chest, perspiration tickles my forehead, and my throat closes over, restricting my breathing. This is it, I have to do it.

"Nate?" The bathroom door swings open, and Leila stands before me. She does a double take of the view in front of her, and a guttural sound emanates from her throat, a sound of horror and disgust. "What the hell are you doing, Nate? Steroids? Since when? How long have you been doing this? How could you? Do you know what this could do to you? Never mind my reputation or Jack's for that matter." She continues to rant and shout at me. Her indignation and anger both repulse me and resonate with me, but her presence at this exact moment simply exacerbates my fear. My sight darkens, and my chest constricts. My whole body shakes until I finally snap.

"Get out. Get out of here, now," I roar at her. She steps away from me, fright evident in her eyes. "I said get out; I don't want you here. Leave."

"Don't push me away, Nate. We can get through this. I want to support you."

"I said leave. In fact... get your stuff and go. I'm not continuing with this farce anymore. I'm breaking our contract. I'm no longer your Substitute. Go home. We're done here."

"We still have another three months left. Don't do this, Nate. I–"
"I am breaking the contract; I will pay the fee for doing so. I just want you out of here," I shout at her coldly. I need her to leave. I can't look at her beautiful face or her story telling eyes, where I know I'll find all the hurt and sorrow my words have brought to her. And I can't bear to tell her the truth.

"Keep the money. This was never about money. If you want me to leave, then fine, I'll leave. I'm taking Missy as agreed."

"That's what I want. I need this to be over."

"Please return my car when you get a chance. I'll call an uber now and leave yours in the garage."

She continues, but as soon as she steps out of the bathroom, I slam the door closed behind her. I'm beyond caring.
I throw the needle into the bin, unable to bring myself to do it. Not after what it has cost me. Now, I'm not only dying of cancer, but I've also broken my own heart too.

## ~ Leila ~

Within a few hours, my life has changed dramatically. After catching Nate injecting steroids, I take my own belongings and Missy and make my way back to my house. My little terrace next door to Arthur in the quiet cul-de-sac on the other side of town. Missy looks around bewildered, and I do too. I don't remember my home being so small. I don't remember the homely feeling it once held. Nothing will ever feel like home, not after Nate.

Having pre-empted that our arrangement wouldn't be long-winded, I knew I would be back here at some point. I just didn't realise my heart would hurt as much as it does. I love him like I've never loved anyone or anything before. My soul is shattered, and once I settle Missy with a bed and a water bowl, I curl up in a ball on the sofa, too numb to even cry.

What am I going to do? I think my career is over at Redvale. Everything about it will remind me of Nate now, plus I disrespected the coach in front of the whole team. That is enough to have me instantly dismissed.

A lot of thoughts go through my mind as I wallow in self-pity. I could go back to my mother's. However, I'm about to give her a tongue lashing too, which will affect how welcome I'll be afterwards. I also torture myself with the reason why Nate helped me to save my job if he was going to end it like this. He is making it clear that he cannot stand to be around me, so how can I continue to work there now? This is counterproductive to what we've been doing these past few months. I don't understand, and it's killing me inside, right down in my gut, because something doesn't make sense, but Nate wouldn't explain anything to me.

The night drags on, and I find myself becoming restless. Anger wars with my heartbreak, and every time I look at my sweet little dog, I'm reminded of Nate and all the memories we made in our short time together. I never in a million years thought it would end like this. If it had to end, I imagined us staying friends. But now that's not even a possibility.

I constantly nurse my hand. I left my engagement ring on Nate's bedside table before I returned to my own home. As much as I love it and wanted the reminder of our time together, that ring was so expensive, and now we are no longer engaged, it doesn't belong to me. My hand feels bare without it, as though a digit has been amputated. The weight of it had once felt foreign, but now my hand is lost without it.

My phone rings and I jump, both praying for it to be Nate and to not be Nate. I needn't have worried; it's only Jack. I let it go to voicemail, unable to face him and his questions. Especially since I called into work and told them I wouldn't be in as I am 'sick'. Technically I am sick, just not in a textbook way.

I've decided to hand in my resignation at work before I am fired, so I can hopefully secure another job at a different club, as far away from Redvale as possible. The thought alone has me welling up. I love my life here in Redvale. My friends, the family I have made and chose. My job. And most of all, despite everything that has happened, I'm going to miss Nathan Cardal. Sadness like I've never known crashes over me, almost bringing me to my knees. My phone rings again. This time I cut it off; I don't need a million Jack's running around promising that 'everything is going to be okay'. It is far from okay.

Missy whines for my attention, reminding me I need to go and buy some food for us both as the fridge and cupboards are empty. The will to face the world has deserted me until I see my sweet little puppy beginning to suffer. I pull out my best Jackie O sunglasses and a baseball cap Nate bought me, and after helping Missy into her doggy jacket and attaching her lead to her collar, I pull on the biggest winter coat I have and brave the rain and wind outside. Halfway to the local shop, Missy refuses to walk any further, and I have to carry her the rest of the way.

The shop is part of a chain, and it is fairly busy. Most people carry on with their business; however, a couple of others recognise me and pull out their phones to take photographs. I put my head down, place Missy into a trolley and go about my business as quickly as possible. The shop doesn't have everything I need, but I manage to buy a few things that will last me a couple of days. I approach the till to pay and notice the newsstand to my left as I do. Redvale's defeat is plastered on a few. I close my eyes to them and continue on with my purchases.

Missy whines again when she has to walk, but with two heavy bags to carry, I am unable to carry her too. "Come on, girl, we all have our cross to bear. We can have extra treats when we get back to the house." Even as I say it, her ears and tail droop. I know it's exhausting her, so I try to lift her again and struggle with the heavy bags.

"Doc. Stop, let me help you. For fuck's sake, you're both drenched through." I look up and see Jack at the side of the road, opening his passenger door wide for us. Missy, upon seeing and recognising Jack, jumps and wags her tail excitedly. "Hello, girl! I missed you too," he says to her, scratching under her ear.

"What are you doing here?" I ask Jack straight. Missy may be glad to see him, but I'm not. How will I ever move on if Cardals keep jumping up at me?

"Looking for you, of course. Let me drive you home." Missy is already in the passenger seat, looking smug. Jack takes my bags from me, and I reluctantly accept his help.

"You do mean back to my house, right?" I remind him. The thought of seeing Sandybank again right now is all too much to contemplate.

"I know you think you know what is going on, Leila, but you are off the mark. Things with Nathan aren't as they seem." I sit quietly in the passenger seat as I listen to him. "Please hear me out. Things might begin to make sense."

"What does it matter? It's over. Nate ended it." A lump rises in my throat, all those unspent tears on the cusp of bursting the banks.

"Do you love him?" Jack asks, when we stop outside my house. "Leila. Tell me the truth, do you love my brother?"

"Yes," I say and finally allow tears to streak down my face. "Yes, I love him, but I'll never know what is going on with him because he never tells me. And now he's discarded me, just as I always thought he would. Like I am nothing to him. As though all this time hasn't meant a thing to him."

"He is cut up over you. He loves you too, and I know he regrets how he acted. He's not on drugs, Leila. Not how you think at any rate. Please give him a chance to explain," Jack pleads with me, but as far as I can see, he is pleading with the wrong person. I gave Nate the chance to explain, and he ended things with me, sent me away. This isn't my problem to fix. This time, Nate has to fix it, and I don't believe he wants to.

"Jack, I appreciate your passion and effort, but I can't fix this." I wipe my face dry and return to looking at him. "Please leave me alone to rebuild my life," I add, opening the car door and gathering Missy and the grocery bags.

"Leila. Will you hear him out?" he shouts through the window to me as I usher Missy down my path. "You'll understand once he explains."

"He doesn't want to explain anything to me, Jack. Please stop, you're torturing me," I shout at him, opening my front door and slamming it shut behind me before crumbling into a pile on the floor. If only Nate was as active in wanting to fix our relationship as Jack is.

## ~ Nate ~

Sandybank has been my home for well over a decade. I have lived here both with Jack and without him, but it's never felt as empty as it does right now. It's not just the house either, my whole life is meaningless. It's the first time that I have ever thought about allowing cancer to win. I have nothing left to live for. The beacon in my life that has kept me strong all these months now thinks I'm a junkie, and probably wants nothing to do with me. I am inconsolable, and just when I couldn't possibly feel any worse, Jack comes home to jubilantly tell me all about Leila standing up to the gaffer.

"You should have seen her, Nathan. Honestly, I got goosebumps! Where is she? She left the ground ages ago," he asks me, looking out into the games room and the formal dining room, trying to locate Leila.

"Gone." I reply simply, unable to bring myself to tell him what I said to her. Unable to recount how I pushed her away so I didn't need to tell her that I am sick and dying.

"Gone where?" he continues, still not completely taking on what I am saying. "When will she be back? I want to thank her for what she said about me. And apologise for worrying her when I disappeared." Once he reaches the end of his sentence, he finally looks at me, and I bite the bullet and give him the news.

"She won't be coming back. I ended it with her," I say bluntly, and although I try to maintain a front, the lump in my throat is so big that I think I'm going to choke on it.

"What? You ended it? Why? Why would you do that, Nathan. I thought you loved her." His voice rises until he shouts the final words at me.

"I do, but it's not going to work out. So, you don't have to worry about keeping my secret now. It's none of her business or anyone else's either." Thinking that'll put an end to his questioning, I begin to walk away from him; however, Jack isn't done torturing me.

"So, you don't mind if she sees other people then?" My guts twist in agony at the thought of my Leila dating some other person.

"It's none of my business who she dates," I spit out at him in annoyance.

He raises his eyebrows at me in mock surprise before retorting, "Even if it's me? I wouldn't mind a second pop at it if you're no longer interested of course."

Involuntarily, my hackles rise. "Don't even think about it, Jack. I am fucking warning you."

"You don't want her, so what's the problem? I could make her happy for a short time." He takes out his phone and begins tapping on the screen, and panic rips through my body. What if he asks her out?

"I do want her. I'll always want her," I admit. "I love her. But I can't do this. She deserves to be with someone who can give her everything her heart desires in life. I can't. I'm dying. And even if I can beat it again, I won't be able to give her a family or the promise that I won't get sick again."

"She deserves to be with the man who loves her and the man she loves back, because she does, Nathan. She adores you. Stop pushing her away and give her some credit. Give her the opportunity to choose if she wants to stick around or not." It's only when he kneels next to me that I realise I have fallen to the ground. My loss hits me all at once. I might never hold a child of my own. I may never get to make Leila my wife. I could die without ever telling her what she means to me.

"She thinks I'm a druggy. She walked in on me when I was trying to inject the steroids the doctor gave me." If I had been honest and had told her the truth, none of this would be happening right now. She would know why I have been prescribed that sort of medication. I have brought this all on myself.

"So, tell her the truth. Tell her and give her the choice of staying or leaving. You are disrespecting her right to make an informed decision about her own future and happiness. You asked her to marry you; you obviously see a future with her. Don't throw it all away because you're scared of being vulnerable." Jack makes a good argument, and I wonder when he became wise and balanced.

"I said some horrible things to her, Jack. I don't know if she'll ever forgive me." I remind him. "I told her I was done, that I didn't want her here anymore. That I needed this to be over."

"So, you're a dick. I'm sure she already knows that. You still need to try and apologise. If she tells you to fuck off, then at least you know where you stand." Although his argument has some validity, there is still the nagging doubt in my mind because he obviously doesn't know about the contract that bound Leila and I together in the first place. I don't have the guts to tell him about it or the patience to suffer through his incessant questioning about it.

"I'll think about things. Maybe the space will do us both good," I tell him, but deep in my bones, I know the longer I leave Leila without an explanation, the less inclined she'll be to forgive me.

---

Jack barges into my office and his brash loudness grates on my nerves thanks to the lack of sleep I got last night. I tossed and turned all night, and the small amounts of sleep I did get were fraught with tortured images of Leila.

"You are going to lose her. Is that what you want? Why haven't you explained to her what is going on? How can she decide for herself if she wants to be on this ride or not if you don't tell her the truth?" I sigh because I really thought he would leave us alone after last night. "I've just been to see her, and she's a mess. You've completely broken her heart, and if you don't do something soon, Nathan, it's going to be too late. Do you understand? There is a time limit on this, and you are cutting it fine."

"It's a bit more complicated than that, Jack. There are things you don't know about. Important things!" I don't volunteer the information. The truth is I don't want to tell him, or explain how this all started because of what he did in the first place.

"What things? This is crazy, Nathan. I know you two belong together. Why can't you see it?" he shouts at me, making my temper rise, and before I can stop myself, I shout right back at him.

"It was all a contract. It wasn't real. I agreed to pose as her fiancé after you almost destroyed her career." Jack stares at me. "She's not in love with me, and we aren't meant to be together. It was all a show to save her job."

"I don't believe you. You were photographed together before I thanked her. I saw it."

"I don't know what to tell you, Jack. The first time I met her was two days after your display. The day we were photographed on the dock was actually moments after we agreed to our contract." I look at him to assess his reaction.

"Are you fucking kidding me? She was in your bed, naked, the following day." I nod to him.

"Yes, she was, but we didn't sleep together, not that time. It was all a set up to make you believe it all so we could save her job. Looks like it worked." I end my confession with a tight smile.

"So, what changed then? Because I know you, and I've never seen you like this with anyone before. You might not have started off conventionally, but you fell in love all the same, didn't you?" The rage I expected from him doesn't come, instead he has probed me with more questions.

"I couldn't help it. She's amazing, and I fell for her. We never spoke about beyond the end of the contract, but I hoped she'd make it official and marry me once the contract expired, but I fucked it all up and ended the contract and pushed her away."

"Just talk to her, Nathan. Please. Before it's too late and you lose her for good. If you love her and you want her in your life, then tell her. For what it's worth, she's in love with you too. She told me that she loves you, but she expected you to discard her, and now you have." He storms out of my office, and I sit with my head in my hands.

"There is a call for you, Mr Cardal." Reluctantly, I accept it. It's Gavin, one of the board members from the football club, and internally, I groan. This is the last thing I need.

"You could have given us the heads up, Nathan. I mean, the way she spoke to Juan Carlos was bad, but her being your fiancée gave her a degree of immunity. She's dropped us with very little time to replace her–"

"I've got absolutely no idea what you are talking about, Gavin." I interrupt his rant before he can continue.

The line is silent momentarily, then Gavin stutters. "You're fiancée, the Doc. She's just emailed her resignation with immediate effect. She is leaving Redvale."

## Chapter 21

### ~ Leila ~

Once I stop crying and compose myself, I do what I can to regain some control. My bank balance has grown a lot since I started living with Nate. Apart from my usual mortgage payment and utilities, I have hardly spent anything. And that is without accepting anything Nate has offered me. I have enough money to tide me over for around six months. Which gives me plenty of time to secure a new job. With that settled, I compose my letter of resignation and send it to human resources, telling them I want to leave with immediate effect. After I send the email, I burst into fresh tears. There is no going back now.

Missy doesn't know what to make of all my crying. She whines and sits on my lap, licking away the salty tears that leak from my eyes. "It looks like it's just you and me, girl," I say to her, cuddling her close to me. In a sadistic sort of way, I'm thankful to have her, my final link to Nate. She'll always be a reminder of my time with Nate and all the memories we made together.

My heart beats faster when my phone rings, and I'm a little disappointed to see it's Claire calling me and not Nate. I suppose I had best get used to it not being Nate. I tell Claire everything that has happened, ending with the news of the demise of my engagement. "We are a sorry pair, aren't we, Ley? I'm up the duff with some playboy's baby, and you've had your heart broken by a billionaire douchebag."

Her analysis makes me laugh, and although I'm still down, I know with my friends behind me, and Missy by my side, I'm going to be okay. A little broken maybe, but I will be alright. "Why don't you come over? We can commiserate together," I ask her.

"Yeah, sure. But only if we can order pizza. I can't get enough pizza at the moment." After promising her that we can order pizza, I pull out fresh clothes from my wardrobe. I need to clean myself up before Claire sees the state I'm in. She will bring holy hell on me for getting into such a mess over a guy.

Before I turn on my shower, my phone rings, making my heart leap again. This time it's Redvale human resources, who want to ensure that I am certain I want to tender my resignation. I assure them that I have made up my mind and wish to utilise any outstanding holidays to ensure I can leave as soon as possible. They accept my resignation and tell me they will contact me with my official leaving date. As simple as that, my time at Redvale is at an end.

I have only just finished getting dressed when the doorbell rings. I bound downstairs two at a time so that Claire isn't waiting outside in the cold for too long. "That was quick!" I shout to her as I swing the door open, but it feels as though I've been kicked in the gut when I look up and see Nathan Cardal standing at my front door, looking tired and as devastated as me but still absolutely gorgeous.

"Hey," he says simply.

"I thought you were Claire." My voice sounds strange, strangled. As though the sight of him has physically knocked the wind out of me.

"Can I come in?" he asks me. His voice sends shivers throughout my body, and a ferocious yearning builds in my tummy. Missy, who must have heard Nate's voice, runs out of the house and barks excitedly at his feet. "Hello, girl. I've missed you too," he tells her when he picks her up.

With Missy in his arms, I step aside and let him in. My heart pounds. Why is he here? "Would you like a drink?" I ask him formally, not really sure on how to handle our situation now we are no longer in a fake engagement.

"No. I came to explain myself and to apologise for the appalling things I said to you and the way I said it." I point to the sofa, inviting him to sit down. "You have the right to know, more than anyone, that I have been keeping something private. Something that I haven't wanted to tell you."

This is probably where he is going to confess his drug problem, and part of me hopes he will. Maybe we will have a chance. He can get help, and I could support him.

"It's not what you think, though, Leila. I'm not an addict... I'm sick."

Frowning, I have a little understanding about addiction and I know that it's an illness, but Nate seems to be accepting he is ill but disregarding that he is addicted.

"I've been hiding this from you because, well, the truth is... I love you, Leila. I am madly in love with you. I wanted the chance for you to know me without my condition interfering. The side effects of the treatments are pretty gruesome, and this is only going to get worse before it gets better."

"What treatments?" I ask starkly, foreboding tingling up my spine.

"Radiotherapy, chemo, bone marrow transplant and steroid therapy... which is what you saw..."

Everything seems to fall into place. The tiredness, the weight loss, the injection, which I can now accept was not drugs but for treatment for his illness. "You have cancer?" I whisper the question, not knowing if it really is a question or a realisation.

"Yes. Technically, I have leukaemia. I have been in remission for a few years, but it has returned. I need to undergo intensive treatment, and this time, I will need a bone marrow transplant too. But first I need a short course of steroids," he tells me calmly. I sit and stare at him, really looking at him, and I notice his pallor, the dark circles under his eyes, and how thin his face has become.

"Oh my god. Are you going to be okay?" I ask, tears springing from my eyes. "Why didn't you tell me?"

"I didn't tell you because I wanted to give us a chance to experience a normal beginning to our unconventional relationship. I wanted you to see me as me and not as a patient," he tells me, tears filling his own eyes too. "And I don't know if I'm going to be okay; I don't know what the odds are this time."

"Why did you push me away? I don't care how much time we have; I want to spend it with you," I tell him through my tears.

"You are everything I have ever wanted and more. You deserve so much more than this. If there was anyone in the world that I could spend my life with, it would be you. I'm in love with you and I have been for a long time. The contract merely complicated what I wanted." He holds my hand as he wipes away my tears before continuing. "I don't have anything to offer you. I can't promise you your whole lifetime of love and commitment, but I promise it for my whole lifetime. Please forgive me and come home."

## ~ Nate ~

Leila weeps at my news, but at least she is listening to me, and before my gumption deserts me, I tell her everything: how I feel about her, what I want from the future, what my prognosis is. It's only as I say the words out loud to her that the magnitude of my situation begins to dawn on me. I've been such an idiot. I should have just told her from the start and none of this would be an issue now

"I've been in denial. I could lie and tell you that I covered up to protect you, but the truth is, I think I have been lying to myself too because I'm frightened. I've got everything to lose now that I've found you." I continue pouring out all my feelings so she knows exactly where I stand with everything.

"So you want to continue with the contract?" she finally asks me with a small frown forming right between her eyebrows, and I realise she still doesn't understand I don't want a fake engagement anymore. I want the real deal.

"No. No contract. Well, not that type. I want you to marry me. Properly. I want us to be husband and wife. I love you, Leila, and I want to spend whatever time I have left with you."

Banging on the front door distracts us both, and hysterical shouting breaks up our little heart-to-heart. Leila jumps away from me as though she has been caught doing something she shouldn't. "Leave her alone, you big oafs. If she doesn't kick your asses, I will. Pregnant or not. LEILA? Is everything okay in there." The shrill voice of Claire permeates the room as she shouts through the letterbox. "Let me in! I need to pee!"

Leila rushes away from me to her friend's aid, while I brace myself for Claire's onslaught, and as predicted, I hear her before I see her. "You've got some nerve showing up here like this–" She stops and looks at me, really looks at me, then looks at Leila. "Fuck a duck! You look terrible, Nate. In fact you both do. Quick, out of my way, I really will pee myself," she tells us earnestly, raising a smile from the both of us.

Having said my piece, I stand up to go, and I can see the panic forming in Leila's eyes. "I know this is a lot of information. As much as I don't want to leave you, I want to give you the space you need to make your decision," I say to her, taking her face in my hands. I will never tire of holding her, of looking into her mesmerising eyes. I just hope this isn't the last time. "I'm sorry for everything I've done wrong, darling. I'll give you all the time you need, but I want us to get married. I want us to wake up next to each other. I want to make all your dreams come true."

Tears stream down her perfect face, and I hate that I have caused them, but I also hope that it means she feels that same way about us. "Nate, I've done something that might change your mind. I resigned from my job. I couldn't stand the thought of working so close to you and us no longer being together."

Laughing a little, I tell her I already know. "It doesn't change my mind, but it does make the present I have for you all the more plausible. Just don't worry about your job; I think I've found a better way to achieve your career goal, and this time there are no strings or clauses attached."

Surprise and intrigue fill her face. "Even if I say no to your proposal?"

Although I wince, I have no hesitation on my answer. "Even if you say no, I still hope you will want to be involved in the foundation. You don't need to marry me for that to happen, though." I kiss her on her forehead, wanting to sweep her up and never let go but settling for a modest amount of affection despite desiring so much more. "I miss you so much. Don't give up on me, darling."

"I love you and I want us to be together, but I can't stand all the lies and secrets. I found out when we got back from Italy that my mother was divorcing my dad when he died and that he was living alone in torment because he was denied access to me." The anger and annoyance in her voice reminds me of her fire and passion as well as her hurt and vulnerability. "I do not want history to repeat itself. I can't live a lie. I will think about what I want, but if I agree, I want complete honesty from this point onwards. I don't think that's too much to ask."

"Are you okay?" I ask her, knowing it's a stupid question but still needing her to know that I am thinking of her. The information about her parents is bound to have upset her.

"It's been hard, Nate. I needed you, and you pushed me away. You needed me, and you pushed me away. I can't live like that, being pushed away all the bloody time. If you won't let me all the way in, then we may as well call time now." My heart pounds. I don't want to lose her, and what she is asking for is the bare minimum. "You're sick, and I want to support you through it because I love you and want to be with you, whether that be for another day, or the rest of my days. But I can only do that if I can trust that you are committing as much as I am. That includes being honest."

Nodding to her, I gulp but feel unable to swallow. This means everything to me, but I sometimes find it hard to be so open. For the longest time, I have had to protect my feelings and information. There has always been someone lurking, looking for a story or an angle, and my privacy has come at a premium. It is a luxury I have protected by any means. However, I want to share my life with Leila, and that means trusting her with stuff I have never trusted anyone with. "I want to be honest with you, and I want to commit as much as you are. I do find it hard to let go, but for you, I will make the effort to be more transparent. I promise you that."

"Okay, well I'm going to spend the evening with Claire as planned, and I will phone you when I've had time to think everything over." I nod to her and reluctantly turn to leave. "Nate? I do love you, and I'm gutted to hear that you're not well. No matter what happens, I'll always be here for you if you need me."

Having dreaded seeing her pity, I instead find her empathy soothing and comforting. I should have had more faith in her. As I walk to my car, I pray Leila can soften her heart towards me one last time, because if I get one more chance with her, I'll never ever let her down again.

All I need is just one more shot so I can prove myself to her.

## ~ Leila ~

Claire walks into the living room with a towel in her hands, drying them. "Where's he gone?" she says as she looks around me, expecting to find Nate hiding behind my sofa.

"He left," I tell her, my voice thick with emotion.

"Ah shit, you're gonna cry, aren't you? Then I'm gonna cry because my hormones are all over the place." Claire's bottom lip wobbles, and her eyes glisten with unshed tears. "Ley, is there no way you guys can work stuff out? You're obviously in love and miss each other."

Thinking about her question before I answer, I wonder to myself what is holding me back. "He wants me to come back home. He asked me to marry him."

"Well, durr! He already asked you, remember?" And that's it right there. Maybe if I tell Claire the real circumstances, I might feel cleansed from all the lying.

"No, not really. It was a set up at first to save my job," I whisper to her, unable to gauge her reaction as she wipes the tears from her eyes from the last upset.

"I KNEW IT!" she shouts victoriously. "You were fuming with Jack that night, but there was no one else in the pipeline. I knew you couldn't hide a man from us!"

"You can't tell anyone, it was all contracted... but, I fell for him, Claire. He's an amazing person, someone I really respect and admire. The sex, the feelings, all of that was never part of the deal. Nate suggested he become my Substitute as compensation for Jack almost destroying my reputation. It was all meant to come to an amicable end once the season was over." While I explain to her, everything seems to make more sense to me. I've been so busy hiding my true feelings from Nate that I didn't see or accept that he felt the same way too.

"He fell for you too, Ley. That was a broken man sitting here just now. So he just proposed and you said you'll think about it?" I shake my head to her, trying to remember the exact wording.

"He said he didn't want to leave, but would give me the time and space I need to think about what I want. I told him we are either both all in, or we should call it quits, that I needed to know that I can trust him to give as much as I do."

"But you love him and want to be with him?" Her question is more rhetorical, a statement of my feelings in fact.

"Yes. I love him. Yes, I want to be with him. I want to marry him and spend the rest of our lives together." The last words sting my throat, knowing that every moment away from Nate is a moment we will never get back. It is time that is precious and wasting it is surely taking his presence in my life for granted. "I have to go and tell him," I say to Claire, grabbing my bag and coat then looking for Missy's lead.

"Yeah you do. Leave the dog here with me... I've been thinking, would you rent your house to me? Louise and her fella are so noisy in the bedroom, and I think I need to start planning for the future." I hug her close to me. "Leave Missy here; you'll want some doggy-free banging when you make up, and I could do with the company while I test run my new home!"

"Thanks, Claire. Thank you for helping me see sense. I gotta go." She throws her car keys at me and reminds me not to forget to return them. "I will get Jeremy to return them as soon as I can."

Claire's car is what I refer to as 'an old man's car'. It's a long saloon type that is usually driven by older men with chips on their shoulders. Claire says they drive it to compensate for their little willies. She drives it to show she wants all the big willies, and the medium ones too. The unfamiliar car makes my journey feel ten times longer than it normally is. I panic when I arrive at the gates to Sandybank. I know the keycode obviously, but what if Nate changed it? Maybe I should buzz to give him some notice of my arrival. In the end, I punch in the code and hope for the best. I'm sure Nate has an alarm anyway.

When the gates open, I am relieved to realise he didn't change the code. That must surely count for something. Slowly, I make the trip up the driveway and pull up in the courtyard.

"Leila?" I hear Nate say from the front door that is now open wide. "Darling?"

"I love you! I don't want to miss a second of what we have because even a million lifetimes together wouldn't be enough." He jogs down the steps to me, and I throw myself at him, kissing him with every drop of love and passion that I have for him. "No more cover-ups, Nate. We both have to agree to be completely open from now on."

"I promise to let you all the way in; I won't be covering anything," he murmurs to me in between kissing me and stroking my hair off my face. "I love you so much. I want to do this properly."

He gets down on one knee, and from his pocket, he pulls out a ring. This time, it's a different ring, and I wonder where my old engagement ring is. The new ring is a princess cut diamond, flanked by two smaller diamonds. "It's beautiful."

"The other ring was a substitute. It's yours to keep, to wear, to sell. But I felt a new ring was in order to mark the new phase of our relationship. I hope you like it." He looks up at me, and this time, his proposal is heartfelt and emotive. "Leila Monrose, you have completely flipped my life upside down. I wasn't looking for you, for the one, but that was exactly when I finally found the piece of me that has been missing. You complete me, and there is nothing I want more than to spend the rest of my days, however many that may be, loving you and being loved by you. Will you marry me?"

As tears of joy stream down my face, I nod my acceptance, unable to speak after such a moving speech. "Is that a yes, darling?" he asks me as he shields his eyes from the winter sun, looking up at my face.

"Yes, in sickness and in health, I want to spend every minute we have together. I love you, Nate. I'll always love you." He pushes the ring onto my finger and then stands back up, sweeping me off my feet before placing me back down so he can kiss me. "I don't want to wait, can we do it soon?"

"As fast as we can. I don't want to wait either," he replies in between kisses. "I want you to be Mrs Cardal as soon as possible."

"Erm... Mrs Monrose-Cardal," I reply to him, which makes him laugh.

"Fair enough, I don't give a fuck what you call yourself as long as you are my wife. Mine forever."

"For always, Nate. My heart will always belong to you."

⚽♥⚽

No one is at home, and Nate has a gleam in his eye. "You're up to something!" I guess out loud, and he nods slowly in response. "What do you plan to do with me?"

"We are going to test out some of the other rooms in the house. I've texted Jack and told him to stay away tonight, because we are making up." I bite my lip as visions of Nate and I in the steam room, in the jacuzzi and on the indoor pitch pop into my mind.

"The games room first."

Wow, there's so many rooms in this place I forgot that there is a games room. It's quite a decent sized room with a billiards, a computer console area and replica pub bar in the corner, where refreshments are always on tap.

"On the table?" I ask, scattering the balls by mistake.

"No, definitely not! The bar. I want to fuck you on the bar, over the bar, behind it." He has already told me about this fantasy before, but Jack always seemed to pop up at the most inconvenient of times or we would have a house full of visitors or staff. This really is the ideal time to give Nate a glimpse of his wildest dreams.

The bar is sophisticated; the top is a wood and resin mix filled with personal items relating to Redvale. There are ticket stubs from both Nate's and Jack's first matches, emblems, bottle caps and a couple of medals too. The resin is the Redvale colours of deep red, black and white, and the dark, solid wood compliments it perfectly. It is polished smoothly, like silk between your fingertips. I'll be getting no splinters in my backside tonight!

Nate stalks me, assessing me before making a plan in his head of what he wants us to do. The excitement has my body humming, and the yearning for him that has ebbed and flowed the past few days sits like an angry beast in my tummy, radiating downwards, making me hot and impatient for satisfaction. "I've missed every millimetre of your body and now, I'm gonna worship all of it. Please take off all your clothes and get comfortable on one of the bar stools."

My core pulses in anticipation while I take off my clothes as requested. Nate removes his shirt, leaving his pants on. He drops to his knees and starts at my toes, kissing each one. He slides his tongue over the top of my foot, sending tingles up my leg. Then he sucks my ankle. The feel of his lips against my skin leaves me needing more. He trails his fingertips over my calves and up to my knees, light, tickling strokes that send shivers all the way up to my spine.

Then he spreads my legs wide. Settling between my open knees, he bites my thighs as he grips tight on to them. I yelp out as the sensation overwhelms me, thrilling me and leaving me needing more in equal measures. "Do you want me to stop, darling?"

"Never stop, Nate. Give me everything you've got," I tell him breathlessly, as he continues to tease me. Thank god for the longevity of waxing; my pussy is splayed open for him, still looking shipshape and shiny. He licks over my pubic bone and traces the contours of my lips, avoiding the very place I want and need him. "Nate!" I groan in warning to him.

"Shush, baby. Be a good girl for me and take everything I give you. Can you do that?" I nod to him, clamping my mouth shut to stop myself from squealing.

From nowhere, a cold gush hits me right on the clit, causing me to jolt in surprise. My eyes snap open, and I find Nate kissing my upper, inner thighs again, but in his hand is the soda gun. Once he makes eye contact with me, he briefly presses the trigger on the gun, sending a short spray of soda that hits my clit again. The sensation is unbelievably exquisite. The coldness of the soda, the bubbles bursting on my clit long after the gun stops spraying, the pressure so different from Nate's tongue and fingers. All of it combines into a wave of pure pleasure.

"Do you like it?" Nate asks me before doing it again.

"I love it. Please do it again." With a wicked grin, he clicks the button for the briefest of moments and allows the shortest spray of liquid out of the gun, followed by a longer attack and three consecutive tiny blasts. The cold soda, which had been wonderful at first, stimulating my sensitive clit, begins to sting me, biting into my tender folds. "Ahh" I cry out, as I squeeze my eyes closed.

"Are you okay, darling? Has it become too cold?" I nod to him, thankful he understands my discomfort. "Don't worry, I've got you."

He sprays the soda directly into his mouth and swirls it around before spitting it on my pussy. The fluid is now warm from his mouth, and the bubbles continue to pop and thrill me. He does it one more time, but this time he doesn't spit it out; he presses his mouth up to my clit and allows the warm soda to seep out. He rubs it into my clit using his tongue, and the rough and warm feel of his tongue against me now pushes me to the peak of orgasm. My legs begin to shake in need and overstimulation. Nate presses his finger deep inside me, while keeping up his pace on my clit with his tongue. The sensation is astonishingly brilliant, and as my body splinters apart, he doesn't let up; he continues to lap up my juices.

"You look so fucking perfect when you come. I want to see it again. Can you do that for me?" I nod to him, unable to talk as my body shudders with the aftershocks of the orgasm he just gave me. "I want you to use me. I want you to grind on me until you come again."

I pull the lever on the stool I am still sitting on and lower it; I instruct him to take off his pants and sit for me. With the chair lower, I am able to squat over him. The tip of his swollen, engorged cock pushes against my clit, sending more shivers of desire right down my spine, forcing me to clench my buttocks so I don't come there and then; there would be no fun in that. I have to make this last a bit longer.

Not realising that Nate kept hold of the soda gun, it comes as a shock when the cold soda hits my nipples. The sensation, agonisingly exquisite, tests my resolve to hold back, but I'm having so much fun with Nate that I never want it to end. "Do it again!" I demand, craving the vibrations, the tingling, the stinging coldness of the soda that contrasts beautifully with Nate's warm mouth and tongue across my delicate skin. Nate laughs against my breast, releasing my nipple from his mouth with a pop.

"You best hurry up; I'll end up coming just from your reactions. I've not even fucked you yet." Against my better judgement, I press his cock against my entrance, yearning for his cock to stretch me wide. Nate smacks my ass. "No, naughty! Not until you've come one more time. Use me, but I'm fucking you, not the other way around."

Groaning in indignation, I lift away from him and grind my clit on the moist tip of his dick. "That's it, that's my good girl. Take what you need from me; show me you can look after yourself." His words and evident enjoyment turn me on even more until I am bouncing on his cock, moaning and squirming "You're so close, darling. You can do it; come for me." And as though on command, my second orgasm thunders through me, taking my breath away. "Yes, that's it, baby. You've done it, my beautiful, wonderful girl. You are a sight."

Opening my eyes, as the pleasure recedes slightly, I catch Nate watching me as I convulse and spasm in delight. He beams in pride at me, and an overwhelming affection for him chokes me up. "I love you so much. I thought I'd lost you," I tell him honestly. In the heat of the moment, all my defences are burnt to the ground.

"Never. I'll never let you go!" He promises me passionately, lifting me up to another tall stool. "Lean back for me and wrap your legs around me." I follow his instructions, praying I don't have to wait much longer for him to be inside me.

My prayers are answered as Nate presses inside me, satisfying me in a way nothing else ever could. Already I can feel a third climax beginning to build. I think Nate can feel it too, because he sets a punishing pace, giving my body everything that it craves for another round of fulfilment. "I'm gonna come again, Nate." I warn him.

"Good. Come again for me. Let your body tell me how much I please you." From nowhere, another spray of soda hits me across my pubic bone and over my nipples again, causing me to cry out in surprise and pleasure. "That's it; cry for me. You're so tight and warm and perfect for me," he adds. His eyes are closed, and he thrusts faster and faster into me, assuring me that his own release is imminent. I take the soda gun from him, and using one hand, I spread my pussy open, giving me access to my clit, and let a continuous stream of soda hit me there. "Fuck!" Nate shouts. It must hit him too, and we come together, the soda gun clattering to the floor as I contort around Nate's deep pumps inside me. He groans above me as he thrusts for the final time.

We both pant and gasp, but as my body relaxes, completely fulfilled and satisfied, I know I could sleep for a week now that I'm back with Nate. "Don't worry, darling. I've got you," he whispers to me, as he carries me through the house and up to our bedroom.

He cleans me up and then settles me in the bed. "Nate?" I murmur through my exhausted haze. "Thank you for taking care of me. It made me feel so loved, respected and cared for. I hope you'll let me do the same for you."

"If anyone must, I wish it to be you and only you," he whispers back to me as he strokes my hair from my face. "Will you help me with my injections? I am terrified of needles and haven't been able to take the steroids the doctor prescribed."

"Yes, of course, I will. I am honoured you trust me enough to help you with this." A lump forms in my throat at the thought of our new normal and the challenges Nate is going to face; however, I will be with him every step of the way now, and he will never be alone with this. "Together we will get through this, Nate. I've got you too."

# CHAPTER 22

## ~ Nate ~

Sharing everything with Leila makes me stronger. All this time, I have worried that her knowing about my illness would make me weak and unappealing to her, when I couldn't have been more wrong. Two will always be stronger than one, and with Leila by my side, encouraging me and supporting me, I am confident I can beat this disease once and for all.

We sleep peacefully now we are back in each other's arms, and the next day, Leila helps me with the steroids as promised. With her help, I get my much-needed medication, and the terror doesn't seem half as bad as she narrates every step to me. I'm very grateful to her, and when I tell her so, she assures me that it is her privilege to help me. Wanting to be completely open and honest with her about everything, I book another appointment with my oncologist for us both to attend so that they can explain everything and answer any questions Leila may have. The first appointment I could get is this afternoon, so while we wait, I decide now is the time to show Leila the plans I have for her foundation.

"The Frankie Monrose Memorial Foundation will be a multi-agency support for players who suffer a career ending injury and their families. Not only will you be able to train people in the field about sports injuries, treatments and rehabilitation, but you can offer mental health support and careers advice." I almost stop when she gasps and tears fill her eyes. "There will be practical support such as job training, accommodation and mediation. Everything that would have benefited your father after his devastating injury will now be offered across the whole English Elite Football League." I pause momentarily, becoming self-conscious that I have over-stepped once again. "Darling? It's just initial plans; you can mould this into a service you want to run."

"I can't believe you've done this! Nate, this is everything I have ever dreamed of for my father's legacy. It could help so many people," she tells me, her voice thick with emotion. She tells me all the information she found out about her father prior to his death and her mothers response too. I pull her into my arms and try to shield her from all the hurt it causes her, but in reality, all I can offer is the same as what she has offered me: my undying love, my empathy and compassion and the knowledge that I am with her every step of the way.

"There is one more thing I need your help with. Shane McAllister has been playing on my mind. If it's true that my mother made him a scapegoat, then I don't blame him for freaking out when he found out who I am." I had a feeling this would be coming up; my fiancée has a pure heart and no matter how much she denies it, I know she feels guilt and remorse for the way things ended with the old team manager.

"We can go to see him now before our appointment, if you like?" I offer her. I know where Shane McAllister lives, and my status will ensure an audience with him. "I'm sure, now that the dust has settled, he'll be more inclined to hear you out."

"I think this is something I need to do, if only for my own piece of mind," she tells me, and I agree with her, smiling as I organise for us to make Shane McAllister a visit. "We have to have breakfast first, though. We both need to take care of ourselves now, no excuses!" I stand and kiss her, my sweet girl, who is a tower of strength.

After a breakfast of poached eggs and wholemeal toast that Leila prepared while I made arrangements with Kim and Eileen on the phone, we make our way to the garage. "Do you want to drive?" I ask her, giving her the option of what she would prefer.

"No. Can you, please? I'm a little nervous about seeing Mr McAllister again," she tells me truthfully. I take her by the hand and kiss her before opening the passenger door for her.

"You don't need to be nervous. If Shane doesn't want to listen, we can leave. The only thing you can do is try and explain to him, but you don't owe him it. He behaved terribly." She nods to me, accepting that I am correct, but the worry doesn't leave her face.

While we drive to Mr McAllister's house in the town, we talk about our living arrangements for the future. "I'm happy at Sandybank, and I hate moving. Plus, I've sort of promised Claire I would rent her my house if I moved."

"Were you seriously going to move away? I'm so sorry for freaking out like I did. I should have just been honest with you." The thought of Leila not being here, of her feeling that she had to move away, tears me up inside.

"Shhh. It's all over with now, Nate. And to be honest, your phobia of needles probably pushed you over the edge. I just appeared at the wrong time," she reassures me, but it's going to take a long time for me to forgive myself for treating her that way. "Are you happy at Sandybank? I want you to be comfortable and content wherever we live."

"I don't care as long as it's with you. Do you mind that Jack still lives with us?" I ask her, and although I crave for us to have alone time, I would also miss the chaos that Jack brings to the house. He is loud and obnoxious, but he's my brother and I love him.

"Not at all, I think it would be weird without him. Is Sam still coming once school is finished?" Sam will be training with Redvale this summer, and he is looking forward to staying with me despite my mother's protests.

"Yes. Though I may need to talk to my mother before then if there are no bone marrow donations that match in the database." I still have to find a donor. I know Jack will be the first to volunteer, but I don't want him to do anything that will interfere with his career. I will ask my mother and some distant cousins, but my best bet is probably going to be an anonymous donor.

"We should do something to raise the profile of the bone marrow donation register. I bet more people would consider donating if they were more aware of its importance," Leila says to me, already pulling out her phone and researching, one of the traits about her that I love, her thirst for knowledge and desire to help others. "I will obviously get tested too. Imagine if I am a match for you– someone should make a movie about that!" She laughs at her joke, while I feel warm inside that she is considering donating because of me.

"Thank you, darling. We are almost at the McAllister house. Are you ready?" I ask her, bracing her for what is to come. She puts her phone back into her bag and breathes deeply. We pull up outside a modest detached house in a residential area, and I point out number 3 to her. "That's his house. Shall we go?" She nods to me and unbuckles her seat belt, so I turn off the engine and get out of the car.

We are just about to open the gate to the McAllister house when his voice catches us both by surprise. "What do you two want? Why are you here?" he asks defensively. Wearing a straw hat and gardening gloves, he is tending to his rose bushes.

"Mr McAllister. I was hoping you would hear me out and we could talk. There are things you don't know, things that I didn't know either until recently," Leila says to him.

"Your mother destroyed my life. I never meant to hurt anyone. Your dad was my pal, and for twenty-five years, I have hated him because of what that witch did," he shouts back at her, and I step to intervene, but Leila holds me back.

"I knew nothing of you, of the court case, of my mother blaming you. I didn't use my father's name to get the job because it hurts me to think of him dying alone, feeling unloved and unsupported. I also wanted to right the wrongs of the past by offering injured players better support, but I wanted the victory to be mine, to earn it, to know for definite it was me making that difference," Leila tells him passionately. I let the two of them continue; I'm here to support my girl and I'll only interfere if things get out of hand. "I'm sorry for what my mother did. I have no excuses for her, because she won't even tell me what happened. I promise you, I never meant to hurt you with my presence or remind you of what you lost too."

"I almost lost everything. I couldn't play because every time I walked onto the pitch, Frankie's mangled leg flashed before my eyes. I never meant to hurt him; I overstepped, and it went badly wrong." Tears roll down his face as he explains. "Then the press began to scrutinise every aspect of my life. My girl left me. I was dropped from the international team and then I lost my spot at Redvale too. I thought when the court case against me was thrown out, it would all stop, but it followed me around like a bad smell for years."

Leila cries with him, and her ability to push aside her own pain to comfort the man in front of her leaves me in awe. "I'm so sorry, Mr McAllister. It must have come as quite a shock when you found out who I am and that I had been right under your nose all this time, but I promise you, I didn't know. I have never searched deeper than what I was told until recently."

"Realising you were Frankie's daughter... I'm not going to lie, I hated you. I thought you were spying on me, plotting my downfall. Everything from back then all bubbled up to the surface, and I couldn't cope with it all." As Shane pours his heart out to Leila, I notice the curtains twitching inside his house and a woman peeking out. I smile to her and indicate for her to come out to us. "I'm sorry about your dad, and I'm sorry for reacting the way I did when I found out."

The front door opens and a woman in her fifties steps outside. "You must be Frankie's daughter? My brother has been in turmoil for most of his life about what happened to your father. I hope you can both get some closure and peace."

"Nate is helping me set up a foundation for players with career ending injuries and their families, and I want you to be on board with me. I think your experience will be invaluable with establishing a holistic view of who is affected and how we can support them," Leila tells Shane, taking me by surprise. I think it's a fabulous idea, though, and Shane, though grouchy and somewhat rude at times, is an invaluable resource in players' services. He will be a great asset to the foundation if he agrees.

"You're offering me a job, after everything I've done?" Shane says to her, stunned astonishment filling his face.

"Everyone deserves a second chance, and if you can forgive yourself after all this time, and me too, then I have no issues letting bygones be exactly that."

"Why don't you come inside for a cup of tea and tell us all about it," Shane's sister adds to us, opening the door wide to invite us in. The tension in her shoulders has gone, and relief is evident in her eyes.

"That would be lovely. We have a bit of time before our next appointment," I tell them all. Overall, this has gone far better than I expected.

## ~ Leila ~

Relief sweeps through my body when Mr McAllister's sister invites me into their home for tea and cake. My heart, although still sore for my father, feels as though it is healed ever so slightly by righting the rift between his former friend and me. I sincerely mean him no harm and I'm happy he now accepts that.

We only stay for half an hour; in the back of both our minds is our impending trip to Nate's oncologist. As much as I don't want Nate to be sick, or need treatment, he does. Now that I know, I want to address what we do to fight it. There is no way on this earth, after everything we've been through to find each other, that I am giving him up without a fight.

I take over from driving, noticing that Nate is becoming nervous. "Are you sure you're happy for me to talk to your doctor? You know there is no coercion; this is your information and if you'd rather keep it private, that's okay," I remind him, wanting to give him the opportunity to think about the consent he is giving me.

"We are in this together. If you know as much as me, I know we can fight this as a team." While my hand is on the gear shift, he holds on to it. "I have nothing left to fear, nothing more to hide, Leila."

We arrive at the hospital, which is a private establishment that is covered by trees and flowers. There are a few celebrities and politicians using the facility, but no one has any true idea why each one of us is here. We are escorted to a comfortable waiting room with large comfortable seats and an abundance of popular, up-to-date magazines. If I didn't fear seeing myself, I probably would have read one, but that's not my life any longer. An assistant brings us cups of coffee, and I cannot help drawing comparisons to what is available in the National Health Service to what I'm witnessing right now. This is light years away from the service others in Nate's position will experience. I'm thankful that the love of my life will have the best chance thanks to his money and privilege, but the thought of another fiancé without the same advantages also following this path hurts my heart.

"Mr Cardal. The doctor is ready for you." The receptionist points us in the direction of a consultation room as we both stand together.

We discuss Nate's diagnosis, and the doctor gives me the breakdown of his proposed treatment plan. "So, his best chance at fighting this is six weeks in hospital having intensive chemo before his bone marrow transplant?" I ask, and when the doctor confirms, I turn to Nate. "That's what you have to do then."

His denial is the last thing I expect. "No. I don't want to spend six weeks locked up in here, away from you. I'll be in complete isolation, Leila," he tells me. "I'll do daily treatments."

"No. Don't fight me on this, Nate! You need to come in and take this seriously. Do you want to die and leave me alone here forever?" I shout at him.

"You know I don't," he shouts back.

"I'll do it with you. We'll drive each other crazy. I'll do the isolation and treatment right here with you." He looks at me stunned.

"You'd do that for me?" he whispers.

"Nate, I would do anything for you. I love you. It's only six weeks." I turn back to the doctor to ask about my plan. "Would that be permitted?"

Nate laughs at my question. "With enough money, darling, anything is permitted."

The doctor nods their agreement. "As long as you aren't pregnant, I have no issue with this."

We arrange for Nate to continue taking his steroids at home before being admitted onto our private isolation ward that we will live in for six weeks. After which, the doctor hopes to have identified a positive bone marrow match for Nate to complete a successful transplant.

Nate drives us back home, and I mull over everything I have found today. "Are you okay, darling? You're very quiet," he asks me in concern.

"I'm just thinking about what the doctor said. There are less than two thousand people on the register waiting for a transplant, but every year they fail to get a match for all of them. With a population the size of England, I think that's shocking." Nate nods to me as he drives. When we arrive home, he holds on to my hand after parking the car.

"You've opened my eyes to my own ignorance today. I never considered how others are affected by the same illness as me. I think I'm in a unique position of being able to influence a positive change." I smile at him, proud of his selflessness, proud of his strength, proud to be his fiancée. "I think we should make it public that I am ill, and ask for able people to consider making a bone marrow donation. We could ask a charity such as Anthony Nolan to collaborate with us."

Tears fill my eyes. "Nate, that is an amazing idea. Are you sure you are okay with making this public?" He nods to me and smiles.

"Ever since I told you, and now knowing you'll be there with me for every step of the way, I don't feel the need to hide it anymore. It's real now, and talking about it doesn't make it any scarier than it already is." I lean forward and press my lips against his, a gentle, fleeting kiss. "I was scared of looking weak, of being weak, but I actually feel stronger and more able to fight this now I'm not worrying about hiding it. That's all thanks to you."

"I can think of a way you can thank me," I whisper to him. "If Jack still isn't home, I'd like to try out the indoor football pitch," I add. Nate kisses my neck and groans in aroused frustration.

"If Jack is home, I'm sending him out. An hour should be enough," he adds jokingly.

Our plans are trashed when we reach our home and find Nate's mum, Drea, her husband, Olivier, and Sam in our home. Drea greets us as though we are late to entertain her, but we had no idea she planned to visit, and while I find it nice that they can make themselves at home, it's also a little intrusive.

"I sent that horrid boy out; I hope he can arrange to stay elsewhere, Nathan."

With anger soaring within me, I reprimand Drea. "You sent Jack away? This is his home. If you cannot be civil to him, I'd appreciate it if you could actually find somewhere else to stay. Nate does not need this right now." She looks at her son for reinforcement.

"Leila is right, mum. She is the lady of this house, and it's rude of you to just turn up, assume you can stay and send one of the people that live here away." Nate threads his fingers through mine. "I'm glad you're here; I have something to tell you and I didn't want to do it over the phone."

Drea smacks her hands to either side of her face dramatically. "I knew it. Didn't I say she was looking a little plump? You're pregnant, aren't you?"

"Mum. No. She doesn't look plump. She isn't pregnant. I'm sick. The leukaemia is back." Nate raises his voice to her and tells her more coldly than I think he intended. Drea gasps and sits down in the chair behind her. Her hands shake and her face has become deathly white.

"How bad is it?" she whispers to the room. Everyone stares at Nate, and I step in front of him, maybe to protect him, but also to give him the time he needs to answer his mother's questions.

"He needs intensive chemo and a bone marrow transplant. He starts the chemo next week. We need to find a match as soon as possible." I take pity on Drea. Tears swim around her eyes, that are the same colour as Nate's, and I know she is as devastated as me about Nate's diagnosis.

"I'll get tested straight away. If only your father was still alive, I know he would have stepped up too," Drea adds. Her husband continues to sit quietly in the corner of the room, offering her no support or comfort.

"I want to get tested too." My head snaps around to Sam. At sixteen years old, I hadn't even considered him as a possible donor.

"Samuel. NO! You're too young," Drea shouts at him, and part of me understands and somewhat agrees with her.

"I said I want to, Mum. And you and him can't stop me. I've made up my mind," he replies firmly. "I want to help my brother." With his solid, unyielding argument, he makes it clear that this is what he wants, and for that alone, I will treasure my new little brother-in-law. His sacrifice could save my love.

"I'll call Jack and tell him to come home. Nate needs his family right now."

While Nate is busy informing Mrs Claybourne, Baxter and Giovanni of our guests, his mother introduces me to her husband, Olivier; however, my first impression of him isn't great. The guy gives me the creeps, and I wonder how the hell a sweet kid like Sam came from them two.

Once the staff has finished preparing the guest suite, I thank them each individually, giving Nate time to show his family to their rooms; however, Sam sticks around, and I tell him we'll find him a room in the main house away from his parents, which he thanks me for. "Please make yourself comfortable; I'm just going to call Jack."

## ~ Jack ~

When Nate's mother and her husband showed up at the house, I knew it would only be a matter of time before I got asked to leave. I don't know where she gets off, but it annoys me that Drea thinks she can come in here and treat me like something she's trod in.

After packing an overnight bag, I spin off from the garage to her judgemental eyes. I swear to god I've never done anything to that woman for her to despise me as much as she does. Usually I would call on one of my friends, crash with them and make a night of it, but all I can think of is Lucy and her peaceful farm. She said I would always be welcome there, that she would leave a light on for me, but I wonder if she meant it, or if she says that to all the beaten and damned who roll up at her safe haven.

Before I can think too much about what I am doing, I follow my trail back to her. Perhaps she could come and have dinner with me? Or I could help her plant seeds or something. I don't really care what we do; I just desire some time alone with her so my soul could feel complete again.

The drive takes longer than last time, and the dark evening is beginning to fall. When her battered farmhouse comes into view, my heart flutters because the light is on in the upstairs bedroom window. Maybe it's her bedroom? I don't know. All I know is I have never felt this need before. The need to be close to another living being, not just anyone, but her.

As I crunch up the path towards her house, uncertainty washes over me. What if I am overstepping the mark? What if she said she'd keep the light on to be polite. Will she be put off by my forwardness?

All my questions are pushed aside momentarily when I hear crying coming from the barn. In a trance, I follow the sound and find Lucy sitting on the floor amongst the hay. She weeps quietly and with dignity, but my entire being fills with the hurt and sorrow she is feeling.

"Lucy? Are you okay?" I ask her, not wanting to creep up on her and alarm her.

She looks around the dimly lit barn, looking for where the voice came from. She squints when she finds my form. "Jack?" she says in a breathy whisper. "Is that really you? I didn't know if you'd come back."

"Why are you crying?" I ask her bluntly. I can't fix it if I don't know what has upset her and I want to fix it as soon as humanly possible. Her being sad and upset is unacceptable.

"I lost a lamb," she tells me with a sad smile. It seems like a silly thing to be crying over, but I want to make her happy, so I suggest a solution.

"Let's go look for it then. I'll help you." She laughs a little with tears still in her eyes.

"No, Jack. It was a premature lamb. It died. It's so sad; the poor little thing didn't stand a chance." She sniffs as a fresh tear leaks from her beautiful eyes and slowly licks her face.

"Oh, I get it. I'm sorry, Luce." She waves me and my sympathy off.

"You must think I'm ridiculous. I'm a farmer, for Christ's sake. Life and death are an everyday occurrence here." I kneel down next to her and using my thumb, I wipe away her tears.

"I don't think you're ridiculous. I think you're amazing," I murmur to her, shocked at my own openness. "Can I take you to dinner to cheer you up?" I ask her, wanting it to be so much more than that, but my own nerves get in the way.

"Uh, I'd love to, Jack, but I have so many chores left to do. Besides, I have a stew in the oven for supper," she tells me, wiping the rest of her tears away on the back of her sleeve before standing up.

"Then, let me help you. What are we doing?" We go deeper into the barn, and Lucy tells me to change my shoes for wellington boots.

"I've brought all the sheep that are in lamb inside so I can keep better tabs on them. That means they don't have access to the food they are usually free to eat, like grass, hay. Until they are safely delivered, I will have to provide it and bring it to them." At the end of the barn, the overwhelming smell of sheep poop hits me full force. "And yes, from the look on your face, the smell has just hit you. You are no longer in Kansas, city boy. Are you sure you can handle this?" She has a gleam in her eye, and her playful, teasing nature is like music to my ears.

"I can handle anything you throw at me," I tell her, and as we work together, Lucy instructing me, and me trying my best to make her proud, I can honestly say this is a lot more enjoyable than I ever imagined possible.

"Will you stay for some supper?" Lucy asks me shyly when we have finished bedding down the sheep. I nod enthusiastically. "Cool, let's go and wash up then."

We walk back to the house in companionable silence, when my phone ringing breaks the calm. "It's my sister-in-law. Do you mind if I take this?" I ask her, and she tells me to go right ahead.

"Hey, Doc. I'm just visiting a friend. I'm not sure what time I'll be back," I say into my phone, allowing Lucy to hear my conversation.

"We've just got back from the hospital, and I have told Drea to leave if she cannot be civil to you. This is your home, Jack." My face flames as Lucy frowns at what Leila has said.

"Yeah, well Drea made it clear I wasn't welcome, and so I didn't hang about. How is Nathan doing?" I ask, knowing his information is safe here: Lucy doesn't even know I play professional football, she doesn't know who Leila or Nate are.

"He needs intensive treatment and a bone marrow transplant. We need to talk to you, but you'll definitely be back by tomorrow, right?" She knows we have a football match and that I have to report for duty. "It's just Nate wants to talk to you before the match about something."

"Don't worry, Doc. I'll do it. If I'm a match, I'll be his donor." The line goes quiet, deathly still, and I can hear sniffing in the background.

"Thank you, Jack. You don't know how much it means to me, and how much it'll mean to your brother that you've offered. However, Nate is very determined to explore all other options before asking you. He said that you are at an important part of the season and he doesn't want to interfere with your career if he can help it."

"Yeah, that sounds like Nathan. We'll get him through this. I'm so glad you guys have each other and have worked through all your stuff. You are meant to be."

After I say goodnight to Leila, I wait for Lucy's interrogation. However, she asks me something that I don't expect.

"So, your life is ruled by seasons too? It looks like we have more in common than I first thought, city boy." I laugh at her quip. She is so sweet and funny. "So who is the Doc?" she asks, and I tell her an outline of my family and work, leaving out that my brother is a billionaire and that I am a professional footballer earning millions every year.

"I'm sorry about your brother, but I was kinda proud of you, stepping up like that, Jack. You're a decent man, you know."

Her assessment of me is music to my ears. I have a long way to go to convince Lucy to be more than my friend, but at least she can see the potential in me at long last.

She invites me inside the O'Dowell house, which is warm and filled with light. Inside a redheaded boy sits at the table with an oily engine part. "Jared, I've told you, not at the table! We are going to eat here!"

The young man scowls at his sister as he collects all his parts and tools. He barely glances at me, but when he does, I'm sure there is a flicker of recognition in his eyes. "Dad's still in bed, Lucy. He said his chest is still hurting something fierce." I notice the immediate concern crossing Lucy's face.

"Is everything okay?" I ask her.

She replies with a tight smile. "Yes. Daddy has been feeling a little under the weather today. I had hoped he would be feeling better tonight. Looks like a visit from the doctor tomorrow. With the sheep being penned, I could do with all the extra help."

Feeling torn, I want to stay and help her, but I can't. I have to work too. "Are there any locals that can help?" I ask, worrying for her and desperate for a solution.

"We had to let the farm hands go; we couldn't afford to pay them," she adds quietly. "Don't worry, Jared can help me if he can put his wrench down for an hour."

"I have to go back for work; I'm already in trouble, but I can come back. How much would it cost to get help for a couple of days, Lucy?" She shifts uncomfortably. "Please let me help. I'll sell my car and get a less pretentious one," I tell her in jest.

"It's eighty pounds a day, Jack. That's if I can get the help." I pull out my wallet and lay the cash I have in there out on the table. For me this is pocket change, nothing. But it can make a big difference to her life right now.

"There is two hundred and ninety-six pounds there. Please use it." Her eyes widen in fascination.

"What about you? You must need that money too?" she whispers. She's shy but grateful.

"Call it payment for the cake and tea, and the hope you gave me. And for my supper this evening, which smells so good," I tell her, inhaling the wonderful scent of her home cooking.

"That's not even worth twenty pounds, and you know it," she adds with a smile.

"Yes, I know the monetary worth, Lucy. But for me, this time with you is priceless. I'm more than happy to help." I don't push my luck; I don't want Lucy to let me kiss her because I've helped her with money. I want her to give me all her kisses because she'll combust if she doesn't. This is the long game, I know, but my reward will be so sweet in the end if it results in me getting the girl of my dreams. It's a challenge, because I want her so bad, but as she said earlier, both of our lives are ruled by our own seasons, but maybe together we could weather it all.

# CHAPTER 23

## ~ Nate ~

It's half-time at the Redvale versus Everglade football club match. It is a local derby, so the match is fraught with rivalry and unsettled scores stemming back decades. Two sides of one city come together to cheer for their beloved teams. Will the Redvale Lionhearts win or the Everglade Blue Socks? It'll be a battle to the end, but right now, as I stand in the centre of the pitch with Leila, ready to address the stadium that is packed to capacity, it seems as though my battle will begin first.

"Please welcome to the stage Redvale City Football Club's CEO, Mr Nathan Cardal, and his fiancée, Ms Leila Monrose." Leila looks amazing but completely out of place. She is not wearing her usual medical staff uniform; instead, she is here in an official capacity as a member of the board. In her red fitted work dress and black high heels, she looks stunning. Graceful, tasteful and all mine. The crowd cheers as they return to their seats. Half time is the ideal time to relieve the bladder or buy a pie or a pint; however, as the start of the second half approaches, most people ensure they are back to their seats so they don't miss a single second.

"Hello, everyone. Thank you for your warm welcome. Since I was a young boy, this has always been by far my favourite match: The Redvale Derby. We are rivals, and yet, when it comes to all other teams, we have each other's backs because we are one city with two places of worship." I pause momentarily, edging towards my announcement. "That is why I thought today would be the ideal time to make the following announcement. I have a secret, and although I want to keep that to myself, the needs of others, not only in this city and in England but across the globe too, make my right to privacy a selfish choice."

Leila grips my hand in support, and it's all I need to push through. "Most of you know me as Mr Cardal or Redvale's CEO. Today, I want you to know me as Nathan, a man who is fighting leukaemia." The eerie silence reverberates around the stands. You would hear a pin if it were to drop. "I have been diagnosed with an acute illness that requires intensive treatment, and after that, if I'm lucky enough, they will find a suitable donor so I can receive healthy bone marrow to replace my faulty marrow. However, to do this, people have to volunteer to be tested. There are less than two thousand people in the UK today on the Bone Marrow Registry looking for a suitable match, but there aren't enough donations for all of them to get a match. I'm imploring you all today to be selfless and consider being tested. Most of you will never have to do more than that. There will be a select few who will be suitable matches and will then be given the honour of saving someone's life."

There is a rise of murmuring among the crowd, hopefully a whisper of support. I suppose time will tell. "Some of you may look at me and think, he's wealthy, he doesn't haven't to worry, but diseases such as cancer and mental illness are not discriminative. They don't care how much money I have, or what plans I have for the future. Fundamentally, apart from circumstances, I am the same as you, and it is my vow now that I will give back to this city in any way, shape or form that I can. Can you help me, please?"

The crowd remains silent for a few moments, then one voice, one single song of hope, echoes across the pitch. "We've got you, Nathan!" I smile, trying to single out my champion; however, before I can find them, the whole stadium chants, "We've got you, Nathan. We've got you, Nathan." Over and over again. Tears of pride at my team's supporters and our rival team too sting the corners of my eyes. I have bared my soul to them, and they are giving me an equal measure of theirs right back. I will never stop repaying this debt.

"Thank you," I call out to them. "Thank you for supporting me." However, my words are lost in the uproar of support that continues to pour down from the fans. On the screens all around the pitch is the sign-up information for the Bone Marrow Donation Register. "My fiancée and I are no strangers to adversity, and my first new investment will be a foundation led by her. The Frankie Monrose Foundation will be a support for injured players and their loved ones. There will be more football focused initiatives to come; however, the community-based ones will start immediately as a thank you to you all for being the best fans in the world."

When I look to the side lines, I see Jack waiting patiently with the rest of his team. I indicate to him to kick the ball to me; however, Leila intercepts, bringing the ball to a stop with her high heels. "Is everyone ready for the second half?" she shouts to the crowd, riling them up for what they came for: A clash of rivals! "It's time to play ball!"

As soon as I leave the pitch, my phone rings. It's the charity leader I made contact with. "Mr Cardal, our lines are jam packed. We cannot cope with the demand right now. Since your announcement, we've had over five thousand applications to become a donor online and the phone hasn't stopped!" Leila hears every word, and we both stare at each other, filled with pride that we were able to make a difference.

After hanging up, I take my love's hand and walk her to the executive box. "There's no point in wasting the facilities; we'll be in isolation next week and wishing we had stayed for the rest of the match."

"Let's have a little fun," Leila suggests with a sparkle in her eye. I cannot resist one more day of laughter with her. Hopefully, once I have had my treatment, we will have all the time in the world to fulfil all our dreams together.

## ~ Leila ~

If I told you six weeks with Nate was easy, I'd be a big fat liar. There were times when I wanted to walk out of that hospital, but deep down, I knew my frustration would ease and any rash decisions I made would instantly be regretted.

Yes, there were times when it felt like we were in a relationship pressure cooker, but overcoming the difficulties ensured I knew that we could make it through anything. Plus, it wasn't all bad. We completed Netflix. Even all the trashy programmes. We caught up with every football match that was televised. We even managed to make a twenty-thousand-piece jigsaw, which I promptly dropped by accident. We played scrabble so much Nate believes he has inadvertently read the whole oxford dictionary. He never let me get away with my made-up words, which would send me into a sulk.

We had an entire suite to ourselves, which meant we could spend time apart as well as together. I worked on programmes for the foundation while Nate rested after his chemo, and when he was feeling well enough, we planned our wedding together.

When I was a little girl, I would often dream of my wedding day. A large meringue dress, several bridesmaids and a groom that wept with joy when he saw me floating down the aisle towards him. However, my dad would always be at my side, giving me away rather reluctantly, deeming no man good enough for his little girl. As I grew older, I became aware that my dad would never be able to do that, and my dreams for my wedding became less elaborate until I just stopped thinking about it and desiring it.

Now, I'm marrying the love of my life. My dad still won't make it, and I no longer want a dress that resembles a sugary dessert, but none of that matters. The hope of a future with Nate is all I care about now. All the dresses in the world could never take its place, and deep down, I know both my father and Nate's will be with us in spirit.

With Claire and Louise as my bridesmaids, and Missy adorably accessorised as my 'flower dog', we become husband and wife on the First of June. We thought it would be a cute wink to where we started and how it evolved.

There had been a couple of points during his treatment when I feared that Nate wouldn't make it. He was so poorly and frail that I worried another treatment may kill him off. Yet, as I stand in the chapel, surrounded by our loved ones, giving my solemn oath to Nate for better or for worse, for richer or for poorer, I know our love will live forever. Now he stands before me, stronger than ever with his grey eyes burning with passion, filled with the life that is now rejuvenated.

Nate is far from out of the woods, but as far as we can see, his treatment has been successful. Thankfully, Sam was his match and his bone marrow has been received well and the healthy cells are growing in response. It's more than we could have hoped for.

Of course, the rest of the football season went ahead as usual. Life didn't stop for everyone else just because it took a short detour for us. However, in between injuries and personal problems with Jack, Tyson and a couple of other players, the team didn't play well enough to win the league, settling once again for second place. I know the team and the fans were disappointed, but work has already begun on strengthening the team for next year, and not all was lost, finishing second in the league guaranteed European football next year, so we have everything to play for once again. Maybe next year will be more settled, and the lads can finally bring home a trophy or two.

We could have had a massive wedding, a star-studded event with no expense spared, but none of that mattered. All we desired was to be husband and wife, and so in the early summer sunshine, we made our vows and then invited our friends and family back to Sandybank, where we celebrated with a traditional English afternoon tea, complete with mimosas and live music. Such a perfect way to end my Substitution Clause.

"Ladies and gentlemen, it is my greatest pleasure to present to you the new Mr and Mrs Cardal!" Jack announces to our guests when we take to the makeshift dance floor for our first dance.

"Monrose-Cardal," Nate reminds his brother, making us all laugh. "At long last you're all mine," he whispers to me as we sway together in time to the music.

"I've always been all yours, Nate, and now, I always will be," I reply to him. His hair is beginning to grow back. It seems darker and curlier than it was– it's so cute.

I look around in time to see Tyson approach Claire, who is now almost six months pregnant and evidently showing it. This will be the first time they've spoken since Tyson told her he didn't want to be involved. Her bump must make everything more real for him, because I see them shake hands, and then when Claire invites him to touch her bump, he does. Maybe they can work out something amicable for the little miracle growing inside her. I hope so.

"I'm so glad we managed to bank my sperm before the treatment. Hopefully, in the future, that'll be us," Nate murmurs against my head, and I share his sentiment. The thought of us having a child together, too, makes my heart fill with excitement.

"Me too. I'd love a little Neila or Lathan," I tell him in agreement, gaining another laugh from him.

"Hey, lovebirds, mind if I cut in for a dance?" Jack asks after tapping Nate on the shoulder, and upon seeing Claire standing on her own again, I send Nate to her. "I'm so happy for you both, Leila. Thank you for not giving up on him and for being his rock through all of this."

Jack has come a long way from that brat who turned my life upside down almost ten months ago. I have a lot to thank him for. "I wouldn't have it any other way, Jack. I love him. He's my world. I suppose, without your antics, none of this would have been possible. In a way, you brought us together and helped us create all this."

He laughs at my comments. "It was my pleasure," he says uncertainly. "I just have to secure my own 'Mrs Cardal' now," he adds with a wistful look in his eyes.

"I thought you were going to bring a guest today?" I gently prod him, hoping he'll open up to me.

"Yeah, she couldn't make it. Responsibilities took priority," he adds, not expanding further or giving me any more information than what I have already gathered myself.

"And you didn't fancy bringing one of the other girls that would chop off their leg for a chance to date you?" I ask him in good fun, but I know something has changed for him... I think Jack is in love!

"Nah, I don't want anyone else. I just don't know how to get her to want me back. I'm trying to be patient; I know she has responsibilities. I do too." I stay quiet, hoping he'll continue. "She thinks being with someone like me will change the life she already has. A life she loves."

"Well, you'll just have to show her how you will only enhance the life she has now. You don't want to take that away from her, you want to enrich it." As though my words open a box in his mind, a look of determination takes the place of the uncertainty that looked so foreign before.

"You're right. I want her to be exactly what she is. I need to show her that. Thanks, Doc." He safely returns me to my new husband, who is appreciating a kick from Claire's baby.

"He's definitely a future Redvale star, Claire. When he can sign a contract, bring him straight to me," Nate tells her.

"It's a boy?" Tyson's strangled voice carries over to us. "We are going to have a boy?"

"No, Tyson. I'm having a boy. You've still got to prove that you're going to be there for the long haul before you get to say that," Claire tells him sharply, putting Tyson right back into his place.

"It looks like there is still a lot of drama to come, darling."

"We have years of it to look forward to," I reply, smiling at our makeshift family and at the trials and tribulations that are inevitable. Life has never felt so good!

- **The End** -

# ELITE ENGLISH FOOTBALL LEAGUE 2023-2024

| Place | Team | Played | Win | Lose | Draw | Goal Difference (+/-) | Points |
|---|---|---|---|---|---|---|---|
| 1 | All Saints FC | | | | | | |
| 2 | Bedfordshire FC | | | | | | |
| 3 | Broadwater FC | | | | | | |
| 4 | Central London FC | | | | | | |
| 5 | Charing Cross FC | | | | | | |
| 6 | Coastal Palace FC | | | | | | |
| 7 | Everglades FC | | | | | | |
| 8 | Kensington Manor FC | | | | | | |
| 9 | Midland FC | | | | | | |
| 10 | Milltown City FC | | | | | | |
| 11 | Newton United FC | | | | | | |
| 12 | Redvale City FC | | | | | | |
| 13 | River Hadrian FC | | | | | | |
| 14 | Robinwood United FC | | | | | | |
| 15 | Saint Marks FC | | | | | | |
| 16 | South Peak AFC | | | | | | |
| 17 | Steel Meadow FC | | | | | | |
| 18 | Stonehenge FC | | | | | | |
| 19 | Westcastle United | | | | | | |
| 20 | West Midlands United FC | | | | | | |

PROPERTY OF CLAIRE RIPPON

# THE FULL CHECKLIST OF LOVER TYPES

The documented proof, reported sightings and sexual encounters of all types of man.

From
Emma Lee-Johnson's
AN ENGLISH ELITE FOOTBALL LEAGUE ROMANCE
SUBSTITUTION
*Clause*

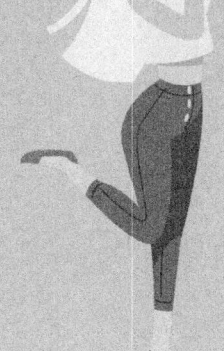

# CLAIRE'S PDF

Hi, everyone, my name is Claire Rippon. You'll learn more about me if you read Substitution Clause and Season Challenges (coming soon). The existence of this PDF made the news, and so I thought, for the sake of women all around the world, I should share it.

Having no luck when it comes to men, I decided to collate a bible dedicated to the men I encounter, the men I have heard about and the ones I cannot wait to meet and their styles. In addition, some of my friends have also added their findings too. If you encounter a new breed of lover type, please, please, please leave the information in the comments, and I'll add it to the document. This is for the good of womankind.

Now, please bear in mind, this is not intended to offend anyone; it's a bit of harmless fun, and unfortunately, due to me being hetero, the document is heavily evidence from my hetero experiences. However, I hope people from all orientations will contribute and maybe this will become a bible of everyone and their technique.

## Cottoncandyman

Very gentle and considerate, strokes her face gently and constantly asks if she's okay and for permission to touch her. Fluffy and excessively sweet.

## Dumbbellboy

Muscular and strong and eager to please. But ultimately thick and dull.

## The Sprinter

No prep, only one goal in mind. Reaching the finish line as quickly as possible. Also referred to as **two pumps and a squirt.**

## The Daddy

Will treat you like his little princess but has no issue with disciping you.

## Viva Voce

Oral specialist

## The Politician

Talks the talk but is completely useless in bed.

## The Mechanic

Very good with his fingers and makes you "purr" after working on you.

## The Painter

He paints fabulous images of your future together but has no money.

## The one-time pleaser

Good in bed, knows what he is doing. Gets off on your pleasure. But has a no repeats rule.

## The Explorer

Adventurous, desire to try new things

## The Lecturer

Teaches you new things, gives you homework

## All Purpose Fellow

Acts as bodyguard - protects you and your secrets.

## The Driver

Takes you wherever you want to go, especially in bed.

## The vacation romantic

Met while on vacation. Perfect romantic. You did all the dates and romantic things. But after vacation he went back to where he lives and her back to her life

## The Monk

Waits until marriage, then only to procreate.

## Mama's boy

Gallant and polite, considerate and generous. However, no one will ever live up to his mama and he is well and truly tied to the apron strings.

## The Jockey

Is small in the trouser department, but will ride you hard and sometimes uses a whip or crop.

## The Tag-Team

Wants his friends in on the action, loves DP and sharing. Even better is the **Triple Threat!**

## The One That Got Away

The one who took your virginity and/or broke your heart for the first time

## The Bro'

One of the boys, his friends always come first. They dress the same, use stupid vocabulary and inside jokes.

## The Destroyer

Always looking for a sub.

## The Twitcher

Likes to watch

## Headliner

Likes being watched, also known as **The Thespian**

## The Narrator

Very vocal about his likes and dislikes, loves dirty talk. (Includes sexting)

## The Golden Retriever

Will do what you command and demand. Aims to please.

## Silent but Deadly

Doesn't say much, but when he does, it's enough to bring you to your knees.

## The Enemy

Annoys the fuck out of you but you are sizzling between the sheets.

## The boy-next-door

Sometimes referred to as **boy bestfriend.** He's secretly liked you for a long time, you didn't see him as more than a friend until he planted the idea firmly in your head.

## The Boss

Evokes deep feelings of wanting to please him and make him proud. Occasionally disciplines you if you're naughty. Loves a Good Girl.

## The Chef

Constantly looking for ways to add spice to your sex life, a new technique, a new herb, a new frying pan.

## Shy Guy

Quiet and reserved in public, people believe him to be innocent, but once in bed he destroys the ever loving hell out of you. Also referred to as **geek/nerdy type.**

## The Cop

Strictly implements the law (his rules) and doesn't hesitate to lock you up- either in his arms, or in his bed. Frequently uses his handcuffs and truncheon.

## Santa's Elf

Has lots of toys and likes to share them in bed.

## Mr Au-Naturale

Beard and pubes galore, all pleasure is derived from him and his technique, nothing silicone allowed! Sometimes referred to as **The Yeti.**

## The Goof Ball

Always joking, pranking and messing around, never ever serious.

## Mr Possessive

Especially when it comes to guy friends

## The Cinnamon Roll

Sweet, supportive and kind.

## The Jock

Fit and athletic, all about his sport and fitness but not intellectual beyond sports rules.

## The Grump

Even when he cums, he sounds annoyed

## The Game Geek

Skilled with his fingers and knows how to use his joystick.

## The End-Game

The one.

### Emma Lee-Johnson

A happily married mum of three, originally from Liverpool, UK. Now a self-published author of Paranormal, Contemporary, sports and Mafia romances that are hot and sweet!

I am a hopeless romantic, with a gutter mind and a potty mouth, but I promise my heart is pure gold!

## Books by this Author include:

- The Alpha's Property
- The Alpha's Heir
- Festive Flings
- More Than Just a Fling
- Festive Wedding
- The Hidden Queen of Alphas

## Coming Soon:

## Books

- The Hidden Strength of a Luna
- Season Challenges (Book 2 Elite English Football League Romance)

## Novella

- A Substitution Christmas (Substitution Clause short story)

*Emma Lee-Johnson*

Romance Author

a https://viewauthor.at/emmaleejohnson

instagram.com/author_emma_lee

tiktok.com/@emmaleejohnson

facebook.com/profile.php?id=100064632064511

# Follow me on social media for exclusive content and updates.

Amazon: viewauthor.at/emmaleejohnson

Ream: https://reamstories.com/chilliandchocolate

Facebook Page: Emma Lee-Johnson

Facebook group: Emma's Angels with Attitude

facebook.com/groups/656345582368378

Instagram author_emma_lee

TikTok.com/@emmaleejohnson

Goodreads Emma Lee-Johnson

Ko-fi.com/emmaleejohnson

Emmalee-johnson.com

linktr.ee/emmaleejohnson

If you have enjoyed reading Substitution Clause, please leave a review.

**Thank you for reading!**

# THE ALPHA'S PROPERTY

Eva: I used to dream about love at first sight and being swept off my feet. Instead, I have a husband who constantly humiliates me and puts me down, and has literally left me stranded at the side of the road. Life seems pretty grim until I walk into the car dealership and the most handsome man I've ever met tells me I belong to him.

Aiden: I've been waiting a long time to meet my mate, and I could never have imagined it would be someone like Eva. She's human, for a start, and she's already married. But dammit, the moment I laid eyes on her I knew I needed her. If there's even a chance for us to be together, I'll do whatever it takes to make her mine.

When Eva and Aiden's worlds collide, it's more than just their relationship at stake: there's Preston, Aiden's Beta, whose mate refuses to commit; Amber, Aiden's sister, whose trust issues prevent her from embracing the happiness her mate bond could bring; Salma, Eva's best friend and a Mafia princess who's being pushed into a marriage to keep her position; Alejandro, Salma's intended who wants a lot more from her than to share her throne; Melanie, whose eyes are gradually opened to the kind of man her lover is; and Ryan, Eva's husband who doesn't want her but doesn't want anyone else to have her too.

Lives intertwine and secrets are revealed as Eva comes to terms with Aiden's claim on her heart and soul: is she really ready to be The Alpha's Property?

## Available now on Amazon on ebook, paperback and hardback.

## Free to read on Kindle Unlimited.

a mybook.to/thealphasproperty

# FESTIVE FLINGS

Set in the festive weeks before Christmas and New Year, Festive Flings follows the intertwining romantic lives of 6 people at different stages in their lives and sexual experiences.

Recently dumped Jamie is ready to move on in time for the holidays, unaware that her boss has been secretly pining over her. Their colleague, Tim, meets the woman of his dreams, but her nightmare of a family has left her self-confidence in tatters. And Jamie's sister, Billie, is hoping for a Christmas miracle to rekindle the passion in her marriage, where kink has been replaced with kids.

Fun, fetishes and frolicking combine in an intertwining tale of spicy British romance in the weeks leading up to Christmas.

All you need for Christmas is... a festive fling!

This book is extremely hot and should be read with caution! Reported side effects reported include: involuntary Kegel and spontaneous pantie-wetting incidents. Read at your own risk... And pleasure!

**Available on Amazon ebook and paperback and Hardcover, read for free on Kindle Unlimited.**

**https://mybook.to/festiveflings**

Deep in the werewolf kingdom, one devout and pious pack continues to live by the ancient teachings and scriptures of the Moon Goddess, but not everyone is happy about it.

Sweet and innocent Soraya wants more from life than her mother and sisters settled for. As an unmated female, she must live a pure and chaste life until she finds her mate or face being shunned as a Scarlet Woman. She dreams of being free, but her life is thrown into uncertainty when she finds her mate on her eighteenth birthday. Which path should she choose?

Her best friend, the feisty and determined Fallon, is the daughter of the strict and unyielding Alpha. She has no idea how much danger her life is in until she starts to search for the truth behind her older sister's disappearance. Will Fallon's curiosity and concern lead her to the same fate of the sister whose name is no longer spoken?

Full of intrigue, mystery, passion and love... are you ready for The Hidden Queen of Alphas?

## Available on Amazon ebook and paperback and Hardcover, read for free on Kindle Unlimited.

https://mybook.to/THQoA

# The Hidden Strength of a Luna

Declared the new Alpha and Luna of the Utopian Wolves Pack, Brandon and Soraya now have a million problems on their plate. Knowing it is only a matter of time before their kingdom is discovered, they must prepare their pack for war.

Maimed and betrayed by his brothers and sister, Clayton will stop at nothing to seek vengeance. Named the new Alpha of the Reverent Moon Pack, he has no qualms about upholding the pack's teachings and values, even when it means mistreating his newly found mate.

Tied to the most powerful and sinister man in the pack, Brianna faces a life of hardship and loneliness.

Will Clayton's siblings come to his mate's aid or will her association with him keep them away? After all, they know all about Clayton's desires for revenge. Or does Brianna have the strength to save herself?

## Coming to Amazon 12th January 2024.

Pre order your eBook now: mybook.to/THSoaL

# Acknowledgments

As always, I would like to thank my husband and sons for supporting me on this unexpected journey. Do you guys know how much I love you? Becoming a writer is a dream come true, but I'll never love anyone or anything as much as I love you all. Thank you for all the input with regards to football, especially the tournament structures and the offside rule... what is it again?! LOL.

To Liverpool Football Club. My team. The inspiration that started this extraordinary journey for me. I wanna quote YNWA but I'm skint. Soz lol.

Anthony Nolan is a UK charity that supports people with blood cancers. They work tirelessly to help people all around the world. You can donate or join the stem cell register, or find further information on their website: www.anthonynolan.org

MIND is a Mental health charity in the UK that offers a variety of information, support and training to anyone in need. For more information, refer to their website: mind.org.uk

For my wonderful friends that helped me with Claire PDF... I'm forever in your debt, thank you for tickling me with your contributions: Melody, Mariarosa, Ally, Emm, Steph and Katie, thank you, thank you. Thank you xxx

Katie is also the provider of sparkly things. If you want resin, check out her Facebook group: Katie Gwilt Creations. Thank you for allowing me to be one of your magpies.

Any book would be pointless without readers, and I have been fortunate enough to have plenty of readers who have positively challenged me and supported me in equal doses. A special call out to Ginger, Debra and Brandi for supporting me throughout this journey.

Thank you to my co-author, Melody Tyden for encouraging me on my self-publishing journey. Her faith in me demonstrates that I have a lot to contribute to the author world. I'm still fangirling though. Check out our joint subscription on Ream: Chilli & Chocolate

Finally, to my amazing editor, Steph. She had to learn all about football especially for this book and if that isn't the mark of an amazing woman, I don't know what is. Thank you so much for everything.

**To everyone who dreams a dream... go out there and grab it!**

Printed in Great Britain
by Amazon